The Agincourt Bride

Joanna spent twenty-five years at the BBC writing and presenting for radio and television. Her first book, *Rebellion at Orford Castle*, was a children's novel set in East Anglia. This was then followed by *Island Games* and *Dubious Assets*, set in her adopted homeland of Scotland and published under the name of Joanna McDonald.

Gripped by Shakespeare's history plays, Joanna originally began researching Henry V's 'fair Kate' as a schoolgirl and the story of Catherine de Valois and the Tudor genesis has remained with her throughout life. Inspired by a chronicle description of Catherine's 'damsels of the bedchamber', the schemes and treacheries of medieval royal courts are brought to life through the eyes of 'Guillaumette', the narrator of *The Agincourt Bride*.

Joanna Hickson lives in an old farmhouse in East Lothian and is married with an extended family and a wayward Irish terrier.

Follow Joanna on Facebook or Twitter @joannahickson.

JOANNA HICKSON

The Agincourt Bride

HARPER

This novel is entirely a work of fiction.
The names, characters and incidents portrayed in it are
the work of the author's imagination. Any resemblance to
actual persons, living or dead, events or localities, is
entirely coincidental.

Harper
An imprint of HarperCollins*Publishers*
77–85 Fulham Palace Road,
Hammersmith, London W6 8JB

www.harpercollins.co.uk

A Paperback Original 2013
2

A catalogue record for this book
is available from the British Library

ISBN: 978-0-0074-4697-1

Typeset in Birka by Palimpsest Book Production Limited,
Falkirk, Stirlingshire

Printed and bound in Great Britain by
Clays Ltd, St Ives plc

MIX
Paper from
responsible sources
FSC www.fsc.org **FSC˚ C007454**

ACKNOWLEDGEMENTS

Some of the people I would like to acknowledge are dead, inevitable when you're transporting the reader back six hundred years. If I could, I would personally thank Catherine de Valois for living such an extraordinary life and, for contemporary accounts of fifteenth century France, the marvellous chroniclers Enguerrand de Monstrelet, Juvenel des Ursins and Jean Froissart. How I wish I could meet them! And there are many historians of subsequent centuries whose work I have shamelessly cherry-picked – too many to name – but to whom grateful thanks are due and of course any factual errors made are my own.

Expert medical advice regarding the possible causes and symptoms of Charles VI's madness came from Bill and Janie Riddle, psychiatrist and psychotherapist respectively, and I gleaned vital information from a string of patient curators and librarians on my research trips to Paris, Picardy, Normandy, Champagne and the Île de France, during which I was inevitably forced to consume some gorgeous French food and wine. So I thank all of them, except perhaps the proprietors of an Algerian restaurant in Poissy where I was served a Couscous Royal from which my figure has never recovered!

And dear reader, *The Agincourt Bride* would not have reached your hands without passing through those of some wonderfully encouraging (and obviously very discerning!) people. They are, in order of handling, Scotland's literary agent *sans pareille* Jenny Brown, friend and novelist extraordinaire Barbara Erskine and the crème de la crème of Harper Fiction – Kate Elton and Sarah Ritherdon, editor *par excellence* Kate Bradley and copy-editor *magnifique* Joy Chamberlain. I am extremely grateful to all of them and also to the team of designers, publicists, marketeers, distributors and printers. I tremble with fingers crossed in the wake of their expertise but if you enjoy it, dear reader, it will have been well worth our while, so thanks to you most of all for picking it up or, in this digital age, downloading it.

Twitter: @joannahickson

☺ Joanna

For Ian and Barley – the two who share my life,
thank goodness.

The HOUSE of VALOIS

Charles V m. Jeanne
(d. 1380)   of Bourbon

Louis   m. Yolande
Duke of Anjou   of Aragon

The Anjou Line

Charles VI m. **Isabeau**
of France   of Bavaria
'The Glass King' 'The Queen'

Louis   m. Valentina
Duke of Orleans   of Milan
(d. 1406)

Charles   m. 1) Isabelle of France
Duke of Orleans   2) **Bonne** of Armangnac

Jeanne
(dy)

Charles
(dy)

Jeanne m. Jean
of France   Duke of
            Brittany

Isabelle m. Charles
of France   Duke of
              Orleans

Charles
Dauphin of
France (d. 1401)

Marie
(a nun)

Michele m. **Philippe**
             of Burgundy
             (Duke from
             1419)

Philippe   m.   Marguerite
Duke of Burgundy   of Male

Jean   m.   Jeanne
Duke of Berry   of Armangnac

Jean 'The Fearless' m. Marguerite
Duke of Burgundy   of Bavaria

Marie   m.   Charles
Duchess of   Duke of
Bourbon   Bourbon

Philippe   m.   **Michele**
Duke of Burgundy   of France

Marguerite m. **Louis**
of France

Louis m. **Marguerite**
Dauphin   of Burgundy
of France
(from 1401)
(d. 1415)

Jean   m.   Jacqueline
Dauphin   of Hainault
of France
(from 1415)
(d. 1417)

Charles m. Marie
Dauphin   of Anjou
of France
(from 1417)

Catherine m. **Henry V**
of France   of England

Phillipe
(dy)

'It is written in the stars that I and my heirs shall rule France and yours shall rule England.

Our nations shall never live in peace. You and Henry have done this.'

Charles, Dauphin of France

NARRATOR'S NOTE

January 1439

Respected reader,

Before we embark on this story together, I think I should explain that I am not a historian or a chronicler or indeed any kind of scholar. I did not even read Latin until my dear and present husband undertook to teach me on dark winter nights by the fire in our London house, when a more dutiful goodwife would have been doing her embroidery. Luckily my days of being dutiful are behind me. I am now fifty-two years of age and I have had quite enough of stitching and scrubbing and answering becks and calls. I have been a servant and I have been a courtier and now I am neither so I have become a scribe, for one good reason; to tell the story of a brave and beautiful princess who wanted the impossible – to be happy. Of course, here at the start of the tale, I am not going to tell you whether she succeeded but I can tell you that some momentous events, scurrilous intrigues and monstrously evil acts conspired to prevent it.

Two things encouraged me to write this story. The first was those Latin lessons, for they enabled me to read the second, which

1

was a cache of letters found when I used a key entrusted to me for safekeeping by my beloved mistress, the aforementioned princess, to open a secret compartment in the gift she bequeathed to me on her untimely death. These were confidential letters, written at turbulent times in her life, and she was never able to send them to their intended recipients. But they filled gaps in my knowledge and shed light on her character and the reasons she chose the paths she followed.

Sadly, for the most part, she was powerless to shape the direction of her own life, however hard she tried. But there were one or two occasions when she, and I too by extraordinary circumstance, managed to steer the course of events in a direction favourable to us both, although this was never recorded in the chronicles of history.

I do not have much time for chroniclers anyway. They invariably have a hidden agenda, observing events from one side only, and even then you cannot trust them to get a story right. Some are no better than the ink-slingers who nail their pamphlets to St Paul's Cross. One of them got my name wrong when he recorded the list of my mistress' companions back in the days of Good King Harry. 'Guillemot' he called me, if you can believe it! Who but a short-sighted, misogynistic monk would saddle a woman with the same name as an ugly black auk-bird? But there it is, in indelible ink, and it will probably endure into history. I beg you, respected reader, do not fall into the trap of believing all you read in chronicles, for my name is not Guillemot. What it is you will discover in the story I am about to tell . . .

2

PART ONE

Hôtel de St Pol, Paris
The Court of the Mad King
1401–5

1

It was a magnificent birth.

A magnificent, gilded, cushioned-in-swansdown birth which was the talk of the town; for the life and style of Queen Isabeau were discussed and dissected in every Paris marketplace – her fabulous gowns, her glittering jewels, her grand entertainments and above all the fact that she rarely paid what she owed for any of them. The fountain gossips deplored her notorious self-indulgence and knew that, like the arrival of all her other babies, the birth of her tenth child would be a glittering, gem-studded occasion illuminated by blazing chandeliers and that they would effectively be funding it. Paris was a city of merchants and craftsmen who relied on the royals and nobles to spend their money on beautiful clothes and artefacts and when they did not pay their bills, people starved and ferment festered. Not that the queen spared a moment's thought for any of that, probably.

For my own part, when I heard the details of her lying-in, I thought the whole process sounded horrible. It's one thing to give birth on a gilded bed but at such a time who would want a bunch of bearded, fur-trimmed worthies peering down and making whispered comments on every gasp and groan? With the notable exception of the king, it seemed that half the court was present; the Grand Master of the Royal Household, the Chancellor of the Treasury and a posse of barons and bishops. All the queen's ladies attended and, for some arcane reason, the Presidents of the Court of Justice, the Privy Council and the University. I do not know how the queen felt about it, but from the poor infant's point of view it must have been like starting life on a busy stall in a crowded market place.

Being born in a feather bed was the last the poor babe knew of luxury though, or of a mother's touch. I can vouch for that. In the fourteen years of her marriage to King Charles the Sixth of France, Queen Isabeau had already popped out four boys and five girls like seeds from a pod, which was about the level of her maternal interest in them. It was questionable whether she even knew how many of them still lived.

Once all the worthies had verified that the new arrival was genuinely fresh-sprung from the royal loins and noted that it was regrettably another girl, the poor little scrap was whisked away to the nursery to be trussed up in those tight linen bands the English call swaddling. So when I first clapped eyes on her she looked like an angry parcel, screaming fit to burst.

I did not take to her at first and who could blame me? It was hard being presented with all that squalling evidence of life, when only a few hours ago my own newborn babe had died before I was even able to hold him.

'You must be brave, little one,' my mother said, her voice

hoarse with grief as she wrapped the tiny blue corpse of my firstborn son in her best linen napkin. 'Save your tears for the living and your love for the good God.'

Kindly meant words that were impossible to heed, for my world had turned dark and formless and all I could do was weep, great hiccoughing sobs that threatened to snatch the breath from my body. In truth I wasn't weeping for my dead son, I was weeping for myself, swamped with guilt and self-loathing and convinced that my existence was pointless if I could not produce a living child. In my grief, God forgive me, I had forgotten that it was He who gives life and He who takes it away. I only knew that my arms ached for my belly's burden and desolation flowed from me like the Seine in spate. So too, in due course, did my milk – sad, useless gouts of it, oozing from my nipples and soaking my chemise, making the cloth cling to my pathetic swollen breasts. Ma brought linen strips and tried to bind them to make it stop but it hurt like devil's fire and I pushed her away. And so it was that my whole life changed.

But I am getting ahead of myself.

I have to confess that my baby was a mistake. We all make them, don't we? I'm not wicked through and through or anything. I just fell for a handsome, laughing boy and let him under my skirt. He did not force me – far from it. He was a groom in the palace stables and I enjoyed our romps in the hayloft as much as he did. Priests go on about carnal sin and eternal damnation, but they do not understand about being young and living for the day.

I am not pretending I was ever beautiful but at fourteen I was not bad looking – brown haired, rosy-cheeked and merry-eyed. A bit plump maybe – or well-covered as my father used to say, God bless him – but that is what a lot of men like, especially if they are strong and muscular, like my Jean-Michel. When we tumbled together in the hay he did not want to think that I might break beneath him. As for me, I did not think much at all. I was intoxicated by his deep voice, dark, twinkling eyes and hot, thrilling kisses.

I used to go and meet him at dusk, while my parents were busy in the bake-house, pulling pies out of the oven. When all the fuss about 'sinful fornication' had died down, Jean-Michel joked that while they were pulling them out he was putting one in!

I should explain that I am a baker's daughter. My name is Guillaumette Dupain. Yes, it does mean 'of bread'. I am bred of bread – so what? Actually, my father was not only a baker of bread but a patissier. He made pastries and wafers and beautiful gilded marchpanes and our bake-house was in the centre of Paris at the end of a cobbled lane that ran down beside the Grand Pont. Luckily for us, the smell of baking bread tended to disguise the stench from the nearby tanning factories and the decomposing bodies of executed criminals, which were often hung from the timbers of the bridge above to discourage the rest of us from breaking the law. In line with guild fire-regulations, our brick ovens were built close to the river, well away from our wooden house and those of our neighbours. All bakers fear fire and my father often talked about the 'great conflagration' before I was born, which almost set the whole city ablaze.

He worked hard and drove his apprentices hard also. He had two – stupid lads I thought them because they could not write or reckon. I could do both, because my mother could and she had taught me – it was good for business. All day the men prepared loaves, pies and pastries at the back of the house while we sold them from the front, took orders and kept tallies. When the baking was finished, for half a sou my father would let the local goodwives put their own pies in the ovens while some heat still remained. Many bakers refused to do this, saying they were too busy mixing the next day's dough, but my father was a kind soul and would not even take the halfpenny if he knew a family was on hard times. 'Soft-hearted fool!' my mother chided, hiding a fond smile.

He was not soft-hearted when she told him I was pregnant though. He called me a whore and a sinner and locked me in the flour store, only letting me out after he had visited Jean-Michel's parents and arranged for him to marry me.

It was not very difficult. No one held my lover at knife-point or anything and afterwards Jean-Michel said he was quite pleased, especially as it meant he could share my bed in the attic above the shop. He had never slept in a real bed because until he went to work at the king's stables, where he dossed down in the straw with the rest of the boy-grooms, he had slept on the floor of his father's workshop with his three brothers. The Lanières were harness-makers and operated from a busy street near Les Halles, where the butchers and tanners plied their odorous trades, making leather readily available. With three sons already in the business, there was no room for a fourth and so, when he was old enough, Jean-Michel was articled to the king's master of horse. It was a good position for he was strong and nimble, but also kind and gentle-voiced. Horses responded to him and did his bidding.

The royal stables were busy day and night and inevitably the apprentices got all the worst shifts, so after we married we only shared my bed when he could wangle a night off. Otherwise it was a tumble in the hayloft or nothing – mostly nothing as I grew larger. When my father sent a message that my birth-pains had started, Jean-Michel rushed from the palace, hoping to hear the baby's first cry but instead he wept with me in the mournful silence.

Men don't feel these things the same as women though, do they? After an hour or so, he dried his eyes, blew his nose and went back to the stables. There was no funeral. I wanted to call the child Henri after my father, but when the priest came it was too late for a baptism and Maître Thomas took the tiny body away to the public burial ground for the unshriven. I know it is foolish but all these years later I sometimes shed tears for my lost son. The Church teaches that the unbaptised cannot enter heaven but I do not believe it.

It must be obvious already that I was an only child. Despite ardent prayers to Saint Monica and a fortune spent on charms and potions, my mother's womb never quickened again. Perhaps because of this, when my baby died she thought I might have lost my only chance of motherhood so, when she could no longer bear the sound of my sobbing, she walked along to the church and asked the priest if there was any call for a wet-nurse.

It so happened that Maître Thomas had a brother in the queen's household, and later that day the appearance in our lane of a royal messenger brought all the neighbours out to gawp at his polished ebony staff and bright-blue livery with its giddy pattern of gold fleur-de-lis. When my mother answered his impatient rap, he wasted no time on a greeting, merely demanding imperiously, 'Does your girl still have milk?' as if he had called at a dairy rather than a bakery.

The first I knew of anything was when my mother's moon-face rose through the attic hatchway, glowing in the beam of her horn lantern. 'Come, Mette,' she said, scrambling off the ladder. 'Quick, get yourself dressed. We're going to the palace.'

Still befuddled with grief, I stood like a docile sheep while she squeezed my poor flabby belly and leaking breasts into my Sunday clothes and pushed me out into the daylight.

The route to the king's palace was familiar from my frequent love-trysts with Jean-Michel. We walked east along the river where the air was fresh and the sky was a bright, uncluttered arc. In the past I had often lingered to watch the traffic on the water; small fishing wherries with fat-bellied brown sails, flat-bottomed barges laden with cargo and occasionally, weaving between them, a gilded galley bedecked with livery, its crimson blades dripping diamond droplets as it ferried some grandee to a riverside mansion.

It was in these leafy suburbs close to the new city wall that

11

many imposing town-houses had been built by the nobility. The highest tower in Paris was to be found there, rising brand-new and clean-stoned above the Duke of Burgundy's Hôtel d'Artois. In the shadow of the ancient abbey of the Céléstins lay the impressive Hôtel de St Antoine where lived the king's brother, the Duke of Orleans. Neighbouring this, however, and over-looking the lush meadows of the Île de St Louis, was the king's magnificent Hôtel de St Pol, the largest and most sumptuous residence of them all. It sprawled for half a league along the north bank of the Seine, the spires and rooftops of a dozen grand buildings visible behind a high curtain wall of pale stone which was fortified with towers and gatehouses constantly a-flutter with flags and banners.

Old men in the market-place told how the present king's father, King Charles V, distraught at losing eight consecutive offspring in their infancy, had eyed his nobles' airy new mansions with envy and went about 'acquiring' a whole parish of them for himself around the church of Saint Pol. Then he had them linked with cloisters, embellished with Italian marble, surrounded with orchards and gardens and enclosed within one great wall, thus establishing his own substantial palace in a prime location and leaving his disgruntled vassals to rebuild elsewhere. This regal racketeering was justified on the grounds that the king's next two sons survived, born and raised in much healthier surroundings than the cramped and fetid quarters of the old Palais Royal.

For my trysts with Jean-Michel I used to slip into the palace by a sally gate in the Porte des Chevaux, where the guards came to know me, but the queen's messenger led my mother and me to the lofty Grande Porte with its battlemented barbican and ranks of armed sentries, his royal staff acting like a magic wand to whisk us unchallenged through the lines of pikes into a vast courtyard. Men, carts and oxen mingled there in noisy confusion. I was kept so busy dodging rolling wheels and piles of steaming dung that I failed to notice which archways and passages we took to reach a quiet paved square where a fountain played before a fine stone mansion. This was the Maison de la Reine where the queen lived and held lavish court and where, presumably, since she'd produced so many children, she received regular visits from the king, although rumour had it that he had not fathered her entire brood.

The grand arched entrance with its sweeping stone staircase was not for the likes of us, of course. We were led to a ground-level door alongside a separate stone building from which belched forth rich cooking smells. The heat of a busy kitchen blasted us as we were brought to a halt by a procession of porters ferrying huge, loaded dishes up a spiral tower-stair to the main floor of the mansion. The queen's household was dining in the great hall and it was several minutes before we were beckoned to follow the final steaming pudding up the worn steps to a servery, where carvers were swiftly and skilfully dissecting roasted meats into portions. The aroma was mouth-watering even to my grief-dulled senses and my mother's long, appreciative sniffs were audible above the noise made by the hungry gathering on the other side of the screen that hid us and the carvers from them.

We were ushered through a door beyond the servery and down a narrow passage into a small, cold chamber lit only by a narrow shaft of daylight from a high unglazed window. Here our escort brusquely informed us that we should wait and then departed, closing the door behind him.

'What are we doing here?' I hissed to my mother, stirred at last into showing some interest in our circumstances.

'Not being fed, obviously,' she complained. 'You would have thought they could spare a bit of pudding!' Huffily she sank onto a solitary bench under the window and arranged her grey woollen skirt neatly around her. 'Come and sit down, Mette, and compose yourself. You want to make a good impression.'

Gingerly I lowered myself onto the bench beside her. It was not many hours since I'd given birth and to sit down was painful. 'Impression?' I echoed. 'Who should I make an impression on?' My breasts throbbed and I was becoming distinctly nervous.

'On Madame la Bonne, who runs the royal nursery.' Now that she had got me here, my mother risked divulging more information. 'She needs a wet-nurse for the new princess.'

'A wet-nurse!' I echoed, wincing as I recoiled along the hard bench. 'You mean . . . no, Ma! I cannot give suck to a royal baby.'

My mother drew herself up, both chins jutting indignantly from the tight frame of her goodwife's wimple. 'And why not, may I ask? Your milk is as good as anyone's. Better than most probably, for you are young and well-nourished. Think yourself lucky. If they take you, you will have drawn the top prize. It might have been a butcher's baby or a tax collector's brat.'

I opened my mouth to protest that a baker's daughter could

hardly despise a butcher's baby but swallowed my words as the door opened to admit a thin, erect woman of middle age and height, dressed in a dark wine-coloured gown with sweeping fur-lined sleeves. The eaves of her black gable-headdress shadowed a pinched, rat-like face and she looked so unlike anyone's idea of a children's nurse that my mother and I were both struck dumb. We stood up.

'Is this the girl?' the woman asked bluntly. Her lip curled. 'Ah yes, I can see it is.'

Following her disdainful gaze, I glanced down and saw that damp milk-stains were beginning to spread over the front of my bodice. Shame and grief sent fresh tears coursing down my cheeks.

'What is your name?' demanded the fur-sleeved lady but any reply I might have made was forestalled as she grabbed me by the arm, pulled me under the beam of light from the window and wrenched my mouth open, peering into it.

My mother spoke for me. 'Guillaumette. My daughter's name is Guillaumette.' She frowned at the crude treatment I was receiving but was too over-awed to object.

Madame la Bonne grunted and released my jaw. 'Teeth seem good,' she observed, aiming her rodent nose at my damp bodice and taking a long investigative sniff. 'And she smells clean. How old is she?'

'Fifteen,' replied my mother, trying to edge her ample frame between me and my tormentor. 'It was her first child.'

'And it is dead, I hope? We do not want any common nurs-ling bringing disease into the royal nursery.' My instantly renewed sobs appeared to convince her of this for she nodded with satisfaction. 'Good. We will take her on trial. Five sous a week and her bed and board. Any sign of ague or milk fever and she is out.' Before my mother could question these terms, the dragon-lady turned to address me directly. 'You should stop snivelling, girl, or your milk will dry up and you will be no use to anyone. The queen was delivered at the hour of sext and the princess needs suck at once. I will send someone to collect you.'

Not waiting to hear whether or not her offer was accepted, Madame la Bonne swept out of the room. My mother stared after her, shaking her head, but the mention of five sous a week had struck a chord. Although my eyes were blurred with tears, I caught the commercial glint in hers as she calculated how much this would add to the family coffers.

'We had best say goodbye then,' she said gruffly, kissing my wet cheeks. 'It is a good opportunity, Mette. Blow your nose and make the most of it. Remember Jean-Michel is not far away. You will be able to visit him between feeds.' Gently, she wiped away my tears with the edge of her veil. 'It will be hard at first but who knows where it could lead? You will get used to it and the baby needs you. You heard the lady.'

I nodded, barely comprehending. When another liveried servant arrived to take me away I followed him without a backward glance. My head was spinning and my breasts felt as if they would burst. Relief from that piercing ache would be welcome, no matter what followed.

They put the baby in my arms and unlaced my bodice. I had

16

no idea what to do but the midwife was there, an ancient crone who must have witnessed a thousand births, and she showed me how to hold the tiny bundle so that my oozing nipple was available to the seeking mouth. At first the infant could not clamp the slippery teat between her hard gums and she yelled with frustration while fresh tears poured down my face.

'I cannot do it!' I cried. 'She does not like me.'

The midwife wheezed with amusement. 'What does she know about liking?' she said, bringing the baby's head and my breast together like a pair of ripe peaches. 'All she wants is to suck. She is a little poppet this one, healthy as a milkmaid and strong as a cobweb. Just you sit quiet now and wait for her to latch on. She will. Oh yes she will!'

She did. Very soon she was fastened to my nipple like a pink leech and I could feel the painful pressure dropping. I stared down at the swaddled crown of her head and noticed a tiny wisp of pale gold hair had slipped between the linen bands. Otherwise, she seemed anonymous, almost inhuman, like one of the gargoyles on the roof of our church. I shivered at the sudden notion that she might be a creature of the devil. Supposing I had been foist with a succubus?

I closed my inflamed eyes and took a deep breath. Of course she was not a demon, I told myself firmly. She was a baby, a gift of God, a morsel of human life that was strangely and avidly attached to my body.

Gradually, I began to feel a steady and reassuring rhythm in the mysterious process of giving suck, a regular swishing sound like the soft hiss made by the surge of the tide on the Seine mudflats. I sensed that the child and I were sharing a universal pulse, joined together in the ebb and flow of life. And as my milk flowed, my tears dried. I did not stop grieving for my lost son but I no longer wept.

2

How can we ever know what life has in store for us? My new situation nearly ended as abruptly as it had begun, because the next morning some of my breast milk oozed onto the white silk chemise that had been pulled over the baby's swaddling in preparation for her baptism. I trembled, awaiting the full power of the rat-woman's wrath, but luckily the stain was quickly hidden under the folds of an embroidered satin christening robe and then, crowned with a tiny coif of lace and seed-pearls, the baby was carried off to the queen's chapel. Later we were told she had been baptised Catherine after the virgin martyr of Alexandria, whose staunch Christian faith had not even been broken by torture on the wheel.

In the beginning I did not really have much to do with Catherine, except to let her suck whenever she cried for the breast. Madame la Bonne insisted on attending to the swaddling herself. She changed it every morning, convinced that only she knew the secret of how to make the royal limbs grow straight. Two dim-witted girls were in charge of washing and dressing and rocking the cradle, which they did with scant care or attention, it seemed to me. After a few days the governess must have decided I could stay, for my straw mattress and Catherine's crib were carried into a small turret room, separated by a thick oak door from the main nursery. I was told that this arrangement was in order to prevent the baby's cries waking the other children but I was far from happy. Terrified of the responsibility of looking after a royal baby alone throughout the night, I became jaded from lack of sleep, home-sick and heart-sick for my own lost son. Yet none of this seemed to affect my milk, which flowed profuse and steady, like the Seine beneath the turret window.

My experience of royal nurseries was nil but even so this one struck me as distinctly odd. Here we were in the palace of reputedly the most profligate queen in Christendom and yet, apart from the pearl-encrusted christening robe which had been swiftly borne away for safekeeping, I could find no evidence of luxury or wealth. There were no fur-lined cribs or silver rattles or chests full of toys, and the rooms, located in a separate tower to the rear of the queen's house, were cold and bare. Although my turret had a small grate and a chimney, there were no fires even to warm the newborn child, no hangings to keep out the autumn draughts and only smoky tapers and oil lamps to light the lengthening nights. Food came up from the queen's kitchen, but it was nothing like the fare I had seen on the day of my arrival. No succulent roasts or glistening puddings for us; we ate potage and bread messes, washed down with green wine or buttermilk. Occasionally there was some cheese or a chunk of bacon but rarely any fresh meat or fish. We might have been living in a monastery rather than a palace.

The reason was not hard to find, for in contrast with her name, there was very little that was good about Madame la Bonne. I quickly understood that her first concern was not the welfare of the royal children but the wealth of the royal governess. I was to learn that any savings she could make on the nursery budget went straight into her own pocket, which was why she had employed me. A courtier's wife would have been more appropriate as wet-nurse for a princess, but a lady of rank would not only command higher pay, she would also have powerful friends, and Madame la Bonne's plans and schemes depended on no one with any connection to power or authority ever coming near the place; none ever visited, not the master of the household or the queen's secretary or chancellor, or even one of their clerks and certainly not the queen herself.

As well as Catherine, there were three other royal children in residence. The oldest was Princess Michele, a solemn, rather plain-looking girl of six who was always trying to keep the peace between her two younger brothers, the Princes Louis and Jean. Louis was the dauphin, the unlikely heir to the throne, a skinny, tow-headed four-year-old with a pale complexion and a chronic cough whose clothes were grubby and too small. However, I observed that he had a quick brain and an active imagination, which often led him into mischief. His brother Jean was a bull-headed terror, a ruffian even at three, darker and sturdier than his brother and more headstrong. You could be sure that if Louis started some mischief, Jean would continue it beyond a joke. After I caught him dropping a spider into Catherine's crib, I decided to keep a very close eye on Monsieur

Jean! I knew that if any harm came to the baby, the blame would instantly be laid on me, not on her infant brother.

Being an only child, I had never had much to do with other children and yet, to my surprise, having been thrown into close contact with these as-good-as-motherless youngsters, I found I knew instinctively how to handle them. Oddly, I felt no similar instinct when it came to Catherine. I could not help nursing a certain resentment that she was alive while my own baby was dead and I could not see past those horrible swaddling bands, which seemed to squash all the character out of her. Sometimes it felt as if I was suckling a sausage. Besides, I grew restless just sitting around waiting to open my bodice, so in between Catherine's feeds I started playing with the older children.

I could see that the boys' naughtiness sprang from boredom rather than wickedness. They were bright and spirited but the two giggling nursemaids were too busy gossiping or sneaking out to meet their lovers to have much time for their charges. They would plonk food on the table but they rarely brought water to wash the children and never talked or played with them. Madame la Bonne had pared their wages to the minimum and, like my mother always said, 'If you pay turnips you get donkeys'.

To start with, the children were wary of me but soon Michele opened up, being touchingly grateful for some attention. A slight, mousy little girl, she had fine, dirty blonde hair that was always in a tangle because Louis had thrown the only hairbrush out of the window in a tantrum and Madame la Bonne had chosen not to replace it. Although outwardly placid, she was terribly insecure, shying at raised voices, assuming slights where there were none and fearful that at any moment she might be whisked away to marry some prince in a foreign land. When I tried to reassure her that she was too young for that, she blinked her solemn sea-green eyes and shook her head.

'No, Mette.' My full name, Guillaumette, was too much for young tongues to master. 'My sister Isabelle was only eight when she went away to England.'

I remembered that departure. I had watched Princess Isabelle being paraded through the streets of Paris at the time of her proxy marriage to King Richard of England, a tiny doll-like figure propped up in a litter, weighed down with furs and jewels, and it had never occurred to me or to any of us in that noisy crowd of citizens how frightened she must have been, being carted off to a strange country to live with a man old enough to be her grandfather. And what had become of that little bride? An English lord named Bolingbroke had stolen King Richard's throne and his abandoned child-queen was still languishing somewhere across the Sleeve, her future uncertain. I realised that Michele was right to be frightened.

The boys took longer to respond to my overtures. Prince Louis' insecurities sprang from a different source but were equally deep-seated. He was haunted by a ghost. At the start of the year his older brother Charles had died of a sudden fever and the whole of France had plunged into mourning. Unlike his younger siblings, the nine-year-old dauphin had been doted on by Queen Isabeau, kept beside her at court, given his own household and showered with gifts and praise. He was shown off to every high-ranking visitor and proclaimed 'the glorious future of France'! Even my down-to-earth mother had joined the crowds cheering him in the streets, raining blessings on his bright golden head.

It was the sweating sickness that carried him off. One day he was riding his pony through the city and the next he was dead, consumed by a raging fever. Queen Isabeau collapsed and the king succumbed to one of his devilish fits. I suppose during the months that followed, the new dauphin might have expected to be whisked off to the life of luxury and privilege that his brother had enjoyed, but this did not happen and so, every time he was reprimanded or denied something, Louis would throw a tantrum, hurling himself to the ground shrieking 'I am the dauphin! I am the dauphin!' This was always a source of great entertainment for Jean, who would squat down nearby and watch with undisguised glee as Louis drummed his heels and screeched. I never saw him try to comfort his brother. Even in infancy Jean was an odd, isolated boy.

Madame la Bonne had devised her particular way of ensuring that the sound of Louis' tantrums did not carry outside the nursery. The first time I heard his blood-curdling yells, I rushed in panic to the big day-room and was horrified to see the governess lift up the screaming little boy, bundle him into a large empty coffer, close the lid and sit on it.

'Madame, really you cannot . . .!' I protested.

'Presumptuous girl!' she snapped. 'Be silent. You are here to give suck, nothing more. I advise you to keep your mouth shut and your bodice open or another wet-nurse will be found.'

Beneath her skinny rump Louis' muffled cries dwindled into whimpers and I was forced to retreat to my turret. It was not until much later, when I was convinced he must be dead, that the governess let the little boy out. Peeping cautiously around the door I saw him emerge trembling and gasping and run to a far corner to press his tear-stained face against the cold stone wall. In his terror he had wet himself but no one offered him dry hose. No wonder he always stank. The governess caught me peeking and gave me another warning glare, so I fled.

A month or so after her birth, Catherine started sleeping for longer periods and I was able to risk my first visit to the stables. Always a man of action rather than words, Jean-Michel greeted me shyly and immediately led me up the ladder to the hay-loft and began shifting bundles of fodder to create a private corner for us, away from the prying eyes of his fellow-grooms. The rows of horses in the stalls below radiated warmth and although at first we talked awkwardly and strangely, it wasn't long before we were exchanging eager kisses. The result was predictable. I am sure I don't need to go into detail. I was fifteen and he was eighteen and after all we were married . . . it wasn't natural for us to remain sad and celibate.

Afterwards we talked some more, carefully avoiding the subject of our dead baby. I told Jean-Michel how Madame la Bonne's greed made life so cold and comfortless in the royal nursery. By now it was early December and the nights were freezing in the turret chamber. Being a kind-hearted lad, he exclaimed indignantly about this and the next time I came he presented me with some bundles of firewood. 'Smuggle them in under your shawl. No one will see the smoke if you burn it after dark,' he suggested.

So when Catherine next woke in the small hours, making restless hungry sounds, I lit a taper with my flint, pulled straw from my mattress for kindling, piled some sticks on top and set the taper to them. As I did so I noticed that her swaddling had come loose and a strip of damp linen was dangling down. On an impulse I pulled it and all at once I could feel her legs begin to kick. In the light of the fire I could see pleasure blaze in her deep-blue eyes and I made an instant decision.

I pulled my bed in front of the hearth, spread the blanket over it and laid Catherine down, eagerly removing the rest of the offensive linen bands. I prayed that no one would take notice of her squalls of protest as I used the icy water from my night-jug to clean her soiled body, and soon the warmth of the flames silenced her cries and she began to stretch and kick, luxuriating in the dancing firelight. Her little arms waved and I bent to smile and coo at her, blowing on her neck and belly to tickle her soft, peachy skin so that she squirmed and burbled with delight.

The previous summer, walking among the wildflowers on the riverbank, I had watched entranced as a butterfly emerged into the sunshine, the full glory of its multicoloured wings gradually unfurling before my eyes. In those first moments by the fire Catherine reminded me of that butterfly. For the first time her big blue eyes became sparkling pools, glowing with life, and her soft mop of flaxen hair, for so long flattened and confined, began to spring and curl. Then, as I bent low and whispered soft endearments into her ear, I was rewarded with a wide, gummy smile.

All the love I had been unable to lavish on my own baby seemed to burst like a dam inside me. I wanted to shout with joy but instead, mindful of the 'donkeys' sleeping in the next room, I swept Catherine up and pressed her little body tightly against mine, whirling her round in a happy, silent dance. I could feel her heart fluttering under my hands and, tiny and helpless though she appeared, she put a powerful spell on me. From that moment I was no longer my own mistress. In the leaping firelight I gazed at that petal-soft, bewitching cherub and became her slave.

When I again wrapped her warmly and began to feed her, giving suck was an entirely new experience. At my breast I no longer saw a pink leech but a rosy angel with a halo of pale hair and skin like doves' down. Now that her limbs were free, she pushed one little hand against my breast and kneaded it gently, as if caressing and blessing me at the same time and under the power of this benison the milk that flowed from me seemed to contain my very heart and soul.

3

'The king's in the oubilette again,' announced Jean-Michel one afternoon when we were alone together. The 'oubliette' was servants' slang for the special apartment set aside to contain the monarch during his 'absences'.

'They carted him off there yesterday afternoon. Apparently he drew his dagger in the council and started slashing about with it wildly, so they had to disarm him and tie him up.'

'God save us! Was anyone hurt?' I asked with alarm.

'Not this time.'

'Have people been injured in the past then?'

'Well, they try to hush it up but one or two chamberlains have mysteriously disappeared from circulation.'

'You mean they have been killed?' I squeaked, incredulous.

'No one has ever admitted it, but . . .' Jean-Michel spread his hands. 'Mad or not, he is the king. Who is going to accuse him of murder?'

I shivered. The closer I got to it, the more I was bewildered by the power of monarchy. Since I had been at the palace I had never laid eyes on the king – at least not as far as I knew. It had been drummed into me by Madame la Bonne that if I should happen to encounter anyone of rank, unless they spoke to me directly, I must avert my eyes and remove myself from their presence as fast as possible. Servants were issued with drab clothing; in my case a mud-coloured kirtle and apron and a plain white linen coif, and like all other palace menials I had perfected the art of scuttling out of sight at the merest flash of sparkling gems and bright-coloured raiment. So, even if I had glimpsed the king I would have been obliged to 'disappear' before I could distinguish him from any other peacock-clad courtier. Of course everyone knew of his recurring malady. One day he would be quite normal, eating and talking and ruling his kingdom, and the next he was reduced to a quavering, raving, deluded wreck, a state which might persist for any length of time, from a week to several months.

'What happens now?' I enquired.

'The queen will pack up and go to the Hôtel de St Antoine,' Jean-Michel said with a sly grin. 'When her husband is out of the way, she jumps into bed with her brother-in-law.'

'The Duke of Orleans!' I exclaimed. 'No! She cannot. It is a sin.'

'Listen to Madame Innocente!' teased Jean-Michel. 'It is treason too, as it happens, but no one says "cannot" to Queen Isabeau. Who is going to arrest her? When the king is ill, she becomes regent.'

Now I was even more shocked. Did God not punish adultery? Did not the fiery pit yawn for the wife who bedded her husband's brother?

'What about hellfire?' I protested. 'Surely even queens and dukes go in fear of that.'

Jean-Michel shrugged. 'I thought you would have realised by now that royalty does not live by the same rules as the rest of us. They can buy a thousand pardons and get absolution for absolutely everything.' His brown-velvet eyes suddenly acquired a familiar gleam. 'You look outraged, my little nursemaid. I like it when you get hot and bothered.' He reached over to pull off my coif for he loved it when my dark hair tumbled down my back and it usually led to other items of clothing becoming disarranged.

I pushed his hand away, softening the rejection with a rueful smile. 'No, Jean-Michel. I must go. Catherine might be crying for me.'

'Catherine, Catherine!' he mimicked, frowning. 'All I hear about is Catherine.' His tone was indignant but a note of indulgence lurked beneath. To look at him you would not think there was anything soft about Jean-Michel but I think he understood that I had come to love my little nursling the way I would have loved our own baby.

I scrambled up, brushing stalks off my skirt. 'I will come again tomorrow,' I promised, giving him a genuinely regretful look, for he was not alone in wanting to linger in our hayloft hideaway.

'One day you must tell Mademoiselle Catherine what sacrifices we made for her!' he caroled after me down the ladder.

As he had predicted, the queen did indeed de-camp to the Duke of Orleans' mansion and their Christmas celebrations set the city abuzz. Night after night bursts of minstrel music drifted up to the nursery windows from lantern-decked galleys ferrying fancy-dressed lords and ladies to a series of entertainments at the Hôtel de St Antoine. Craning our necks through the narrow casement, we could just see the crackle and flash of fireworks and hear the roar of exotic animals, brought from the king's menagerie to thrill the assembled guests. Jean-Michel reported that the taverns were full of minstrels and jongleurs who had converged on Paris in droves, drawn by the promise of lavish purses for those who impressed the queen.

It was a mystery to me why she did not include her children in all this fun. She did not even send them presents. The joy of Christmas barely touched the royal nursery. On the feast-day itself, Madame la Bonne pulled their best clothes out of a locked chest and took the children to mass in the queen's chapel and I was allowed to sit at the back with the donkeys. Otherwise we might not even have known it was Christmas.

Our dinner was even worse than usual, consisting of grease-laden slops and stale bread, which the children understandably refused to eat. Only the Christmas pies I fetched from my parents' bake house gave the poor mites a taste of good cheer.

By Epiphany the palace had ground to a halt. Madame la Bonne had gone to a twelfth-night feast at the house of one of her noble relatives, leaving the 'donkeys' in charge, and they had taken advantage of her absence to make themselves scarce as well. 'You'll be all right on your own, won't you, Guillaumette?' they said airily. 'Just ask the guards if you need anything.'

The next morning the varlets who brought our supplies of food and water failed to turn up. I was alone with four royal children, no food, no warmth and no one to turn to. I was terrified. Only the sentries remained at their posts, guarding the entrance to the nursery as usual.

'Nobody has been paid,' one of them revealed bluntly, when I plucked up courage to ask where everyone was. 'The master of the household has gone with the queen and taken all the clerks and coffers with him.'

'Then why are you still here?' I enquired.

The soldier's sly grin revealed a row of blackened stumps. 'The royal guard is paid by the Constable of France, God be praised – and he is an honourable man.'

'Unlike the royal governess,' I muttered. 'I have not been paid for weeks.'

'Best leave then, my little bonbon, like the rest of them,' he wheezed in a foul-smelling chuckle. 'Fools earn no favour.'

But how could I leave? How could I abandon four friendless and motherless children? I persuaded the guard to fetch us some bread and milk for the children's breakfast and after the donkeys finally returned looking smug and dishevelled, I fed Catherine and left her sleeping while I sped home to the bakery and begged a basketful of pies and pastries from my mother. I told her the king's children were starving in their palace tower.

It was no real crisis because Madame la Bonne returned from her social engagement and the meal deliveries, mean though they were, began once more. But there was still no sign of any laundry and I was sent to the wash-house to investigate. Overwhelmed by the acrid stench of huge bleaching vats overflowing with urine and the smelly heaps of dirty linen turning blue with mildew, I filched an armful of linen napkins when I

32

spotted them and ran. I could wash the napkins daily and keep her clean. Without a supply of clean swaddling, Madame la Bonne could no longer truss the baby up every morning, so Catherine's limbs were allowed to kick free and strong. Meanwhile her blonde curls rioted under the little caps I sewed for her. Ironically, during those dreadful weeks of winter she grew as bonny and plump as a bear cub.

But I felt sorry for the older children. They were cold and hungry and the only thing in plentiful supply was punishment. Whenever mischief flared, which it often did, especially between the boys, some new and vindictive retribution was devised by their governess. On several occasions I saw Jean struggling against tight bonds tying him to his chair, or Louis sitting down gingerly, his buttocks clearly smarting from a beating. I often saw his eyes glinting with resentful anger but he was only four, powerless to retaliate, and if he could have voiced a complaint, who would he have voiced it to? Perhaps the worst thing however, was the fact that their father's oubliette was too close to the nursery tower and the inhuman noises which frequently erupted from that grim place were enough to freak young minds.

The general belief was that the king's madness was caused by agents of the devil. Perhaps living close to the king, Madame la Bonne had been taken over by them as well. Sometimes I was sure I could hear their wings fluttering against the door and I scarcely dared to inhale for fear of contagion.

Jean-Michel told me that in the city taverns, out-of-work palace menials made easy ale-money telling lurid tales of black masses where sorcerers called up flocks of winged demons and sent them flying to infest the subterranean vault where the mad monarch was housed. I often heard the donkeys frightening each other with sightings of these imps. No wonder all the children had bad dreams and Jean wet his bed. As punishment, Madame la Bonne made him sleep on a straw mattress on the floor. At least she ordered the donkeys to wash his bedclothes and not me, but not until they reeked abominably.

The winter was stormy and snow-laden and the children hardly left the nursery for weeks but somehow, with the aid of my father's pies, my stock of family fairy-tales and Jean-Michel's pilfered firewood, we struggled through those cold, dark days. Then, at last, the season turned, the sun began to climb in the sky and the ice melted on the Seine. When the guilds of Paris began their spring parades and the blossom frothed in the palace orchards, the king suddenly regained his senses and the queen came back to the Hôtel de St Pol.

'If she wants to be regent when he is ill, she has to live with the king when he is not,' Jean-Michel observed sagely when I remarked on the speed of her return. 'And believe me, she *loves* being regent.'

Of course she still came nowhere near the nursery, but at least she brought back her coffers and courtiers and Madame la Bonne was forced to start paying servants to bring us food and supplies instead of relying on free hand-outs from my father's bakery. It had not escaped my notice that the rat-woman must have amassed a great deal in unpaid wages over the winter so I summoned my courage and demanded the sum I was owed.

Madame la Bonne simply laughed in my face. 'Four marks!

Whatever made a chit like you think she could reckon?' she mocked. 'Five sous a day do not come to four marks. You are not owed a quarter of that sum.'

Despite my best endeavours, I only managed to prise one mark out of her. When I showed it to my mother I think her anger was more due to the governess' slighting of my education than her act of blatant cheating. 'I suppose we should be grateful to get that much,' she said with resignation. 'They are all at it. Every shopkeeper and craftsman in the city complains about the "noble" art of short-changing.'

As it grew warmer, the palace became like a fairground. The gardens filled with gaily dressed damsels and strutting young squires, laughing and playing sports. Music could be heard drifting over walls and through open windows, and court receptions were held out of doors, under brightly painted canopies. It made life difficult for us menials, as we constantly had to change direction to get out of the way of groups of courtiers making their way to these receptions or to the pleasure gardens and tilting grounds. Often it took me twice as long to get to the stables in order to meet Jean-Michel because I would have to wait with my face to the wall while processions of chattering ladies and gentlemen ambled past me in the cloisters. At least I was able to take the children out to play every day, although Madame la Bonne made it a strict rule that we were only to go to the old queen's abandoned rose garden because we could get there from the nursery without encountering anyone of consequence. She did not want a nosy official querying the state of the royal children's clothing, did she? Nor – heaven forefend – did she want some inadvertent meeting between the queen and her own offspring!

As for the queen herself, as the summer progressed and the August heat became stifling in the city, she set off in a long procession of barges for the royal castle at Melun, further up the Seine. Soon after her departure, word spread that she was pregnant and, in view of the timing, rumour again flared that the child was not the king's but had been fathered by the Duke of Orleans during the last royal absence. I did my own calculations and came to the conclusion that she could just about be given the benefit of the doubt. Perhaps the king did the same because there was no sign of any rift between himself and his brother or his queen.

At about the same time, I began to notice certain changes in my own body. It was popular belief that nursing a child prevented the next one coming along, but this did not hold true for me. My mother put it all down to Saint Monica of course and Jean-Michel boasted to his stable-mates that it took more than a royal nursling to stop him becoming a father!

Madame la Bonne said nothing until it became obvious that I was breeding, when she sniffed and said, 'It's time Catherine was weaned anyway. You can leave at Christmas.'

Remembering the miseries of the previous Christmas, I hastily assured her that since my baby was not due until spring, I could stay well into the New Year. I could not bear to think of Catherine having only the donkeys and Madame la Bonne to look after her, but I knew I had to steel myself for the inevitable parting. Perhaps, had it not been for my own babe, I might have timed

Catherine's weaning so that I could have remained as wet nurse for the queen's new child, but I knew that no lowborn baby would be allowed to stay in the royal nursery or share the royal milk supply. Our time together was drawing inexorably to a close. Soon after her first birthday, Catherine began to take wobbling steps and I started feeding her bread and milk pap, and by February, when the queen's new son was born, I had prepared her as best I could for the arrival of her new sibling.

Far from questioning the paternity of his latest offspring, the king was so delighted to have another son that he insisted he should be called Charles, apparently unconcerned by the fact that both previous princes of that name had died young. Like all his siblings before him, this new Charles popped obligingly from the queens womb, was baptised in silk and pearls and then brought to the nursery, well away from his parents' attention. His wet-nurse was another nobody, like myself, who could be exploited by Madame la Bonne but, I like to think unlike myself, she was a timid individual who took no interest in the older children and confined herself to suckling the baby and gossiping with the donkeys. She was a deep disappointment to me, because I had hoped she might be the motherly type who would give Catherine the cuddles she would need after I was gone.

My little princess now toddled about on dimpled legs, a delightful bundle of energy who giggled and chattered around my skirts all day. I could not imagine life without her, but there was no alternative. It was a beautiful spring day when, forcing a bright laugh and planting a last kiss on her soft baby cheek,

I left Catherine playing with her favourite toy – one of my own childhood dolls. Once clear of the nursery, I became so blinded by tears that Jean-Michel had to lead me home.

I had the consolation a month later of giving birth to my own healthy baby girl who, the Virgin be praised, breathed and sucked and wailed with gusto. We named her Alys after Jean-Michel's mother, who adored her, having raised only boys herself. I loved her too of course but, although I suckled her and tended her every bit as scrupulously as I had Catherine, I admit that I probably never quite let her into the innermost core of my heart, where my royal cuckoo-chick had taken residence.

To many I must seem an unnatural mother, but I looked at it like this: Alys had a father who thought the sun and moon rose in her eyes and two doting grandmothers. She didn't need me the way Catherine did. As the summer passed and the days began to shorten once more, I thought constantly of my nursling. While dressing baby Alys and tucking her into her crib, I wondered who was doing this for Catherine. Was anyone cuddling her and singing her lullabies? Would they comb her hair and tell her stories? I saw her face in my dreams, heard her giggle in the breeze and her unsteady footsteps seemed to follow me about.

No one understood how I felt except my mother, bless her, who said nothing but bought a cow and tethered it on the river bank behind the bakery ovens. When Alys was six months old, I weaned her onto cow's milk and went back to the royal nursery. I know, I know – I am unchristian and unfeeling – but both the grandmothers were delighted to have a little girl to care for and I could no longer ignore my forebodings about Catherine.

Dry-mouthed with apprehension, I approached the guards at the nursery tower. Suppose they did not recognise me, or were too honest to resist the bribes of pies and coin I had brought? Things had not changed in that respect however, and I was soon quietly entering the familiar upper chamber. But how she had changed, my little Catherine! Instead of the sturdy, merry-eyed toddler I had left, I found a moping moppet, thin, dull-eyed and melancholy with lank, tangled curls and a sad, pinched face. When she saw me she jumped straight down from the window-seat where she had been glumly fiddling with the old doll I had left her and ran towards me shouting, 'Mette! Mette! My Mette!' in a sweet, piping voice.

My heart did somersaults as she flung herself into my arms and clung to my neck. I was astounded. How did she know my name? She had been too young to speak it when I left the nursury and surely no one else would have taught it to her. Yet there it was, spilling joyfully off her tongue. Tears streaming down my cheeks, I sank onto a bench and hugged her, murmuring endearments into her shamefully grubby little ear.

I was brought down from the euphoria of reunion by a familiar voice observing with undisguised sarcasm, 'Well this is a touching sight.' Madame la Bonne had been sitting at a lectern under the window with Michele – I had, it seemed, interrupted her reading aloud in Latin – but now the governess moved across the room to stand over me wearing her usual disapproving expression. 'Does this mean you have lost another baby, Guillaumette? Rather careless is it not?'

I stood up and deposited Catherine gently on the floor, where she clung tightly to my skirt. I smiled at Michele. It was difficult to swallow my anger at this heartless enquiry, but I knew I must if I wanted to stay. 'No, Madame. My daughter thrives with her grandmothers. Her name is Alys.' To Michele I said, 'I'm glad to see you are still here, Mademoiselle.'

I exchanged meaningful looks with the solemn princess, who had grown significantly since I had last seen her. No one else appeared to have noticed this fact however, for her bodice was straining its stitches and her ankles protruded from the hem of her skirt.

'We are all still here, Mette. Louis and Jean have a tutor now though.'

'And your lesson should not be further interrupted,' complained Madame le Bonne, glaring down her nose at me. 'If you can keep Catherine quiet, you may take her over there for a while, Guillaumette.' She pointed to the other window recess, where I had played so many games with the children in the past. 'Princesse, let us continue your reading.'

Michele dutifully returned her attention to the heavy leatherbound book on the lectern and I took Catherine's hand and retreated gratefully to the other side of the room. There were two windows in this upper chamber and the depth of their recesses meant that one was almost out of sight of the other.

Almost, but not quite; I could just see the governess sitting poker-faced throughout the next hour, doubtless pondering the implications of my arrival while she lent half an ear to Michele's hesitant recital. Unbeknown to me, one of the 'donkeys' had run off with her varlet lover and my arrival had handed the governess a heaven-sent opportunity.

At the end of the lesson she left Michele and approached us. To my dismay I felt Catherine instinctively shrink from her presence.

'The younger children need a nursemaid, Guillaumette. You can start straight away. Of course you will not be paid as much as you were as a wet-nurse. Three sous a week, take it or leave it.'

I knew that the chances of being paid anything like that sum were slim but I did not care. 'Thank you, Madame,' I said, rising and bowing my head. 'I will take it.' Hidden by the folds of my skirt, I squeezed Catherine's little hand in triumph.

Within a week she was the sunny, laughing infant she had been before I left. Even Louis and Jean seemed pleased to see me. They lived separately from their sisters now, on the ground floor of the tower and were subject to a strict regime of study and exercise supervised by one Maître le Clerc, a supercilious scholar who wore the black robes of a cleric and one of those linen coifs with side flaps, which left his hairy ears exposed. I was intrigued to learn that Louis was already managing to construct simple sentences in Greek and Latin but unsurprised to hear that Jean was constantly being punished for his academic shortcomings. Supervising his bedtime one evening I glimpsed red weals on his legs and buttocks and despised the high-nosed tutor even more. However, at least he had introduced books to

41

the nursery. Most girls of seven might have preferred stories or poetry but quiet, studious Michele was quite content with the worthy, religious tracts that he selected for her from the famous royal library in the Louvre.

I suspected that the governess and tutor might be related. They were certainly cast in the same mould for I soon learned that Maître le Clerc was as adept as Madame la Bonne at filling his own coffers. I confess I closed my eyes to their thieving ways. I had promised Catherine I would never leave her again. The children needed someone who was on their side; someone who would look out for them, encourage the boys not to fight, tell them jokes, bring them honeyed treats from the bakery. So we all rubbed along, playing what effectively amounted to blind man's buff for nearly two years. Then, with the suddenness of a whirlwind, our lives were dismantled.

4

In late August of 1405, a searing heat wave had caused trees to wilt and stone walls to shimmer. In the hope of catching an afternoon breeze off the river, I had taken the children to the old pleasure garden which ran down to a river gate. Planted on the orders of the king's mother, Queen Jeanne, and sadly neglected since her death, it was smothered with overgrown roses which clambered about tumbledown arbours, making perfect haunts for Catherine's imagined fairies and elves. As always when she played, little Charles shadowed her like a small lisping goblin, tottering determinedly on skinny legs in wrinkled, hand-me-down hose. Catherine loved him, though no one else seemed to, always comforting him when he cried.

In her usual quiet way Michele perched sedately on a bench under a tree and immersed herself in Voraigne's *Legendes d'Or* and I am ashamed to say that as I sat with my back against a sun-baked wall, lulled by the murmuring of bees, I drifted off to sleep. I did not doze for long however, because Louis, little menace that he was, took advantage of my lapse to creep up and drop something wriggly and bristling down the front of my chemise. Roused by a stinging sensation between my breasts, I

43

squealed and sprang behind some bushes, tearing open the laces in order to delve into my bodice while the boys screamed with delight. Shuddering, I removed a hairy black caterpillar and tossed it away. An itchy rash had already appeared on the tender damp flesh and, mortified, as I re-tied the laces of my bodice I was already rehearsing the rollicking I was going to deliver to the young princes when their giggling ceased abruptly. Emerging red-faced from my refuge, I stared open-mouthed at the sight that met my eyes.

It was as if a flutter of giant butterflies had alighted in the garden. The guards had rushed to open the old gate that led to a little-used dock on the riverbank and through it was advancing a procession of ladies and gentlemen clad in the height of fashion and chattering and laughing together. The gilded galley from which they had disembarked could be seen bumping gently against the landing stage, while a trio of escorting barges drifted in mid-river, each carrying a score or more of arbalesters and men-at-arms. Rooted to the spot, the children stood gawping like street urchins.

The half dozen ladies of the party wore full-skirted gowns in rainbow hues with high waists and trailing sleeves and they walked with a studied, laid-back gait, carefully balancing an array of architectural headdresses – steeples, arches and gables – glittering with jewels and fluttering with gauzy veils. The men were no less flamboyant, sporting richly brocaded doublets with high, fluted collars and exotically draped hats and teetering on jewel-encrusted shoes with high red heels and spring-curled toes.

In the van of the procession strolled the most magnificent pair of all, locked in animated conversation. I had never seen her at close quarters, but I knew instantly that this must be the queen, linked arm in arm with her brother-in-law the Duke of Orleans.

Queen Isabeau was not slender any more – eleven children and all those succulent roasts had seen to that – but on this stifling afternoon when everything was melting, she glittered like ice. Her gown was of lustrous pale-blue silk so liberally woven through with gold thread that it shimmered as she moved and around her shoulders hung thick chains of pearls and sapphires. On her head an enormous wheel of pale, iridescent feathers was pinned with a diamond the size of a duck's egg.

Her escort was no less resplendent. Louis of Orleans was tall and handsome with a jutting jaw, a long, imperial nose and twinkling speckled grey eyes. To my astonishment there were porcupines embroidered in gold thread and jet beads all over his gown and his extravagently dagged hat was trimmed with striped porcupine quills, which rattled as he walked. It was only later that I learned that the porcupine was the duke's personal emblem. Louis of Orleans liked everyone to know who he was.

I was so mesmerised by these visions of fashionable extravagance that I had forgotten to scamper out of sight and now I could only sink to my knees, for Catherine and Charles had taken shelter behind me and were clinging to my skirt. As it turned out I need not have worried, for I do not think Queen

Isabeau even noticed us. She only tore her gaze from the duke in order to fix it on Michele, who was now standing nervously, clutching her book like a shield.

'Princesse Michele?' The queen beckoned to the trembling girl and I detected a distinctly peevish note in the deep, Germanic voice. 'It is Michele, is it not?'

Well may she ask! I heard my own voice exclaim inside my head. To my knowledge she had not laid eyes on this daughter of hers more than once or twice in the nine years since her birth.

'Come. Come closer, child!' She made an impatient gesture.

The grubby hem of Michele's skirt moved into the scope of my vision and I saw her bend her knee before her mother. For one so young her composure was remarkable.

'Yes, you must be Michele. You have my eyes. And these are your brothers, are they not?' She gestured towards Louis and Jean and nodded at Michele's whispered, 'Yes, Madame.'

'Of course they are! What other children would be playing in Queen Jeanne's garden? But how wretched you look!' exclaimed the queen. 'Have you no comb – no veil? And your gown . . . it is dirty and so tight! Where is your governess? How dare she allow you to be seen like this?'

Michele coloured violently, her expression a mixture of fear and shame. I waited to hear her denounce Madame la Bonne but she merely swallowed hard and shook her head. Perhaps she knew that her all-powerful mother would never believe the truth; that the nursery comb had few remaining teeth, there were no clean clothes and the governess was closeted in her

46

tower chamber counting the coins she had managed not to spend on her royal charges.

'Have you forgotten your manners?' the queen demanded. For a tense moment it looked as if she might explode into anger but then she shrugged and turned to the duke. 'Well, never mind. Young girls are better quiet. What do you think, my lord? Will she polish up for your son? He is only a boy after all. They are cygnets who can grow into swans together!'

Louis of Orleans bent and placed one gloved finger under Michele's chin. The little girl's eyes grew round with apprehension, giving her the appeal of a frightened kitten. The duke smiled, releasing her. 'As she is your daughter, Madame, how could she be anything but perfect? I love her already and so will my son.'

The queen laughed. 'You flatter us, my lord!' Orleans' charm made her forget Michele's shortcomings and the absent governess. She waved the large painted fan she carried. 'Michele, Louis, Jean, follow me. I am glad to have found you in the garden. It has saved us sending men to search the palace. The time has come for you to leave here. It is no longer safe for you. The new Duke of Burgundy thinks he can use you to rule France himself but I am your mother and the queen and I have other plans. You need bring nothing. We are leaving now.'

Her words fell like a thunderbolt in the scented garden. The three named children exchanged astonished glances; Michele with alarm, Louis with excitement and Jean with bemusement. None of them dared to speak.

'We are going somewhere where Burgundy cannot force you

into undesirable alliances. We will foil his schemes and you will have new playmates in your uncle of Orleans' children. Ladies!'

The queen snapped her fan at her attendants, two of whom hastened forward to manoeuvre the long train and voluminous skirt around her feet so that she could turn around. While they busied themselves, she cast another doubtful glance at her children, then leaned closer to Orleans, murmuring, 'Are they worth saving from Burgundy's machinations? They look a sorry bunch to me.'

Orleans made a reassuring gesture. 'Have no fear, Madame, they are of the blood royal. They will polish up.' He turned to address Michele, who still clutched her book fiercely, as the only solid object in a violently shifting world. 'The Duke of Burgundy wants to marry you to his son, Mademoiselle, but how would you like to marry *my* son instead?'

He clearly expected no reply, for the procession was already moving off, back towards the river-gate, and he immediately returned his attention to the queen, missing Michele's eloquent glance in my direction. 'I told you so,' it said, 'I am to be married to heaven-knows-whom and taken to heaven-knows-where!' I crossed myself and whispered a prayer for her. Poor little princess, her worst fears were realised.

'But the dauphin is our first priority,' the queen insisted more forcefully, still within earshot. I saw little Louis flush at hearing himself referred to by the title he had so long desired. 'If he can marry Louis to his daughter, Burgundy will try to rule through him.'

'You are right, as always, Madame,' acknowledged the duke. 'The dauphin, most of all, must be kept away from Cousin Jean. He who calls himself Fearless! What is fearless about stealing children? Jean the Fearless – hah!' The porcupine quills rattled their scorn as the Duke of Orleans tossed his head and cried, 'But you need have no fear, my children! He shall not steal you from your mother. Forward! We are heading for Chartres, with all speed.'

These were the last words I heard because the two remaining infants began to jump and wail beside me as their siblings walked away without a backward glance. Who could blame them? They were confused and frightened. A band of total strangers had invaded their world and within minutes their sister and brothers were disappearing. The river-gate clanged shut. A band of musicians on the galley struck up a merry tune as if nothing untoward had occurred. Sailing off in her cushioned galley, Queen Isabeau was totally unaware of the misery she left behind.

Nor were the day's dramas over. I had taken Catherine and Charles to the seat in the overgrown arbour for a reassuring cuddle, so I did not see a group of men arrive at the palace end of the garden and begin to play some sort of game in the bushes, but the unusual sound of excited whoops and male laughter soon reached us and I popped my head around the sheltering foliage in alarm. We had always had the garden to ourselves and I had no wish to encounter any fun-seeking courtiers or playful lovers who might have strayed there. I wondered if we could escape to the nursery tower without being seen.

Alas, we could not. The strange and disturbing figure of a man was already approaching our hiding-place and had seen me poke my head out. He stopped dead with a smile of childish glee frozen for an instant on his thin, pale face before it turned to a ghoulish grimace of dismay. Strangely, in this palace of smooth-cheeked, neatly-trimmed courtiers, his chin had a growth of straggly brown beard and his lank hair trailed down in a messy tangle to his shoulders. His clothing was rumpled and filthy, but had once been fine and fashionable, the shabby blue doublet edged with matted fur and patterned with a tarnished gold design that might once have been fleur-de-lis. With a fearful flash of intuition I realised that I was now, incredibly, face to face with the ailing king, as if having just encountered the queen were not enough for one day, not to mention having lost three of my charges.

We stood speechless with shock at the sight of each other, but Catherine, whose curiosity never dimmed, stepped past me into the king's path. As she did so, two sturdy men in leather jackets appeared at the far end of the garden – the king's minders. I reached to pull Catherine back, but she wriggled out of my grasp and walked boldly up to the stranger, staring at him enquiringly. 'Good day, Monsieur. Are you playing a game?' she asked sweetly. 'May I play too?'

She did not know, of course, that this might be her father. She had never met him, any more than she had met her mother, and a three year old who is not shy will always be ready to play with someone new, oblivious of circumstances.

For his part, the dishevelled king was provoked into an

extraordinary reaction. Perhaps, whether mad or sane, he was frightened of children. Certainly, he had avoided his own. He threw his arms up to fend Catherine off as if she was a springing lion or a charging bull and he screamed! God in Heaven how he screamed! Hurriedly I picked up baby Charles and held him. The noise seemed to fill the shimmering arc of the burning sky. Through wide-stretched lips and discoloured teeth the king hurled invective at the little girl, releasing sounds from his throat like the screeching of a wounded horse, high-pitched and ear-splitting. There were words contained within the scream which struck me with icy terror and must have traumatised Catherine, standing as she was only an arm's length away.

'Keep away! Do not touch me! I shall bre-e-e-e-eak!'

A look of terror on her face, Catherine spun around and threw herself at me for protection. I could feel her whole body shaking with fear as she buried her head in my skirts and broke into muffled sobs. At the same time the two strong-looking minders arrived panting, having raced down the path at the first sound of the scream. One of them had pulled a large sack out of a pack on the other's back and between them, without saying a word, they pulled it over the king's head, pinning his arms to his side and then picked him up and carried him bodily towards the palace gate, his legs kicking helplessly. Despite the sack he was still screaming, if anything even louder than before.

A third man, similarly dressed in studded leather, appeared from nowhere and panted at us, 'I am sorry, Madame, but he is more frightened of you than you are of him. He thinks he is made of glass. He would not have hurt the little girl. Please tell her he is not an ogre. He is the king and he is ill.'

Not waiting for a response, he touched the edge of his bucket hat and raced after the others. It took several minutes for both children to stop hiccoughing with fear and my heart was still thudding in my chest when I grasped Catherine's little hand and hurried with them both to the relative peace of our tower. I told myself that it would be a very long time before I would venture into Queen Jeanne's garden again.

Back in the nursery the two little children clung to me as if to a rock in fast-rising water. I did not think they had heard what the third 'minder' had said and I was not about to make it worse for them by revealing that the terrifying man they had met in the garden was their father, the king. It was enough that they had suffered his animal screams and would probably see his agonised face in their dreams. More disturbing in the long term was the absence of Michele, Louis and Jean. Their older sister and brothers had been an integral part of their short lives; not always easy or kind but always there, to squabble with, play with or annoy. The nursery was silent and strange without them, a place at once both familiar and frightening.

Catherine was full of questions. Where had the others gone? Why had they gone? What would happen to them? When were they coming back? Was that lady really her mother? Why hadn't she spoken to her? Would she come for her, too?

I had no answers because I had no idea why the queen had taken the older children away, or what would happen to them, or whether they would be back, or why she had completely ignored her two youngest children. Her actions seemed arbitrary and inexcusable, but she was the queen and I supposed there must be some rhyme or reason to it. I had heard much mention of the Duke of Burgundy and his boastful nickname Jean the Fearless, seen Michele's anguish at the sudden talk of her marriage and gathered that Chartres was their destination, but that was the sum of it. I was as mystified as the children. Perhaps it was significant that we all avoided making mention of the screaming man.

Once I'd tucked them up, cuddling each other in one truckle bed, I went to seek guidance from the governess and the tutor, but there was no sign of them. Significantly I found their chamber doors standing open and, on entering, the chests and guarderobes empty. Madame la Bonne and Monsieur le Clerc had packed up and gone and, on further investigation, so too had the latest donkeys, for their meagre bundles of belongings were also missing. I had not grasped then what I soon discovered; that having inherited Burgundy, Flanders and Artois on his father's death the previous year, Jean the Fearless had now set his sights on France and was heading for Paris, scheming to rule in the mad king's name through his son the dauphin, thus ousting the cosy regime of the queen and the Duke of Orleans.

I felt completely out of my depth. Only hours before I had been a sleepy nursemaid in a sun-baked garden and now I was alone with two of the king's children and with little notion of exactly what had happened to the others. Who could I turn to for advice? Would I be blamed for the disappearance of the three older children? Did anyone in authority even know they were missing? Was there anyone in authority still in the palace? It may sound odd, but I felt an urgent need to settle my feelings of panic with some pretence at normality, so I took my basket of mending and sat down in the window of the main nursery to catch the last of the daylight and await developments.

Tired though they were, the little ones could not sleep and before long they appeared hand in hand, eyes enormous in solemn pinched faces. In their crumpled white chemises, they looked like the waifs of the wood from one of their favourite fairytales.

'We are frightened, Mette. Please tell us a story,' Catherine begged.

My heart ached for them. Abandoning the garment I was mending, I opened my arms and pulled them both onto my lap. For a few moments we clung together and gazed out of the open window at the muddy, drought-shrivelled stretch of the Seine which had carried the other children away. The evening sun cast gloomy shadows down the tree-lined banks while across the river on the Île St Louis, weary peasants were stacking corn stooks at the end of a long day's harvesting. There was a lump in my throat as I started the familiar tale of St Margaret and the dragon.

I had just reached the part where the saint tames the fire-breathing beast by raising the Holy Cross when we were suddenly assailed by the sound of manic laughter, harsh and insistent and impossible to ignore. Who knew what new

54

and weird delusion had stirred the poor mad king, now back in his oubliette, but the intrusion of his insane laughter into our cosy little world was like a leper's clapper rattling in a hushed church. Both the children screwed up their faces and covered their ears with their hands, but after a minute Catherine took her hands away and asked, 'Is that the man from the garden, Mette? Is that the king?'

I shook my head, dismayed that she had obviously heard more than I thought of the minder's words. 'Who can tell, my little one? It is a nasty noise anyway. But we can run away from it. Come with me!'

I gathered them up and swept them downstairs to Madame la Bonne's abandoned chamber. Her big tester bed had heavy velvet curtains, which I drew closely around us. As we huddled together in the flickering light of an oil lamp, I made up a story pretending we were fugitives who had sought sanctuary in a secret chapel where only God could find us. The warmth and intimacy of the curtained bed with its feather pillows and fur-lined covers seemed to comfort them for, royal though they were, they had never experienced such luxury and at least the thick hangings deadened the noise from outside. There was no more mention of the manic laughter or the screaming man.

I could find no comfort myself however. When the children had fallen asleep and the lamp had spluttered and died, I lay between them in the stifling darkness, wide-eyed and rigid with fear. Echoes of the king's cackle summoned nightmare images of the tavern stories Jean-Michel had relayed, of winged demons sent flitting through the night by sorcerers. I imagined flocks of malevolent creatures clinging to the bed hangings, carrying the taint of madness on their breath and infecting the black shadows. Convinced that their very breath could send me mad, I buried myself in the bedclothes muttering a string of Aves. It was hours before I slept.

5

The terrors of the night were nothing compared with the horror of waking. Jerked out of sleep by a loud metallic clang, I opened my eyes just as the curtains were hauled back by an armoured figure brandishing a naked blade. My shrill scream was underscored by the panic-stricken wails of the children who instinctively dived behind me into the protective pile of Madame la Bonne's pillows. I am not brave, but in that instant anger overcame my fear and I reared up like a spitting she-cat to confront our assailant. What a pathetic sight that must have been – rumpled linen versus burnished steel!

'In here, my lord!' yelled the anonymous intruder, his dagger aimed at my throat.

I recoiled, clutching at the yawning neck of my chemise and demanding divine protection and information in one hoarse, garbled screech. 'God save us – who are you – what do you want?'

'Calm yourself, Madame,' the man advised. 'His grace of Burgundy would speak with you.'

Even had I dared, there was no opportunity to protest that this was hardly a convenient moment to receive the noble duke, for in that instant an even more terrifying figure parted the curtains at the foot of the bed with a movement so violent it tore the hooks from their rail. His grace of Burgundy, framed in blood-red velvet. I let out another scream.

Encased to the neck in black and gold armour, his presence loomed like an incarnation of the demons of the night. The very smell of him seemed to rob the air of life; not the natural odour of male sweat, but a sweet cloying scent, like rotting fruit. And his face matched his armour, dark in every way; expression grim, complexion swarthy, grey eyes deep-socketed, cheeks shadowed with several days' growth of beard, black brows thick and bristling and a nose hooked like a meat-cleaver over a fleshy, purple mouth.

'Where is the dauphin?' this demon demanded, peering past me at the small legs and feet protruding from the pillows. 'Who are you hiding there? Take a look, Deet.'

The man with the dagger flung me roughly aside and hauled Catherine from her refuge. The brave little girl kicked and fought, but she was as powerless as a fly in a web. Cursing, the knight dumped her at arm's length and reached for Charles, who immediately set up a scream of astonishing volume.

'That is not the dauphin,' observed the duke, raising his voice above the din and eyeing Charles with distaste. 'Too small. You, Madame, tell me immediately, where is the dauphin? Deet, help her to think.'

To my relief, I saw the dagger sheathed but then I felt my arm almost wrenched from my shoulder as I was dragged off the bed and thrown to the floor at the duke's feet. The pain was no more fierce however than his basilisk glare. In that split second he seemed like evil incarnate and I did not believe that such an ogre could have the best interests of the royal children at heart, certainly not more than even the most neglectful mother, as the queen undoubtedly was. Inwardly I resolved to tell him nothing and, in any case, I was trembling with fear and tongue-tied.

'Well?' His gold-tipped metal foot tapped. 'I know who you are, Madame, and your family is no friend to Burgundy, so it would be foolish to make me lose my temper.'

It was suddenly clear to me that the duke had concluded that I was Madame la Bonne. It was an understandable mistake, given that I had been found in the governess' quarters and even in her bed, but it was not an identity I wished to own to, especially in present circumstances.

'I am not Madame la Bonne, sir,' I hastened to reveal, panic restoring my voice. No wonder the governess had fled. God alone knew how she and her family had offended Burgundy, but I did not wish to carry the blame for it. 'She has left. I do not know why, but when I looked for her and the tutor yesterday evening they were nowhere to be found.'

The duke began to pace the floor. For a moment I feared he was not going to believe me, but something obviously convinced him of my ignoble roots. He began muttering, thinking aloud.

'Left, has she? I am not surprised. She fled because she is corrupt and greedy, like all the queen's ladies. However, she will be found and punished for abandoning her charges. But she is unimportant. What I need to know immediately is the whereabouts of the dauphin.' His voice had risen and his pacing had brought him back to me. Almost casually, he grabbed a handful of my hair and jerked my head upwards, forcing me to look at him. 'You can tell me that can you not, whoever you are?'

The burst of pain brought tears to my eyes and I thought my scalp would split. 'No!' I yelped. 'I cannot. I am only a nursemaid. The queen came with the Duke of Orleans and took the dauphin and his brother and sister. I do not know where they went.'

'I do not believe you,' he snarled, hurling me away from him so that I cannoned into the steel-clad legs of the other man. I felt a fearful crunch in my neck as my head whipped back and tears of pure terror began to course down my cheeks.

'Do not do that!' Through blurred vision I saw Catherine hurl herself at the duke's armoured leg, hammering at the gleaming metal with her fists. I shouted a warning and scrambled forward, but I could not reach her before he did, bending to snatch her up and hold her level with his face, her bare feet dangling helplessly. She was stunned into silence, mesmerised by his predatory glare.

'You are a little shrew, are you not, Mademoiselle?' he hissed, eyes glinting with anger.

'Do not hurt her!' I screamed in desperation. 'She is only a child.'

The duke shot me a look of cold venom. 'When the hawk swoops, it does not ask the age of its prey,' he snapped. His eyes drilled into Catherine's, his hooked beak almost touching her nose. 'Now, little shrew, *you* tell me where your brother is. I take it you are the dauphin's sister?'

Catherine stuck out her chin, her mouth clamped shut. His cruel treatment had brought out her stubborn streak and I feared the result. 'She is not yet four, my lord,' I protested. 'How can she know anything? These two are only babes.'

The duke sneered. 'I have children and I know that they understand a great deal more than you think.' He shook Catherine so that her head wobbled alarmingly. 'Is that not so, little shrew? You know where they have gone.'

'Chartres!' Charles' high lisping treble rendered the word almost indecipherable, but it diverted the duke's attention and he dropped Catherine in a heap on the floor beside me. I clutched her to me, sobbing.

Now the ducal gaze focused on Charles whose thumb, as always in times of stress, had gone to his mouth. The duke bent and wrenched it out, gripping the small wrist so fiercely that Charles let out a wail of anguish. 'Silence!' roared Burgundy, pushing the little boy towards his armoured companion. 'Did he say Chartres, Deet? Make him say the word again.'

'No!' I screamed as the man pulled Charles towards him. 'He did say Chartres. The queen said they were going to Chartres! That's all we know.'

With sudden and vicious momentum, the duke swung round and swiped my cheek with the back of his hand in its studded gauntlet. Stars exploded in my head and I fell back against the bed, gasping with shock. 'You stupid slut!' I heard him shout through the ringing in my ears. 'Why didn't you tell us that straight away?' He began to issue orders to the man he had called Deet. 'Get the men mounted immediately. We can be sure that the queen will not hurry. She will have rested overnight at Melun. But they must *not* reach Chartres. We will cut them off at Étampes. Go, man! I will join you very soon.'

My head was still spinning but I managed to haul myself to my feet as Charles was abruptly released and ran to my arms. My cheek was burning and the unfamiliar taste of blood was in my mouth where my teeth had cut the inner flesh.

Behind his hawk-like beak, Jean of Burgundy's grey eyes glittered, fixed not on my face but on my unlaced chemise and my breasts, scarcely covered by the thin cloth. I felt blood dribble from my cheek and mingle with the sweat running cold between them.

'Let that be a lesson to you, slut,' he sneered, moving towards me.

His gaze was like an obscene caress and my skin crawled. Slowly, he removed the gauntlet from the hand which had struck me and from its bristling surface he flicked a scrap of what I assumed was my own torn flesh. Without the glove I could see that his hand was white and soft and I cringed, thinking he was going to grope me. The thick, sweet smell of him was nauseating.

'Name, slut?' The repetition of the insult was effective in reducing me to an object, without free will.

I heard myself say in a croaky whisper, 'Guillaumette,' and immediately regretted it. Why had I told him the truth? The unusual name marked me out. Why hadn't I said Jeanne or Marie and been lost in the crowd?

His let his hand hover over me and a cruel smile twisted his lips as he relished my mounting terror and disgust. Then, instead of reaching downwards to grope my breasts as I feared he would, he let his fingers linger briefly on my battered cheek. When he withdrew them, they were red with my blood. My gorge rose as I watched him push them one by one into his mouth and suck them clean. His action struck me as so revolting that it was all I could do not to vomit over his steel-clad feet.

'Not noble blood but sweet enough,' he conceded, smacking his lips. 'Unfortunately I have no time to savour it now but I will remember – Guillaumette, the slut . . .'

He slipped the gauntlet back on and his mood immediately became businesslike. 'There will be changes here. The king's affairs must be put in order. I will leave a guard on these royal children. See that they do not venture out.' Then he turned on his heel and was gone. His threat echoed in my head, 'I will remember – Guillaumette . . .'

Catherine stared after him, her pretty little face twisted into an expression of loathing. 'Who is that man, Mette?' she asked in a thin, fierce voice.

'That is the Duke of Burgundy,' I told her, struggling to control my voice.

'He is a bad man,' she responded, her voice rising in passion. 'I hate him, hate him, *hate* him!'

Young though she was, I often wondered if Catherine had a premonition about the Duke of Burgundy. It was many years before she was to encounter him again, but his image was to haunt her dreams as vividly as mine.

*

To my surprise, most of the palace servants saw Burgundy's arrival as a boon and it must be said that he did impose some much-needed order. The sight of the Burgundian cross of St Andrew fluttering on every tower and gatehouse alongside the royal lilies made me feel distinctly uneasy, but it held no sinister overtones for the mass of scullions, chamberlains and varlets, who were only too happy to start pocketing regular wages for a change. In the nursery we even received a visit from a household clerk enquiring after our needs and, amazingly, within hours the children received new clothes, two tire-women arrived to scrub the floors and stairways and decent food and hot water were brought to us regularly. Several luxury items were also brought to the children, including a beautiful miniature harp which had apparently been sent to Charles months ago by his godfather, the Duke of Berry. It seemed that Burgundy's agents must have caught up with la Bonne and le Clerc and recovered the goods they had looted. Having felt the violence of the duke's anger myself, I shuddered to think what punishment had been meted out to that thieving pair.

The children liked the new clothes and the better food and didn't associate them with the terrifying encounter in the governess' chamber. They hardly noticed that there was now a double guard on the nursery tower and that armed soldiers shadowed us whenever we ventured out for fresh air, but I certainly noticed these things, for I became a virtual prisoner, unable to visit Jean-Michel or my parents. Consequently, it was some time before I discovered what had been going on in the outside world.

Had I known that the three older royal children had never reached Chartres, but had been abducted from their mother's procession and forced into Burgundian marriages, I might have been more prepared for what was to come. In the event, perhaps ignorance was bliss, because when she asked about her sister and brothers I wasn't able to tell Catherine that Louis had been forced into a binding betrothal with Burgundy's daughter Marguerite and had since been confined in the Louvre with Burgundian tutors, while his sister and brother had been whisked away to live with the children to whom Burgundy had matched them; Michele in Artois with the duke's only son Philippe, and Jean in Hainault with Burgundy's niece, Jacqueline, his sister's daughter. However, I also heard that, far from considering themselves beaten, the queen and the Duke of Orleans had raised an army to confront Burgundy outside Paris. The king remained mad and confined, and the spectre of civil war stalked the land.

For the next three weeks I lived on tenterhooks, happy to have sole charge of Catherine and her little brother, but daily expecting a new governess to arrive and take over in the nursery. One September morning I believed that moment had arrived.

Little Charles had never been much of an eater. Who could blame him, given the awful slops he had been offered during most of his short life? I was encouraging him to finish his breakfast bowl of fresh curds sweetened with honey – a new and delectable treat – when there was a commotion on the tower stair. The door of the day nursery flew open to admit a richly dressed lady shadowed by a large female servant in apron and coif, not unlike my own. I sprang to my feet and hovered protectively over the children, who looked up in fright.

'I am Marie, Duchess of Bourbon,' the newcomer announced, without smile or greeting and only the merest glance to show that her words were addressed to me.

I backed away and dropped to my knees, my apprehension rising rapidly as she continued speaking. 'His grace of Burgundy has requested me to make arrangements for the care of the king's children.'

The mention of Burgundy rang loud alarm bells in my head. 'Y-yes, Madame,' I stuttered.

Catherine heard the name Burgundy and the tremor in my voice and her gaze swivelled in panic from me to the grand visitor. 'No!' she cried, instinctively sensing danger. 'No, Mette. Make them go away.'

Marie of Bourbon glided forward and knelt by Catherine's stool. With a smile and a touch she tried to reassure the trembling child. 'Do not be frightened, my little one,' she cooed. 'There is nothing to fear. Your name is Catherine, is it not? Well, Catherine, you are a very lucky girl. You are going to a beautiful abbey where kind nuns will look after you and you will be safe. You will like that, will you not?'

Catherine was not fooled by a soft voice and a tender touch. 'No! No, I want to stay with Mette.' Like a whirlwind, she jumped off her stool and ran to my side, closely followed by little Charles, curds dribbling down his chin.

Still on my knees, I put my arms around them, tears springing to my eyes. 'I am sorry, Madame,' I gulped, avoiding the lady's gaze. 'There has been much upheaval in their lives lately and I am all they know.'

Marie of Bourbon rose and her tone became brisk as her patience grew thin. 'That may be, but these are no ordinary children. They have been woefully neglected and it is time they were given the training they need and deserve. I will be taking Charles with me now. He is my father's godson and he is to live in his household and receive the proper education for a prince. You are to prepare Catherine for her journey to Poissy Abbey. She will be leaving tomorrow morning.' She waved an imperious hand at her servant. 'Get the boy. We are leaving.'

Before he realised what was happening, Charles was swept up in a pair of sturdy arms. He set up a shrill screech and began to kick and struggle, but the woman had been picked for her strength and his puny efforts were stolidly ignored.

'No! Put him down!' Catherine screamed and ran at the woman, swinging on her arm and trying unsuccessfully to dislodge her brother. With tears of fear and frustration, the little girl turned to me. 'Mette, don't let them take him! Help him!'

Miserably, I shook my head and wrung my hands. What could I do? Who was I against the might of Burgundy, Bourbon and Berry? Our last sight of Charles was of his agonised, curd-spattered face and his outstretched hands as his captor descended the stairs but the sound of his screams persisted, punctuated by Catherine's sobs. Marie of Bourbon's cheeks were flushed and her expression grim as she stood in the doorway and gave me final instructions, raising her voice above the commotion.

'I will come for Catherine at the same time tomorrow. See

that she is prepared to leave. I do not want any more scenes like this. They are vulgar and unpleasant and not good for the children.'

'Yes, Madame.'

I had bowed my head dutifully, but my deference disguised a mind whirling with wild rebellious notions. Could I whisk Catherine off to the bake house and raise her as my own child? Could I flee with her to some remote village? Could I take her to the queen? But even as these ideas flashed through my mind, I knew that no such course of action was feasible. Catherine was the king's daughter, a crown asset. Stealing her would be treason. We would be hunted down and I would be put to death and how would that help her, or my own family? To say nothing of myself! As for taking her to the queen – I did not even know where she was, let alone how to get there.

I suppose I should have been grateful that we had another day together, that Catherine had not also been carried instantly to a closed litter, while Burgundy's guards turned deaf ears to her heart-rending screams. At least I had a few hours to prepare her for our separation and to try and convince her that it was for the best.

How do you persuade a little girl of not quite four that what is about to happen is *not* the worst thing in the world when, like her, you completely believe that it *is*? How was I to make my voice say things that my heart utterly denied? I had heard cows bellowing in the fields when their calves were taken from them and I could feel a thunderous bellow welling up inside me; one that, if I let it out, would surely be heard throughout the whole kingdom. But I knew that I could not – must not – if I was to help Catherine face up to her inevitable future.

At first she wept and put her hands over her ears, screwing up her eyes as she cried, 'No, Mette, no. I won't leave you. They c-cannot make me. I will stay here and you can f-fetch Charles back and we will be happy, like we were b-before.'

I held her tightly in my arms. She was shaking and hiccupping. Wretched though I felt, I had to deny her. 'No, Catherine. You must understand that you cannot stay here and that you and I cannot be together any more. You have to go and learn how to be a princess.'

She broke away from me and started shouting indignantly, 'But why? You are my nurse. You have always looked after me. I thought you loved me, Mette.'

Ah, dear God, it was soul-destroying! Loved her? I more than loved her. She was an essential part of my being. Losing her would be like losing my hands or tearing out my heart, but I had to tell her that although I loved her, I had to let her go. She was not my daughter but the king's and she had to do what her father wished.

'But the king is mad,' she cried. 'We saw him in the garden. He does not care about me. He does not even know who I am.'

Out of the mouths of babes . . .! It was heartbreakingly true. He and his queen may have loved Dauphin Charles, the golden boy who had died, but none of the rest of their surviving offspring could be said to have benefited from one morsel of parental concern.

'But God cares,' I responded, grasping at straws. 'God loves you and you will be going to His special house where His nuns will look after you and keep you safe.'

'Does He love me as much as you do?' Her breath was shuddery and in her little flushed face her eyes were round and questioning. My darling little Catherine. Those enchanting, deep sapphire eyes seemed to hold the entire meaning of my life, even reddened and swollen as they were. The image of them would stay with me for ever.

'Oh yes,' I lied. Call it blasphemy if you like, but I swear that the Almighty could not have loved that little girl as much as I did. 'He loves us all and you must remember His commandment – the one about honouring your father and your mother, which means you must do as they say.'

'But that lady said it was the Duke of Burgundy who sent her. He is not my father. I hate him. I do not have to do as he says, do I?'

Sometimes, I thought, she was far too bright for her own good.

Involuntarily, I touched my cheek, which would always bear the mark of Burgundy's vicious, studded gauntlet and swallowed hard on the bile his name inspired. 'Well, yes, Catherine you do, because he is your father's cousin and helps him to rule his kingdom.'

I could sense her desperate resistance crumbling. Her shoulders drooped and her lower lip began to tremble. 'What about my mother? Does she want me to go away to this place?'

Who knew what the queen wanted? I had heard that she and Orleans had raised an army, but so far no other news of her had reached my ears.

'I am sure the queen agrees with the king,' I answered lamely, casting about in my mind for some way of distracting her. 'Now, supposing we go out for a bit? Shall we go and light a candle to the Virgin and ask her to protect and keep us until we meet again?' I hoped the guards would not stop us going to the chapel and that its peaceful atmosphere might calm us both. I might pray for a miracle, I thought, but in my heart I knew that not even the Blessed Marie would be able to save us from Marie of Bourbon.

I was so proud of my darling girl when she took her leave the next morning. She and I had already said our farewells, exchanging a long embrace and many tearful kisses before I laced her into her new, high-waisted blue gown, ready for the journey. Then I brushed out her long, fine, flaxen hair for the last time and tied the ribbons of a white linen cap under her chin, trying not to let my hands shake and transmit my own churning emotions to her. When the Duchess of Bourbon held out her hand to lead Catherine to the waiting litter, she looked the perfect royal princess; obedient, sweet and decorous. Only two bright pink patches on her cheeks indicated the misery and turmoil beneath the calm façade. Looking back, I think the diamond quality of her character was revealed in that moment.

At the door of the litter the grand lady turned to me with a gracious smile. 'I believe your name is Guillaumette,' she said. 'For one who can have no knowledge of courtly manners, you have done well by the princess. However, I am sure you understand that there is much for her to learn that you could never teach her. Now you may go to the grand master's chamber and collect what is due to you. The nursery is to be closed. Goodbye.'

As the litter swung out of sight through an archway, I longed to run after it and shout, 'I do not want what is due to me! I do not want your blood money! No payment can be recompense for losing my darling girl!'

But I did not. I stood, frozen like a statue, praying. I prayed that Catherine knew my love for her was unconditional, knew that it would never fade and that whenever – if ever – fate brought us together again, she would remember her old nurse Mette. I was nineteen years old and I felt like a crone of ninety.

PART TWO

Hôtel de St Pol, Paris

The Shades of Agincourt

1415–18

6

'I have news that may lift your spirits,' said Jean-Michel as we lay in bed, whispering so as not to wake our children who slept in the opposite corner of the cramped chamber.

'News of what?' I responded dully, too tired to rouse much interest. I was always tired these days – had been ever since returning to the Hôtel de St Pol, after years away. Many highs and lows had led to Jean-Michel and I sharing a bed together in the royal palace and our lives were very different now.

For over eight years I had raised my children in my old home under the Grand Pont. The summer after leaving the nursery, I gave birth to a baby boy and, thanks be to God, he lived. We called him Henri-Luc after both his grandfathers, but he was always just Luc to me. Jean-Michel completed his apprenticeship at the palace stables and was appointed a charettier, driving supply wagons between Paris and the royal estates, which meant he was away a great deal. He was allocated family quarters at the palace, but my mother became increasingly crippled by painful swollen joints and I was needed at the bakery, which suited me fine, because for a time the Duke of Burgundy had kept his hands on the reins at the Hôtel de St Pol and after my terrifying encounter I preferred to stay as far from him as possible.

But city life wasn't easy. No one lived in cosy harmony with their neighbours any more, for after Burgundy's abduction of the royal children, Paris had become a sad and vicious place, its people divided into factions according to which of the royal affinities they supported or were dependent upon. Locked in their battle for power, the Dukes of Burgundy and Orleans lobbied and bribed all the various guilds and in the church and university. As a result, split loyalties tore society apart, causing a succession of riots and murders, burnings and lynchings, which brought terror to the streets. Officially the ailing King Charles still sat on the throne, but for long periods he was unable to command the loyalty of his lieges and, while attempting to rule in his stead, the queen played one duke off against another – as rumour had it both in and out of bed.

It must be said, looking back, that Catherine was well out of it, tucked safely away in her convent in the country, but I missed her like a limb. I knew I should forget her and that I would most likely never see her again, but every new stage of my own children's lives reminded me of her. I loved Alys and Luc, of course I did, and as they grew older it was obvious that they loved me. Under their grandparents' roof and with Jean-Michel coming and going, they were part of an outwardly tight-knit family unit, loyal to each other and loving, but for me they were also the source of an intense heartache, which I could confide in no one, for I knew that no one would understand or condone such maternal ambivalence.

Gradually my mother's illness grew so bad that in the morning she could barely haul herself out of bed and spent most of the day sitting behind the open shutter of the shop telling me what to do and finding fault with my efforts. I knew she could not help it because the terrible pain in her swollen joints made her cry out in agony, but I found it hard to keep my temper with her and I have to confess I often failed. That she only ever scolded me, not my father or the children, did not help. Eventually she started taking a special remedy, which I would fetch for her from the apothecary. It was hard to believe how a syrup made from poppies could affect someone the way that potion affected my mother, but from the day she started taking it she was more or less lost to us. At first I was so grateful that it relieved her pain that I ignored her total lassitude and the vacant look in her eyes, but after several weeks I grew worried and secretly substituted another remedy. However, when she started shaking and vomiting and screaming for what she called her 'angel's breath', I was forced to give in. One night I think she must have swallowed too much of it, or else the mixture was tainted in some way, because my father woke up to find her dead beside him.

We were both devastated, remembering the strong woman she had once been, but we were also thankful that her suffering was over. In some ways she was lucky to die in her bed, for at that time life in Paris was perilous and cheap. People were murdered simply for wearing the wrong colour hood or walking down the wrong alley. Bodies were found in the streets every day with their throats slit or their skulls cracked like eggs.

One freezing November night it was none other than the Duke of Orleans himself who was hacked to death, set upon by a masked gang in the Rue Barbette behind the Hôtel de St Antoine. He had been a frequent visitor at a mansion there, in which a lady, widely believed to be the queen, had been living for several weeks. As royal guards swarmed through the streets seeking the duke's murderers, news spread that the corpse's right hand had been severed at the wrist. Blue-hooded Burgundians declared this to be proof positive that Orleans had been in league with the devil, who always claimed the right hand of his acolytes. White-hooded Orleanists maintained, meanwhile, that the only devil involved in this murder was the Duke of Burgundy who, rather giving credence to this claim, abruptly quitted his coveted position of power beside the king and fled to Artois, destroying strategic bridges behind him. That left a power vacuum, which for the citizens of Paris was the most dangerous situation of all. In the gutters the body count mounted nightly.

My father knew the baker who delivered bread to the heavily guarded house in the Rue Barbette and it was he who told us that the lady the Duke of Orleans had visited so frequently and foolhardily had given birth to a baby and had only just survived. After the murder she too fled, no one knew how or where. The house was just suddenly empty. A few weeks later, a royal pronouncement told us that Queen Isabeau had given birth to another son, stating that the boy had been baptised Philippe and died soon afterwards.

My father and I wore brown hoods and kept our mouths

shut. We managed to stay alive, but it was a daily struggle to keep the ovens fired. The brushwood we burned had always been collected by fuellers in the countryside, but desperate gangs of bandits and cut-throats made the gathering of it too dangerous. Flour supplies were another problem as factional armies were constantly on the move around Paris, purloining food stocks as they marched. Fortunately, Jean-Michel was often able to 'divert' sheaves of dry furze and sacks of flour to the bakery from supplies shipped in by barge to the royal palace. Yes, I am afraid we took to filching royal assets as freely as Madame la Bonne had done. It was the only way to survive.

After years of scheming and struggling to keep the bakery going, a sudden apoplexy carried off my father and even before we had buried him, the Guild of Master Bakers callously informed me that our license was revoked. It was pointless to protest. Women were not admitted into the guild and only guild members could bake bread. Although, as my father's sole heir, I owned the ovens, I could not use them, nor could I safely live alone with my children in lawless Paris. So, lacking any choice, I let the house and bakery to one of our former apprentices and brought Alys and Luc to live with their father at the Hôtel de St Pol.

I was far from happy to be back, but at least Burgundy was no longer in charge. By then the dauphin – little Prince Louis who had dropped the hairy caterpillar down my bodice – had turned sixteen and taken his seat on the Royal Council, aided and abetted by his much older cousin, the Duke of Anjou. Between them they managed to prevent Burgundy and his cohorts from making any successful moves on Paris, but it wasn't all good because the queen had clung onto her position and she and the dauphin had to share the regency. It was a daily feature of life at St Pol to see red-faced emissaries scuttling between the Queen's House and the dauphin's apartments, making futile attempts at building bridges between a mother and son who were constantly at loggerheads.

Not that I was one to talk. I have to admit that it wasn't all peace and harmony between me and Jean-Michel. After the death of my mother, I had grown used to being mistress of my own home and helping to run a business. Now I was once more on servant's wages and living in one damp, dark chamber with no grate and no garderobe. We peed in pots and had to use the reeking latrine ditch behind the stables. I grumbled constantly about my reduced circumstances, so no wonder Jean-Michel was glad to have news to cheer me up.

'Not news of what,' he countered. 'Of who. Of the Princess Catherine.'

I sat bolt upright, wide awake. 'Catherine! What about her? Tell me!'

Until he said her name I had not realised how starved I had been of her, my longing raw and secret, like a concealed ulcer.

'She is coming back to the Hôtel de St Pol.'

'When?' I nearly screeched, rearing round and shaking him by the shoulder. 'When, Jean-Michel?'

'Shh!' I could not see him in the dark, but I could sense the admonitory finger on his lips. 'Sweet Jesus! Simmer down, woman, and I will tell you. Quite soon, I think. One of the grand master's clerks was down at the stables today, making arrangements for her travel from Poissy Abbey.'

My mind was doing somersaults, but I tried to steady myself so that I could ponder this development. 'I wonder why she is coming back now. There must be a reason. My God, Jean-Michel, will you be involved?' There were occasions when he was called on to ride in the teams which carried the royal horse-litters.

'No, no. She is the king's daughter. There is to be a full escort – twenty knights and two hundred men-at-arms – too grand a job for me.' Jean-Michel reached out to pull me down beside him. 'I must find more things to get you excited,' he murmured, nuzzling my ear, and being by now full of pent-up feelings, I reciprocated. But after we had stoked the spark of passion to a blaze and zestfully quenched it, I lay wide-eyed, my mind spinning like a windmill in a gale.

A few weeks previously, an embassy from England had arrived at the French court. A cardinal and two bishops, no less, had ridden in with great pomp and show, parading through the city with banners flying, trailing a huge procession of knights and retainers eager to enjoy the sights and brothels of Paris. It was a surprise to see them come in peace, because up to then we had heard tell that the English king was mobilising to re-claim territories on this side of the Sleeve, which he considered belonged to England. Normandy, Poitou, Anjou, Guienne, Gascony, they were all on his list. I remember wondering why he did not just claim the whole of France, the way his great-grandfather had done. Being a staunch royalist, my mother had told me how seventy years ago King Edward III of England had tried to claim the French throne as the nearest male heir to his uncle, King Charles IV of France, who had been his mother's brother. But thirty years before that, in their own male interests no doubt, the grandees of Church and State had decided that women in France could not inherit land – pots and pans yes, horses, houses and gold yes, land no. They could not even pass land through their own blood line to their sons, pardieu! They called it Salic law, but my mother never explained why. Perhaps she did not know. Anyway, this law nullified King Edward's claim and put Catherine's great-grandfather on the French throne instead. Arguments over sovereignty had been rumbling between France and England ever since.

However, the present argument was not about who sat on what throne. This high-powered English embassy was apparently only interested in settling the dispute over territories, and in sealing the deal by acquiring a French wife for King Henry V of England, who was the great-grandson of Edward III. Well, you didn't have to be a genius to conclude that the return to court of our king's youngest and only unmarried daughter might have something to do with this. I decided there and then that if my darling Catherine was coming back to St Pol to be dangled before the King of England as a prospective bride, then she was going to need help – and who better to help her than her faithful old nursemaid?

Gone were the days when everything closed down if King Charles had a bad turn. From a powerful man with periodic delusions, he had dwindled into a predominantly childlike creature, only occasionally violently mad; a puppet-king to be manipulated by whoever guided his hand to sign the edicts. As a consequence, the palace was brimming with courtiers on the make, all looking to fill any official posts that might put them within reach of the pot of gold that was the royal treasury, which meant that accommodation was at a premium. If you lived in servants' quarters, you had to earn them and therefore our whole family was employed in the royal household, even Luc.

In fact, he was the happiest of all of us, for although he was only eight, he was in his element as a hound boy in the palace kennel. He had grown into a bony-kneed, cheeky-faced lad with an affinity for animals like his father and a stubborn streak like me. I had tried hard to teach him the rudiments of reading and writing, but with an ambition to be a huntsman, he could not see the point. Alys had taken to her letters easily, but now had little time to practice since she worked in the queen's wardrobe, where she hemmed linen from dawn till dusk. How she bore the tedium, I'll never know but she'd grown into a docile, long-suffering little maid and I consoled myself that seaming was better than steaming, which was my unhappy lot. Since females were banned from working in the bake house or kitchens, where I might have used my skills to their best advantage, I was forced to become an alewife – the lowest of the low. I was used to hard work and fermenting barley was no harder than baking bread, but it was different when it wasn't your own business.

The worst thing for me, living in the palace, was being constantly reminded of Catherine. I saw her face at the windows of the nursery tower, heard her laughter in the old rose garden and her footsteps on the flagstones of the chapel cloister. Only her imminent return looked set to stir me out of the deep, persistent melancholy I had been feeling without admitting it to myself.

The day after Jean-Michel dropped his bombshell, I went to the grand master's chamber in the King's House and, mercifully, my powers of persuasion did not desert me. Within minutes, the clerk charged with assembling staff for Catherine's new household had agreed that I was ideally suited for work as her tiring woman and arranged for my transfer from the palace brewery. I would be on familiar ground, for she had been allocated the very rooms in which she had spent the first years of her life. We were both going back to the nursery tower. My feet scarcely seemed to touch the ground as I sped to my new post, gloating over the fact that soon, very soon, I would once more be as close as any mother to the child of my breast.

The first-floor chamber of the tower, once Madame la Bonne's bedchamber, had been turned into a salon where Catherine and her companions would be able to read and embroider and entertain themselves and her visitors. The former governess' crimson-curtained bed had been long ago removed and the chamber walls were hung with rainbow silks and jewel-coloured tapestries. It was furnished with cushioned stools, polished chests and tables and a carved stone chimneypiece framing a deep hearth, where a blazing fire would keep the air a good deal warmer than it had ever been in the old days. It was while I was lighting this fire a few days later, that the door opened without warning and a young lady entered and stood staring at me.

Catherine! I sank to my knees, glad to do so as my legs had turned to jelly. Dumbstruck, I gazed up at a vision of loveliness, dressed in a cornflower-blue gown, her beautiful Madonna face framed by neat little horns of netted blond hair and a filmy white veil.

'Do not look at me, woman!' the vision snapped. 'I will not be gawped at by a servant.'

I flinched and lowered my eyes. A thousand times I had imagined a reunion with Catherine, but this reality jarred alarmingly. Everything looked as it should – the stylish velvet gown neatly trimmed with fur, the small oval face, the royal-blue eyes and the creamy complexion – but the sweet nature I remembered seemed to have vanished, the vibrant, loving spirit of the child had apparently withered into brittle pride. With a sinking heart I was forced to conclude that my darling, winsome girl had become a haughty mademoiselle.

'Who are you?' she demanded. 'What is your name?'

'Mette,' I replied, struggling to control my shock.

'Mette? Mette! That is not a name. What is your full name?'

I was prepared to forgive the fact that she had not known me by sight, but she had known my name as a toddling infant – surely she would not forget it. But I heard the cold scorn in her voice and I neither wanted nor dared to look up and see it in her eyes. Suddenly I was consumed with anger against the nuns of Poissy. What could they have done to destroy the gentle essence of my Catherine?

'Guillaumette,' I gulped and had to repeat the word to make it audible. 'Guillaumette.'

I risked a fleeting glance. Not a flicker of recognition.

'That is better. What you are doing here, Guillaumette?' The lady began to patrol the room, peering at its hangings and furnishings, viewing them without any visible sign of approval.

'I have been appointed your tiring woman, Mademoiselle. I thought you might need a fire after your journey,' I said meekly.

'In future, if you are needed you will be summoned,' she declared, fingering the thick embroidered canopy of a high-backed chair as if assessing its market worth. 'Servants should not loiter in royal apartments. Remember that. You may wait below in the ante-chamber.'

'Yes, Mademoiselle,' I murmured and scuttled for the door, as eager to leave as she clearly was to be rid of me.

I stumbled down the stairs in a state of disbelief. Of course I had considered it possible that Catherine might not remember me after such a long period of separation, bearing in mind how young she had been when we parted, but such an evident change in character was a tragedy. I felt as if my heart was being squeezed in a giant fist.

The ante-room where I had been ordered to wait was on the ground floor, off the main entrance. It had been a bare, cold room when Louis and Jean used to have their lessons there, but now there was a brazier to warm the draught from the door and a tapestry on one wall depicting a woodland scene, with benches arranged beneath. No candles had been lit however and only a few dusty beams of twilight slanted in through the narrow windows.

Such gloom echoed my mood. Angrily dashing tears from

my eyes, I cursed myself for being so foolish as to believe that my former nursling would automatically greet me with warmth and joy. She had been sent to Poissy to be educated as a princess and royalty was used to receiving personal service from noble retainers. Courtiers fought amongst themselves for the honour of pulling on the sovereign's hose or keeping the keys to his coffers. I knew that my duty as a menial servant was to be invisible, performing the grubbier tasks in my lady's absence and, if caught in the act, turning my face to the wall and scuttling out of sight. To gaze directly at a princess and expect her to remember the affection she had shared with me as a child, had been to defy the social order. I might harbour a lifetime's love for the tiny babe I had suckled, but there was no rule which said she must return the sentiment. Quite the reverse, in fact. She was far more likely to have closed her mind to her neglected past and embraced her glittering present. Downcast, I nursed my injured feelings and contemplated a future which seemed once more joyless and bleak.

7

'Mette? It is Mette, is it not?'

I'd been huddled on a bench in the far corner of the ante-room, too wrapped in misery to look up when I heard someone open the door. Then the low, sweet voice startled me to my feet with such an acute pang of recognition it made my very bones tingle. A hooded figure stood hesitating in the doorway, the face in shadow.

'Yes, Mademoiselle. It is Mette,' I whispered, my hands flying to my breast where my heart was leaping and fluttering like a caged finch.

I caught a faint hint of indignation as she eased back her hood and asked, 'Do you not know me, Mette?'

'Oh dear God! Catherine!' Tears swamped my eyes and I must have swayed alarmingly, for she rushed across the room and I felt her arms go around me, supporting me as my knees buckled. We fell together onto the bench.

Even the smell of her was familiar; the soft, warm, delicate, rosy smell of her skin was like incense to me. How could I have mistaken another for her? Every inch of my body knew her without looking, like a ewe knows her lamb on a dark hillside or a hen knows her chick in a shut-tered coop.

'You are here,' she crooned. 'I felt sure you would be. Oh, Mette, I have longed for this day.'

We drew back from our close embrace to study each other. The curves of her brow and lips were like glowing reflections of my dreams and even the gloom of the chamber could not leech the colour from those brilliant blue eyes. I gazed into their sapphire depths and felt myself submerged in love.

'I have crawled on my knees to St Jude,' I cried, my voice breaking on a sob, 'asking him to bring us back together, but I never thought it would happen.'

Catherine gave a little smile. 'St Jude – patron of lost causes. That was a good idea. And, you see, it worked.' She shook her head in wonder, her eyes still roaming my features. 'I have seen your face in my dreams a thousand times, Mette. Other girls at the convent pined for their mothers, but I pined for my Mette. And now here you are.' Her arms slid around my neck and her soft lips pressed my cheek. 'We must never be parted again.'

Her words were like balm to my soul. During those long years when I had secretly kept her image locked in my heart, she had also cherished mine. She was the child of my breast and I was the mother of her dreams. I could have crouched in that shadowy corner for ever, feeling her breath on my cheek, our hearts beating together.

'Ah, you are *here*, Princesse. This lady said you had arrived.'

There were two figures outlined in the doorway against the light of the hall, but it was the aggrieved tones of the lady I would never forgive myself for mistaking for Catherine that shattered our idyll. Whoever she was, she came rushing forward, clearly horrified at finding the princess in close embrace with a servant. 'For shame that this impudent woman should accost you, Mademoiselle! Let me have her removed. I fear she does not know her place.'

With her back to the door, Catherine rolled her eyes, gave my hand a reassuring squeeze and smothered a little giggle; that blessed giggle which had echoed in my head down the years. Then she stood up and turned to face the outraged newcomer. The real Princess Catherine was dressed more plainly – a drab hood and travelling mantle covering a dark robe – than the girl I had thought to be her, yet there was something in her carriage which made the haughty creature in her fashionable attire fall back.

'On the contrary, she knows her place well. Her place is with me,' my nursling told her, casting a hand back to encourage me to rise. 'Her name is Guillaumette. Who are you?'

The haughty girl sank into a courtly obeisance; a skilled crouch which I presumed was of precisely the right depth to honour the daughter of the king. 'Forgive me, Mademoiselle. My name is Bonne of Armagnac. The queen has appointed me your principal lady in waiting. She sent me to welcome you and to command you to attend her as soon as you have recovered from your journey.'

Catherine turned to me with an expression of exaggerated surprise. 'Do you hear that, Mette?' Her voice had suddenly acquired a crystal hardness which startled me. 'My mother wishes to see me. There is a first time for everything.' Then she stretched out her hand to the other girl, who still hovered uncertainly in the doorway, gesturing her forward. 'Agnes, this is Guillaumette – my Mette about whom you have heard so much. Mette, this is my dear friend Agnes de Blagny, who has bravely agreed to accompany me to court. She and I have been close companions for the last four years, ever since Agnes came to Poissy abbey after she lost her mother.'

Agnes de Blagny was dressed like Catherine in a simple kirtle and over-mantle, with a plain white veil. I assumed it to be some sort of school habit worn by all the abbey pupils, but somehow Agnes did not wear it with the same easy elegance as her royal friend. She looked swamped and nervous, but she returned my smile with a shy one of her own.

'There is no time to linger down here, Princesse!' An older and more forceful female presence bustled into the room stirring dust off the flagstones with her flowing fur-lined mantle. 'Court attire has been prepared for you. We will help you dress to meet the queen.'

Fittingly, it had been the Duchess of Bourbon who had fetched Catherine from Poissy, just as she had delivered her there nearly ten years before, and it was she who now made a brisk entrance, greeted Bonne of Armagnac graciously, gave me a dismissive glance, then swept all the young ladies off to Catherine's new bedchamber, the room that had once been a day nursery but which was now transformed by silken cushions and hangings and some fabulous flower-strewn Flemish tapestries.

'Do not go away, Mette,' Catherine had whispered as she

reluctantly left my side. Nothing could have made me leave, but I thought it prudent to keep a low profile, so I took up position on the stair just beyond the entrance to her bedchamber, carefully hidden by a turn in the spiral, and waited patiently, rendered impervious to the cold draughts by the knowledge that I was only a few steps from my life's love.

When I next saw her, I might have been forgiven for not recognising her. She was encased in a weighty jewel-encrusted gown and mantle, her head crowned with gold and stiffened gauze. The stair was hardly wide enough to accommodate her voluminous skirts and the two noble ladies were too busy assisting her descent to notice me peering around the central pillar. The brief glimpse I had of Catherine's face showed me rouged cheeks, stained lips and a wary, closed expression. In less time than it took a priest to say mass, they had turned my sweet girl into a painted doll. Agnes had been found a simpler court costume and scampered after the grand ladies like a little mouse. I did not think the timid school friend would make much of a mark at Queen Isabeau's court.

I had plenty to occupy me as I waited for Catherine's return. The chamber bore all the signs of a major upheaval. Her travelling clothes had been flung to the floor, brushes, combs and hair-pins were scattered on dressing-chests and pots of face-paints and powders had spattered polished surfaces. I set about restoring the chamber to the pristine condition in which I had left it and preparing for the return of what I was sure would be a drained and exhausted Catherine, lighting candles and setting glowing coals in a hot box to warm the bed. Guessing (correctly as it turned out) that the queen would have dined and would not think to offer Catherine any refreshment, I also set some sweet wine and milk to curdle near the fire and put out some wafers. As I worked, I tried to imagine what the conversation would be like between mother and daughter, meeting as strangers.

The candles had burned down several inches when a noise like birds twittering roused me from my sentinel stool. It was the high-pitched chatter of excited young ladies drifting up the stair and I swiftly retreated to my previous hiding place. Catherine's retinue had obviously expanded and fortunately, as they tripped into the bedchamber, they left the door open, so I was able to hear Bonne of Armagnac's authoritative voice begin allocating various tasks concerning Catherine's toilette.

'With your permission, Mademoiselle, Marie and Jeanne will help you to undress whilst I secure your robes and jewels . . .'

Catherine's voice broke in, low and sweet but firm enough to silence her attendant. 'No, Mademoiselle Bonne. You do not have my permission. What I would like you to do is call Guillaumette. She is the one I need to help me.'

'Do you mean your tiring-woman, Mademoiselle?' Bonne protested. 'A menial cannot be trusted to handle your highness' court dress or safeguard your jewels! That is a task for someone of rank.'

I smiled at the steely determination audible behind Catherine's deceptively mild reply. 'Mette is not "a menial", as you put it, she is my nurse. When I was a child she was trusted with my life. I'm sure she can be trusted now with a few rags and baubles. Summon Guillaumette if you please.'

I heard my name called from the doorway and waited a timely minute before responding. Meanwhile Catherine was gently attempting to mollify her affronted lady-in-waiting. 'You are older and wiser than I, Mademoiselle Bonne, but I suspect that even you have a nurse who cared for you in childhood and who knows all your little ways . . .'

'Well, yes,' Bonne of Armagnac admitted reluctantly, 'but I thought . . .' Her voice trailed away uncertainly.

'. . . that mine would have long gone?' Catherine suggested gently. 'But you see my faithful Mette has not gone. She is here . . .' As indeed I was, entering the salon exactly on cue and dropping humbly to my knee inside the door, head bowed to deflect the angry glare of Mademoiselle Bonne. '. . . and I have decided that she and she alone will have full charge in my bedchamber.'

I had to pinch myself to remember that she was not yet fourteen. I sent up a silent prayer of thanks to St Catherine, for it was surely she who had inspired this combination of sweetness and obstinacy in her namesake.

Peeping under the edge of my coif I watched Catherine stifle a yawn and say wearily to the assembled bevy of young ladies, 'I am very tired. There will be much to do tomorrow. The queen seems to have commissioned half the master-craftsmen in Paris to fit me out for court life and I shall need all your advice on the latest fashions. So now I will bid you goodnight and I know you will show kindness and assistance to my friend Agnes de Blagny who, as you know, will be one of your number.'

I felt quite sorry for the timorous Agnes as she was carried off by four court damsels who obviously found the prospect of a day spent picking clothes and jewels so enchanting that their excited chatter died only gradually away down the stair. Bonne of Armagnac remained behind however, sidling up to Catherine and dropping her voice to a confidential murmur. I tactfully retired to the hearth to re-heat the curdled posset, but I have sharp ears and easily caught the gist of her speech.

'Coming from the convent, Mademoiselle, you will need more than just advice on jewels and fashions. The ways of the court are complex. It is easy to make mistakes. The queen trusts me to help and guide you, just as my father helps and guides the dauphin.'

'No doubt she does.' There was a pause as Catherine gazed steadily at Bonne before continuing with the kind of regal assurance that I now believe cannot be taught. 'And you may be sure that I will be as grateful to you as the dauphin is to your father, Mademoiselle. But I must remind you that the queen made an announcement at court tonight which you seem to have forgotten. As the only remaining unmarried daughter of the king, I am to have the courtesy title of Madame of France. I feel certain that you of all people will not want to continue making an error of protocol by addressing me as Mademoiselle. Now I wish you a very good night – and please leave the key to the strong-box.'

It was only later I learned that the key in question was

tantamount to Bonne's badge of office. It hung from her belt on a jewelled chatelaine and for a moment I thought she was going to refuse to hand it over. Then she unhooked it abruptly and dropped it on the table beside Catherine.

'As you wish, princesse. Good night.'

'Good night, Mademoiselle Bonne,' replied Catherine, her painted court face unsmiling beneath the ornate headdress.

The Count of Armagnac's daughter made one of her precise courtesies and stalked out, casting a baleful glance at me and leaving the door deliberately open. As I obeyed Catherine's mute signal to close it, I heard the lady's footsteps halt at the curve of the stairs and guessed that she had paused in the hope of catching some of our conversation. With a grim little smile I ensured that the only sound that carried to her ears was the firm thud of wood on wood.

'Am I to address you as Madame then, Mademoiselle?' I asked Catherine, confusing myself.

To my delight she giggled again. 'Well, you certainly do not need to address me as both, Mette!' she exclaimed. After a moment, she said, 'I think I would rather you stuck to Mademoiselle. I seem to remember that when you called me a little Madame you were usually cross with me.'

'I am sure I was never cross with you, Mademoiselle,' I assured her. 'You were always a good child, and you are scarcely more than a child still.'

She raised a quizzical eyebrow at me.

'You may not know, Mademoiselle,' I said, crossing to the hearth to pour the warm posset into a silver hanap, 'that while

96

you were away there was much political upheaval and at one time the Duke of Burgundy ordered a number of the queen's ladies to be imprisoned in the Châtelet. Mademoiselle of Armagnac was among them. It is said that their gaolers abused them and I know that they were mauled and mocked by the mob on the way there. She can have no love for commoners like me.'

Catherine gazed at me steadily for several moments before responding. 'See how useful you are to me already, Mette,' she remarked. 'Who else would have told me that?'

I placed the hanap on the table beside her and began removing the pins that fastened her heavy headdress.

As I lifted away the headdress, she briefly massaged an angry red weal where the circlet had dug into her brow, then she cupped her hands around the hanap and took a sip. 'Now I will tell you something that *you* may not know, Mette. Mademoiselle Bonne has recently become betrothed to the Duke of Orleans, he who was supposed to marry Michele but ended up marrying our older sister Isabelle. I went to their wedding when I was five but unfortunately she died two years later in childbirth. I prayed for her soul, but I did not weep because, as you know, I hardly knew her. The queen was at pains to tell me all about Bonne's betrothal this evening. Apparently Louis does not allow his wife Marguerite to come to court because he hates her for being the Duke of Burgundy's daughter, so when Bonne marries Charles of Orleans, she will be third in order of precedence after the queen and myself.'

Fast though news spread in the palace, this gossip had not

yet reached the servants' quarters. The present Duke of Orleans was the king's nephew, heir to the queen's murdered lover. His Orleanist cause had benefited greatly from the Count of Armagnac's military and political support, and this marriage would be the pay-back, bringing Bonne's family into the magic royal circle. Mademoiselle Bonne was definitely a force to be reckoned with and I feared that, by showing me favour, Catherine had already irretrievably soured relations with her.

I bent to unfasten the heavy jewelled collar she was wearing and she put down the posset and raised her hand to my face, pushing under my coif to trace the two puckered scars that ran from cheekbone to jaw.

'The Duke of Burgundy gave you these,' she said softly, 'when you were defending me. And my lady Bonne dares to question your trustworthiness!'

'I am surprised you remember, Mademoiselle,' I said. 'You were so young.'

'How could I forget?' she cried. 'Burgundy's black face still haunts me.'

'You should not let it,' I admonished, though I suffered similarly myself. 'You have the queen's protection now. It seems that nothing is too good for her youngest daughter.'

Catherine gave a mirthless laugh. 'A change from the old days, eh, Mette? Do you know, this evening I could not recall my mother's face?' She paused reflectively. 'Yet I should have remembered her eyes, at least, for they are the most extraordinary colour – pale blue-green, almost the colour of turquoise – very striking. I knelt, I took her hand and kissed it as I had been told to do and she raised me and kissed my cheek.'

I began to unpin the folds of her stiff gauze veil and she helped me as I fumbled with the unfamiliar task. 'You must have been nervous, Mademoiselle,' I said, thinking that a mother and her long-lost daughter should have met in private, not conducted their reunion in the full view of the court.

Catherine nodded. 'I was, at first. I had no idea what was expected of me, but then I realised that she did not want me to say or do anything. Just to be there so that everyone could see me. She was very gracious, very effusive. "I declare Catherine to be the most beautiful of my daughters," she announced. "The most like me."'

Catherine's mimicry of her mother's German accent was done straight-faced, but I saw that her eyes were dancing. 'Praise indeed, Mademoiselle!' I remarked, my own lips twitching.

'Then she made me sit on a stool at her side and proceeded to talk over my head. The hall was full of people hanging on her every word. She said, "We must make the most of France's beautiful daughter. I have commissioned the best tailors, the finest goldsmiths, the nimblest dance-masters!"'

I had only heard the queen's voice once before, but Catherine's impersonation was a wickedly accurate reminder of that fateful day in the rose garden.

When she spoke again, it was in her own soft tones. 'I asked after my father, the king, but she merely said that he was as well as could be expected. Then I asked about Louis and she looked annoyed and said that the dauphin was away from court but would be back for the tournament

'They have a huge tourney planned to entertain the English embassy. I am ordered to appear at my most alluring. The queen herself will choose my costume.' Catherine sighed and her voice trembled as she asked, 'What is she scheming, Mette?'

'A marriage, undoubtedly, Mademoiselle,' I said, removing the last pin, finally able to lift away the unwieldy veil.

'Yes, inevitably – but to whom?' She shook out her hair, running her hands through the thick, pale strands. I swear it had not darkened one shade since babyhood.

I saw no need to hesitate in my reply. 'Why, to King Henry of England I suppose.'

Her brow wrinkled in alarm. 'Surely not. He is old! Besides, does he not have a queen already?'

My heart lurched at the sight of her, tousle-haired and doe-eyed in the soft light from the wax candles. Whichever king or duke it was who got her would win a prize indeed.

I began to unlace her gown. 'You have been in the convent a long time, Mademoiselle. The old King of England died more than a year ago. The new king, his son Henry, is said to be young, chivalrous and handsome – and in need of a wife.'

'Young, chivalrous and handsome,' Catherine echoed, rising to discard the voluminous jewel-encrusted court robe. I gathered it up with a grunt of effort and I did not envy her the wearing of it. 'What do you call young?' she queried ruefully, plucking at the ties of her chemise. 'By my reckoning he must be at least six and twenty. Twice my age! That does not seem young to me.'

As she spoke, her chemise fell to the floor. A sumptuous velvet bed gown had been provided for her use and I held it out for her, marvelling at how slim and sleek the limbs that I remembered rounded and dimpled had become. Hugging the robe closed, she ran her hands over the silky fabric. 'This is beautiful – so soft and rich. The nuns would think it enough to put my soul in danger,' she remarked.

'Seeing you without it would put King Henry's soul in danger!' I countered with a twinkle.

This brought a girlish blush to her cheek and I reflected that nubile though she now was, she was still little more than a child. What could she know, fresh from her convent, of the power of her own beauty or the strength of male lust? Mademoiselle Bonne was right; Catherine did need a wise and steady hand to guide her, but I feared the jealous, opinionated daughter of Armagnac was not the right one for the job.

8

With her new-found indulgence towards 'the most beautiful of my daughters', the queen promised Catherine anything she wanted and it turned out that what she wanted most, God bless her, was me. The nuns of Poissy had taught her Greek and Latin and the Rule of St Dominic, but in their strict regime of lessons, bells and prayers there had been no room for love or laughter and, instinctively, she knew where she might find both.

So, in order to keep me close, she gave me two rooms on the top floor of her tower. I do not believe she can have remembered, and I never discussed it with her, but one of them was the small turret chamber where I had lit those secret fires for her as a baby, and the other, the larger chamber adjoining it, was where the infants and the donkeys had once slept. This one had a hearth and chimneypiece, a window overlooking the river and in the thickness of the outer wall, much to my joy, a latrine. In the past this floor of the tower had been used as a guardroom for the arbalesters who patrolled the battlements and so it was accessible from the curtain wall-walk, which meant that once the sentries got to know them, my family would be able to come and go without passing through Catherine's private quarters.

'You will need to have your family around you, Mette,' she told me earnestly. 'I would not like to think that being with me took you away from your own children.' It was no wonder I loved her. I swear there was not another royal or courtier in the palace who would have given a second's thought to the family life of a servant.

Originally the accommodation had been ear-marked for those of Catherine's ladies-in-waiting yet to be appointed and they were rooms that Bonne of Armagnac had counted on filling with some of her own favourites, so when she heard that I was to be given them, she went straight to the queen's master of the household and complained that I was unsuitable for such preferment and would be a pernicious influence on Princess Catherine. Me – a pernicious influence on the daughter of the king! I had certainly come up in the world. It would have been funny if it had not been so alarming. I had seen what happened to servants who offended their lords and masters. I did not want to end up shackled in the Châtelet or even to become one of the mysteriously 'disappeared'.

Luckily Lord Offemont, the wily old diplomat who ran the queen's household, understood only too well the jealousies and machinations of court life and managed to mollify Mademoiselle Bonne with some even more desirable accommodation for her protégées, but the episode further strained relations between me and the future Duchess of Orleans.

When Catherine heard of Alys' sewing talent, she immediately arranged for her also to be transferred to her ever-growing household, which meant that instead of endlessly hemming the queen's sheets and chemises, my nimble-fingered little daughter found herself tending the princess' new wardrobe, sewing fashionable trimmings onto beautiful gowns which, needless to say, she loved.

Ah, those gowns! A score of them were ordered, all truly fabulous; designed and constructed by the best tailors using gleaming Italian brocades, embroidered velvets and jewel-coloured damasks, the hems of their trailing sleeves intricately dagged into long tear-drops or edged with sumptuous Russian furs. Despite their constant complaints about unpaid bills, the craftsmen of Paris clamoured for the patronage of this new darling of Queen Isabeau's court. Tailors, hatters, hosiers, shoe-makers, glovers and goldsmiths flocked to Catherine's tower, filling the ground-floor ante-room with their wares and spilling out into the cloister until it began to resemble a street-market where the fashion-mad young ladies-in-waiting fell over each other to handle lustrous silks and gauzes, try soft Cordovan leather slippers and exclaim over exquisite jewelled collars, brooches and buckles. It was these ladies who decided which craftsmen and traders should be invited to present their wares personally to the royal client and I soon learned that their decisions were not made on merit alone. Even I was promised a silver belt-buckle if I would clear the path to Catherine's door but, although as one of Catherine's key-holders I had recently taken to wearing a belt, I angrily refused the offer and roundly scolded the offender.

My intimate relationship with the princess was a constant irritation to Bonne of Armagnac and flashpoints occurred almost daily. I tended to keep a close, motherly eye on my chick, whereas Bonne's attitude was more didactic, offering copious advice and instruction but often leaving Catherine to flounder in awkward situations.

Entering the salon at the height of the fashion frenzy, I found the princess cowering in her canopied chair surrounded by a bevy of tradesmen all gabbling at once and thrusting samples of their wares in her face. For a young girl only a few days out of the convent, it was a distressing situation and, seeing Catherine close to tears, I inwardly cursed Bonne and her silly court creatures, conspicuous by their absence, being unable to resist the temptations displayed in the cloister.

'Shame on you, masters,' I protested, pushing the men aside. 'The princess will make no decisions while you rant at her like that!' I bobbed a knee before Catherine's chair. 'Forgive me, highness, but it is time to prepare for court. Have I your permission to clear the room?'

'Yes, thank you, Mette,' she murmured and I shooed the importunate craftsmen through the door, still trying vainly to cry their wares. Catherine was visibly shaken, her hands white-knuckled on the arms of her chair. 'That was horrible!' she exclaimed. 'I did not know what to do. They just kept coming. I feel so foolish.'

I was about to point out that she should not have been left without support when Bonne arrived looking flustered. Seeing me, her expression changed abruptly.

'Oh, it is you,' she said coldly. 'The masters said some wimpled hag had dismissed them.' Pointedly turning her back on me, she addressed Catherine in a more circumspect tone. 'Could you make no choices, Madame? It will be hard to dress you adequately for court if no accessories are selected. Did the masters offend you in some way?'

'Yes,' replied Catherine, lifting her chin and fixing Bonne with a suddenly dry and steely gaze. 'There were too many in the room and I should not have been left alone with them. Fortunately Mette came to my aid.'

Colour flooded Bonne's creamy cheeks. 'I crave your pardon, Madame. They were only the most worthy craftsmen. I thought your highness understood that furnishing your wardrobe is a matter of urgency.'

'That may be so, but I do not have to be pestered,' Catherine retorted. 'The queen relies on you to help me, Mademoiselle, and I think she would not be pleased to hear that you left me alone with all those men, however worthy you consider them.'

Bonne had no alternative but to look contrite and murmur another apology, but the most galling thing for her was probably not the reprimand but the fact that it was delivered in my presence.

Of course there were times when Bonne came into her own. Catherine was summoned daily by the queen to attend a meal or an entertainment or be presented to a visiting dignitary. Mademoiselle of Armagnac was an expert on protocols and pedigrees and before each visit was able to relay snippets of useful information picked up from her court-wise father. These coaching sessions intensified as the grand tournament approached, a day Catherine was dreading.

'Oh the tournament, the tournament! The queen never stops talking about it,' she complained one morning, fidgeting fretfully as a gesticulating tailor issued quick-fire instructions to Alys, who was kneeling before Catherine, pinning final adjustments to the magnificent gown ordered for the princess' first grand public appearance. A high-waisted, sweep-skirted style known as the houppelande was the new height of fashion at the French court and Queen Isabeau had insisted that this vitally important example of it should be tailored from cloth-of-gold, which would clearly demonstrate Catherine's high value in the marriage market. I was no expert on fashion but I thought the heavy gold gown threatened to overwhelm her fair, translucent beauty.

'The queen keeps reminding me that the English envoys will be reporting every detail of my appearance and behaviour back to King Henry and that I have the honour of France to uphold. It makes me so nervous that I will probably fall over or come out in spots.'

I overheard this comment whilst busy tidying behind the guarderobe curtain and I immediately wanted to rush out and tell her that there was not a princess in the whole of Christendom more brilliant and beautiful than she, but with Mademoiselle Bonne supervising the fitting I let discretion rule me.

She took a less reassuring line. 'I'm sure the queen only wishes to remind you of how much is at stake, Madame,' I heard her say. 'If there is no marriage there will be no treaty with the

English and war will inevitably follow. My father tells me that the treaty talks are at a crucial stage and Cardinal Langley is a very slippery customer.'

'I cannot think why King Henry sent a cardinal to do his wooing,' Catherine grumbled. 'What does a celibate know about marriage?'

I smiled to myself, hearing the schoolgirl speaking. One day someone would tell her of the many former convent pupils ensconced as the paramours of primates.

Mademoiselle of Armagnac was not put off her stride. 'Cardinal Langley is a diplomat first and a priest second, Madame. When it comes to a royal marriage, the bride is always part of an extended negotiation.' It occurred to me that Bonne might have been describing her own marriage. 'In such circumstances birth and pedigree are of paramount importance.'

'So why does the queen lay so much store by my appearance?' retorted Catherine. 'I am the King's daughter – that is all they need to know.'

Bonne shook her head. 'A queen who charms her lord and husband can influence his actions. The cardinal may not take this into account but the queen certainly does. This marriage is not just to seal a peace between France and England. She wants you to seduce King Henry into making your enemies his enemies.'

Bonne's shrewd analysis of the machinations of diplomacy did not surprise me for she was born to it. Although neither prince nor duke, the Count of Armagnac had nevertheless manipulated himself onto the Royal Council and won his daughter a marriage to the king's nephew. Bonne had clearly observed and absorbed her father's serpentine skills.

However, Catherine's response equally clearly demonstrated that her lady-in-waiting had not cornered the market in clear thinking. 'Yes, I can see how that would benefit the queen,' she mused, 'as long as my enemies are her enemies.'

I could not see Bonne's expression, but her silence was eloquent. I wondered how long it would be before this remark reached the queen's ears.

The Grand Tournament brought Paris out *en fête*. It was held on Shrove Tuesday, the last permitted day before the onset of Lent brought a temporary halt to such war games. Even the palace servants were encouraged to go and watch, so Alys and I joined the throng jamming the streets leading to the royal tourney-ground beside the Seine.

It lay on flat land in the shadow of the Louvre, the ancient fortress of the old kings of France, whose towering battlements and fearsome, impregnable donjon still guarded the royal exchequer. Gaily decked pavilions had been erected along the curtain wall, ready for royal and court spectators and before them stretched the lists, two sandy gallops the width of a field-strip, divided by a stout jousting rail, while beyond the arena a series of railed-off enclosures waited to receive the common herd, and beyond these ran the river Seine with flotillas of boats and barges moored as viewing platforms for extra spectators. At one end of the ground stood the Heralds' Gate, a painted wooden barbican fluttering with flags and banners that marked the entrance from the knights' encampment, a field full of gaudy tents displaying the colours and devices of hundreds of participating knights who had ridden in from every corner of Europe, eager for a chance to win prize money and display their combat skills.

The day was cold and bright and under a clear blue sky the air seemed to vibrate with the sound of neighing horses, whistling grooms, rattling harness and ringing anvils. It was a number of years since Paris had hosted a spectacle of this magnitude and, except for the great festivals of the church, I had never seen such a massive gathering of people. Hawkers manned every vantage point, crying their wares; spiced ale and wine, hot pies, pardons, cures and tawdry trinkets. Bands of musicians played on street corners, their instruments screeching out of tune as each battled to be heard above the next. Hordes of students and apprentices, granted a day off to join the fun, brought their rowdy rivalries out into the squares and fights sprang up without warning. Alys and I held hands tightly so as not to lose each other as we elbowed our way through to the arena reserved for royal servants where we squeezed onto a bench which gave us a clear view both of the lists and of the royal pavilion.

In due course a loud fanfare of trumpets announced the grand entry of the royal party, which processed slowly down a covered wooden stairway, specially erected to give access from the soaring walls of the castle. One by one the king, queen and their eminent guests acknowledged the crowd and then seated themselves on cushioned thrones and benches set under an emblazoned canopy. Heraldic banners fluttered from the pavilion's roof, depicting the personal crests of every seated celebrity and somehow lilies had been grown in mid-winter, which nodded their noble heads solemnly along the parapet. From our lowly viewpoint the royal family and their guests resembled a row of gorgeous dolls, clad in brilliant hues, sable-lined against the cold and so laden with precious stones that they glinted blindingly in the flat February sun.

It was no easy task for Catherine to stand out amongst this muster of peacocks, but in the end her beauty and simple elegance paid off. The fabulous gold gown, flowing and pearl-trimmed, glowed serenely against the scintillating glitter of her parents' showy magnificence, and her gleaming pale gold hair, falling loosely from a pearl-studded circlet, rippled down her back like a silk oriflamme. (And so it should. God knows I had brushed it hard enough!) It was the custom on formal occasions at the French court for unmarried girls to leave their hair loose and uncovered, which meant that beside the queen and the other royal ladies with their elaborately veiled and jewelled headdresses, Catherine looked fresh and nubile and, to put it bluntly, eloquently marriageable. I have to confess that while my heart swelled with pride at the sight of her beauty, my stomach churned at her vulnerability.

'If this king does not get her, then the next one will,' I whispered to myself, brushing a sudden tear from my eye.

'She looks like an angel!' cried Alys, her sweet round face flushed with adoration. 'There can be no lady in the world more beautiful than Princess Catherine!'

'Let us hope the fat cardinal thinks so then,' growled a voice from the row behind. 'Otherwise the English excrement will be sailing up the Seine come September.'

I turned to look at the speaker. He wore the blue and gold livery of a royal chamberlain and was bleary-eyed and stubble-chinned, with a sharp, foxy face and probably a bald head beneath his draped black hat. 'It will not be Princess Catherine's fault if they do,' I countered, adding a smile on the grounds that I had few enough chances to glean palace gossip and did not want to kill the conversation stone dead.

He responded with a meaningful wink. 'Aye, she is a beauty all right. Any man would like to get her maidenhead! . . . What?' He stopped abruptly, warned by my fierce frown and head-jerk in Alys' direction.

Anxious to steer him onto a less prurient topic, I pointed to the red-faced cleric seated on Catherine's left, whose crimson soutane was stretched tightly over his substantial belly. 'I take it that is Cardinal Langley,' I said, 'and they are the king and queen on her other side. We work for the princess but we do not get a chance to see the other royals at all.'

As if to make amends for his vulgarity, the chamberlain became quite voluble. 'There is no mistaking the queen – see all the jewels she wears, three times more than anyone else – and the king beside her, poor devil. He looks all right from here but he is as simple as a six year old. I know this because I empty his bath and he has a fleet of wooden ships that he plays with.' Registering my incredulous expression, he nodded vigorously. 'It is God's truth. The lady beside him is the dauphiness. I am surprised she is here. The dauphin cannot stand her and usually keeps her locked up in a nunnery. He only lets her out when he absolutely has to.'

I stared at the lady in question – Marguerite of Burgundy, a thin, whey-faced creature who looked older than I knew her to be, which was about twenty. She was richly dressed in ruby velvet liberally embroidered with dolphins and daisies. The dauphin might not want her as his wife, but she was defiantly declaring her status by linking his heraldic dolphin device with her own marguerites.

'Is she not the Duke of Burgundy's daughter?' I asked, keen to prompt more information. Fox-face had a wine skin clamped between his thighs, from which, by the looseness of his tongue, he had been drinking freely.

'Yes, that is the trouble. The dauphin hates her father's guts so he wants nothing to do with her. Perhaps she prefers being locked up in a nunnery to being married to him, but it is my bet she prays for the day the Duke of Burgundy comes back to Paris!'

I chose my next words carefully. 'I hear that he still has many followers in the city.'

A grin split the chamberlain's narrow face and he nodded vigorously. 'So he does and they say that he is wooing the English as well, offering his own daughter, Catherine, as bait. Hey, look – the fun is about to start!'

Another loud blast of trumpets announced the first joust, a contest between the dauphin and the Earl of Dorset, the English king's uncle who was leading the embassy. The two contenders cantered up to the royal pavilion to make their salute. It was the first time I had clapped eyes on Prince Louis since he had quit the palace garden as a nine year old boy and frankly I was shocked.

Now eighteen, he could only be described as fat. No – he was obese! I had been expecting an older, taller version of the lanky boy who had dropped the caterpillar down my bodice. It hadn't occurred to me that the deprivations of his youth might have turned him into a glutton. Only a half-blind sycophant could have called him handsome, for his features were blurred by puffy jowls and multiple chins, his eyes appeared mean and small, sunk into the flesh of his cheeks and his hair was shaved high up the back of his head in the mode currently favoured by young men-about-court, exposing thick rolls of fat on the back of his neck. Only his aquiline Valois nose remained distinctive, unmistakably declaring his lineage. In his huge suit of armour his body was a vast metal hulk covered with a blue and gold surcôte and squashed into a high-cantled jousting saddle. Somehow a horse had been found strong enough to bear his weight, but getting him onto its back must have required substantial lifting-gear. Even from afar he did not look well. If he had still been in my charge I would have prescribed a strong purge and a prolonged diet of bread and water.

Although in boyhood Louis had been the brighter of the two princes, it was Jean who had excelled with the sword and, now that he was a man, Louis still showed little skill at knightly pursuits. To the disappointment of the crowd, he was trounced by the considerably older Earl of Dorset whose lance scored a direct hit on the first pass, such as would have lifted a normal man out of the saddle but which barely nudged the elephantine heir of France. My garrulous neighbour informed me that the rules of chivalry stipulated that the loser in a joust must forfeit the price of his armour, which in the dauphin's case must have been a considerable sum, so it was hardly surprising that Prince Louis was puce with anger when he joined his family in the royal pavilion to watch the rest of the tournament.

Over the next few hours the cream of French and English chivalry rode against each other in a blur of colours, dust and glinting steel. It was a brutal spectacle and more than once I regretted bringing Alys along. Numerous armoured men had to be dragged from the ground on hurdles, their helmets so badly dented that their skulls must have burst within them, and right in front of us a magnificent horse suffered a crashing fall, snapping its foreleg. The poor beast screamed and thrashed for many agonising minutes before it could be bludgeoned out of its misery and hauled away across the sand. During this incident Alys hid her face against my shoulder and I looked anxiously across at Catherine expecting to see a similar reaction on her part, but her expression remained rigidly schooled, as if such stomach-churning sights had been a daily occurrence at Poissy Abbey!

The grand finale of the day was to be a mêlée, when the jousting rails were removed and the French and English knights staged a mock battle in the open arena, challenging each other at random until the heralds judged which side had won. I wanted to take Alys away from what I feared might be another bloody spectacle but, just as we were about to leave, the Earl of Dorset rode up to the royal stand. 'If the beautiful daughter of France will grant me a favour for the coming trial I will carry it on behalf of my nephew King Henry,' he declared gallantly.

The crowd roared its approval of a gesture made in the true spirit of chivalry. I could see Catherine glance at the queen who nodded indulgently but, as she leaned over to pluck a lily from the floral display, the dauphin moved to restrain her.

'No favours for the English!' he bellowed, rising to his feet. 'Not while they plot to snatch France from its rightful heirs!' He had a voice to match his bulk and his words echoed clearly around the lists. 'Go back to your nephew, Dorset, and tell him that his dream of possessing my sister founders on his daydream of stealing my father's lands. You may have won in the lists, my lord, but I vow before God and St Denis that that is the last victory England shall have over France!'

Dorset's reply was lost in the general hubbub that followed, and some of the French and English knights, who had been swapping rude gestures and insults ahead of the mêlée, decided to forego ceremony and clash swords before the trumpet sounded; instantly a war developed which the heralds had no chance of controlling.

In the palace viewing arena many of the male servants began to join in the fun, standing on their seats and shouting encouragement with wine-fuelled gusto, among them the foxy-faced chamberlain. 'There goes your lady's marriage!' he yelled at me as I pulled Alys away. 'If English Henry wants her, he will have to come and get her!'

9

'This is the last straw!' exclaimed Bonne, furiously pressing all her weight against the door of Catherine's bedchamber. 'Either you admit me to the princess' presence instantly or I will go straight to the queen and demand that you be removed from her highness' service immediately.'

I am a sturdy body and had no difficulty keeping hold of the door, but I cannot pretend that her words did not send cold shivers down my spine. I reckoned that, influential though her family was, Bonne did not have the clout to actually demand such a thing of the queen, but a sly remark, dropped at the right moment, would have the same effect. By thus barring her entrance, it was possible I could find myself in the Châtelet by evening, or at the very least expelled from the palace. Nevertheless, I held firm.

'Believe me, Mademoiselle, it is for your own safety that I respectfully suggest that you do not enter,' I insisted in a far from respectful tone of voice. Bonne had managed to wedge her foot in the door and our conversation was conducted through the narrow gap. 'The princess has a fever and until we know the exact nature of the illness she gave orders that no one else is to come near her. The physician has been sent for, but meanwhile she asks that you and her ladies pray that it is not serious or infectious.'

For a moment the sliver of Bonne's face that was visible to me expressed doubt, swiftly replaced by firm resolve. 'This state of affairs has been allowed to go too far,' she said with cold finality. 'It should not be some ignorant, jumped-up tire-woman who decides whether or not the princess has a fever and who takes it upon herself to send for the physician, it should be the queen's appointed lady-in-waiting. I shall remain here until the physician comes, and then I shall accompany him to her highness' bedside and inform the queen of his conclusions. I shall also inform her of the dangerous position of influence a common creature from the back streets has been allowed to assume over her daughter.'

'You must do as you think fit, Mademoiselle,' I responded, suddenly pushing the door hard against her foot in its soft leather slipper. There was a squeal of pain as she jerked it back and I closed the door with relief, inserting the peg which locked it against further entry. I had fulfilled my promise to Catherine not to let anyone in, but at what cost? This time I feared serious repercussions.

It was two days since the tournament. Immediately after its ignominious ending, Catherine had been witness to a terrible row between the queen and the dauphin over his high-handed and very public sabotage of the Anglo-French treaty. Queen Isabeau had accused Louis of ruining France's prospects of peace and prosperity out of mere pique at being bettered in the lists, and Louis had countered by calling her faith in King Henry's goodwill naive and foolish.

'Henry is a bully, Madame,' the dauphin had thundered, 'who will stop at nothing to grab lands, titles and treasure in order to build himself an empire. How you can even contemplate giving Catherine in marriage to such a greedy, ignoble creature is beyond me. All he wants her for is to get his foot on the steps of the French throne. You want to kiss the cheek of a man who would lock my father away, humiliate my sister and disinherit me. I have not ruined any chance of peace. I have thrown down the gauntlet to a glory-seeker and told him that peace is not for sale. We will not buy off his aggression with vast tracts of land, a pair of blue eyes and a two million crown dowry. If he fancies himself as Emperor of the World he will have to fight and, God willing, die for it!'

Queen Isabeau had retorted, 'It is you who is naive, Louis. King Henry is not a bully, he is a warrior. He will not retreat from your bombast as you hope, he will pick up your gauntlet and march against France and we cannot rely on our lieges to defend us. You have not taken control of your destiny, you have thrown it to the wolves!'

It was a thoughtful and distracted Catherine who had described this confrontation to me in detail as I helped her out of the gold gown. Then she sat and regarded me for so long without speaking that I feared she was about to reproach me for something. It was, however, the very opposite.

'I can absolutely trust you, can I not, Mette? In fact, I think you are the only person I *can* trust.' She said this so gravely and

120

sorrowfully that I sank to my knees beside her, took her hand and kissed it.

'I would give my life for you,' I said softly. 'But even more dreadfully, I would live my life without you if that would serve you better.'

'God forbid that,' she breathed. 'Not again. He could not be so cruel.'

Despite her apparent maturity she still possessed youth's need for reassurance and the instinctive optimism of a child. With cynicism born of bitter experience, I was far from certain of the Almighty's benevolence in this matter.

She stood, took my hand and pulled me to my feet, steering me towards the hearth where her canopied chair was set. 'You sit there, Mette,' she said, pushing me gently into the chair and perching herself on a nearby stool. 'I will tell you my thoughts and you can tell me afterwards what you think.'

Feeling distinctly awkward with our positions reversed in this way, I found myself wondering what Bonne would say if she could see my common backside sullying the royal cushions. However, all such petty thoughts were soon banished as Catherine broached her subject.

'What I am going to tell you must never go beyond these walls,' she began cautiously, 'for some might call it treason. But the longer I am at court, the less I find myself able to trust my mother.'

My involuntary exclamation made her raise her hand to cut off any protest. 'Please do not say all the things I would hear from others, Mette. I know I am young and I may not fully

121

understand what she says and does but I am not a simpleton. I could give you many examples of her dishonesty, but it is only necessary to give you one. She professes to loathe the Duke of Burgundy for his involvement in the murder of Orleans, but that is just words. In fact, she hates the Count of Armagnac, whom she professes to admire. Whenever they are together it is easy to detect the animosity between them. Nor is there any love between her and Louis, as you know. Publicly she embraces the Orleanist cause, but in fact she schemes with Burgundy.

'This would not matter so much if she was loyal to the king, but she is not. She sits beside him at formal occasions but otherwise she shuns him. She only wants him alive because as his queen she has the power of regency. When my father dies Louis will be king and she will be powerless, so she secretly treats with the Duke of Burgundy, paving the way for him to return to the king's side. Why? Because Burgundy controls Jean. In alliance with him, through the son she sent into exile ten years ago, she could continue to rule France.'

'But only if Louis were dead!' I exclaimed.

'Exactly.' She leaned over to lay a finger on my lips. 'Ssh. I only tell you all this because I want you to understand why I am going to ask you to help me. I need to speak to Louis without my mother knowing. I want you to take a message to him, Mette, asking him to come here secretly. He could come via the wall-walk and we could meet in your chamber, while we put it about that a sudden fever confines me to my room. You would have to keep my ladies at bay, for they all report to the queen in one way or another.'

'Especially Mademoiselle Bonne,' I murmured. 'And it won't be easy to fend her off. She already hates my guts.'

Catherine looked apologetic. 'I know. She is liable to complain against you, but do not worry. If anyone threatens your removal, I will just throw a real fever and show no sign of recovery until they bring you back to me.' I was far from convinced that this ploy would succeed, but she grasped both my hands excitedly, forestalling any objection. 'I need to see Louis, Mette. He is so isolated, caught between our mother who wishes him ill and Armagnac who professes loyalty, but serves only his own interests and is shackled to a wife who is the daughter of his sworn enemy. I must let him know where my loyalties lie.'

I was all at sea, floundering in affairs that were way above my head. 'What about your own interests?' I felt bound to ask. 'The dauphin has already ruined your chances of being Queen of England.'

She shook her head. 'Actually, I thank him for that. The marriage would have put me in an impossible position. As I said at the start, it is a matter of trust. I must marry whoever is chosen for me, I know that. But who will do the choosing? My father is too feeble and I do not trust my mother. I would rather put myself in the hands of my brother.'

I had said I would die for her and if this scheme went wrong it looked as though I very well might, but I had to help her – how could I not?

Having barred the door against Bonne, I waited in Catherine's bedchamber for what seemed like hours, trying to busy myself with small tasks; tidying her toilet chest, pounding Fuller's Earth for robe cleaning and replenishing the sweet-smelling herbs on the guarderobe floor. As I worked, I pictured Louis and Catherine conversing earnestly in the chamber above, where I had placed the largest chair available by a good fire, and below me I imagined Bonne of Armagnac pacing the floor of the salon, waiting for the physician who would not arrive, for the simple reason that he had never been sent for. I constantly expected to hear a hammering on the door as Bonne grew impatient, but to my surprise none came.

Eventually Catherine descended, her forehead knitted in a frown. I was aching to know how the meeting with Louis had gone but was forced to wait.

'I must pray, Mette,' was all she said, going straight to her prie-dieu. 'Please keep the door a little longer.'

I promised I would, but now that Catherine was back in her chamber I thought it safe to slip down the stair to check on Bonne, whose silence I considered more ominous than her anger. As I descended, I encountered a page wearing the Armagnac cross of Lorraine climbing the stair towards me. 'I have a message for the Princess Catherine,' he announced.

I held out my hand, my heart racing, certain this was the first sign of Bonne's backlash. 'Her highness is indisposed,' I said. 'I will take it to her.'

He removed a sealed letter from the purse on his belt and gave it to me before retreating down the stair. I was sorely tempted to destroy the letter there and then, but prudence prevailed for I reasoned that if Bonne was working against me the sooner Catherine knew of it the better. When I re-entered her bedchamber, she made the sign of the cross and rose from the prie-dieu. The Virgin gazed benignly down from the candlelit triptych revealing nothing, but I noticed that whatever intercession had been asked of Her, the creases had not been smoothed from Catherine's brow.

Silently I handed her the letter and, when she broke the seal and opened it, I saw that it contained several lines of script. I waited while she read it, imagining I could already hear the stamp of the guards' heavy boots advancing up the stair to arrest me.

When she raised her head, Catherine's eyes were wide with surprise. 'It is not from Bonne, it is from her father the count,' she said, re-folding the parchment. 'In view of the failure of the English treaty, Armagnac and Orleans have decided that the marriage between Bonne and the duke should take place immediately. The count deeply regrets that his daughter's duty in this matter takes her away from my service, but he hopes I will understand and wish her well.' Catherine laid a gentle hand on my arm. 'So you can stop twitching, Mette. Mademoiselle of Armagnac is no longer a member of my household.'

My sense of relief was short-lived as I realised the news was bad as well as good. 'But very soon she will be Duchess of Orleans,' I pointed out, 'more powerful and even more alarming.'

'And much too busy and important to concern herself with us,' Catherine reasoned. 'Meanwhile, she is not here so let us sit together, while I tell you about my meeting with Louis.'

I stirred up the fire and we sat by the hearth, this time with her enthroned under the canopy and myself on a stool. Outside the wind howled and driving rain rattled the shutters, but the candlelight and blazing logs enfolded us in a flickering intimacy.

'Thank you for leaving the wine and the sweetmeats in your chamber, Mette,' Catherine began with a smile. 'You certainly know the way to Louis' heart.'

I shrugged. 'I remember how he used to fall on the pastries I brought in from my father's bake house. He was always hungry as a boy.'

'That has not changed. He consumed everything you left.' Catherine made a face. 'He is so greedy!'

'It is making him ill,' I commented. 'He has too much black bile.'

'Is that so? It is a pity because he needs to be fit and healthy. France has suffered too long from an ailing monarch.'

There was a pause while she considered the dire truth of this.

'Perhaps I should not ask, but what did you pray for when you returned?' I probed gently. 'You seemed so troubled.'

She shook her head as if to clear it. 'I felt confused. Sometimes when you pray, things become a little clearer.'

'Yes,' I said, unable to think when prayer had done the same for me. 'And did they?'

'No. Not really.' Her eyes found mine then and I saw that they were full of tears. 'Oh, Mette! I feel so lost.'

Impulsively I took both her hands in mine, feeling the prick of tears in my own eyes. But I did not press her to confide in me. Instead I tried to be reassuring. 'You can never be entirely lost when I am here.'

She squeezed my hands then let them drop, settling back and

clearing her throat. 'I have to make a decision, Mette. Telling you about my dilemma might make it seem less daunting.'

I nodded encouragement and gestured towards the triptych. 'You know that I will remain as silent as the Virgin.'

Catherine's brows lifted in mild censure. 'I think sometimes that you are too irreverent, Mette,' she said reproachfully.

I occurred to me to remind her that I did not have the advantage of a convent education, but instead I tried to look contrite and receptive at the same time and said nothing.

'I was never happy at the convent,' she observed, as if she had read my mind. 'But I am grateful to the nuns for showing me right from wrong. It is a shame that no one did the same for my mother and brother.'

I must have looked surprised at this outburst because she went on hurriedly. 'It is true. They are as bad as each other. At least, I think they are. I am not absolutely sure about Louis yet. I know he is not being straight with me, but I feel I should not judge him until I know why. I was praying to be shown the reason.'

A log shifted on the fire, throwing up a cloud of sparks and heralding a rush of words from Catherine.

'He told me that he had stopped my marriage to King Henry because he did not want to see me tied to a godless libertine. Stories had reached him from England that Henry lived a debauched life and he, Louis, wanted to save me from shame and humiliation. Well, of course, I thanked him very much, but I also asked if Henry's demands for land and money had nothing to do with it. He looked irritated and said that these had been only minor considerations. When I expressed concern that the failure of the treaty might spark an English invasion, he laughed and told me that Henry would never dare to invade France and, if he did, he would be chased back into the sea. Then he said: "England is a paltry little country and Henry is an apology for a king. His father was a usurper and he will pay the price for it. I would not give him a parcel of tennis balls, never mind my sister in marriage!"

'I could not believe my ears, Mette. I was there when he told our mother that he sabotaged the treaty because Henry was power-crazy and only wanted to marry me in order to claim the French throne. There was no mention then of saving me from the clutches of a libertine. It was more a case of saving his own inheritance. Not that I blame him for that, but why is he not consistent?'

'So did you tell him of your suspicions about the queen?' I asked.

'No, not in so many words, but I did formally pledge my allegiance to him as the heir of France, and he seemed very touched when I knelt and kissed his hand. He said he understood that as a female I was obliged to obey my mother, but to remember that he always had my best interests at heart. I think he has his own suspicions about the queen. It is clear that he does not trust her, but then he obviously does not trust anyone. What a mess! It seems that everyone is working to their own secret plan, but all of them involve me in some way or another. I feel like one of Louis' tennis balls, being hit in all directions with no power over where I will land.'

I nodded sympathetically. 'I can only say that wherever you do land, Mademoiselle, if you call me I will come to you.'

I felt her arms go around my neck and her soft kiss on my cheek. 'Oh, Mette, you are more to me than mother, father and brother! I will always want you with me no matter where I go. I wonder what England is like. To be honest, I am beginning to believe that any marriage, even to "an apology of a king", would be better than having to live in the perfidious House of Valois!'

10

Bonne's marriage to Charles of Orleans was the social event of the spring season, taking place immediately after Easter. Lacking the charisma of his dead father, the young bridegroom was said to be sensitive and serious, much taken with poetry and music. On the other hand, the Count of Armagnac was ambitious, dynamic, politically able and willing to lead the Orleanist faction. So when the Duke of Orleans installed his new duchess in the Hôtel de St Antoine, her parents came too and the four of them proceeded to set up a showy and magnificent court, which swiftly began to draw aspiring nobles away from the Hôtel de St Pol.

Meanwhile, Catherine began to discover the frustration of being powerless. 'If the queen and the dauphin would only stop arguing with each other, they might be able to exert their royal prerogative,' she exclaimed one afternoon, returning from a fruitless visit to her brother's apartment. 'They've had yet another row and Louis has stormed off to Melun, calling on all the other princes of the blood to meet him there. This pointedly excludes the queen, so of course she is furious and to get back at him she is bringing Marguerite back to court and expects me to be nice to her. But if I am nice to her, Louis will accuse me of treachery, so there's only one thing for it, Mette – get out the physic bottles; it's time to feign illness again.'

I think if Catherine had been able to leave court, she would have followed Louis to Melun but, without the Queen's permission, she could not so much as commandeer a horse. So, as good as her word, she retired to her bedchamber, refusing admission even to her confessor and insisting that only I attend her.

Word obviously reached the queen because the next day a black-robed doctor arrived and announced himself as Maître Herselly, an appointed royal physician. Catherine was half-minded to refuse him entry, but she was eventually persuaded to accept a liberal dusting of white-lead face-powder and to lie back looking ashen and weak in her curtained bed while the doctor attended. Fortunately, having assiduously tasted and sniffed a sample of the patient's urine and questioned her briefly from a safe distance, he went away declaring that she had a bad attack of the flux, probably brought about by eating green fruit. For such an august man of science he seemed woefully ignorant of the fact that it would be some weeks before the spring blossom yielded any sort of fruit, but at least his report won Catherine a few days' absence from court.

Suddenly the queen announced her intention of joining the dauphin at Melun and insisted that the dauphiness go with her. Queen Isabeau may have hoped to bring about a reconciliation, but Louis was having none of it. Minutes after his mother's barge was sighted approaching the river gate at Melun, he and his knights galloped out of the main gatehouse riding headlong towards Paris. Catherine, having made a surprise 'recovery' in her mother's absence, was startled by her brother's precipitous arrival, spattered with mud and in a towering rage.

'Give me wine!' the dauphin exclaimed, striding into the salon, scattering us all into corners and making the room seem suddenly small. Picking up a silver flagon from a side table, he took a huge gulp from it before spitting it out in a great shower. 'Ugh! That is horse piss! Bring me good Rennish wine, and something to eat. I have been riding for hours.'

Catherine signalled me to obey the order for refreshment and I left as Louis was flinging off his riding heuque and gauntlets and bawling at her flustered ladies, 'Leave us! I want to be alone with my sister.'

By the time I had collected a flagon of the requested Rennish wine from the queen's cellar and a heaped platter of spiced cakes from the kitchen, I returned to find Catherine standing patiently by the fire, while the dauphin held forth at full volume, pacing the floor. When I entered, as unobtrusively as I could, he came to an abrupt halt, glaring at me.

'Do not worry about Mette,' Catherine told him hurriedly. 'She is my oldest and most trusted friend – and yours too. Perhaps you recognise her, Louis.'

Snatching the flagon from my hand, the dauphin endeavoured to take a deep draught of the wine while keeping his porcine gaze fixed on my face. Remembering the correct deference, I sank to my knees, glad to avert my eyes as the ruby liquid dribbled down his numerous chins. At length he smacked his lips and flicked the wine carelessly off his jowls with the back of his hand. 'We had a nursemaid once called Mette,' he remarked, lowering the flagon.

'Yes,' nodded Catherine. 'This is she.'

But Louis' attention was distracted by the platter I held before me. 'Ah, food! I am famished!' Grabbing the dish, he flung himself down in Catherine's canopied chair and I winced inwardly as he splashed wine carelessly over the delicate silk cushions. His great thighs in their tautly stretched hose were heavily mired from his hectic ride, further sullying the brocade. I smothered a rueful sigh and rose to move a table within his reach. As he put the platter of cakes down on it and selected one, I inadvertently caught his eye and ducked my head again, my colour rising.

'I remember you, Mette!' he cried, spitting crumbs. 'You used to bring us pies and pastries from your father's bake house. They were the only things that kept us from starving. So now you are my sister's trusted maidservant. Good. Even so, I would rather you were not here. Leave us.'

Behind the dauphin's back Catherine jerked her head in the direction of the guarderobe arch, which was covered with a heavy curtain. She made a downward motion with her hand and her eyes rolled upwards and I understood from this dumb show that she wanted me to stay close by, wary perhaps of her brother's unpredictable temper. Behind the curtain I hugged the inner wall inside the arch and strained to listen, trying not to think what the dauphin might do to me should I be caught eavesdropping.

133

'I cannot stay long, Louis,' I heard Catherine say. 'I am due to attend Mass with the king.'

'Why have you not gone with the queen to Melun?' he asked.

'I have not been well. She took your wife with her for company.'

'Bah!' I heard Louis spit loudly and hoped he was not expelling food but expressing an opinion. 'They deserve each other, my wife and my mother, for both serve the same cause.'

'What cause is that?' asked Catherine.

'Why Burgundy's of course,' growled Louis. 'Surely you have been at court long enough now to realise that our mother is a two-faced Janus who is diverting royal funds to Burgundy's agents in the city. I have sent men to seize treasure and coin she has hidden in various houses around Paris, waiting for Burgundy's arrival. She plots to bring him back because she thinks he will share power with her and block me out. She is wrong, of course, because he is even more treacherous than she is. Anyway, she will find it is all to no avail because I have decided to pre-empt them both – and all the scheming princes of the blood. While they are at Melun, I intend to disband the Council and declare my sole regency. Edicts will go out in the king's name ordering all the princes to retire to their estates. The queen I shall order to remain at Melun and I shall escort my wife back to her nunnery at St Germain-en-Laye. If I split them all up it will bring an end to their tiresome conspiracies and let me get on with ruling the country.'

After these momentous announcements there was a prolonged

silence. My heart skipped a beat as the dauphin's heavy tread creaked on the wooden boards close to my hiding place, then faded away as he prowled back across the room.

'Why do you say nothing, Catherine?' he demanded. 'Do you doubt my motives or my powers?'

'Neither,' she assured him. 'But will the princes do as you say? Why should Anjou and Berry and Bourbon not join forces and advance on Paris?'

'Because they know I have the right!' Louis' voice grew strident. 'I am the dauphin. Besides, those posturing princes cannot agree with each other long enough to raise a flag, let alone an army. Constable D'Albrêt commands the royal guard and he is loyal to the throne and therefore to me. From now on, none of our vassals will enter Paris or approach the king without his or my permission. Let them go to their neglected estates and order their affairs there. Come – do you not agree with me, Catherine?'

'You know you have my total support,' responded Catherine faintly.

As if she had any other choice, I thought, cowering behind my curtain. Did her brother forget that at her age he was still in the schoolroom?

'That gives me great satisfaction,' declared Louis approvingly. 'And you are to remain here with me in Paris, not go to the queen, even if she asks for you.'

In the guarderobe I put my hands to my head in despair. Poor Catherine! Less than three months out of the convent she had become a hapless pawn in the power-struggle between her brother, her mother, her uncles and her cousins. It would not have surprised me if she had fled back to Poissy in despair but then, thinking about it, how could she even do that?

For once, the squabbling princes did as they were told. Perhaps they were tired of all the arguments; I know I would have been. Burgundy, of course, was already in Flanders, but the Duke of Orleans took his new duchess and her parents to his castle at Blois, the Duke of Berry went to Bourges, the Duke of Bourbon to Bourbon and the Duke of Anjou to Angers. Many lesser nobles followed their overlords' example and with them went their families, baggage, servants and retainers. Jean-Michel reported that driving the regular supply-train back from the royal estates had been a nightmare because all the roads out of Paris were jammed with long columns of horsemen, carts and litters going in the opposite direction.

In the absence of the queen, Catherine relaxed noticeably. Most of her ladies-in-waiting had retreated with their families, leaving only Agnes and a couple of low-ranked baronet's daughters to attend her. So since she was no longer obliged to spend long, tedious hours attending court, she could occupy herself however she chose. For the first time in years, the countryside was relatively peaceful and, with the dauphin's authority, Catherine was able to command horses and escorts to make excursions beyond the walls of Paris. She liked the exercise of riding, but on the first day of May she insisted that Alys, Luc and I should join her on a trip to the Bois de Vincennes and that Jean-Michel should drive us there in one of the royal supply wagons.

'It will be a May Day holiday, Mette,' she said excitedly. 'You can organise a picnic for us.'

The castle of Vincennes was a royal hunting lodge surrounded by forest outside the east wall of Paris where the king often went to pursue deer and boar when he was well enough. Hunting was one adult activity he could still enjoy; although Jean-Michel said the Master of Horse only mounted him on a pony these days, rather than one of the spirited coursers on which he had galloped after prey as a young and healthy man. For me it was like a taste of paradise to wander through groves of great oaks where bluebells carpeted the clearings and to do it in the company of all the people that I loved most in the world. It was perfect spring weather and when the sun had climbed to its highest, we gathered in the dappled shade on the bank of a stream and ate cold capon and May Day sweetmeats and afterwards Catherine and her young ladies took off their shoes and hose and ran barefoot through the lush green grass, hitching up their silken skirts like harvest-maids. When she grew breathless, Catherine ran to sit beside me on a fallen log where I was watching Alys and Luc laughing and splashing in the gravel shallows.

'How did you celebrate May Day as a girl, Mette?' she puffed.

'You will stain your gown,' I protested, seeing the folds of daffodil-coloured silk already sullied by the fresh green moss that grew on the log.

'Oh never mind,' she shrugged carelessly. 'Tell me!'

I relented of course. 'We used to climb the hill of Montmartre at dawn and wash our faces in the dew. They say that if you kiss a boy with the May Day dew on your lips he will be yours for ever.'

'What a shame that the sun has dried the dew or else we could have tried it!' Catherine teased, twinkling at gawky Luc whose cheeks blushed bright scarlet. Dumbstruck by such close proximity to a flesh-and-blood princess, I do not think he managed to utter a word in her presence all day.

Even so, that excursion marked the start of a new and dangerous closeness between Catherine and my family. Dangerous, not because in itself it was daunting or threatening – it was a joyous thing – but because of how others might have viewed such a friendship, forged across the yawning social gulf that divided us. Simply sitting beside Catherine and sharing her food was breaking strict protocol and I knew there were plenty at court whose jealous natures would seek to punish such presumption. I just hoped they were all too far away for it to come to their attention.

A few days later, having dressed Catherine in full court finery to dine with the dauphin, I went up to tend my own fire and sent Alys to see if Jean-Michel and Luc were free for a family meal. We sometimes managed to snatch an hour or two together in this fashion and earlier I had wheedled a mess of pease and bacon from the king's kitchen and set it to warm over the fire. The four of us were settling down to eat it, exchanging companionable banter, when the door creaked gently open and there to our intense surprise stood Catherine, her ornate robes clashing incongruously with the homespun simplicity of our tower-top chamber.

She hovered in the doorway, a wistful look in her eye. 'I heard your talk and laughter and I wondered if I might share your fire for a while.'

Suppressing an oath, Jean-Michel sprang to his feet, pulled off his hood and began to shuffle awkwardly from one foot to the other, uncertain how to receive such an august visitor. I hastened to offer Catherine his vacated chair. 'Oh no,' she said shaking her head and smiling at Alys and Luc who had risen shyly from their bench beside the hearth, 'I will not steal your father's seat. I would rather sit with you, Alys, if there is room. Can you squeeze me in?'

She edged onto the bench, but with her thick embroidered skirts bunched up around her there was scarcely room for three, so Luc happily squatted down on the floor with his bowl and stared up at her, mesmerised by the wealth of gold and gems that gleamed at her throat and brow.

'That smells very good,' she remarked, sniffing the steam rising from the small cauldron hanging over the fire. 'Do you have a spoonful to spare, Mette?'

'Take this, Mademoiselle,' I said immediately offering her my own bowl. 'I have not yet tasted it.'

'Thank you,' she said, accepting it with both hands. 'I would not deprive you, but I can see there is more in the pot. I must admit I am hungry.'

Taking the horn spoon, she began to eat in small, delicate mouthfuls, then paused to beg Jean-Michel and me to sit down. 'I shall wish I had not come if you are uncomfortable,' she pleaded. I resumed my stool, but Jean-Michel could not instantly persuade himself to sit in the presence of royalty.

Not only was I astonished by Catherine's arrival, I wondered at the reason for it. 'I hope you were not waiting for me to attend you, Mademoiselle,' I ventured, pouring ale from our jug into a wooden cup and passing it to her, adding apologetically. 'I am sorry, we do not have wine. Since you were dining with the dauphin, I presumed you would not need me for several hours.'

Catherine took the ale with a smile of thanks and shrugged. 'I went to the dauphin's hall at the usual time, but dinner cannot be served until he is ready and that depends on when his high and mightiness deigns to get out of bed. Today he chose not to rise until after dark and I became impatient waiting, so I left. That is why I am hungry. I feel sorry for his courtiers, who sometimes have to wait hours for their meal and then may be kept at table late into the night while course after course is served. The dauphin insists on huge banquets every day of the year and he certainly *does* have wine. He also drinks some fiery spirit made from apples in Normandy. I don't know what it is called but it smells vile.'

'Ahem.' Jean-Michel cleared his throat nervously, but his urge to impart knowledge when he had it overcame his shyness. 'They call it *l'eau de vie* your highness – the water of life. I have drunk it in the taverns in Rouen but it makes you feel like death the next day.'

'Perhaps that is why my brother stays in bed so long,' frowned Catherine. 'I wish he would not drink so much of it. He says he can rule France alone, but I do not know when he attends to any business if he sleeps until dusk.'

'Ahem.' Jean Michel coughed again and, gathering fresh courage, decided to resume his seat at last. 'His grace sends messengers out in the dead of night,' he confided. 'We have to supply horses from the stable at a moment's notice and couriers ride in at all hours too. It is well known that letters arriving in the early hours will be received, but for a courier to come at noon is fruitless.'

Catherine nodded. 'He turns night into day. Let us hope he can turn the country around too, as he says he will. What do your fellow drivers think to that, Jean-Michel?'

A deep flush spread over my husband's face and neck. 'Well, highness . . .' he began.

I cut in, knowing his forthright opinions and fearful of what he might say. 'I would not pay heed to that bunch of oafs, Mademoiselle,' I said. 'These days anyone who drives a cart thinks he can run the country!'

Jean-Michel glared at me resentfully and blurted out his opinion without even coughing. 'If you want the truth, they all think that war is inevitable.'

'War with whom?' Catherine asked. 'With the English?'

'Yes Mademoi – er . . . Madame,' Jean-Michel nodded vigorously. 'Yesterday a messenger came in from Boulogne and told us that strings of new hulks were sighted being towed across the Sleeve to England. King Henry has commissioned them from the shipyards of Zeeland to build up his royal fleet and there are no prizes for guessing why.'

'But if that is the case, why has Louis sent the princes away? Surely he will need them to raise an army?' Catherine's expression was so flatteringly earnest that Jean-Michel became quite loquacious.

'Some think he is blind to the English danger. That he reckons King Henry is a usurping dog who barks a lot but has no bite and will not dare to confront the might of France. So he can ignore what he calls "the petty English threat" and it will go away.'

Catherine leaned forward, looking intently at Jean-Michel. 'If only some think that, what do the others think?'

My husband licked his lips anxiously. For several moments he seemed uncertain whether to answer her truthfully and then committed himself in a rush. 'They think he is more fearful of Burgundy's ruthless ambition and actually hopes to make an alliance with King Henry to cut the duke out. You may not know this, but some pretty important people left court this week – the king's secretary and his confessor, the Archbishop of Bourges – not the sort to leave their posts without good reason. I helped to harness their baggage train. They were bound for England.'

'You are right. I was not aware of that.' Catherine's gaze swung from Jean-Michel to me, her brow knitted. 'No wonder the dauphin insists that I remain in Paris. It is no good sealing an alliance with a marriage if you are not in possession of the bride.' She took a sip of ale and lifted her chin defiantly. 'Well, all I can say is, if I *am* essential to my brother's plans, the least he could do is get out of his bed to give me dinner!'

Had it not been for Jean-Michel's stable-gossip, Catherine would never have known that she had once again been used as diplomatic bait in treaty negotiations. Nothing seemed to come of it however; a few weeks later the secret embassy came back as quietly as it had left, marked for us only by Jean-Michel's report of the return of the horses to the stables.

Paris began to sizzle in the summer heat, but beyond the walls the uneasy truce between the two main rivals paid dividends. Freed from armies of Orleanists and Burgundians constantly skirmishing and foraging over the Île de France, the peasants were able to tend the crops unmolested and Jean-Michel came back from his supply runs describing fields golden with grain and orchards groaning with fruit. For once I did not feel the need to fret over his safety while he was gone.

Then, just as the harvest was in and the barns were full, we heard that King Henry had embarked in his new fleet of ships and sailed across the Sleeve with twelve thousand men, landing at the mouth of the Seine and surrounding the fortress port of Harfleur with guns and siege engines. Dining in the dauphin's hall, Catherine heard the herald's report and watched aghast as, instead of issuing a call-to-arms as she expected, the dauphin called for another barrel of *eau de vie* and applauded loudly as his fool sang a satirical ditty about 'a motley band of English apes'.

'Louis says that Harfleur is well-armed and well-supplied and will easily withstand any assault,' she told me as I helped her to bed. 'He is treating the siege as an entertainment and declares he will give twenty crowns to the knight who brings back the most amusing account of it. He refuses to see the need for a counter-attack, declaring that the English are led by a decadent baboon who will soon give up and go home.' She stamped her foot in anger. 'That "decadent baboon", as my dear brother now calls him, is the same King Henry to whom, only a few weeks ago, he sent an archbishop to make peace and broke a marriage with me!'

September brought a violent change in the weather and it poured with rain for days on end. Contrary to the dauphin's sanguine boasts, the English took Harfleur.

'*Eau de Vie!*' cried Catherine in despair. 'It should be re-named *Eau de Folie.*' Constantly under its influence, Louis had ignored warnings that a bloody flux, which ravaged the English army, had also decimated the defenders of the beleaguered port. Starving, sick and discouraged by lack of royal support, the garrison had surrendered.

Paris slammed shut again as rumours began to spread that the English were sailing up the Seine. Suddenly heralds and messengers were galloping in all directions carrying the king's *arrière-ban,* his summons-to-arms, to all his scattered vassals. Meanwhile Paris was in uproar as weapons were distributed to civilian militias and the dauphin and Constable d'Albrêt led a hastily assembled force out of the city towards Picardy where the lieges were to muster. I found myself in a constant state of anxiety about Jean-Michel because every available charettier was employed supplying this army, driving to and from Paris with loads of arms and provisions through territories where the latest reports suggested that the English king was now leading his men on what the soldiers called a *chevauchée* – a 'sack and burn' march to wreak havoc and gather plunder.

The sellers of pardons, relics and amulets were doing a roaring trade ahead of what was seen as inevitable war with the English. On a rare trip into the centre of Paris, Alys and I visited one of their stalls and bought a St Christopher medal for Jean-Michel, hoping that the patron saint of travellers and wayfarers would guard him in his dangerous work. It was not made of precious metal, but we chose it because there was a slight fault in the casting which made the saint look like he was smiling. When Luc saw it at dinner time he even said he thought it looked like Jean-Michel himself. I decided that a glimpse of it on a chain around his neck might be a temptation to snatch-thieves, so during one of his brief overnight rests I sewed it into the padded lining of his boiled leather jacket, next to the heart.

'Surely now we must attack,' fretted Catherine. 'Louis cannot let the English ravage Normandy without retaliation. We are certain to hear of some action soon.'

We were all frustrated by the lack of news for there was no one left in the palace to whom a herald might bring tidings. The queen was still at Melun and at the beginning of October even the king was led away on his pony to lend the stamp of regal authority to a council of war in Rouen. In Catherine's salon the talk was all of knights and battle, and any royal retainer who set foot in the palace was asked for news of the gathering chivalry, even my Jean-Michel, who staggered off the wall-walk into our tower chamber one October night, utterly weary and soaking wet. He hardly had time to change into dry clothes before news of his arrival had filtered down to Catherine, who sent Agnes de Blagny hurrying upstairs.

'The princess says she has a fire and food and would dearly like to hear your news,' she begged Jean-Michel, 'as would we all.'

The very idea of a common groom entering Catherine's private salon would have sent Duchess Bonne into apoplexy, but Bonne was in Blois and Catherine was happy to turn a blind eye to protocol. Jean-Michel however, had a more conventional attitude and had to be persuaded to accept the invitation. When he did descend to the salon, his eyes grew wide at the opulence of the furnishings. I hid a smile as I saw him self-consciously trying to polish the scuffed toes of his bottins against his hose while he squirmed, awkward and tongue-tied, on the stool placed for him near the fire. Wisely, Catherine bade me pour him a large cup of wine and by the time he had halved its contents and consumed most of a venison pie, his confidence was sufficiently bolstered to set him off.

'I have been sent back to fetch a new consignment of royal banners,' he confided. 'The dauphin is worried that men who have so recently been fighting each other will be confused about who is friend and who is foe. He wants every French captain to add the fleur-de-lis to his standard.'

'Will there definitely be a battle then?' asked Catherine eagerly. 'What size of force has the dauphin managed to raise?'

Jean-Michel scratched his head. 'I could not say, Madame. I drive between different camps but I do not see them all. And there is another thing. While I was delivering a load of crossbow bolts to Count d'Albrêt's camp, Artois Herald rode in to warn the constable that if he moved troops any nearer to the Flemish border, the Duke of Burgundy would regard it as an act of aggression against his domains and respond accordingly. The duke's army is poised between the dauphin and the English and you could toss a coin as to which side he will join.'

'Burgundy will serve Burgundy as always,' observed Catherine acidly. She, like me, still came up in goose bumps at the mere mention of that name, although fortunately the devil duke had not set foot in Paris for over seven years. 'What about the English army, Jean-Michel? How big is that?'

'Well, they left a garrison at Harfleur and sent a few thousand sick and injured back to England, so now they reckon King Henry has maybe eight thousand men,' replied Jean-Michel upending his cup. 'Not nearly enough to withstand the might of France.'

'Perhaps Henry reckoned the dauphin wouldn't be able to rally the might of France,' said Catherine. 'Heaven knows, we all wondered about that!'

'They say the English hoped to make a quick dash for Calais, gathering what plunder they could, but they were caught short after the constable cut all the Somme River crossings. Now, unless Burgundy takes England's part, they say King Henry is caught like a rat in a trap. Around the camp fires our men are laying wagers that he will either be dead or a prisoner by Crispinmas.'

Catherine was intrigued by this forecast. 'King Henry a prisoner . . .' she mused. 'Perhaps they might bring him to Paris and we will all get a look at him. Just think, he might have been my husband. They say he is handsome but stern. I wonder if he ever smiles? Do pour Jean-Michel more wine, Mette.' She waved me forward with the flagon, adding, 'When will the dauphin attack, do you suppose?'

I poured a little more wine with some trepidation. The cup was a large one and it was stronger drink than Jean-Michel was used to. His cheeks were already flushed and his speech a little slurred. 'Not before I return with the royal banners anyway,' he declared grandly, taking another large gulp. 'A squire I met on the road told me that by the rules of chivalry, King Henry has been allowed to cross the Somme so that the two sides can face each other on dry ground in Picardy. Not that anywhere is truly dry after all this rain.'

Catherine gave a snort of disbelief. 'He has been allowed to cross the Somme? This is supposed to be war not a tournament! Surely if we had the advantage we should have attacked them as they crossed.'

'Oh we have the advantage all right,' chuckled Jean-Michel, all deference banished in a haze of wine. 'King Henry has only five hundred knights. Most of his men are common archers. They do not even have boots. That is why we call them apes, because they fight barefoot and their only armour is a leather jacket. They will be dog meat after our first cavalry charge. A massacre; that is what it will be. The plains of Picardy will be soaked in English blood.'

This was all getting a bit gory in my opinion, so at this point I thought it politic to remind Jean Michel of his early start the next day. After only a short battle of wills, he reluctantly bowed himself out and let me push him up the stair to bed.

I returned to find a buzz of excited chatter in the salon and stole a quick glance at the wine flagon, for Catherine's cheeks were quite pink but it was as I had left it. However, Jean-Michel's blood-thirsty predictions had obviously stirred a warlike streak in the princess.

'I *wish* we could *see* the battle!' she exclaimed. 'It will be such a spectacle! Imagine – our French chivalry lined up row on row with their armour glinting and horses prancing and the heralds galloping to and fro between the captains and above it all the Oriflamme streaming in the wind.'

She was a girl, with all a girl's romantic fantasies and no concept of the realities of war. In truth, I knew little of it either, aside from the effect it had on prices. However, I had no faith in Catherine's bloodless vision of prancing steeds and streaming banners, so after my husband left my side at cock's crow next morning, I went to light a candle to St Christopher, to reinforce the power of Jean-Michel's medal and pray for his safe return. Travelling on the king's business, he constantly risked ambush and accident but never before had he driven off to a battle.

11

For many years, the last days of October had hung heavy with me. Inevitably, on the anniversary of my first son's birth and death, I would find myself mourning him, and Catherine's absence on each birthday while she was at Poissy with the nuns would plunge me further into dejection. On the day she turned fourteen, I cherished the joy of being able to celebrate with her.

Looking back on the events of that memorable day, it seems extraordinary that she was only fourteen. I recalled myself at the same age, when I had thought I was so grown up and ready for all the thrill and romance my racing blood demanded. Now, of course, I realised that I had been almost a child when I satisfied the call of my youthful lust by returning Jean-Michel's burning kisses and urgent embraces. By contrast, Catherine had until recently lived under the scrutiny of virgin nuns, and now she suffered all the restrictions and expectations of the life of a princess, with the entire royal court watching her every action. Ever since returning to St Pol, she had been so much at the centre of state schemes and crises that she had not really had much chance to be either the child she still was or the

150

blossoming nymph she promised to be. At this time there were no young lords or squires for her to flirt with because they had all answered the *arrière-ban*, but nevertheless I hoped that this birthday would be an opportunity for Catherine to enjoy some light-hearted fun.

A feast was held in the great hall of the Queen's House, decorated for the occasion with coloured ribbons and garlands of autumn leaves. Of course Queen Isabeau had been invited, but Catherine was neither surprised nor disappointed when she sent word to say that she could not make the journey. And word was all she sent. No gift to mark her daughter's birthday.

'She is displeased with me,' Catherine shrugged. 'I have not rushed to be with her at Melun so she believes I have sided with Louis. I doubt if he has told her that he will not allow me to leave Paris.' She did not admit relief at avoiding the queen, but I sensed this to be the case and that she believed Louis' tales that linked their mother to Burgundy's cause.

Most of the palace cooks and supplies had been commandeered to feed the army so the menu for the feast had to be relatively simple. However, nobody noticed that there was one less strutting peacock in the queen's pleasure garden and, roasted and re-feathered, it made a magnificent centre-piece for Catherine's birthday banquet. Since no feast could be considered complete without it, I had prevailed upon one of my father's old guild-fellows to create a marchpane subtlety especially for her, while a minstrel had been commissioned to compose and perform a lay in her honour. It told of a young princess whose beauty and purity were renowned and who rejected a dozen noble suitors for love of a humble squire, who naturally turned out to be a prince in disguise. Catherine was thrilled with the story and the song and rewarded the handsome young singer with a well-filled purse, exchanging sidelong glances with her ladies and hiding girlish giggles behind her hand as he bowed low and flashed his brilliant white teeth in gratitude.

The lack of noble guests meant there was room at the feast for Catherine's servants, albeit well down the board. But I was perfectly content to sit with my own children and study from afar the child of my breast, caught in beguiling transience like a dewdrop in a cobweb, not yet quite a woman but luminous with promise. Troubadours still sang of how at the same age her mother, then an obscure German princess, had so enraptured the seventeen-year-old King of France that he had insisted on marrying her within a week of their meeting. Looking at Catherine, it was easy to imagine history repeating itself.

For her celebration she wore a gown of pale azure and silver and on her head one of the frivolous gauzy cones that had become so fashionable among the court damsels. Sewn with tiny crystal stars, its veil sparkled like sea-spray in sunlight and I proudly nursed the secret that only the day before I had plucked her hairline back to emphasise the smooth expanse of her brow and accentuate the high planes of her cheeks. As applause died for the minstrel's lay, a team of liveried pages too young to be at war began to parade the marvellously crafted subtlety which depicted a Catherine wheel – what else? – standing proud in a sea of marchpane 'flames'.

However, before this masterpiece could complete its circuit

of the hall, there was a disturbance at the main entrance and the buzz of conversation died as a royal herald stumbled through the great carved arch, his embroidered tabard hanging tattered over a mud-stained hauberk. With the rolling gait of the saddle-weary, he approached the high table, sank to his knees and waited for the company to fall completely silent. When he spoke, the high-flown language of heraldry sounded at odds with the hoarseness of exhaustion in his voice.

'His Grace the Prince Louis, Dauphin of Viennois and Duke of Guienne sends greetings to his beloved sister Catherine, Princess Royal of France. He commands me to inform you that two days ago, on the feast of St Crispin and St Crispianin, the lieges of France engaged in battle with the English at a place called Agincourt.'

I saw the colour leave Catherine's face and her clasped hands sprang to her breast but she did not speak as the herald waited for the inevitable hubbub to subside before continuing. 'I regret to report that France has suffered a calamitous defeat. Many noble lords are dead and injured. You must prepare for great mourning and tribulation.' The herald's voice quavered with emotion and he fell silent, shaking his bowed head.

Catherine rose slowly to her feet, her knuckles white as she gripped the edge of the board for support. She gazed down at the messenger. 'You are Montjoy Herald, are you not, sir? Your tunic is so dreadfully torn I was not certain. Thank you for performing your terrible duty. Can you give us any more details? We must give thanks to God that the dauphin's life has been spared, but who is numbered among the dead?'

The herald shook his head. 'Regrettably I do not know, Madame. The list is being prepared but it will take many days. There has been much carnage . . .' His voice broke on these words and he hung his head, physically and emotionally drained.

'You are exhausted, sir, I can see.' Catherine beckoned stewards to his side. 'Help him to refreshment and rest. When you are recovered, sir, I would hear more of these terrible events.'

She watched as he nodded wordlessly and was helped to his feet. All around the hall there were murmurs of distress and disbelief, but silence quickly fell as Catherine cleared her throat to address the assembly, all joy and merriment wiped from her face.

'There can be no more celebration. This feast is over. We must pray for France and for the fallen. God have mercy on us all.'

I found myself clutching Alys and Luc tightly to me as we watched her disappear through the privy door, her birthday gown with its silver bells and baubles suddenly appearing tragically frivolous. 'What about Pa?' Luc asked, his dark eyes wide. 'Do you think he was involved in the battle?'

His question echoed what had been my own instant dread. 'How can we know?' I responded faintly, unable to offer reassurance. 'As the princess said, we can only pray.'

Exchanging muttered comments, the diners abandoned their meal and began pushing towards the great door. Wedged among this morose crowd, I was taken by surprise when a liveried page suddenly appeared at my elbow.

'The princess is asking for you,' he said, edging close to make himself heard. 'I am to take you to her.'

I hesitated, loyalties painfully divided. My overwhelming

desire was to pray with my stricken children for the safety of their father, but as ever in my life Catherine's call took precedence. I nodded reluctantly. 'One minute,' I said and pulling Alys and Luc away from the tide of moving bodies, I took their hands and pressed them together. 'Look after each other. Go to the church and pray for your father, then wait for me in our chamber. I will come as soon as I can.'

Against the flow of the crowd the page struggled to clear a path to the dais, behind which imposing double doors led to the queen's private apartments. As we approached, two liveried guards threw them open but, before entering, the page paused, a perplexed frown creasing his brow. 'The princess said you would advise me what to fetch,' he murmured. 'She said the dauphin needed comfort and you would know what that meant.'

I did not hesitate. The message could only mean that Prince Louis was in the palace, unable or unwilling to appear in public but, as at all times of stress, thirsty and hungry. 'Fetch pastries and any meats from the feast. And some Rennish wine from the queen's cellar. And do not stint. Where is he?'

'With the princess. Come.'

We passed down a short passage to reach a carved door and faintly through its timbers came the dauphin's voice, keening what sounded like some ritual chant, over and over again in a high, wailing monotone, 'I should have been there. Dear God, I should have been there!'

'Fetch the refreshments immediately,' I urged the page. 'Go – quickly! And make sure the wine is from Anjou – he will not drink anything from the Duke of Burgundy's estates. Go!'

155

A huddle of Catherine's ladies was gathered nearby, wringing their hands and whispering together. 'The dauphin made us leave,' Agnes de Blagny told me anxiously. 'Princess Catherine is alone with him and he is very troubled. What shall we do?'

'Nothing,' I said flatly. 'If the dauphin has dismissed you, there is nothing you can do. When the food and wine come, I will take them in.'

There was a pause in Louis' chant long enough for Catherine to interject, but I had to strain to hear her soft voice through the thick planking of the door. 'Why were you not there, Louis? You are the Captain-General of France. Who was leading the army?'

'The constable!' responded her brother vehemently. 'He said it would be a rout. There were only a few thousand English in the field – too insignificant a skirmish to honour with my presence. Hah!'

'And what does the constable say now? How does he explain the defeat of so many by so few?' Even muffled, I could hear the scorn in Catherine's voice.

'He says nothing for he is dead!' cried the dauphin in an anguished screech. 'Dead in the first charge – smothered in a sea of mud along with thousands more of our greatest nobles and knights. I galloped to the field as soon as the news came. It was a sight to make the angels weep!' I could feel the floor shake as Louis stamped out the level of his distress.

Catherine tried to calm him. 'Will you not sit, Louis? You must be exhausted. You should rest.'

'How can I rest when the flower of France lies rotting in a

ploughed field?' The dauphin's pacing grew more frenetic. 'The whole dynasty of Bar is wiped out – the duke and both his sons – Alençon is dead and Brabant and Nevers . . .'

'Burgundy's brothers!' Catherine interjected. 'My God, so they were there. And what of Burgundy himself?'

'Burgundy never came,' replied Louis dully. 'He was only a few miles away and he kept saying he would but he never did.'

'What a surprise! So much for Jean the *Fearless*!' exclaimed his sister with biting sarcasm. 'Charles of Orleans – what of him?'

'Taken prisoner, along with Bourbon and many others, but at least they are alive to be ransomed, unlike half the French prisoners who were put to the sword on the order of English Henry, against the laws of chivalry! Why did he do that when we had let him cross the Somme? He is a monster! Jesu – so many are dead. I wish I was one of them!' I heard in this cry the voice of the cowed and terrified little boy who had emerged from the nursery punishment chest in the despot days of Madame la Bonne. Life had treated Louis harshly. The frightened child was never far from the surface.

'Thank God you are not!' I heard Catherine exclaim. 'France needs you now more than ever.'

I missed the dauphin's response to this, for the page arrived with the wine and a dish of remnants from the abandoned banquet. He looked grateful when I relieved him of them. 'I will go in,' I said, determined to do my best to protect Catherine against her unpredictable brother if it should prove necessary. 'Open the door.'

157

At the sound of my entrance Louis swung round, ready to spit out his fury at the unwanted intrusion, but his gaze fell on the contents of the dish. 'Ah, food!' he exclaimed, pouncing on a piece of meat pie and biting into it.

'Blessed Virgin! How can you eat at such a time?' demanded Catherine incredulously. 'It is grotesque!'

'How dare you!' Her brother turned on her, pastry flakes falling like snow from his mouth. 'I eat because I must. How else am I to fill the emptiness I feel? But you wouldn't understand that, Catherine, standing there in your little pointed hat and your little pointed shoes.' He sneered at her as he chewed. 'I suppose you do not realise that all this death and destruction is down to you?'

'Me?' echoed Catherine, staring at him in astonishment. 'Merciful God! How can you suggest that?'

'Because you are a witch – an enchantress!' Louis exclaimed, reaching for the cup of wine I had poured ready for him.

The only light in the room came from the flickering flames of the fire and a single candle on a buffet-board. Smothering a gasp of shock at the dauphin's outburst, I laid the food and wine down beside the candle and crept into a dark corner. No one ever forgot the king's dreadful malady or that Louis was his son. Judging by her expression, Catherine was as fearful as I that he, too, might lose control. He had certainly lost all awareness of my presence.

'Have you no idea what beauty like yours does to men?' he persisted between hectic gulps of wine. 'That impious libertine Henry of Monmouth came lusting over to France, desperate to possess your soft, white virgin flesh – and now ten thousand Frenchmen lie dead . . . dead, at *your* little feet!'

'Ten thousand – Jesu!' Catherine whispered, half to herself. I saw the blood drain from her face at the scale of the losses and I prayed that the dauphin was exaggerating in his distress. 'That is a terrible number. However you are wrong, Louis!' she went on bravely, in a firmer tone. 'King Henry does not lust after *me*, but after France. I am not the territory he wants, I am the wretched scapegoat who is tethered to it. I am glad you did not fight because at least you remain alive to lead us out of this mess. Without you, power might fall to his *dis*grace of Burgundy, which God forbid! His motive for not fighting is glaringly obvious, is it not? He is saving his men to move on Paris.'

'Well!' Louis paused between mouthfuls to glare at Catherine, fury replaced in his expression by grudging respect. 'You are not just a pretty witch, are you, sister?' he acknowledged. 'But what you do not know is that our charming mother has already actually *sent* for Burgundy, promising him a hero's welcome in Paris and a place at her right hand. My agents intercepted her messenger and I have ordered the gates closed against him.'

Catherine crossed herself, looking alarmed and distressed at this latest bombshell.

'Holy Marie! I will never understand our mother! But who is to hold the gates?' she demanded. 'If the constable is dead and the army is scattered, what forces can you call on to hold the city?'

'I have sent for the Count of Armagnac. He is on the way from Gascony.'

'Which means he missed the battle also!' Catherine made an

exasperated noise. 'You cannot trust him, Louis, any more than Burgundy.'

'I have no choice,' muttered the dauphin, draining his cup. 'I need men; Armagnac has men. The king needs protection; Armagnac will protect him. It is Armagnac or Burgundy – the bandit or the devil – and of the two I prefer the bandit.'

'But can you be sure he will come?' pressed Catherine. 'If he could not bring his men to Picardy in time to fight the English, why should he bring them to Paris in time to forestall Burgundy?'

'Because I have promised to make him Constable of France if he does,' said Louis.

'Ah, yes. That should bring him. And what about King Henry? Will the English army not also march on Paris?'

'Now there is one blessing.' The dauphin poured himself another cup of wine. 'The pernicious Monmouth is so short of men that he can do nothing but march post-haste to Calais!' His voice cracked on a cry of indignation. 'I ask you, how in Jesu's name did he manage to win?'

'Meanwhile, where is our own king?' Catherine asked with sudden anxiety, ignoring the prince's rhetoric. 'Tell me our father is safe from Burgundy's clutches!'

'His litter was right behind me on the road with an escort of five hundred men. He should be here within the hour. But I have not told him about the battle. It would break his heart.'

'Undoubtedly,' said Catherine bleakly, her face expressionless as she watched her brother gulping down another cup of wine. 'It has certainly broken mine.'

*

It was hours before I was able to share the fears and prayers of my own children, for when the flagon of wine was empty and the dauphin had departed, Catherine's admirable self-control, which had remained so strong in Louis' presence, broke down and she began to weep uncontrollably, her tears soaking the bodice of her birthday gown.

'I d-did not want to cry in f-front of my br-brother,' she hiccupped, doubled up on a stool in her grief, 'but oh, Mette, – all those d-deaths! Ten thousand! What a w-waste! How could it happen? It is t-terrible. It hurts me here, l-like a knife in the stomach.'

I called her ladies in and we accompanied her, still choking back sobs, to her own apartment but it was not grief alone that caused her pain. After refusing any food and attending a special Mass in the royal chapel, she let me help her to bed, still red-eyed and complaining of stomach pain and we both immediately noticed bloodstains on her chemise.

'Blessed Virgin!' she whispered, staring at the marks in horror. 'There must be demons gnawing at my belly, Mette! Louis said I was the cause of the battle and I am being punished for it.'

'No, no, Mademoiselle!' Impulsively I threw my arm around her shoulders, berating myself for failing to warn her of this mundane and inevitable development. I should have realised that, for their own very different reasons, neither the nuns nor her mother would have done so. 'It is a terrible time for this to happen, but you are becoming a woman. All grown women bleed with the cycles of the moon. It is the curse of Eve.'

'The curse of Eve? Then I *am* bewitched?'

'No, Mademoiselle, not at all! I will explain – but first, a napkin to staunch the flow.'

Having hastened to supply the necessary item, I did my best to explain God's punishment of Eve for giving Adam the fruit from the Tree of Knowledge, but even in her despair at the carnage of Agincourt she found the Genesis story hard to believe. 'Can that really be true?' she asked. 'God placed this curse on women so that they should all bear Eve's shame?'

'That is how the Church interprets it,' I nodded.

She looked incredulous. 'The nuns never taught us that. Did the Holy Mother suffer the curse of Eve?'

'I suppose so. Perhaps you should ask a priest. I only know what my mother told me.'

'That all women bleed for one woman's misdeed? Surely God is not so unjust!'

I pursed my lips. She was not the first to question the Church's teaching in this respect, but it was inviting a charge of heresy to do so. 'I suppose it is not for us to question the Almighty,' I said tactfully. 'And the curse is not constant. It only comes once a month for a few days.'

'And it had to start today!' I saw Catherine shudder and close her eyes, clutching her belly. 'France bleeds and so do I. God has cursed us both.'

When Montjoy Herald presented himself the next morning, Catherine's salon was already shrouded and shuttered and she and her companions sat in semi-darkness, attired in sombre clothes and black veils like novice nuns. By candlelight, one of the king's chaplains had been intoning a passage on sin and suffering from the book of Job, but he closed the book when the herald arrived. From somewhere, he had found a black surcôte and hose and came freshly shaven and bare-headed, bending his knee on entering. Rested after his hectic ride from Picardy, he looked younger than he had the previous day and I caught the two baronets' daughters exchanging sidelong glances, apparently not so overwhelmed by grief that they did not coyly relish the presence of a handsome man.

The formalities of greeting over, Catherine bade her visitor sit and tell them in his own words what he could of the calamitous battle that had plunged France into deep mourning. His account was a harrowing one, and he gave it with due gravity. It is the job of a herald to observe the whole theatre of chivalry, but in my opinion at times he over-dramatised things.

'Constable d'Albrêt had chosen to deploy the French force at one end of a shallow valley with thick woods on either side,' he began, 'and the English king drew up his army at the other end – if you could call it an army for it was a pitifully small band of men compared with our thirty thousand, maybe five or six thousand. It would not be overstating the case to compare the confrontation to that of David and Goliath.'

Agnes and the other two young ladies, who had not heard the dauphin's agonised cries of incredulity at France's losses as Catherine and I had, reacted with gasps of amazement at the enormous difference in numbers.

'If you do not know the countryside of Picardy, Madame,'

the herald continued, spurred on by the audience reaction, 'let me tell you that it is very lush and green, and there are few hills of any size, but we French held what high ground there was, beside the castle of Agincourt. Our cavalry was mustered across the whole valley, thirty companies of armoured knights mounted on caparisoned coursers with banners flying, packed spur to spur as thick as stitches in a tapestry and the scarlet Oriflamme raised high in the van, streaming in the breeze.'

Now he had the ladies' full attention. They were all young girls after all, avid for stories of gallant knights and chivalry, their imaginations fired by the vivid picture Montjoy was painting, even though they already knew the appalling outcome. In truth, I could not blame the herald becoming infected with their excitement and warming to his descriptive task.

'Mercifully, the rain had stopped overnight and we could see the English gathered below us, less than a mile distant. They were all on foot. They did not appear to have any horsemen, although it turned out there were a few hundred hidden in the woods. Their foot-soldiers were mostly armed with longbows, except for two companies of dismounted knights and men-at-arms deployed on either flank. In front of one of these a huge standard billowed, goading us, insolently emblazoned with the combined arms of England and France – the lions and the lilies. Beside it we made out the figure of the English king, wearing his crown over his helmet as if to say "Behold! Here I am, come and get me!" Well, Madame, I must tell you that in our ranks were eighteen hand-picked knights who had sworn a vow to do just that.'

'Are you sure it was him?' interrupted Catherine. 'I have heard that kings have been known to confuse the enemy with doubles dressed like them and wearing crowns.'

Montjoy looked indignant that his word might be doubted, but was also anxious not to offend the daughter of the king. 'I assure you, Madame, it was Henry of England. I had delivered a message to him from his grace the dauphin only the day before.'

Catherine leaned forward, fascinated despite her best efforts to display dispassionate calm. 'So you spoke to King Henry! Pray, tell me how he looked. Was he anxious, frowning, fearful?'

The herald shook his head. 'No, not at all, Madame. My task was to relay the dauphin's invitation to surrender himself for ransom and thus save his army from destruction. But Henry of England smiled and shook his head. He declared that his cause was just and God would therefore favour it and that God's will would be done. Then he bade me take that message back to the dauphin. He looked serene and untroubled, but as I rode away I could see that his men were without shelter, cold and wet. Yet none deserted or refused to fight.'

'Perhaps because they had nowhere to go,' remarked Catherine, 'and nothing to lose.'

'Nevertheless, at the start of the next day, as our forces mustered, I heard the constable say to the dauphin that he still believed there would be no battle and that the English king would surrender as soon as he saw the great might of the French host. That was when the dauphin rode away, telling Count d'Albrêt to bring him the son of the usurper in chains.'

I saw Catherine bite her lip at that and guessed she was

remembering how loudly on the previous evening the dauphin had deplored his absence from the field of Agincourt. Watching the king of arms continue his narrative, I considered the job of a herald. He was not pledged to fight, but only to convey orders, note the activity of arms-bearers and, ultimately, to count and record the names of the dead. Just the noble dead of course – those permitted to bear arms and entered in the register of chivalry. Once again, as I had so many times already, I pondered the fate of my Jean-Michel, wondering where he was and if he was still alive. If he was not, would his name appear on any list? Meanwhile the herald's story was reaching its climax and still commanding the ladies' rapt attention.

'For what seemed like hours, nothing happened,' he went on. 'Bread and ale was distributed to our men and the constable pointed out that the English had no supplies and would starve unless they either attacked or surrendered. And then a single knight strode out of the English ranks towards us, but he did not carry a white flag. He walked slowly to the centre of the valley, saluted each army with his warder and then hurled it high into the air. It was a signal for battle to begin and a ragged cheer went up from the English ranks. However, they did not move so our cavalry, which had been champing at the bit, launched the first charge and a great line of armoured horsemen thundered down the valley between the trees. To a man the English foot-soldiers turned and ran and all around me our soldiers laughed and jeered, jerking their first two fingers in the air, the same ones they had orders to hack from the English archers' hands when France was victorious.

'But the English did not run far; only far enough to reveal what their bodies had been hiding from us since dawn – a forest of sharpened stakes, which had been hammered into the ground at just the right angle to impale a galloping horse. Then, on a signal, the archers notched their arrows and began to fire. In seconds the air was thick with missiles falling like rain on our advancing horses. I watched with horror as, funnelled by the trees, our first charge had nowhere to go; they could not stop or turn back because, blind to the trap that loomed ahead, another charge was already galloping close behind, and another behind that. They had no choice but to ride on, into the hail of arrows and onto the bristling wall of stakes. Within minutes the lush green valley had become a quagmire, churned into deadly mud by ten thousand horses' hooves with, at the English end, a screaming, bloodstained mound of mangled men and horseflesh growing ever higher with every charge.'

At this point the herald's voice broke and he passed a shaking hand over his eyes as if to brush away the nightmare vision. Blinking back tears, Catherine hastily signalled me to bring the man a cup of wine.

'I am sure it is extremely painful to recall, Monseigneur,' she sympathised, 'but it is important that I understand exactly what occurred on that bloody field. If the queen were here, she would require it too.'

The herald took a gulp from the cup I handed him, cleared his throat and nodded. 'I understand, Madame. I beg you to excuse my weakness. I am ready to continue.'

However, his flowing language seemed to desert him at this time and his narrative continued in jerky gasps.

'English archers shoot fifteen arrows every minute and their shafts can pierce steel plate. Many of our knights were killed or wounded in the volleys and, in their heavy armour, unseated riders could not get to their feet in the mud. Loose and wounded horses panicked and trampled them. Bodies lay writhing and others fell on top of them. The pile was shoulder high and ever-growing and soon the English archers stopped firing and moved in to pick them off with their daggers and maces, dancing over the mud and bodies in their light leather jackets and bare feet, agile as goats. The English king fought his ground on foot among his retinue, somehow keeping his footing. One by one, our hand-picked knights attacked him and he fought them off. I saw him battle for several minutes over his wounded brother, the Duke of Gloucester, until squires managed to carry the duke to safety. I can only say, Madame, that he wields his broadsword like an avenging angel; he is a fearsome knight.'

Catherine could not let that pass without comment. 'But a stranger to the laws of chivalry, according to the dauphin,' she observed. 'Did he not order prisoners killed?'

'Some who had surrendered were put to the sword,' agreed the herald dolefully. 'The Duke of Brabant galloped late into the field and French prisoners began to break their oaths and pick up captured weapons to fight again. Henry of England is an implacable enemy and he quickly realised that the prisoners outnumbered his army. It seems that chivalry bows to necessity in such circumstances.'

'When will the names of the dead be known?' It was Agnes who spoke, in a voice hoarse with anxiety. 'My home of Blagny is not far from Agincourt. I am sure my father would have fought on the day.'

Montjoy Herald raised his shoulders and spread his hands. 'I do not know when, Mademoiselle. The list is long – very long.' He stood up, putting down his empty wine cup. 'I should return to the field, Madame,' he added, bowing low to Catherine. 'There is much for a king of arms to do.'

She nodded sadly and, not forgetting her royal obligation to reward good service, reached out to pick up the cup. It was fashioned of gilt and set with precious stones. 'The cup is yours, Monseigneur de Montjoy. We thank you for your dreadful duty. None of us will ever forget your account of the field of Agincourt. Although the battle is over, I fear our woes have just begun.'

12

The Count of Armagnac won the race for Paris, galloping in at the head of a horde of tough Gascon horsemen only hours before Burgundy and his Flemish thugs arrived. Behind him, as the dauphin had ordered, the city gates were slammed shut, leaving Burgundy to kick his heels fuming under the ramparts. Both Catherine and I sent up heartfelt prayers of thanks, for although we had no reason to trust Armagnac, time had not reduced our mutual fear of the black Duke.

The palace, Paris, the whole of France, was in a state of shock. When heralds delivered the list of Agincourt casualties, their recitation filled the three hours between the holy Offices of Tierce and Sext. The names of the dead were inscribed on fifty rolls of vellum. Hardly a noble family had escaped loss. Poor Agnes, who had been fretting about her father ever since the battle, discovered in the most heartless possible way that he was listed among the dead. No more than that, just a name read out in the formal, dispassionate tones of Bon Espoir Pursuivant, one of the junior royal heralds, but in that instant Agnes discovered she was an orphan. Most of us listening had become mesmerised by the seemingly endless recitation of names and, being unaware of his Christian name and rank, had not even noticed the inclusion of Percival, sire de Blagny. But Catherine had and caused a pause in proceedings as she left her place on the royal dais to comfort her school-friend, who had slumped back against the wall of the great hall, her hands covering her face.

I was loath to leave the recitation and take a weeping Agnes to the Church of St Pol for comfort and prayer, because I knew there would be no mention of the fate of servants and commoners; even had there been there was no knowing how many names would have been on it for no one knew how many ordinary men had died. Across the land thousands of families like mine could do nothing but wait and pray for news of their husbands, fathers, sons and brothers who had followed their lords and masters to an unknown fate in Picardy. Since Jean-Michel's brief stop-over before the battle, it was as if he had vanished from our world. Each day I went to the stables to enquire after him, but the visits gave me little solace. A score of royal drivers were missing and the occasional straggler who fought his way through continual rain and hock-deep mud told frightening tales of narrow escapes from bloodthirsty outlaws.

Then, a fortnight after the battle, Luc came to me in tears. A convoy of six battered wagons had just returned from Picardy and one of the drivers had at last brought news of Jean-Michel. 'Pa's been injured,' Luc sobbed. 'H-he was hit by an-an arrow and he's in some monastery somewhere. I must go to him, Ma!'

I hugged my distraught son and shuddered at the thought of losing him as well. 'Oh my brave Luc! Much as you love your

171

father, you are too young to face the terrors of the road. Come, let us find Alys and you can take us to the man who brought the news.'

The bearer of these terrible tidings was one of Jean-Michel's fellow charettiers, a sturdy man from Brittany called Yves. His story did not make easy listening.

'After the battle we were heading for Abbeville with carts full of wounded when a few opportunist outlaws attacked us, looking for loot, and unfortunately Jean-Michel took a crossbow bolt in the thigh. We managed to fight them off, but the wound quickly turned putrid. Most of those bandits' weapons are rusty and I am sorry to say that Jean-Michel was raving by the time we got to Abbeville. He must have tremendous strength because many of the battle-wounded died en route. The monks have much skill with healing so we thought it best to leave him there, but I am afraid you may have to wait some time for further news. It is too dangerous to go back at present. Burgundy's army is swarming all over Picardy and gangs of those outlaw cutthroats are in every forest. Besides, anyone leaving Paris now has no guarantee that Armagnac's guards will let them back in. Even with our royal passes we had difficulty in gaining entry to the city.'

I had no heart to hear more at that moment and thanked him weakly. Almost without thinking, I found myself steering the children towards the familiar refuge of the stable hayloft, seeking comfort in its scented peace. As a couple Jean-Michel and I did not always see eye to eye, but I was nevertheless greatly fond of my stalwart husband. He may have been a man of few refinements, compared with the liveried pages and mannered men-servants I encountered in the royal apartments, but he was as straight as an arrow and as plucky as a buck hare and he still had the power to make my pulses race. Also, although he was quicker to laughter than endearment, I was aware that he loved me and our children, which Heaven knew was a rare thing in these violent, godless times. Teeth clenched, I did not allow the tears to come, telling myself that I would weep only when I knew he was dead.

Being young, Alys and Luc were not as stoical as I. They wept freely and I tried to comfort them with my own belief that he still lived and would come back to us, but my encouragement lacked total conviction. The loss of ten thousand on the field of Agincourt had barely moved me; I could feel no horror at the 'Death of Chivalry' as the nobles called it. To my mind the only thing that truly mattered was the life of one insignificant charettier whose life hung by a thread and so, there in the hayloft where they had been conceived, I hugged my son and daughter and prayed for God to lend His strength to their absent father. I did not voice my doubt but in my inmost thoughts there was no denying the truth. Yves had said the wound was putrid – and putrid flesh was a killer.

As the days passed without further news, I made enquiries about getting to Abbeville myself but Yves informed me that there were presently no supply convoys leaving the palace and even if I survived the journey, I would gain no admittance to the monastery.

'No females allowed in there,' he said flatly, 'and the road is no place for woman or man. We call the forest outlaws *les Écorcheurs* – the Flayers – because even if you have nothing to steal they will flay the skin off your back and sell it to the tanners for leather. Take it from me – Jean-Michel is safe in Abbeville and you are safe in Paris. When he recovers he will find his way home.'

His use of the word 'when' was kind, for the look in his eyes said 'if'.

The Hôtel de St Pol had become a place of sadness and gloom to everyone save the king. Locked for many months now in a delusion of childhood, King Charles remained blissfully unaware of France's disastrous defeat and traipsed about the policies with his guardians, playing 'blind man's bluff' in the cloisters or 'seek me' in the gardens. In other circumstances it might have been a comic sight to see tough, muscular men dodging between pillars or hiding behind bushes while the king ran to and fro giggling, but observers did not smile, for his terrible malady was recognised as the original and chief cause of France's woes. Catherine still occasionally had vivid flashbacks to her terrifying childhood encounter with her father's man-of-glass delusion, but she nevertheless regularly shared Mass with the king, determined to establish some form of relationship with him and hoping that he might, on his better days, show some shadowy awareness of her love and loyalty.

As he had promised, the dauphin made Armagnac Constable of France and Count Bernard more or less took over the government, gathering Orleans' supporters around him at the Hôtel St Antoine while Louis shut himself away in his

St Pol apartments and avoided affairs of state as much as possible. Whenever Catherine went to visit him she either found him, comatose or incoherent, surrounded by equally drunken acolytes.

'There is only one sober person there, Mette; a strange new secretary who is permanently at Louis' side, no matter what his state. Louis must have brought him back from Picardy. His name is Tanneguy du Chastel and he dresses like a lawyer, but he wears a sword. He tells me that Louis is ill but it seems to me that he is simply drowning in strong drink.' Catherine made an exasperated sign of the cross. 'Mother of God! France is falling apart and the dauphin is falling-down drunk. Any moment now, the queen will come back and start double-dealing again.'

And that is exactly what happened. The queen returned to Paris, bringing Marguerite of Burgundy with her, an event which drove Louis even further into his reclusive ways, to the extent that he refused to attend council or meet with any of its members, especially the queen.

Although of course she did not decline into drunkenness, Catherine shared her brother's deep depression and Agnes' mourning for her father. The two friends began behaving more like nuns than girls of fourteen, spending hours at prayer and refusing all suggestions of exercise or entertainment, preferring to immerse themselves in a series of dusty books, sent from the Louvre library. I almost wished that the queen would summon Catherine to her court, as she had previously done on a daily basis, but it seemed that 'the most beautiful of my daughters' was still severely out of favour.

'She now prefers Burgundy's daughter to her own,' Catherine observed sourly. 'What does that tell us?'

I could do nothing to cheer her, being sadly down-hearted myself, hovering between hope and despair over Jean-Michel. I confess that when I told Catherine of his desperate circumstances, I found her reaction disappointing. She offered no words of comfort, listlessly expressing relief that he was still alive but failing to show any appreciation of his mortal danger. As I went about my duties we exchanged only commonplace remarks and despite my initial fondness for Agnes I found myself experiencing stirrings of jealousy as she became the focus of all Catherine's compassion. For soon after hearing of her father's death, Agnes's woes were compounded by a letter received from a lawyer acting for her father's second wife, a stepmother she had never met.

'Agnes has been dispossessed, Mette,' Catherine told me indignantly. 'She was not aware that this new wife had recently given birth to a son who is now heir to her father's whole estate. The lawyer wrote to inform Agnes that she could no longer consider the manor of Blagny her home and that all the dowry money due to her had been paid to Poissy Abbey for her care and education. Poor Agnes is not only an orphan, Mette, but apart from what she receives from the royal purse for her services to me, she is destitute. Surely this cannot be fair!'

Listening to gossip among the ladies of Catherine's household had taught me that Agnes' story was not uncommon. If a girl of gentle birth found herself with no family support and no dowry she was indeed destitute unless she could find a husband, but even among the lesser nobility no man would take a wife without a dowry and so, more often than not, the only escape from penury was to become someone's mistress. I did not think Agnes possessed either the looks or the inclination to make this her route to salvation, but she did have an advantage over many of her fellow sufferers.

Perhaps with a touch of sour grapes, I took the pragmatic view. 'At least she has your friendship, Mademoiselle,' I pointed out. 'So I imagine that, barring the unlikely possibility that a besotted suitor may emerge who would make no demand for a dowry, you can safely assume that you have a companion for life.'

Catherine regarded me askance. Her no doubt well-deserved remonstration was couched in language she must have heard from the Mother Abbess.

'Such an unkind and unchristian attitude does not become you, Mette,' she said, frowning fiercely. 'I am going to seek legal advice on Agnes' behalf and I know precisely the man who can help me. I shall pay a visit to my brother and since Agnes is in no fit state to do so, you will accompany me.'

It took us several minutes to walk through courtyards and cloisters to the Dauphin's House and when we reached the main entrance it was shut and barred. In answer to my loud knocking, the porter yelled through a small iron grille in the door, 'No one is to be admitted. The dauphin is ill.'

'Then he will welcome a visit from his sister.' Catherine raised her own voice to carry through the grille. 'And if you cannot take it upon yourself to open up, Monsieur, then pray call Maître Tanneguy du Chastel.'

That name appeared to have some effect, for the porter's face disappeared but we were still subject to a frustrating wait until we heard the sound of bars being lifted and bolts drawn. The heavy nail-studded door swung slowly open to reveal a tall, black-clad figure, which I assumed to be the secretary. He was, as Catherine had described, a mysterious-looking character, high-browed and broad-shouldered, with the bearing of a soldier and the ink-stained fingers of a clerk.

'I apologise for the delay, Madame,' he said with a low bow. 'We are under the dauphin's orders not to admit visitors but in your case . . .'

Catherine swept past him wearing her most regal expression. 'I have heard that my brother is ill, Monsieur. Please take me to him.' Her words bore the tone not of a request but an order. It was my day for discovering that Catherine could be as imperious as her mother when she put her mind to it.

'His grace *is* indeed indisposed, Madame,' Maître Tanneguy ventured politely. 'He is in his bed . . .'

'In that case we can help,' insisted Catherine. 'My nurse here is skilled at healing.'

I hid my astonishment at hearing myself thus described and bowed my head solemnly in tacit acknowledgement of the lie.

'Very well, Madame,' du Chastel acquiesced and it occurred to me that he might possibly be grateful to share responsibility for the dauphin's condition with another member of the royal family, however young and powerless. 'I will take you to him but I warn you that if you mention the queen or the dauphiness, he will order you to leave. Please follow me.'

We followed him into a panelled lobby and up two flights of an impressive stone stairway. Towards the top we began to smell the dank, sour aroma of sickness.

'I did warn you that my lord is ill . . .' murmured Maître Tanneguy, noticing Catherine lifting the sleeve of her gown protectively to her nose as we arrived at the door of a chamber. Several guards were slouching against the wall, but sprang to attention when we appeared.

'The princess royal is here to see my lord dauphin,' du Chastel told the squire of the chamber who had risen from a stool placed nearby.

'Please tell his grace at once that I am here,' Catherine demanded, her voice muffled by the fabric of her sleeve. 'Is there someone looking after him?'

'Oh yes, Princesse. In a manner of speaking,' replied the secretary.

I noticed Maître Tanneguy's eyebrow twitch on this remark and the unspoken comment was explained when, within a few seconds of him entering, a young woman emerged, flustered and dishevelled and wrapped in a crumpled chamber-robe. She made a sketchy bob in Catherine's direction, murmured a few indecipherable words and disappeared down a nearby passage. Catherine flashed a glance at me and I wrinkled my brow in return. That Louis had a mistress was no great secret, but she had not previously revealed herself in person to his sister.

Presently Maître Tanneguy re-emerged, bowed punctiliously to Catherine and said, 'His grace will see you now, Princesse.'

We soon discovered that there was nothing gracious about the dauphin's state. He lay among rumpled and stained covers on a large, crimson-curtained and canopied bed and beside it there knelt a boot-faced squire holding a silver bowl, the contents of which were undoubtedly the source of the stench. A platter of half-eaten meats was flung carelessly among the bedclothes and alongside Louis an indentation in the mattress indicated the recent presence of a second occupant of the bed. It occurred to me that if his mistress was of noble blood she did not have very fastidious habits or indeed any concept of nursing the sick. Louis himself was propped on pillows wearing a stained linen chemise and an expression that was a blend of irritation and discomfort. Compared with the last time I had seen him he looked bloated rather than fat and his complexion was an alarming shade of yellow.

'I am not well, sister,' he complained in a hoarse voice. 'I hope your business is important.'

'The most important thing is your health, Louis,' responded Catherine with genuine concern. 'What is wrong with you? Has your physician diagnosed any particular malady?'

'Bah! Physicians! I would rather consult a soothsayer,' replied her brother. 'It is obvious what is wrong with me – Agincourt.' He heaved himself further upright, noticed the brimming bowl as if for the first time and waved the kneeling squire away. 'Remove that disgusting thing, you fool! The princess does not want to see that.'

The retainer backed off and scurried away, a look of intense relief on his face. I caught sight of what was in the bowl and was horrified to see clear signs of blood among the vomit. I was not the healer Catherine boasted of, but I knew enough to realise that Louis was suffering from something more serious than a hangover.

'I do not think Agincourt would make you vomit blood,' remarked Catherine, as sharp-eyed as myself. 'Perhaps a good deal less of that – what do you call it? – *eau de vie* – would help,' she added daringly.

Louis gave a weak laugh. 'On the contrary, sister, it is my cure.' He clutched at the sheets covering his stomach. 'It deadens the pain I have here, where the demons gnaw me. But you did not come to discuss my problems. I am curious. What made you come? Let me guess – it is something to do with our mother – our glorious queen!' His lip curled as his tone hardened into sarcasm.

Catherine pulled Agnes' lawyer's letter from the sleeve of her gown, shaking her head. 'No. I have not seen the queen.'

'Good. I am glad,' said Louis with satisfaction. 'The less we all see of her, the better. So, what *is* your business with me?'

'It is this.' Catherine handed over the letter. 'Not every victim of Agincourt is a man, Louis.'

The room was dim and the dauphin held the parchment up to catch the light from a hanging lantern. The letter was not long and he read it quickly, then he rolled over, his face contorting, thrusting the letter at Tanneguy du Chastel and groaning, 'Ahh, the demons! Tanneguy this is one for you. Now leave me. And call my chamber-squire quickly!'

Maître Tanneguy grabbed the letter and chivvied us out of the room, barking an instruction at the squire who was hovering outside the door holding a fresh basin. 'See to his grace – go!'

'Poor Louis,' fretted Catherine. 'He looks so ill. What do you think ails him, Mette?'

'Yes, let us have the opinion of your wise woman, Princesse,' broke in Maître Tanneguy, stepping up close behind us. 'What are your thoughts, goodwife?'

I hesitated. Being called goodwife was one thing, but the tag of 'wise woman' was a two-edged sword. Some people admired the skills of a healer, but many condemned them as sorcery.

'The dauphin is right,' I replied cautiously. 'Something is gnawing at his guts but it is not demons. He has too much black humour; it is poisoning him. Perhaps the *eau de vie* is causing it,' I added without conviction.

'What else could it be?' queried Maître Tanneguy. 'His food and drink are all tasted before he consumes them.'

'You think someone may be trying to poison him?' Catherine's interjection was shrill with dismay and she paused at the top of the stair, looking back at the secretary. 'Who would want to do that?'

'I'm afraid there are always people who wish harm to great men,' observed du Chastel. He turned to me. 'Do you know of any remedy we might try, goodwife?'

I paused again to consider my words, distinctly uneasy at finding myself asked to pronounce on the health of the dauphin.

'I was a children's nurse, Monsieur,' I prevaricated. 'I know only about childish ailments. When a child has too much bile we withdraw all red and green foods and feed only white until the yellow colour leaves his skin. Also, that which his grace calls his "cure" definitely is not, I would say.'

Maître Tanneguy gave a resigned sigh. 'Mm. It is one thing to withdraw certain food from a child and quite another to deny it to a man, especially a prince. However, I will tell the dauphin what you say. I know he respects your opinion.'

My expression then must have been a picture. I could hardly believe my ears. The boy who had dropped a caterpillar down my bodice had grown up to respect my opinion! I found it hard to believe.

'Now, please consider the letter, Monsieur, which was sent to my lady of the chamber, Mademoiselle de Blagny,' Catherine reminded the secretary, stopping at the top of the stair. 'You are a lawyer, I believe. Is the information in the letter correct?'

Maître Tanneguy perused the contents of the letter swiftly before folding it neatly and handing it back. 'The information conveyed to the lady is legally correct, Madame. Land can never be inherited by a female, although sometimes it can pass through her to her son if there is no direct male heir. But here obviously there is. As far as a dowry is concerned, if the amount of money bequeathed to a daughter in dower has already been paid, for instance to a religious house as would seem to be the case in this instance, then no more is due. Perhaps the abbey in question will receive the lady back when her service with you is completed. That is the best she can hope for. It might have been better if she had never left.'

Catherine fixed Maître Tanneguy with a royal glare. 'If that is the law, then the law is unjust. What do you think, Monsieur?'

'I am afraid that whatever I think will not change it, Madame,' Tanneguy bowed apologetically, 'I do not recommend it, but if your lady in waiting wishes to fight this case then I would be happy to suggest an advocate. At present my own chief concern is the health of your brother, the dauphin.'

He had couched it in gentle terms, but there was no denying that this was a blunt dismissal of the matter. Catherine turned abruptly away and recommenced her descent of the stair, but her face was flushed and I could sense her bitter frustration. She was royal, a princess and the daughter of a king, yet it seemed she was as powerless to help Agnes as I was to help Jean-Michel.

I do not deny that the injustice of Agnes' situation made my female hackles rise. Women have to be careful not to rail against the precedence of men because the Church calls it heresy, but frankly this was a piece of God's will that passed my understanding. The fact that a girl like Agnes could be robbed of her inheritance because of a baby brother she had never met or even knew existed and that the boy's mother could legally deny her the dowry that might have bought her some security was an outrage. At least I was getting rent from my father's bakery, even if I could not bake the bread.

On our return to Catherine's tower we were informed that the Duchess of Orleans had sent a message asking if she might visit the princess royal that afternoon. I would have preferred to avoid an encounter with the former Bonne of Armagnac, but Catherine begged me to be present.

'You know her, Mette, and you always supported me in her presence before. Agnes is too upset to be there. You cannot leave me friendless now.'

So I took a seat well in the shadows of the shrouded salon, hoping that Bonne would have business that was more pressing than the settling of old scores. She arrived swathed in mourning veils and entirely focused on Catherine at whose feet she threw herself, neglecting the formality of greeting.

'Princesse – dear Madame – only you can save my lord!' she cried, hands clasped beseechingly before her. 'I beg you to help me.' The young duchess' fair beauty was obscured by the veil, but the shrill timbre of her voice still had the power to set my pulses fluttering in alarm.

'Of course I will help you if I can,' Catherine responded. 'You have no need to beg. Please rise, Madame. Sit. Tell me what I can do.'

In a rustle of black silk, Bonne arranged herself on a cushioned stool placed ready for her. 'You must be aware that my lord is a prisoner of the English,' she ventured. 'A victim of the dreadful events of Saint Crispin's Day.'

'Of course I am aware!' Catherine cut in. 'I am as devastated as anyone at the terrible toll of Agincourt, but I understand that at least the duke is in good health.'

Bonne made the sign of the cross, her slim white hand flickering from forehead to breast before returning to twist at the silk kerchief she held in her other hand. 'God be thanked he suffered only minor injuries, but he is not of a robust constitution. There is no knowing how his health will stand up to his present living conditions. He is held in the Tower of London, did you know that? A dreadful fortress, where many have died incarcerated.'

'But I believe the tower is also a royal palace,' remarked Catherine gently, 'where the King of England often resides. Is there any indication that the duke, your husband, is not being held in circumstances befitting his high rank?'

Through her shadowy veil it was just possible to see an angry flush suffuse Bonne's pale cheeks. 'There is every indication, Madame! Ransom negotiations are underway for all other prisoners of rank, but our envoys from Blois have been repeatedly turned away unheard. Henry of Monmouth has declared that he will never ransom Orleans while France refuses to cede Guienne and Normandy to England.'

Catherine looked troubled at this revelation. 'I am sorry to hear that,' she said. 'Your husband is a very important prisoner of course. Perhaps King Henry's attitude will soften in time.'

Bonne lifted her veil to dab at her eyes with the kerchief. 'That is the problem, Madame,' she sniffed delicately. 'We do not have time. I must confide to you that I am *enceinte* and expect the child in early summer. If you do not help me, I fear the heir of Orleans may never see his father.'

I thought her bold assumption that her child would be a son and heir was typical of Bonne, who would naturally expect fate to bend to her will in such a matter.

Catherine beamed at her visitor, ignoring her final remark.

'Congratulations! How fortunate to have the consolation of a child to soften the hardship of your separation. God has swiftly blessed your marriage.'

'Yes, but you see how urgently I need your help!' A note of irritation crept into Bonne's voice, which I had an inkling would not assist her suit. 'I am certain that a plea from you on my behalf will move Monmouth to change his mind. After all, he faced the might of France to claim you as his bride.'

Her final point did not go down well with Catherine, whose smile faded. 'If that is the case, then why has he not done so? To the victor the spoils, is that not how it goes?' She sat back in her chair and paused to arrange her hands neatly in her lap. 'Instead, King Henry has returned to England, presumably to gather reinforcements for another invasion. Which implies that our French territories are rather more important to him than marriage to me, do you not think?'

In the blink of an eye the body language of both young ladies had changed from companionable to combative.

Bonne did not immediately respond, but her previously rest-less hands became clenched and still. 'Nevertheless, the world knows that he covets you as his bride,' she said at length, with a forced smile. 'I am certain that if you were to make a plea for my lord's release, Henry of England would be sure to grant it.'

There was a prolonged silence while we waited for Catherine's response. 'I suspect you may be wrong about that,' she said slowly, 'but I am afraid we will never know. Only queens can beg indulgences of kings. The dauphin has made very clear his trenchant opposition to any territorial claim by the English on

French lands and therefore there is no question of my making any plea to King Henry. I am sorry, Bonne.'

Shocked by such an outright refusal, Bonne launched herself from her stool to her knees, snatching so violently at the hem of Catherine's gown that her kerchief fell and lodged in a fold of the skirt. 'But we are friends Catherine!' the duchess cried, her voice rising. 'I helped you when you first came to court. In common humanity, how can you refuse me this small favour in return?'

Catherine's reply was delivered in a calm even voice. 'Because it is not a small favour, Bonne. Even if your father's agents could carry a letter containing such a request to England, I would not write it. France and England are at war. I would be treating with the enemy. It would be disloyal to my father, the king, and to my brother, the dauphin, and it would undermine his cause, which is to preserve the crown and territories of France at all costs.'

Bonne released her hold abruptly and sat back on her heels, but Catherine went on in a firm voice. 'I am sorry if you are angry. I would help you if I could, but this is not a personal matter, it is a matter of state.'

Seeing Bonne struggle to rise, Catherine leaned forward to help her and, catching sight of the abandoned kerchief, scooped it up and held it out. 'I am truly pleased for you about the coming child, Bonne. I hope news of it may reach the duke and give him cheer. Let us pray that King Henry is more chivalrous than at present appears and will release your lord before too long.'

Bonne snatched the kerchief and jerked herself upright, rejecting Catherine's assistance. 'Do not forget that your ancestor, King Jean, remained a prisoner of the English for many years,' she snapped, all evidence of weeping vanished. 'My son could be a grown man before he sees his father. I hope you do not live to regret your decision, Madame.' Somehow she achieved a curtsey, stiff with repressed anger.

As Bonne turned for the door, her glance briefly registered my presence, retired among the billowing black mourning drapes. 'I see you still keep a common servant among your intimate companions, Madame. Does the queen know of this, I wonder?' The question was delivered over her shoulder, but it made its mark.

Catherine caught my eye and gave me a rueful shrug, of little reassurance to one who in the past had only narrowly escaped the consequences of Bonne's wrath. Now that the princess no longer basked in the queen's approval, how easy might it be for Bonne to achieve my dismissal in revenge for Catherine's rejection of her plea?

13

Rain had persisted through the autumn and the paths around the palace were consistently muddy. On the morning following Bonne's visit, I accompanied Catherine to the king's chapel and waited outside in a cloister to help her fasten the pattens that kept her feet above the mire. Even after the queen returned to the Hôtel de St Pol, Catherine had continued to hear Mass daily with her father and, on this occasion, I was astonished to see her emerge at his side, apparently engaged in conversation with him. The king was smiling and animated and fashionably turned out in a luxurious black fur-lined houppelande, wearing a magnificent gold collar around his shoulders and a modish turban hat with an erect folded 'comb' at the crown. He looked suitably regal except for the cup and ball toy he carried, with which he must have been distracting himself during the service. I could not hear what passed between them, but I saw him take Catherine's hand at one point and swing it playfully to and fro like an excited boy. I noticed a plainly dressed man hovering discreetly in the background, clearly an assiduous guardian, sharp-eyed for any change in the king's condition.

After the king left her to enter his house, Catherine came over to me, almost skipping with excitement. 'Did you see, Mette? My father spoke to me!' She was pink with excitement, her eyes wide and shining. 'He asked me where I lived and if I played ball games and told me he liked my brooch.' In her beaver hat she was wearing a pin shaped like a shield with an enamelled fleur-de-lis in the centre. As she spoke, a frown creased her brow. 'He did not know my name and when I told him, he ignored what I said and called me Odette, which was strange.'

I drew a sharp breath as I knelt to fasten the wooden pattens over her soft slippers. The name may have been strange to her, but to almost everyone else in the palace it would have been instantly familiar as that of the king's mistress, Odette Champdivers, who for the last eight years had remained commendably faithful and discreet throughout her lover's mercurial alterations of mind and character and, rumour had it, even borne him a daughter. So far Catherine had been spared knowledge of this relationship and, fortunately, at that moment a royal page appeared carrying a folded note bearing the queen's seal and addressed to Catherine, which she immediately opened and read. When I heard its content I almost fell off the iron hoops of my own pattens.

'I am required to attend the queen after she has dined,' Catherine revealed, refolding the parchment. 'And she also requests me to bring my nurse. You are to meet the queen at last, Mette.'

Only days before, I had been hoping there would be just such a summons to relieve Catherine's depression, but now I was terrified by the instruction that I, too, should attend the queen's court. Count Bernard had established himself in such a position of power that, however much she might secretly favour Burgundy's cause, Queen Isabeau was bound to heed any complaint made by Armagnac's daughter.

'I – I am honoured, Mademoiselle,' I managed to stutter. 'Was any reason given for this – er – privilege?' I rose, pressing my hands together to stop them shaking.

'No, none at all,' she replied, glancing around at courtiers still leaving the chapel and passing within earshot. 'Perhaps she thinks it is time she met the woman who nursed her youngest daughter – and there is no doubt that it *is*.' She laid a hand on my arm, fingering the sleeve of my plain-spun bodice. 'It is unfortunate that household servants were not issued with black clothes after Agincourt,' she observed. 'It would not be wise to go to court clad as you are. You had better see if you can find some mourning garb in the wardrobe to fit you.' Ten months at her mother's court had taught her that appearance counted for everything.

Given the difference in our sizes, what she suggested was not an easy task and by the time I had selected the loosest and plainest of her black gowns and got Alys to make a few necessary adjustments to the seams, I was almost sick with nervous panic. The one item of mourning that had been issued to servants was a black coif and mine covered my head and neck. When I had donned a clean white linen wimple and buckled on my belt with its heavy iron chatelaine, I must have looked more like a Dominican nun than a nurse. Nun – nurse

– whatever I looked like, I felt like death, for I knew that just one word from the queen could mean banishment from her daughter's side. The agonising prospect of that merely added to the burden of anxiety I already felt for Jean-Michel.

From Catherine's tower it was a short walk to the Queen's House via a cloister and a rear turret stair. No clumsy pattens were necessary and by this route we were able to enter the great hall behind the dais, saving us, God be thanked, a public parade down the length of the room to reach the throne. The meal was over and the boards had been removed, so a few dozen courtiers were standing in groups – nobles and their ladies and a sprinkling of clerics – talking quietly together. In the background subdued music wafted from a band of minstrels hidden in the gallery above the screen. At this time of deep sorrow there was none of the noise and bustle of entertainment for which Queen Isabeau's court had always been famous, so the arrival of Madame of France provided a welcome diversion. Muted conversations ceased abruptly and then rapidly resumed, our presence providing a new talking-point. As we sank to our knees I hid at the back of the small group of her ladies while the princess moved forward to make her obeisance to her mother.

My first glimpse of the assembled court made me deeply grateful to Catherine for lending me the mourning gown, for I realised that the horror of Agincourt had plunged everyone into black, even the stewards and pages who, in normal circumstances, would be in gaudy liveries of royal blue and gold. However, amongst all this crow-like drabness the queen was transcendent, seated high on her throne under a silver-tasselled black canopy, her breast glittering with diamonds and jet and her headdress a startling gold-horned contraption veiled in shimmering black gauze. I noticed that she did not offer Catherine a seat, although a lady wearing lesser-horned headgear and only slightly more discreet jewellery, whom I took to be Marguerite of Burgundy, occupied a stool close beside her.

'We have been too long without your company, Catherine.' Queen Isabeau's voice rang clear into the rafters, loud enough for the entire assembled company to hear. Despite thirty years at the French court, she still spoke the language with a pronounced German accent. 'Illness and tragedy has kept us apart, but families should support each other in times of trial, as our dear daughter the dauphiness has so loyally demonstrated.' At this point a look of complicity passed between the two horned ladies, which spoke more about the present direction of the queen's favour than any words.

Catherine bowed her head. 'Indeed, your grace. It is good to see you back at the Hôtel de St Pol. I hope your health is improved.'

'A little thank you, but I suffer,' declared the queen mournfully. 'I suffer for France and for all our bereaved families and I pray for them.' Hands clasped in demonstration of this piety, she continued with a swift and disconcerting change of subject. 'Yesterday I received the Duchess of Orleans as, I believe, did you.'

'Yes, Madame,' nodded Catherine, still standing below the dais and having to raise her voice to be heard. 'I found her naturally distraught at the imprisonment of her husband, but she gave me the happy news that she is with child, which I am sure will bring much-needed joy to the house of Orleans.'

'And she asked if you would intercede with the King of England for the release of the duke, did she not? – Your ladies may rise, by the way.'

As we got to our feet, the queen swept us with her gaze and I felt her sharp scrutiny like the prick of a dagger.

'She did ask me to intercede, your grace, but I was unable to agree.' Catherine's chin jutted as if she was expecting censure and she was clearly surprised at the queen's positive response.

'So I heard and I am glad. France cannot be seen to beg anything from England. However, I am bound to observe that King Henry's denial of a ransom to our nephew of Orleans shows a sad lack of royal dignity. He would do well to remember that he may have won a battle, but he is far from achieving the prizes he sought to gain by war.'

All were aware that the queen intended Catherine to recognise herself as one of those unredeemed prizes. 'Indeed, Madame,' she agreed. 'Naturally I sympathised with the duchess, for she is very unhappy, but I fear my refusal also made her very angry.'

'Yes, it did and we have all heard about it!' exclaimed her mother grimly. 'Did you bring your nurse with you as I asked?'

Only Catherine and I knew that this question was less out of joint than it sounded.

'Yes, Madame. Have I your permission to present her?'

At the queen's brief nod, Catherine turned and beckoned me

forward with an encouraging smile. Offering a silent prayer, I stepped up to the dais and I felt a jolt of surprise as Catherine used a name I had never before heard on her lips.

'Your grace, may I present to you Madame Guillaumette Lanière.'

Bless her, I thought. God bless her for making me sound grander than the bourgeois baker's daughter I really am.

I hid my work-worn hands in my sleeves as I knelt before the throne. My back was to the room, but I could hear a wave of murmurings from the crowd of curious onlookers. Close up, I could see that the queen's cheeks were smoothed alabaster white with paint, bringing into stark contrast the eyes which had scarcely faded from the vivid turquoise I had found so remarkable in the old rose garden ten years ago.

Disconcertingly, she fixed them on my face and studied me in silence. 'You are younger than I expected,' she observed at length. 'You can have been little more than a child yourself when you entered the royal nursery.'

I licked my lips. Under her Medusa-like gaze my mouth had gone so dry that I found myself unable to form words but Catherine spoke for me. 'She was fifteen, Madame, and had just buried her stillborn son. Her sad loss was my undoubted gain.'

'And her own, I would say,' remarked the queen dryly. 'However, I remember hearing good reports of you from the Duchess of Bourbon, after Catherine left for the convent.' She leaned forward in her throne, signalling me to rise and move nearer and when she next spoke her voice had dropped to a level not intended for other ears. 'She said you had shown skill and devotion beyond your station in bringing Catherine through her early years. At the time I paid little heed to her opinion, but perhaps that was unwise . . .' She paused, her guttural tone curiously unsuited to muttered confidences. Then, her voice rising again, she made another of her disconcerting subject swerves. 'I gather that you went with my daughter to see the dauphin recently, Madame Lanière. Pray tell us – tell the dauphiness, who is very concerned about her husband's health – what is your opinion of his condition?'

I gulped and flashed a look at Marguerite of Burgundy sitting prim and silent, her expression void of any evidence of her feelings. What should I say to the abandoned dauphiness about her husband? What could I tell the Queen of France about her son? That he was either being poisoned or was a fat glutton who was eating and drinking himself to death at not quite nineteen years of age? And how did Queen Isabeau know that Catherine and I had visited Louis? Surely Tanneguy du Chastel would not have told her? Her spies must be everywhere. My mind raced, searching for a reply that would not see me leaving the hall under arrest.

I opted for the way I had answered Tanneguy. 'I was a children's nurse, your grace. I have little experience of treating adult ailments, but the dauphin does seem extremely distressed by the events of recent weeks.'

Obviously this did not impress the queen, who frowned deeply, but her dissatisfaction turned out to be with Louis rather than with me. She spread her heavily ringed hands and almost trumpeted with indignation, 'Well! We are *all* distressed, but we must think of France at this time. We should not allow our personal feelings to rule us.'

I bowed my head, unable to suppress memories of the queen's lavish Christmas celebrations with Louis of Orleans, while her children went hungry and the king languished in his 'oubliette'. Whose 'personal feelings' ruled then? I wondered, hiding such treacherous thoughts behind lowered lids.

'You cared for Prince Charles too, when you were in the nursery, did you not?' enquired the queen. 'So you may be interested to know that we have persuaded the Duke of Anjou to lend us his wise counsel. He is bringing his household to Paris, which of course includes our son Charles.'

I was filled with such profound relief that I had not so far been accused of gross insolence or even treason that this announcement scarcely seemed to register, but there was no mistaking the thrill in Catherine's voice as she greeted the news. Until now, her persistent loyalty to the dauphin had somewhat eclipsed the deep affection she clearly still felt for their younger brother, the lisping companion of her infancy.

'Charles is coming to Paris?' she echoed excitedly. 'That is marvellous, is it not, your grace?'

Plainly the queen did not share Catherine's elation. 'I am surprised that you remember him, Catherine. You were both so young when you parted,' was all she said before turning to me with pursed lips. 'I understand that he did not speak very clearly as an infant. Was that so, Madame Lanière?'

This jerked me into thinking that I may have felt relief too soon. Was I now to be blamed for Prince Charles' lisp? 'Er – yes, Madame, he did have a slight speech impediment, but I am sure it was a childish thing, which he will have grown out of long ago.' Out of sight up my sleeve, I crossed my fingers.

'Well, let us hope so.' The queen made it abruptly clear with a shooing movement of her hand, that I was dismissed. As I backed gratefully away, I noted that she was calling for a stool for Catherine. Perhaps my princess was back in favour.

I never really understood why Catherine loved her younger brother. I suppose she felt protective of him; certainly in the nursery she had always taken his part against the merciless teasing of his older brothers. Prince Charles had been a timid, tetchy infant and although at the time I had felt sorry for him, as I had for all the neglected royal children, now that he was almost twelve, I discovered that he'd developed into a tricky youth, irritable and suspicious, hard to please and quick to take offence, yet Catherine hardly seemed to notice this.

He had been betrothed to nine-year-old Marie of Anjou, two years before, a match arranged by the dauphin to counteract the marriage ties which the Duke of Burgundy had forced on himself, his sister Michele and his brother Jean. I knew that Louis saw his own union with Marguerite of Burgundy as the blight of his life. He had once confessed to Catherine that he would never father an heir because he could not bear to lie with Burgundy's daughter or stomach the notion of his arch-enemy's descendents on the throne of France.

'There is such animosity between Louis and the Duke that I suspect there is more to it than an unhappy marriage,' Catherine had observed at the time. 'He has never spoken of the two years he was confined in the Louvre under Burgundy's governorship. I often wonder what forms of discipline Louis' tutors were instructed to use.'

Certainly fate had dealt Charles a better hand than Louis in the marriage stakes. It had been a stipulation of his betrothal that he should leave the stifling care of his elderly godfather the Duke of Berry and travel to Angers, there to share his life and education with his future wife and her brothers, a lively and intelligent family, well nurtured by their powerful mother, Yolande of Aragon

The day after he arrived back in Paris, Prince Charles attended Mass in the king's chapel. The December weather was cold and blustery, but to his credit he had felt an immediate duty to bend the knee to his sick father, even though he was treated to a frightened whimper and instant recoil for his pains. Afterwards, having reassured Charles that this was the king's usual reaction to strangers and that things would improve in time, Catherine invited her brother back to her apartment to share her breakfast.

'Mette will serve us, Charles,' she told him as I took their fur-lined mantles, 'just as she did when this room was our nursery, do you remember?'

'No I do not,' he said brusquely, ignoring me entirely as he took his seat at the place I had hurriedly prepared for him. 'Nor do I care to. My only recollection of those years is bare walls and constant hunger.'

At least they had not turned Charles into a glutton like his brother. The first thing that struck me was that he bore very little resemblance to either Catherine or Louis. He was puny and diffident and had neither Catherine's grace nor Louis' swagger, but being only twelve I suppose he had time to grow in stature and bearing. Fortunately his baby lisp had disappeared, but he still pronounced his Rs like Ws and doubtless always would. He was a wary individual who seemed to trust animals more than humans and had insisted on bringing with him into Catherine's salon, his two huge white deer-hounds, Clovis and Cloud. They were well-trained dogs, which was fortunate considering they stood shoulder high to their master, but the fact that they gathered mud freely on their shaggy coats and shed white hairs all over the black hangings did not endear them to me.

Conversation at the meal began somewhat stiffly, which was hardly surprising between siblings separated since infancy.

'How was your journey from Angers?' Catherine asked as I held a bowl of warm water for Charles to wash his hands. 'I hear that bands of outlaws lurk in every wood.'

'If they do we saw nothing of them,' he replied. 'But they would steer well clear of a procession like ours, with an escort of a hundred men-at-arms. All I can tell you is that we were on the road for over a week and it grew quite tedious.' He wiped his hands on the napkin I offered. 'I am much more interested in what has been happening here in Paris. Have you seen Louis? I hear he is ill.'

I moved around Catherine's chair with the bowl and napkin

and she nodded as she dipped her fingers. 'Yes he is. I saw him a few days ago. He says he is cursed because of Agincourt and that demons are gnawing his stomach, but I think it is too much strong drink.'

I placed cold meats on the table before them and began to offer wine.

'Or else it is poison,' said Charles matter-of-factly.

'Oh no, I do not think it can be,' his sister retorted and turned to me. 'Tell Charles what Maître Tanneguy said when we went to see the dauphin, Mette,' she urged. 'That all his food and drink was being tasted. He did say that, did he not?'

'Yes, Mademoiselle,' I agreed, 'and because of that he did not see how poison could be administered without detection.'

'There you are, Charles!' exclaimed Catherine. 'It cannot be poison.'

'Poison does not have to be contained in food or drink,' insisted her brother. 'It could be put on his clothes or his bed-sheets or even burned on the fire to produce poisonous smoke.'

'Have you been reading too much Pliny, Charles?' Catherine asked teasingly, causing an indignant flush to spread over her brother's face. 'Louis drinks vast amounts of *eau de vie*, which is a horrible fiery spirit from Normandy. His guts cannot take it. That is all.'

Charles obviously thought little of this argument. 'Men *do* drink a lot, Catherine,' he said witheringly, taking a large gulp from his own cup as if to illustrate his point. As he put it down he cast me a sharp glance, which told me he knew immediately that the wine had been watered. Then he went on, 'I have seen my uncle of Berry sink three flagons of strong wine at a sitting and he has survived to a ripe old age. No, I do not believe it is drink that is making Louis ill.'

'All right, so who is poisoning him and why, in Heaven's name?' demanded Catherine.

Charles answered her with a question. 'Did I hear you mention a Maître Tanneguy?'

'Yes. He is Louis' new secretary who came back from Picardy with him after Agincourt. His proper name is Tanneguy du Chastel.'

Charles' face assumed an irritatingly smug expression. 'No, I think you will find his proper name is Tanneguy, the *Seigneur* du Chastel – a man of some nobility, however humble a secretary you might think him. And he is a sworn vassal of Orleans. My uncle of Anjou held a big council last spring and I saw your Maître Tanneguy there in the retinue of the Duke of Orleans. He was constantly at the duke's side. I remember him particularly because he looks like a crow – always in black and with that big beak!'

Catherine's brow furrowed. 'Noble or not, are you saying that Tanneguy is the one who is poisoning the dauphin?'

'No, but I am saying that he reports everything Louis does to the Hôtel de St Antoine. And if a spy for Orleans can be so intimate with the dauphin, then a Burgundian agent might be just as close. One of his chamber squires for instance, or even his mistress. I hear he has one.'

Catherine leaned back in her chair and gazed at her brother

curiously. 'I must say, you seem to know an awful lot about what goes on in Paris, Charles, considering you have only just arrived!'

Charles shrugged. 'I learn from the Duchess of Anjou. She is the cleverest person I know. She understands about spies because she has armies of them herself. If the Count of Armagnac was sensible, he would take counsel from her rather than from her husband. You should meet her, Catherine, then you would see what I mean.'

'I would like to. I learn only from dull priests and greasy dance masters. Oh, and the queen of course. You wait till you see *her*!'

Charles made a face. 'We are commanded to honour our mother *and* father, but Duchess Yolande has no such qualms. I know *exactly* what she thinks of the queen and I share her opinion.'

Catherine was not immediately to learn what that was however, because a page suddenly burst through the door looking flustered. Clovis and Cloud instantly woke from their slumbers and crouched growling, ready to spring, but a word from Charles stayed them.

'The Seigneur du Chastel is here, Madame,' the page said and had hardly got the name out when the man himself shouldered him out of the way, entered and made a sketchy bow. Bundling the page outside, he firmly closed the door before speaking in a hushed and urgent tone. 'Highnesses, I fear I bring bad news – his grace the dauphin is dead.'

'Dear God!' Catherine's hand flew into the sign of the cross and I saw the blood drain from her face. Hastily I picked up her wine cup and placed it in her hand. She sipped from it, trembling.

Charles seemed comparatively unmoved. 'Dead of what, Monseigneur?' he asked steadily.

Du Chastel shook his head. 'Who knows, Highness. He has been ailing for weeks.'

'So I heard. But you would know if it was poison, would you not?'

Maître Tanneguy shook his head. 'No, not without the word of a physician.'

'Has no physician been called?' demanded Catherine, her voice shrill with distress. 'Why not?'

'Because as soon as I found him dead I sealed the room and came straight here, Madame,' explained the secretary. 'I was told by the captain of the palace guard that his highness Prince Charles had been to Mass and was visiting the princess royal. I particularly wanted to inform you both of your brother's death before it became official knowledge. It will give you time to prepare.'

'Prepare?' echoed Catherine, puzzled. 'Prepare what?'

'Yourselves, Madame.' Tanneguy approached the table. 'Have I your permission to sit down?' At Catherine's perplexed nod, I pulled a stool to the table and poured him a cup of wine from which he sipped neatly. 'Whatever the cause, the death of your brother has profoundly changed the balance of power. Young though you are, you must realise this and make the necessary adjustments. You must know who to trust, for people will try to use you for their own ends.'

'Why should we trust you, for instance?' Catherine interrupted. The colour had returned to her face and she looked grave and alert.

Tanneguy nodded approvingly. 'That is a good question, Princesse, and I will answer it as briefly as I can. As a youth I swore my oath of allegiance to the house of Orleans and when your Uncle Louis was murdered, I swore another oath to bring his murderer to justice. The dauphin shared this desire and he was our hope for France's future –' he slipped suddenly from his seat and went on one knee before Prince Charles '– but now that hope must rest with you, Highness. You are not the legal dauphin, but I fear that your brother Prince Jean has been for too long under the influence of Burgundy and so, while my lord of Orleans remains a prisoner in England, I must now pledge my oath of allegiance to you.' Dramatically he grasped Prince Charles' hand and pressed it to his lips. 'I am your liege man in life and limb, as long as you pursue the interests of France and oppose the power of Burgundy.'

Charles looked bemused but also gratified and allowed his hand to be kissed without protest. Conscious that my presence might be untoward, I kept myself a shadow in the background but Maître Tanneguy turned to fix me with a look and said, 'You are witness, goodwife, to that solemn oath. I will do everything in my power to further the cause of both Prince Charles and Princess Catherine.'

'But what shall we do now?' demanded Charles impatiently. 'Surely we must tell the queen that Louis is dead.'

'Indeed we must, Highness.' Tanneguy stood up and bowed solemnly to both young people. 'Please accept my profound condolences on the death of your brother. I will go now and call the court physicians and summon Montjoy Herald to convey the news,' he told them. 'These things are best done by the appointed people.'

Even so, it was two days before the public announcement was made that the dauphin had died of a sudden fever. No further details were given as to the cause of death and, by then, all the arrangements had been made for a magnificent funeral Mass at the Cathedral of Notre Dame, followed by a funeral procession behind the coffin to the royal basilica at the abbey of St Denis. Catherine accompanied the king and queen to these obsequies in taxing conditions of wind and freezing rain and returned shivering and red-eyed, but I soon discovered that her tears were not only for the brother she had just buried.

'Bonne is dead too, Mette,' she revealed as she dropped her sodden fur-lined mantle from her shoulders. 'She was to have represented the house of Orleans at the funeral, but a messenger came to tell us that she had died in the night. It is terrible – so much death and sorrow!' She sank down into the cushions of her chair, reaching her hands out to the fire, as if silently beseeching solace from the licking flames. Agnes slipped onto a stool beside her, murmuring a prayer.

'How did this happen, Mademoiselle?' I asked, shocked to

the brink of tears myself at this unexpected event. Bonne and I had hardly been on the best of terms, but I would never have wished her dead.

It was a tale too often heard. Bonne had miscarried her baby, suddenly and violently, in the middle of the night. Although she had cried out for help, no one had been able to stop the bleeding. Poor Bonne had died in a bloodbath every bit as gory and tragic as any casualty of the battle of Agincourt.

14

If, like a monkish chronicler, I was to set down a full and proper history of those times, I would record in detail the major events of every year as they took place, but this is the story of Catherine and the extraordinary way her life and mine entwined together and for the next two years, frankly, there were no events of any note – at least not compared with what had gone before and subsequent developments. New faces came and went among the small corps of Catherine's ladies-in-waiting but Agnes de Blagny remained ever present, faithful, quiet and unaffected, compliant and devout and, if I am completely honest, a bit insipid. However, their shared past gave them a sense of kinship and they complemented each other – the lustrous and the matt, the lively and the steady, the white hart and the lamb. Together they read and embroidered, attended court, attended Mass, rode in the park, learned to fly hawks and occasionally, at Prince Charles' instigation, hunted with them in the Bois de Vincennes.

Catherine's brother remained a close companion and, when the mourning periods for Agincourt and the dauphin's death were over, surviving members of noble families flocked back to court, including numerous young lords and ladies raised prematurely to high rank by the Agincourt deaths, some of whom inevitably formed a 'set' around the princess royal and Prince Charles. There was dancing and entertainment, flirtations and frivolities, but no talk of Catherine's marriage and no romances. Hers was a regulated and privileged existence, governed by court protocol, church rules and social taboos. Looking back, she was marking time – we were all marking time.

However, although Armagnac's tight control of the city gates and guard meant that Paris remained relatively quiet, things were far from ordered beyond the walls. King Henry lurked across the Sleeve, raising another large force to invade Normandy, and the Duke of Burgundy tramped an army through Picardy as predicted, marching on Paris. When he failed to bully his way back to power at the king's side, he took revenge by occupying the town of Compiègne and seizing several other royal castles. All this violent but inconclusive warmongering had the usual dire effect on life among the common people – towns were ransacked, women raped, villages plundered and once again the poor peasants who managed to stay alive were unable to plant crops or raise stock, so that when winter came everyone went hungry.

And it was a very, very cold winter. Even the River Seine, the lifeline that normally brought supplies to Paris from the less battered valleys to the east, froze over. There were bread riots as prices rose and we were constantly led to expect incursions, either from the English or the Burgundians. The riots were crushed and the gates held, but the city seethed under siege and curfew, while the Count of Armagnac argued constantly with the queen and tyrannised a council weakened by a lack of powerful and experienced members.

Having been officially declared the new dauphin after Louis' death, Prince Jean stubbornly refused to travel to Paris from his wife's home in Hainault, despite promises of safe passage. The closest he came was to Compiègne, the once-royal citadel in Picardy which had fallen to Burgundy. In an effort to lure her son into French-held territory, the queen travelled as far as Senlis, a day's ride away, but the nearest she came to contact with Jean was a visit from his wife, Jacqueline of Hainault, and her mother who was the Duke of Burgundy's sister. Burgundy's grip on the new dauphin was apparently unshakeable.

Unwillingly, Charles had accompanied the Queen to Senlis. 'Jean does not trust our mother any more than we do,' Charles murmured to Catherine at one of their breakfast meetings soon after his return from the abortive trip. 'While we were in Senlis, I sent Tanneguy to Compiègne in secret, with my pledge of allegiance to Jean, but he still refused to come and meet us. His response was to tell me to come alone next time. He would not treat with a Jezebel.'

Catherine appeared slightly uncomfortable at hearing her mother so described. 'Did Maître Tanneguy say how he looked?'

'Fierce was the word he used,' replied Charles succinctly.

'No, I mean was he in good health? Did he seem otherwise happy?'

Charles shrugged. 'As to that I do not know but I met his

wife Jacqueline. She is beautiful and will bring him a large chunk of the Lowlands in her inheritance, so he cannot be too unhappy.'

Catherine glared at her brother, unimpressed by this display of male bigotry. 'You cannot grumble, brother!' she exclaimed. 'You have just been granted the Duchy of Berry. Not a bad fourteenth birthday present!'

The previous year the old Duke of Berry had died in his bed and since he was survived only by daughters, the council had approved his wish that his titles and estates should pass to his godson, Prince Charles.

'True,' admitted Charles smugly. 'Suffering a childhood with a cranky old godfather had some compensations after all!'

Then, unexpectedly and shockingly, we heard that Dauphin Jean, too, had died. The report delivered to the queen by the Hainault herald said that doctors had been unable to relieve a putrid abscess in his ear, which had driven him demented with pain before finally sending him to his maker shortly before Easter. Poor Jean, he was only eighteen, and I am sure the young thug of the nursery would have wanted a more glorious end. There was a rumour that he had been poisoned by Orleanists who abhorred his affinity with Burgundy, but of course there were always rumours after a sudden death. Then I remembered Tanneguy's dramatic vow of allegiance to Charles on the day Dauphin Louis died and wondered if the mysterious secretary's visit to Compiègne could possibly have had any connection with Jean's death, but I did not discuss it with Catherine. Sometimes it seemed wise to keep my thoughts to myself.

Whether Tanneguy du Chastel had any hand in the death or not, his wish was granted and Prince Charles duly became dauphin. Then the council appointed him governor of Paris. How a mere boy was expected to govern a starving city, riddled with factions and under external threat from two hostile armies, was a mystery to me but, with Tanneguy as his guide and mentor, Charles took the job very seriously.

Death and its consequences stalked the royal family in this period. A few months later, a sudden apoplexy carried off the Duke of Anjou and as a result Queen Isabeau found herself without friends in council. To Catherine's utter shock and surprise, the Count of Armagnac grabbed the opportunity to rid himself of his *bête noir* and produced a royal edict, signed by the king, which accused the queen of treason by dint of an adulterous affair with a nobody of a knight called Sir Louis Bourdon. There was no trial. Within hours the hapless Sir Louis was arrested, tied into a weighted sack and thrown into the Seine and the queen was forced into a closed litter at sword-point and carried off to be confined in the royal stronghold of Tours, a hundred leagues from Paris.

The dimmest of wits knew that the king was incapable of fastening his own doublet, let alone comprehending the crimes and punishments he had put his name to, but no one was prepared to take the queen's part against the devious Armagnac. Even her son showed no inclination to help her.

'The king signed the edict,' Charles shrugged, when Catherine pleaded with him. 'I am only the dauphin.'

I had never seen Catherine so angry.

'He says he owes her nothing, Mette. She abandoned him as a child and he will do nothing for her now. But she is his mother and this is a totally spurious charge! I doubt if the queen ever even met Sir Louis Bourdon. You know how she is about precedence and protocol. If she did commit adultery – and it is a big if – she would not do so with anyone of lower rank than a count. Yet look what happened to that poor knight. He didn't stand a chance. And what will they do to *her* when she is out of sight in Tours? We are none of us safe, when bullies like Armagnac think they can play monarch.'

'Only last week you told me that you feared the Queen would succeed in bringing Burgundy back to Paris, Mademoiselle,' I reminded her. 'At least we may be spared that now.'

'Yes and that is the real reason why Charles does not intervene. Tanneguy makes sure he is terrified of Burgundy, but the truth is we are all at the mercy of whoever holds the Royal Seal and the Constable's Sword. Oh, Mette, if only my father were not ill, if only Louis had not died! Dear God, the queen may not be good, but at least she is sane and she is strong. That is why Armagnac wants her out of the way and that is why we need her back.'

I was astonished that the day had come when Catherine was defending her mother, but there it was . . . uncertainty can induce strange alliances.

As to my own family affairs, I no longer knew whether Jean-Michel was alive or dead. My regular enquiries at the stables did bear some fruit when a royal scout who knew of my plight returned from a dangerous sortie into Picardy, having made a point of sheltering at the monastery in Abbeville. There the monks revealed that in the spring after the battle of Agincourt, Jean-Michel had recovered enough from his leg wound to limp off down the road towards Rouen, where he intended to find river transport to Paris. They had tried to persuade him to wait for a royal convoy or join an armed party of travellers, but he had insisted that he would make his own way and that was the last anyone had seen of him. I had heard enough stories of banditry and violence in the countryside to make me fear the worst. Whilst at last allowing myself to weep for his loss, I also scolded my husband's ghost for walking out into danger. Perhaps he had reckoned that a solitary limping vagrant would be of no interest to the *écorcheurs*, but as time went on it became obvious that he had been fatally wrong; poor, dear, stubborn Jean-Michel. Even so, a tiny spark of hope remained before I could completely resign myself to widowhood and Alys and Luc still harboured desperate hope that their father might one day return. War can pin people down for long periods when towns and cities come under siege or are occupied by a new power. The faint possibility remained that Jean-Michel was caught up in the civil unrest that had displaced so many.

Unlike her brothers and sisters, who had all been married as children, Catherine celebrated her sixteenth birthday if not free, at least single. With Paris under virtual siege, marriage to anyone seemed unlikely, least of all to King Henry who at that time was busy storming one Norman stronghold after another.

It was my Alys who gleaned the first inkling that our lives

215

were about to tumble into the abyss. She was still the apple of her Grandmère Lanière's eye and she paid regular visits to the harness-shop. One day she returned looking unusually troubled.

'The guilds are arming themselves,' she told me. 'My uncles talk of nothing else and I noticed that they all have the cross of St Andrew sewn under their hoods.'

Alys was nearly fifteen now and although quiet and gentle, she was nobody's fool. Her very placidity meant that people often forgot she was there and consequently she heard much that she may not have been intended to hear.

I felt my stomach lurch. 'Burgundy's badge!' I breathed. 'They want him back.'

Alys nodded vigorously. 'Yes. And it's not just the guilds. They say the university has swung over to Burgundy as well. And there's a rumour that the duke has rescued the queen from her imprisonment at Tours.'

'What!' I almost squeaked in my alarm. We were trying to keep our voices down for fear that we might be overheard, even though we had locked ourselves in my rooftop chamber, where few people came. I crossed myself and clasped my hands together. 'Holy Mother save us, if that is true what will Catherine do? She wants her mother back, but not under Burgundy's banner!'

'The story being spread in the city is that the queen feigned sickness and the castellan at Tours was so frightened she would die that he allowed her a litter to take her to a local holy well to seek a cure. She must have been in secret communication with Burgundy because he appeared at the well with a large force of men and took her to Melun.' Alys frowned. 'They say she will return to Paris when the guilds open the gates to Burgundy. And they will, Ma, I am sure they will.'

As soon as Catherine heard the rumour, she tackled Prince Charles with it. Despite their differences, their friendship persisted and they still broke their fast frequently together after Mass.

'I hear that the queen has finally thrown in her lot with Burgundy,' she remarked as soon as they had washed their hands. 'And that he has rescued her from Tours. Is this true?'

I was serving them as usual, but everything they ate had been tasted by the dauphin's cup-bearer, a taciturn individual appointed by Tanneguy du Chastel.

'Yes, it is true,' Charles nodded, spearing a preserved plum with his gold-handled knife. Each fruit in the dish bore a small scar where the taster had sampled it. 'Our beloved mother now lives under the protection of the cousin who murdered our uncle.' He raised his gaze to meet Catherine's. 'What a fine family we come from and what fine people we have for parents do we not? A madman and a traitor. Do you ever wonder who you take after? I know I do.'

Catherine ignored the question. 'You may call her a traitor, Charles, but Armagnac forced her into it, did he not? What else could she do?'

'Throw herself off a tower perhaps. There must be plenty of them at Tours,' Charles replied coldly.

Perched on his high-backed chair, his skinny physique encased once more in black mourning for his father-in-law, the Duke of Anjou, I could not help thinking he resembled a jackdaw on a chimney-pot. Earlier in the year, shortly after his fifteenth birthday, he and Marie of Anjou had been married, but although she shared his household, as she was not yet fourteen they had not been bedded. Surveying the Dauphin's undeveloped frame I wondered if he had reached the necessary maturity himself. Certainly his voice showed little sign of breaking.

'And commit herself to eternal hellfire! How can you say that?' protested Catherine. 'Are you suggesting that is what I should do if Burgundy forces his way back to the king's side?'

Charles dipped his plum in a bowl of cream. Cows grazed the orchards of St Pol and cream was one of the few luxuries still available in the palace. 'No, though you may wish you had,' he replied grimly. 'Certainly I see no future for myself under his aegis and I do not suppose the queen has much love for me either. Not since we found the gold she had stashed away at her house in the city and returned it to the Treasury.'

Catherine looked astounded. 'What gold? When was that?'

'Soon after she was taken to Tours. She will say it was owed to her, but we know it was stolen to bribe the guilds to admit Burgundy to the city.'

'Well, it looks as if the butchers may admit him anyway. What will you do if they open the gates?'

'Run for my life.' He popped the creamy sweetmeat into his mouth and chewed it thoughtfully. Then he placed a hand on his sister's arm and added earnestly. 'Will you see that my dogs are cared for?'

She eyed him balefully. 'I thought you advised me to throw myself off a tower. I can hardly do both.'

A rare smile creased her brother's cheeks. 'I said you may wish you had but I know you will not. You are too stubborn – and too devout.'

When the dauphin had gone, Catherine asked my opinion of this conversation, adding, 'Be honest, Mette, for I know you have a low opinion of Charles.'

'Not low, Mademoiselle,' I denied hastily. 'I mistrust him because he shows little concern for you. As children you were his refuge and support but now that he is your only real protector, he is more concerned for his dogs!'

'Oh but, Mette, he says he does not remember our childhood,' objected Catherine. 'And although he is the dauphin, he is still only a boy. If you think about it, he and I have only each other to rely on. All our other brothers and sisters are either dead or allied elsewhere. I am sure that, *in extremis*, Charles would not let me down.'

I bowed my head to hide the doubt in my eyes. 'If you say so, Mademoiselle. He did not offer to take you with him if he flees, however.'

She acknowledged that, but still refused to condemn her brother. 'I would be quite a hindrance, would I not? He truly believes he would be fleeing for his life. He is the last dauphin, and with him out of the way Burgundy could declare himself Heir of France. Poor Charles, he has much to contend with.'

'So do you, Mademoiselle,' I reminded her. 'Have you forgotten the cruelty of the Black Duke?' I fingered the scar on my cheek. 'The Count of Armagnac has always left you alone. I doubt if Burgundy would do the same.'

She lifted her chin. 'Burgundy frightened me when I was a child, but I am a woman now and the queen will protect me. I have nothing to fear.'

Brave words, I thought, but I spied the doubt in her eyes.

Easter came and went and nothing happened. The city was eerily quiet. There were none of the usual spring parades when guild members carried the effigies of their patron saints through the streets singing carols and dancing. Even the students, who normally went crazy on Mayday, remained diligently at their desks. Then, at the end of the month, on the feast of St Germain, monks and students dropped their pens and craftsmen and apprentices downed tools to escort the effigy of Paris' patron saint to the Hôtel de Ville, where priests prayed long and loud, imploring the saint to preserve the city from tyranny and strife. It was all too evident whose tyranny they meant, for Armagnac's guards trained crossbows on the crowd from the battlements of the Châtelet. Mercifully none was fired.

All the Lanière men, Jean-Michel's father and three brothers, attended the gathering and at the end of the day, Alys hurried off to the harness shop for news. Darkness had fallen before her return and as the Compline bell rang from the Celestine Abbey, I grew desperately anxious for her safety.

'You need not have worried, Ma,' she chided, at last slipping into our chamber from the moonlit wall-walk. 'Grandpère came with me to the palace gates and he whispered something very odd as he left me. *"Sleep behind locked doors tonight, Mignonne,"* he said. What do you think he meant?'

My blood froze. Mignonne was her grandfather's pet name for Alys and there was no doubt that this was some kind of warning – as far as he dared go to protect his beloved granddaughter. Taking her hand, I pulled her after me down the spiral stair towards Catherine's salon. 'I do not know precisely what he meant,' I muttered grimly, 'but I do know we must tell Mademoiselle immediately.'

Catherine and her ladies were in light-hearted mood, laughing over some remark one of them had made and she did not look pleased at our interruption.

'I am not nearly ready to retire yet, Guillaumette.' Her use of my full name was always a sign of irritation. 'I will call you when I am.'

I bent my knee and felt Alys do the same behind me. 'With your permission, Mademoiselle, we must speak with you. Alys has urgent news.'

I suspect that the desperate wringing of my hands told her more than my words, for she rose instantly, asking her ladies to leave. When the three of us were alone, she became less formal. 'What is it, Mette? Is there danger?'

When Alys told her what her grandfather had said, Catherine's cheeks blanched. 'Something is planned for tonight then? But what?'

I lifted my shoulders. 'We do not know. Perhaps the old man is right. We should all lock our doors and pray.'

Catherine made an impatient noise. 'No. First we must warn the king and the dauphin. I will go to the king. He will not understand, but at least his grand master can take precautions. Mette, can you go to Charles?'

'Of course, Mademoiselle, at once.' As I made for the door, I heard Alys at my heels and turned back to stop her. 'If the dauphin is not in his chamber, I will have to go searching for him. There is no point in us both risking danger.'

Catherine spoke up at once. 'No indeed. Alys can stay here with my ladies. We will all go to the king's hall. I am sure my father will not be harmed, whatever happens.'

Alys looked mutinous, but I kissed her quickly on the cheek and bade her obey the princess. 'Thank you, Mademoiselle,' I said gratefully. 'God be with you.'

'God be with *you*, Mette,' said Catherine earnestly. 'If anyone stops you, just say you are on an errand for me. It might be unwise to mention the dauphin.'

I took the route so often used by Jean-Michel and Luc – through the door at the top of the tower and along the wall-walk to the kitchen gate where steps led down to the rear of the Dauphin's House, now the home of Prince Charles and Marie of Anjou and their household of retainers and officials. No one stopped me for I was a familiar figure to the sentries on the battlements and even in darkness the pale gleam of my coif and apron easily identified me. Between the crenellations of the parapet I caught glimpses of bright moonlight shining off the river and heard the gentle slap of water far below against the curtain wall. It was a luminous May evening and the scene was one of peaceful calm. Only the sound of the sentries' boots stamping out their beat broke the tranquility. As I hurried along, I anxiously considered the possibility that I might have triggered a false alarm.

15

As soon as I stepped through the archway at the base of the kitchen gate, I knew it was no false alarm; during the minute it took me to descend the stair from the battlements, the peace of the night had been shattered. Raucous shouts and heavy thuds were now echoing over the rooftops and the sentries could be heard running towards the main gatehouse, their studded boots scrunching on the pavement of the wall-walk. The atmosphere had soured as fast as milk in a thunderstorm and a sense of approaching menace filled the air.

Heart pounding, I sped across the cobbled court to the king's cloister, at the far end of which a rear entrance led into the undercroft of the Dauphin's House. The stout, iron-bound door stood open, but the guard was lounging inside, deaf to the sounds that should have alerted him to trouble.

'Bar the door!' I ordered with as much authority as I could muster. 'And go and tell the guards at the front to do the same. Strangers are at the gates.'

Perhaps it was the urgency of my tone, perhaps he recognised me as the princess royal's nurse or perhaps he could see no harm in taking precautions even though the warning came from a bossy female in an apron. For whatever reason he took the requested action, sliding the heavy wooden beam into metal brackets on either side of the door. I picked up my skirt and raced up the spiral stairs ahead of me, which I assumed must lead to the upper apartments.

At the top I found myself in a vaulted vestibule from which several doors and archways led. I hesitated, trying to decide which to follow but none appeared more likely than another. Torches set into sconces emitted a weak flickering light, casting deep shadows which set my skin prickling. Instinct told me that time was too short to waste on futile searching, so I resorted to the quickest way of locating my quarry, yelling at the top of my voice. 'Attention! My lord dauphin! Danger!'

Almost instantly I heard the sound of running footsteps and Tanneguy du Chastel appeared panting from an archway just as several liveried men arrived from another, all brandishing naked blades. To my relief, Maître Tanneguy immediately called the others off, sheathed his own fearsome-looking poignard and grabbed me by the elbow. 'I know you,' he growled, peering close to identify me in the dim light. 'It is Madame Lanière. What is this danger? Tell me as we go.'

I explained as quickly as I could, despite the pain of his vice-like grip on my arm as he hauled me up a wider stairway at breakneck speed. 'I believe the guilds have opened the city to Burgundy's men, Monseigneur,' I panted. 'From the noises outside they are already at the palace gates. My father-in-law is a member of the butchers' guild and he warned my daughter

225

to expect trouble tonight. Princess Catherine has gone to the king and she sent me to warn her brother.'

'Bravo to the princess and bravo to you!' Reaching an upper floor, Maître Tanneguy swept me through a door and into the chamber beyond, where we were greeted by alarming snarls and the bared teeth of the dauphin's hounds.

'Back Clovis! Down Cloud! Maître Tanneguy, in the name of God what is it? What is happening?' Scrambling down from his magnificent curtained bed, Prince Charles looked ashen-faced but his voice rang out surprisingly forcefully, sending the dogs into a snarling crouch. My own heart was thudding like a barge-master's drum.

Tanneguy's immediate action on entering had been to unlock a heavy, iron-bound chest and extract a small leather pouch. It must have held something very precious for he buttoned it swiftly and carefully into the front of his doublet. 'Burgundy's men are at the gates, my lord,' he replied. 'We must leave instantly.' As he finished speaking, he began racing around the room collecting necessities – a sword and belt, a pair of boots, a fur-lined heuque.

'But I am in my chemise,' Charles protested. 'Surely there is time for me to dress!'

Tanneguy shook his head. 'No, your grace. You must come at once. Better to be naked and free than clothed and in chains.'

To his credit, Charles did not argue but asked one pertinent question. 'If the enemy is at the gate, Tanneguy, how do we leave?'

'Over the roof,' replied his mentor. 'I have established a secret route whereby we can get all the way to the Bastille, where the captain is a loyal friend.' By now he stood impatiently at the door, motioning the young prince forward. 'Come, highness. At once! I will show you.'

In the doorway Charles looked back at his hounds and then at me. His expression was anguished. 'Look after Clovis and Cloud for me, Mette. I will send for them when I can. Take them to your son Luc. Please!'

'Please' from a royal prince! His expression of desperate entreaty coloured my last impression of the dauphin – a tousled, frightened lad in a billowing chemise, his bare legs and feet showing white and vulnerable in the flickering lamplight. And then he was gone.

I stared around at the abandoned chattels of a princely life. A portable altar bearing a carved and gilded crucifix, a pile of leather-bound books clasped and hinged in gold and a jewel-encrusted harp with ivory keys but in the midst of all these lay Charles' most treasured possessions – the two long-nosed, lean-flanked white hounds, which he had consigned so urgently to my care. They crouched like heraldic beasts, regarding me intently as if I might be their next meal.

It was then that I heard the sound of conflict grow nearer and louder than before, so loud that it had to be coming from the very entrance to the Dauphin's House and I guessed the insurgents must have penetrated the main gate. My thoughts turned anxiously to Catherine and Alys. Were they safe? Surely Burgundy would not allow his men to harm defenceless girls? I felt sick with apprehension, knowing that the opposite was probably the truth.

Trying to appear calm so as not to alarm the hounds, I scanned the room for their leashes and spied them hanging from a hook beside the hearth, the jewelled thongs glinting in the glow of dying embers. Gingerly I crossed the chamber to collect them, half expecting the animals to make any movement an excuse to pounce. However, perhaps the sudden departure of their constant companion had subdued them for, to my surprise, they became quite docile, allowing me to fasten the leashes to their gem-studded collars. I even felt a moist lick of submission as I tugged them gently to their feet.

With the two white dogs trotting obediently beside me, their noses nudging my elbows, I set out to leave by the route I had come. When I reached the main stair the sound of irregular thumping indicated that the invaders had resorted to some sort of ram to batter down the main door. Strangely the hounds seemed unperturbed, but it scared me into a scurrying run. I had no wish to be found in the vicinity of the dauphin's empty chamber when the assailants inevitably managed to break through. The guard had abandoned the door in the undercroft but, after a brief struggle, I managed to remove the heavy bar and drag it open. I could not secure it after me, but since the bird had already flown there seemed no need. Pulling the dogs through the narrow doorway, I allowed myself a brief smile, perceiving the irony of the Burgundians battering away at the front entrance while a door stood wide open at the back. To my shame I never gave a thought to little Marie of Anjou in her apartments above, by then probably terrified by all the banging and shouting. Nor, I realised later, had her husband, racing for his freedom along the battlements and rooftops of St Pol. He had expressed concern only for his dogs.

The cloister leading along the rear of the building stretched away empty and quiet, oddly striped along its length due to the pattern of shadows cast by the bright moonlight slicing between its pillared arches. I was still intensely aware of possible danger but, emboldened by the company of the hounds, I let them lead me off down the flagged passage, praying that at the other end I would find Catherine and my little Alys safe in the king's hall.

We had taken no more than a dozen paces when the dogs suddenly stopped dead. In the moon's glare I could see the hackles rising on their necks. A duet of deep, angry growls swelled from their throats as, a few yards ahead, two burly figures stepped out of a black shadow into the white moonlight. Their faces were hidden under dark hoods but moonbeams glinted wickedly off the broad blade that each held in his right hand. My blood froze and I let forth a strangled cry, my gaze fixed on these glimmering shafts of evil. There was no mistaking their purpose. They were meat cleavers, crafted to hack through flesh and bone at a stroke. So there was no mistaking their owners either. Butchers – members of the trade guild which only five years before had been almost entirely responsible for 'The Terror' which had stalked the streets of Paris.

'Here's a sight to stir a man's cock,' growled the larger of the two faceless hulks. 'A nice meaty heifer, ready for the bull.'

In a busy alehouse or crowded city street such lewd talk might have merited a toss of the head and an angry riposte, but at night, in a deserted place, it was fraught with ugly intent.

Beside him the other man let out a long, lecherous snigger, a chilling sound crackling with bigotry, brute force and lust.

Fear flooded through me like molten metal, raising the hairs on every inch of my skin. Sensing my distress the hounds tugged their leashes free and surged forward, their snarls rising ferociously in pitch as they flung themselves at the two men with fangs bared. For one foolish moment I thought they might be my saviours.

I could not have been more wrong. Far from being daunted by a hundredweight of howling hound, both men roared with glee, swayed back on their heels and swung their cleavers with practised ease. Growls turned to yowls and then whimpers, which diminished to an unholy silence as two hairy bodies crumpled to the ground and quivered into lifelessness. Blood flowed from deep wounds in their white pelts, gathering in gleaming black pools in the moonlight. Appalled by this barbaric slaughter, at the moment when I should have turned on my heels and run for my life, my feet remained rooted to the spot and all I could do was gasp in horror, like a landed codfish.

The larger man advanced and I tensed automatically, waiting for the slashing blow that would pitch me headlong into eternity like the dauphin's poor hounds, but instead he fixed me with a sneering grin, grabbed a fold of my skirt and calmly used it to wipe the blood from his blade. I watched the stained cloth drop from his hand, a gaping cut showing where the razor-sharp edge had sliced through the fabric. Only then did I start to move, backing away like a hind at bay.

But escape was impossible. From being frozen with fear, my mind suddenly went into full spin and I saw with awful clarity the scene I had pictured every time I heard that another village in the countryside had been plundered and another wretched batch of peasant-women raped. Now the terror and violence had come to me, in all its hideous reality.

My attacker's hood had slipped back revealing fleshy bearded jowls, a bulbous nose and a mane of greasy hair. 'We were hoping for a royal ride, but I see all we have here is a common drab.' His voice was rough and harsh, laced with sneering venom.

He reached out with his free hand and grabbed my coif, pulling it roughly from my head as he pushed his face right up to mine. His breath stank like a latrine ditch. I felt my gorge rise and jerked away, but by now I was backed up against the wall of the cloister. At last I summoned up enough presence of mind to scream and let out two full-blooded shrieks before there was a clang of steel as my tormentor's cleaver fell to the ground and a grimy hand clamped over my mouth.

'Shut up, bitch!' the fiend snapped, cracking my head back against the hard stone so that stars exploded behind my eyes. 'Here, Hugh, you hold her and I will go first.'

Rolling my eyes wildly to the side I saw the second butcher put down his cleaver and move in beside his mate. 'Get her down, man,' he said roughly. 'More fun.' With a grunt he aimed a kick and his booted foot thudded into my knee, which instantly buckled. I struggled desperately but in seconds I was sprawled on the flagstones, arms flailing, trying vainly to land a few telling blows anywhere I could. Their answer to that was to pull my heavy woollen skirts up over my head and pin me down by them. Two brawny knees crushed my shoulders into the pavement, pulling the thick fabric tight over my face so that I could scarcely breathe. My senses swam, my limbs went weak and all the fight went out of me.

I do not know how long my ordeal lasted. It might have been minutes or it could have been half an hour. In my state of blind suffocation I felt as if my body was divided in two; my head and shoulders remained pinioned and paralysed as I struggled to suck air through the thick fabric of my woollen skirt and block out what was happening to the rest of me.

It felt as if a battering ram was pulverising my private parts, thudding and grinding at me like a huge pestle in a disintegrating mortar. It didn't seem possible that my body could take such an onslaught. At its height I thought my womb must burst up through my belly, forced from its roots by an impaling force that made my guts explode in agony. On and on it went, violent thrusts accompanied by brutish grunting and hoarse yells of triumph, as if I was some age-old enemy being gloriously conquered, instead of a poor lump of female flesh being bludgeoned and pounded into a wretched pulp.

When at last the 'battle' ended I was sightless and half-senseless and at the same time suffused with shame and pain. I felt the crushing weight leave me as the second of my self-satisfied 'victors' presumably stood up. 'Better finish her off,' I heard him say gruffly.

At first I hardly grasped his meaning, so grateful was I that the suffocating layers of cloth had loosened over my face, allowing drafts of air to reach my burning lungs. I sucked greedily at it, spitting the gagging fabric from my mouth. Then I heard the deadly ring of steel on stone as one of the men retrieved his cleaver from the cloister pavement. A sudden clear understanding stirred my cramped and battered limbs into action and I managed to raise my torso, push down my skirts and roll away from where I sensed the slashing blow would fall.

It never came. There was a warning shout from one man to the other and both my assailants suddenly scampered off down the cloister as fast as their craven legs could carry them, whilst from the other end of the passage came the thud of approaching footsteps.

Several pairs of feet stopped in my field of vision, which was confined to a small area of moonlit flagstones. I had neither the strength nor the will to lift my head and see who it might be, certain that whoever it was could only have scorn and derision for a female used as I had just been. I feared that perhaps the assault would begin again with a fresh onslaught, but I could not summon the strength to flee. Slumped into the right-angle where the wall met the floor, I fervently wished I could crawl down a crack in the mortar. The intense pain in my body's core was matched by a burning sense of self-loathing. I felt like the slime left by a passing slug.

'What has been going on here?' demanded a clipped voice which sounded more used to issuing orders than emitting oaths. 'You three – follow those men and try to apprehend them. I do not like the look of this.'

Three pairs of leather-clad feet disappeared, leaving behind two pairs more grandly clad in plated armour; a knight and his squire perhaps. I was too dazed to care.

'Here, let me help you.' The same voice spoke again and a hand appeared, offering me assistance to rise. I shrank away from it and tried to force my trembling legs to support my own weight by grabbing at the rough stone of the wall. Gradually I hauled myself upright but I kept my head down, refusing look at the speaker. All I could see was the yellow chevron device on his jupon and the riveted joints at his steel-plated elbows.

'Who are you?' he asked and to my surprise I detected a note of compassion in his voice. 'What has happened here?'

I shook my head. Even under torture I could not have found words to describe my recent ordeal.

'Is this yours?' The knight's companion had retrieved my coif and held it out so that I could see it. It was dusty and crushed, but to my addled wits it represented a desperate scrap of decency. I grabbed it gratefully and pulled it over my head but the effort nearly sent me crashing back to the ground. My skirt hid the bloodiest of the damage but my legs were juddering with shock and my shoulders still heaved with the effort of trying to force air into my starved lungs. A terrible moisture ran down the inside of my thighs.

'Who are you?' The knight repeated and this time a hint of impatience tainted the pity in his tone. 'What is your name?'

I shook my head once more. My mind had cleared enough to prompt caution. I would trust no man again.

'Do you work here at the palace? Are you a servant perhaps? Who do you work for?'

I remained silent. Now that a tiny measure of my strength was returning, I itched to be away. However chivalrous this anonymous knight might appear to be, he was a Burgundian and no good came with him.

Nevertheless he persisted, mouthing words at me slowly, as if to a dim-witted child. 'We are looking for the dauphin. Do you know where we might find him?'

His companion had been examining the mangled corpses of the hounds. 'Look, my lord, they are white hounds. I have heard that the dauphin possessed a pair of pure-bred deerhounds.'

Now I knew I had to get away. Being found in the proximity of these poor princely appendages definitely implied knowledge of their master's whereabouts. I tensed against the wall, ready for flight.

'Are these the dauphin's hounds? What has happened to their master? You know something, do you not? Tell me!' The knight's voice vibrated in my ears and I shook my head violently, as much to rid myself of the questions as to refute them. Suddenly I could not take any more. Whatever the cost, I had to get away. I clapped my hands over my face, turned blindly and stumbled off down the cloister in a shambling, uncertain lope, hardly knowing which direction I took. I heard the metallic ring of armour plate as the squire made to follow me, but the knight's next words halted him.

'Let her go. The woman has been badly abused and her wits are addled. We will get no sense from her and we are wasting valuable time.'

Intent on fleeing, as much from myself as from the Burgundian knight, I blundered on, bumping into corners and tripping over uneven flagstones until, when I finally took my hands from my face, I found myself in the kitchen courtyard, without really knowing how I got there.

Returning awareness brought an agonising resurgence of pain, both physical and mental. My whole body throbbed and the flesh between my legs seemed to sizzle and burn. All I could think about was quenching the fire and with that in mind my eyes fixed on the huge stone cistern which collected the rainwater from the palace roof, where scullions dipped their pails to replenish the kitchen water-barrels. Whimpering, I hobbled across the yard and heaved myself recklessly over the edge of the tank, lowering my legs into its dark, blessed depths. My skirts blossomed around me, lifted by trapped air, and the cold water brought instant sweet relief to my burning private parts. For many minutes I stood waist deep, while the chill numbed my ravaged flesh until I could no longer feel any sensation. But it could not still the whirling of my mind. Fear and self-disgust spun into a maelstrom of rage and humiliation, crystallising as an all-consuming hatred. The identities of my individual attackers I might never know, but the core of my loathing centered not on them but on another; the man who had seared his name on my mind the day he scarred the flesh of my face and who I knew was truly responsible for the evil that had descended upon us. Jean the Fearless, Duke of Burgundy.

16

In the king's great hall the royal party made its way onto the dais and a loud cheer rose up from the assembled crowd of onlookers. Standing silent among them, I felt my stomach clench; for the first time since his mailed fist had scarred my face fifteen years before, there before me stood the devil duke. He was garbed all in black as I remembered him but, instead of armour, he wore a magnificent flowing houppelande gown edged with sable and liberally patterned with the bizarre personal emblem that so eloquently declared his vaunting ambition – a carpenter's plane. Here was a man determined to shape the world to his own design.

Working themselves up to a frenzy of excitement, the crowd began to chant his battle-cry – *'Jean sans Peur! Jean sans Peur!'* – and he raised an arm in salute like a victorious general. An elaborate turban-hat added inches to his stature so that he dwarfed the shrunken figure of the king, who scuttled into the hall a fraction ahead of him wearing a gold coronet slightly askew and a blue ermine-trimmed gown, which seemed to have been made for someone much larger. I noticed the duke's hand go to the king's elbow, a gesture which appeared to offer deferential support, but actually ensured that the feeble-minded monarch did not stray from his new protector's side. Behind this ill-matched pair came the queen, as flamboyant and glittering as ever, followed by Catherine, graceful but ghostly pale, swaying in her heavy court robes like a willow-wand hampered by the weight of its leaves.

As they took their seats at the board, the triumphant smiles of the queen and the duke reflected the brilliance of the gleaming gold plate displayed on the fine damask cloth. The King perched between them, corralled in his high-backed throne, twitching like a trapped coney and Catherine sat on the duke's left, isolated at the end of the table where the resplendent new Burgundian grand master of the king's household stood directing proceedings with his silver staff. For this was no ordin-ary repast. It was a public banquet, an occasion when the people of Paris were allowed into the king's great hall to watch their monarch dine and, on this occasion, to witness the advent of a new regime.

I stood with Alys, jostled and pushed by the crowd, mostly of men who alternated between cheering their hero and quarrelling over the best vantage points. Judging by the roars of adulation, there were few among them whose skin crawled as mine did at the sight of the new regent of France, as Jean the Fearless now styled himself. To a man they welcomed him, hoping for the restoration of order and the end of anarchy and shortage.

I saw the duke incline his head towards Catherine to make a remark and noticed her flush deep red in response, but whether from anger or embarrassment I could not tell. Burgundy's expression was unreadable.

'Keep calm, my sweet girl, keep calm,' I willed her silently.

I kept my own feelings well hidden these days. Inside I had become a wobbling mass of hatred and disgust but during the blood-soaked weeks since the palace gates had opened to Burgundy's thugs, I had perfected the art of deception, had even managed to conceal all evidence of the bodily harm and the loathsome horror inflicted on me by the two predatory butchers. It was the only way I felt able to hold my head up and survive. It is a sad commentary on our skewed society that nothing but disdain and disparagement is offered a woman known to have been violated. I had been unlucky but I was not dead and I did not wish to be disparaged. I considered that my secret was safe with me and me alone. Anyway, to describe it to anyone would have been to release the dreadful demons that threatened to overcome me every time I had a flash of recall and I feared that if I let them loose I would succumb completely, like the poor, mad king. Mercifully, only a few days after the attack I was blessed with Eve's curse, for I think to have found myself with child to a nameless thug would have been a burden impossible to bear.

At the time, after the freezing water in the kitchen cistern had sufficiently numbed my battered body, I had dragged myself to my quarters and made liberal applications of a witch-hazel salve and changed into dry clothes. Then, scared by the sudden and very raucous sounds of looting in Catherine's apartments below, I had scurried out onto the wall-walk, praying it would be deserted, and forced myself to brave the perils of stairway and cloister, ducking out of sight from every possible encounter until I reached the king's great hall. There, to my intense relief, I found Catherine and Alys huddled among a frightened group of court ladies on the steps of the royal dais, claiming whatever sanctuary was to be found in the shadow of the anointed monarch, who sat bewildered on his throne, uneasy but defiantly wearing his crown and court mantle. Whoever had dressed the king in these potent symbols of his sovereignty had shown great foresight for they gave him a much-needed air of regal authority over the Burgundian commander of the insurgency, who had placed hand-picked guards on the entrance to the great hall, insisting that the rabble be excluded and the king and his daughter be treated with due deference.

'Thank God you are safe, Ma!' Alys had exclaimed, hugging me fiercely and too overcome with joy at my arrival to notice me wince with pain. 'Did you have any trouble?'

'No,' I lied. 'But there have been looters in your chambers, Mademoiselle. I heard noises there but I did not investigate.'

'Nor should you have done!' Catherine whispered indignantly. 'May God reward you for your courage tonight, Mette. Were you successful in your chief endeavour?'

I nodded briefly but emphatically and was rewarded by a squeeze of the hand and a triumphant little smile. It was at that moment that I resolved to consign my own nightmare experience to the deep recesses of my mind, where it kept company with the faint hope that one day Jean-Michel would walk back into my life. Only later, when I woke from deep sleep, sweating and kicking and desperately gasping for breath was it brought forcibly home to me that I had as little hope of erasing those terrible memories as I had of celebrating the return of my husband.

The next day, God be thanked, Luc managed to make his way to my tower-top quarters and I quickly learned that his first concern had been for his canine charges.

'Some weird guys came to the kennel waving meat cleavers but luckily they took no interest in the dogs,' he recounted. 'They only wanted their jewelled leashes and collars. I'm very worried about the dauphin's deer-hounds though. They seem to have disappeared.'

I had no intention of revealing that I knew the fate of the deer-hounds. It would provoke too many questions that I had no wish to answer. 'We heard that the dauphin managed to escape from Paris, so perhaps he took them with him,' I said, quickly adding on a warning note, 'And you, Luc? Are you keeping that loose tongue of yours under control? You do realise that now is not the time to start answering back or offering your opinion on anything? Just do your work and say nothing.'

He looked at me pityingly. 'I know how to look after myself, Ma,' he protested.

'Perhaps you do, but these are exceptional times, Luc. We must all be extra careful,' I insisted, inwardly affirming my own vow of silence because a boy only recently turned twelve should not have to deal with his mother's rape.

My words of warning were timely, for in the following weeks Paris was subject to wholesale murder. Anyone who was known or discovered to oppose Burgundy, paid the penalty. One of the primary victims was the Count of Armagnac, betrayed by a member of his household as he was attempting to flee Paris. Along with the king's grand master, chancellor and secretary, he was paraded in chains to a makeshift scaffold outside the Hôtel de Ville and, without charge or trial, unceremoniously hanged before a jeering and hate-filled mob. I took care not to venture out of the palace, but we were told that their bodies still dangled from the gibbet three months later, mutilated and raven-pecked. The Countess of Armagnac had also been arrested and questioned, and she remained under close confinement in the Louvre. Only after the riots and killings had died down and the streets had been cleaned up, did the Duke of Burgundy make a grand procession into the city with the queen at his side. The following day heralds proclaimed their joint regency at every market cross.

With both the king and the queen under Burgundy's control, Catherine was completely at the mercy of the man we were now too frightened to call 'the devil duke', even in the privacy of her bedchamber. Immediately after her first encounter with him, I could see the change in her. She returned pale-faced and clearly troubled. She did not confide what had passed between them, but it was evident that even formal contact with such a master manipulator had begun to undermine her self-confidence.

Overnight all Catherine's Armagnac-appointed ladies-in-waiting had vanished, either arrested or fled from Paris with their families. Only faithful Agnes de Blagny remained, having no connections and therefore judged to be no threat. The new sentries posted at Catherine's tower were total strangers and unpleasant ones at that. Not only did they question every exit and entrance, but they spied on us blatantly and we knew that everything was relayed to Burgundy's agents.

A word or a message from Charles might have boosted her morale, but there was none. After his disappearance over the roof-tops we heard nothing of him except that an attempt led by Tanneguy du Chastel to retake Paris through the Porte St Antoine had been swiftly repulsed.

Then the new joint regents issued an edict stripping Prince Charles of the dauphincy and declaring him an outlaw, a traitor and a bastard.

Having heard this edict read in the king's hall, Catherine marched angrily into her bedchamber snatching pins from her elaborate court head-dress and scattering them wildly about, as if she couldn't rid herself quickly enough of all connection with the court and its leaders.

'The queen has gone mad!' she exclaimed. 'Does she not realise that in declaring her own son a bastard, she condemns *herself* as a traitor and an adulterer? No doubt Burgundy will soon be calling himself the heir of France. Who knows what he would have done to Charles had he not fled. I thank God and his angels that you and Alys warned us in time, Mette. At least there is one member of our family who is not caught in the devil's thumbscrew.'

In the midst of this tirade I rushed to close the door. 'Take care, Mademoiselle,' I warned. 'Ears are everywhere.'

'All right, Mette, I will whisper,' Catherine agreed, dropping her voice so that I had to strain to hear her. 'Let me tell you the latest scheme at the court of double-dealing. My brother is betrayed utterly. Peace negotiations are to resume with King Henry of England – the queen and Burgundy will be looking to King Henry to destroy Charles, and I am crucial to their success!'

She sank her head in her hands and I thought the anger would turn to tears.

Instead, she said, 'I am to have my portrait painted – again! An artist arrives tomorrow to begin the picture.' To my surprise she looked almost pleased at the prospect.

Intrigued by the change in her, I murmured, 'Is that so, Mademoiselle?' and picked up the hairbrush, exchanging puzzled glances with Alys who was crawling around the floor retrieving the scattered hair-pins.

Catherine sat on her dressing stool and leaned her head back to let me run the brush down the full length of her pale-gold tresses in the way that always relieved her tensions. She closed her eyes but her murmured confidences continued. 'I think it possible that if I marry Henry I might persuade him otherwise. Besides . . .' her eyes opened and she raised a hand-glass to consider her reflection, '. . . I have decided that marriage may be my only way of thwarting the devil's lechery. If I am being offered as the future Queen of England, surely even Burgundy will not dare to tamper with the goods.'

There was a short pause in my brush strokes as I caught my breath, confounded by this last remark. I looked down at the beautiful face in the glass and thought of the girl she had been at her fourteenth birthday banquet, before the battle of Agincourt had changed everything. Then she had been a young damsel, now she was truly a royal lady, with a guarded intelligence in her once-guileless blue eyes. It had been weeks since I had seen her smile and in that moment I knew that she had been keeping as much from me as I was keeping from her.

'Are you telling me that he has propositioned you, Mademoiselle?' I asked with deep concern.

Catherine shook her head. 'Oh no, Mette, but his every glance is charged with a vile contempt for women. Poor little Marie of Anjou is brought down to dinner by an armed escort, otherwise she would not enter the duke's presence. Of course she scarcely eats a thing. I know Charles could not take her with him, but what is to become of her? Today she begged the queen to be allowed to go to Charles in Bourges, but Burgundy said to her that the pope would not hold her to an unconsummated union with a bastard and that he would find her a real man to bed with. How could the queen let him speak like that?'

Every aspect of Catherine's portrait was supervised by Burgundy, starting with the choice of artist, Maître Henri Bellchose, who had painted the duke's likeness the previous year. Although it was August and searingly hot, he was adamant that Catherine should be pictured in full court regalia, complete with heavy gold coronet and ermine-trimmed mantle. Stressing the need for haste he also insisted the sittings were long and so for days on end she emerged from them prostrate with the heat. I thought

245

the resulting portrait showed the strain she was under, depicting a lady who, although beautiful, looked considerably older than Catherine's sixteen years. It was displayed for several days in the king's hall before the Bishop of Beauvais carried it off to a meeting with King Henry, who was still besieging Rouen as the climax of his conquest of Normandy.

'Very convenient, him being only fifty leagues away,' remarked Catherine with cynical irony. 'They are going to arrange my marriage to the sound of English guns dismantling the walls of one of my father's most loyal and beautiful cities.'

But the walls of Rouen held; there was no treaty and no marriage. King Henry insisted that King Charles' signature on any document must be counter-signed by Dauphin Charles, publicly declaring Burgundy 'not eligible to dispose of the inheritances of France'.

To impart this news to us, Catherine had dismissed her unwelcome posse of Burgundian ladies, pretending to go to her bedchamber and instead climbed the stair with Agnes to find me and Alys eating supper by our own hearth. Her visit took us by surprise because she had not done this for many months. She did not, as hitherto, take a seat beside Alys on the bench, leaving that place to Agnes and instead letting me install her in Jean-Michel's old chair.

'You could have heard a pin drop in the great hall while the herald read King Henry's response to the treaty proposals,' Catherine began. 'I did not know whether to laugh or cry, especially when it came to the bit about Burgundy's ineligibility to sign. I have never seen the duke's expression so black. I thought he might have an apoplexy. Obviously my portrait made no difference whatsoever. King Henry intends to take what he deems to be his by force of arms.' She shook her head at my offer of a cup of wine. 'Meanwhile, the duke has announced that the court is to move to Pontoise. He says it is to avoid the plague in Paris. I have not heard of any plague, have you, Mette?'

'No I have not, although there are always rumours of some epidemic or other. Pontoise is nearer to Rouen, of course, but if he is intending to attack the English, why is he taking the whole court?'

'Because he is not going to attack the English – he is going to double-deal as usual,' she replied. 'Burgundy will do what he is best at – playing two sides against the middle – and guess who is the scapegoat, tethered between the howling wolves?' She paused for a moment, staring into the fire before continuing her tale of affairs at court.

'The queen told me today that Charles has also offered my hand in marriage to King Henry, as part of *his* peace negotiations. Well, good for Charles! I prefer to be offered to the enemy by my brother than by Burgundy. However, my scheming mother believes *she* can save the whole situation by bringing the lost sheep back to the fold. To that end, Marie of Anjou is to be allowed to go to Charles in order to persuade him to return to his father. I think the Queen believes we can all be one big happy family – herself, Burgundy, Charles, King Henry and me. Sometimes I am not certain which of my parents is the craziest! How can she not know that Charles would rather throw himself on his sword than come within fifty miles of Jean of Burgundy?'

Perhaps it was her own powerlessness in the midst of this political turmoil that led Catherine to begin her practice of writing letters to her brother. I was not aware that she was doing this until many years later, although once or twice I spied her pushing folded papers into a concealed compartment in the base of her travelling altar and locking it with a small silver key, which she kept on a neck-chain hidden under her chemise. Sadly, as all court couriers were in the employ of Burgundy and her companions and servants were closely watched, there could never have been an opportunity for her to send a letter, especially to the outlaw, traitor and bastard that the new Council of Regency had decreed her brother to be.

From the Princess Royal, Catherine of Valois, Daughter of France,

To my dear and well beloved brother Charles, Dauphin of Viennois,
I am resolved to write down everything I can of events following your departure from the Hôtel de St Pol, so that when you are come to your inheritance, that is to the throne and crown of France, you will be fully appraised of the crimes and atrocities perpetrated on the king, his court and the people of Paris by Jean, Duke of Burgundy, his affinity and accomplices.

Among these the murder by lynching of the king's chief ministers, including Constable Armagnac and the grand master and other officials of the royal household.

Our mother the queen has signed the decree declaring you illegitimate and stripping you of the dauphincy, though such an infamy also makes her a traitor and an adulterer. The devil duke has her in his power, it is said, because you failed to go to her aid when she was imprisoned at Tours on charge of treason. These are dreadful times when ties of blood unravel and I hope and pray that will never happen between us.

It has come to my knowledge that your ministers have proposed a peace treaty with Henry of England, to be cemented by a marriage between him and me. How willingly I would agree to such an arrangement if at the same time it removed the Duke of Burgundy from the King's side and established you as the rightful dauphin and Regent of France.

I thank God that Marie has at last been allowed to come to you, but you should know that she suffered great humiliation at the hands of the duke. Meanwhile, for me the humiliation continues. The duke has no regard for Christian morals and constantly plagues me with lewd insinuations.

I cannot be sure when or if I will be able to send this and future letters, but at least they will serve to chronicle the grisly circumstances presently surrounding

Your loving sister,
Catherine

Written at the Hotel de St Pol, Paris, this day Monday the 25th of July 1418.

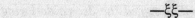

PART THREE

From Chateau de Pontoise to Troyes
Burgundy's Reign of Terror
1418–20

17

At thirty-two years of age, I had never slept a night outside the walls of Paris, but during the next two and a half years we – that is Catherine and her little entourage – became like nomads, constantly on the move. Despite some apprehension about travelling into the unknown, it felt good to leave Paris – good to leave the fear and the rivalries and the danger in the streets.

Pontoise was one of a score of royal castles built to defend the city approaches. It lay on the road to Rouen, in an area of forest and farmland called the Vexin. In good weather one man on a horse could reach it in a few hours, but moving the whole court was a different matter and our journey took two long days. Alys and I travelled on an oxcart laden with chests full of clothing and linen and this cart was followed by several more containing bedding, hangings and furniture, including the prie-dieu and Catherine's precious altar with its triptych of the Virgin and Child. Her bed, dismantled and stacked, travelled on a cart of its own.

'Do they have no furniture at Pontoise?' I grumbled to the clerk of the household who came to supervise this exodus.

'None suitable for a princess,' he responded testily, all the while scratching an inventory on a long roll of parchment. 'You had best get used to packing and unpacking, for his grace of Burgundy thinks that the royal family should be seen more outside Paris.'

With the duke prominently at their side no doubt, I thought sourly. Watching the clerk make his inventory, I decided it might be prudent to make one myself when the carts were unloaded in Pontoise. If anything went astray, I wanted to be the first to know about it.

Catherine left Paris several days before us, travelling down the Seine by barge with the queen. Agnes went with her, as well as her four new Burgundian ladies-in-waiting who Catherine had already secretly christened 'the Flanders mares'. En route they were to stay at Poissy abbey, the convent where Catherine and Agnes had been educated and where Catherine's older sister Marie, who had been enclosed there for twenty years, was due to be installed as the new abbess. There being no place for men on such an occasion, the Duke of Burgundy escorted the king separately by barge to Pontoise.

As we trundled laboriously through open country with the city vanishing behind us, I was relieved that Catherine was not travelling with us. From her barge I hoped she would not be able to see, as we did, league after league of weed-choked fields, burned-out villages and fire-blackened orchards. It was like travelling through purgatory. Tales had been reaching us for years of successive armies tramping over the Île de France causing havoc and devastation, and now we could see the evidence with our own eyes; one abandoned village after another with empty hovels falling to ruin around the walls of crumbling, roofless churches.

On the second day our way passed through thick forest and the road was narrow, leaving no room to avoid the deep ruts, baked like stone in the August sun. Alys and I were soon so bruised and battered from clinging to the bucking oxcart, that we decided to get down and walk. In the shade of the trees it was much cooler and happily it afforded us the chance to talk freely to each other without being overheard.

Luc had remained with the royal hounds in the kennel at the Hôtel de St Pol and Alys fretted about his safety. 'He is a bit of a dauphinist at heart. That is why I wonder if he will be all right, although he does know he has to keep very quiet about it.'

'I did not know he had any particular loyalties – apart from to us, of course,' I said faintly.

'That is another thing,' Alys went on. 'I think that whoever the princess marries, Luc is more likely to want to go and join the dauphin than come with us. He thinks that if the dauphin arranges a marriage to King Henry that is one thing, but if the Duke of Burgundy arranges it, it will be a betrayal.'

I walked in silence for a while, brow knitted. I hardly dared to ask my next question. 'What about you, Alys. Are you having second thoughts?'

She turned to me with a smile that lit up her brown eyes and a lump came to my throat as I suddenly saw how much she resembled her father. 'No, Ma. I will stick with you – and the princess of course. Luc will go his own way.'

With a little difficulty I returned Alys' smile and tucked my arm in hers. I thought of myself at her age, unrepentantly pregnant and heedless of what the future held. She seemed so much steadier, less foolish. 'We will have to wait and see. I hope one day you will find a man who will want you to go his way.'

'Perhaps,' she said. 'But at least I will have a choice. I wouldn't like to be the princess – handed over like a prize filly – even if I was wearing fine silks and jewels and marrying a king.'

I laughed at that and jokingly pulled her coif down over her face with my free hand. 'Oh, Alys, Alys,' I teased, 'you are such a little *bourgeoise* – with a mind of your own. No king would know what to do with you!'

When we reached Pontoise the sun was burning like a brazier on the horizon, dramatically illuminating our first glimpse of the castle, a mighty fortress built high on a rocky outcrop over the River Oise. To reach it we had to cross a stone bridge and pass through the town, a prosperous-looking habitation tucked protectively behind stout walls and boasting several market places and a scattering of stone churches. Our driver told me there had been a fortification at that point since ancient times, guarding the river-crossing. 'They say the present castle is built on the vaults of a much older one,' he added. 'It sounds risky to me, but it looks solid enough.'

To my eyes it looked daunting. Monumental towers of grey stone gathered us into their long black shadows as we neared the outer drawbridge and Alys and I exchanged doubtful glances. This was vastly different from the wide courtyards and elegant cloisters of the Hôtel de St Pol and there was little sign of a welcome in the bristling ranks of bowmen on the battlements. However, apprehension gave way to anger when I saw the accommodation allocated to Catherine. It was in a two-story stone building adjacent to the great hall and the rooms were small, damp and cheerless with unadorned walls and meagre windows, but the chief fault was a crucial one. In this fortress full of rough soldiers, Catherine would need her entourage of young ladies around her to act as chaperones, but there was no room for them. Furious at this glaring omission, I set out immediately to seek redress.

After asking directions I found the grand master's office on the first floor of the main gatehouse. In a room scattered with ledgers and piles of scrolls and papers, several clerks were perched at high desks, busy with ink and quill, and two apprentices were stacking parchment rolls in a heavy ironbound chest. Judging by the richness of his garb, the only other occupant of the room was of a higher social rank. He looked no more than twenty, but he had a definite air of command, aided by a handsome, square-jawed face and bright-blue eyes. Approaching him purposefully, I made a polite bob and waited for him to speak.

'Is there something you want?' he asked curiously, his manner brisk but not unfriendly.

'Yes, if you please, sir,' I nodded. 'I am woman of the bedchamber to the princess royal and I have just been shown the apartment allocated to her. I regret to say that it will not do.'

The young man lowered the letter he had been reading and raised one of his arched eyebrows. 'Indeed? Why not, may I ask?'

'Before I explain, may I know whether I am speaking to someone in authority?' I persisted, irritated by the suppressed amusement I detected behind his outward courtesy.

To my surprise he swept me a bow, waving the hand holding the letter in an exaggerated flourish. 'Guy de Mussy at your service, Madame, loyal squire to the Duke of Burgundy and presently seconded to the grand master of the royal household.'

I had never seen or heard of him before, but there were many in Burgundy's retinue who were new to their tasks and most were a good deal less personable than this young man. I decided that reason rather than protest would be the wisest approach. 'Well, Monsieur de Mussy, the lodgings allocated to the Princess Catherine simply are not big enough. There are only two chambers and one guarderobe, which, I am sure you will agree, is an insult to offer to the king's daughter.'

'Why, how many guarderobes does she need?' the squire asked, his eyes twinkling. 'No, I am sorry, let me explain. There is a shortage of accommodation within the inner defences of the castle, where his grace has ordered that the royal family should be lodged for their protection. The king and queen have no more rooms than the princess. Chambers have been allocated elsewhere for their companions and retainers, so I assure you, Madame, that you will not be obliged to sleep in the great hall with the men-at-arms.'

I drew myself up indignantly. 'It is not my own security I am concerned about, Monsieur, it is that of the princess royal. I am sure you will agree that in a fortress such as this, where many knights and soldiers live cheek by jowl with those they serve, a lady of her beauty and nobility should be well protected from any – er – nuisance.'

The young man inclined his head and his piercing blue gaze told me he understood my meaning. All hint of mirth had vanished. 'I have been instructed by the duke himself to make it my personal duty to ensure her highness' comfort and safety. I shall be in constant attendance and if you will come with me now, Madame, I will show you the additional accommodation set aside for the other ladies. You will see that it is not very far from the princess' and that it, too, is well protected.'

Pontoise Castle was built on old-fashioned defensive lines, with a great hall and donjon within an inner wall and other houses and outbuildings ranged within a sprawling outer curtain. After murmuring instructions to one of the clerks, the squire ushered me across the outer bailey to a substantial stone house situated beside the tunnel gateway, which was the only access to the inner defences. When royalty was in residence in the donjon, this lodging accommodated the constable of the castle and his lady and also contained several upper rooms which Guy de Mussy said would suitably house Catherine's companions.

'And the constable's servants will attend to their needs and protection,' he added.

One thing still gave me cause for concern however. 'What happens when the inner gate is shut and the portcullis lowered?' I asked. 'The ladies would be on the wrong side of it.'

De Mussy smiled reassuringly, showing a complete set of enviably straight, white teeth. 'The inner gate is only shut if the castle comes under attack and in that unlikely event you can be sure that there would be alarms and warnings and plenty of time for all the ladies to take shelter in the keep. Now, shall I escort you back to the princess' tower, or can you remember the way?'

I took the hint, thanking him for his help and assuring him that I could find my own way back. As he strode away across the cluttered bailey, I watched the youthful swagger of his gait and the proud set of his shoulders and wondered what Catherine would make of him. It was not long before I found out, for when she arrived at her new lodgings it was Guy de Mussy who escorted her there.

He had obviously explained the restrictions on accommodation, for Catherine did not show any surprise when she crossed the threshold. In fact, she made no comment at all but sat down and languidly began to wave her fan in front of her face. 'Monsieur de Mussy, is there a garth or pleasure garden anywhere in which we might escape the heat a little while we are here? That would be a great boon.'

The young man looked doubtful. 'There is a small garden, Princesse, but I believe it has been earmarked for the queen. Would you like me to enquire whether . . .'

Catherine cut him off with a smile and a snap of the fan. 'Oh no, please do not put yourself in an awkward position with the queen. I will ask any favours of her myself. Perhaps it might be possible to ride out into the countryside for some fresh air, if you were to be kind enough to arrange an escort for me.'

Guy de Mussy bowed. 'With your permission I will

accompany you myself, Madame. There are some shady places to ride along the river but it is necessary to check first with the constable of the castle that there have been no reports of trouble in the vicinity. Things have been peaceful lately, but there is always the possibility of incursions.'

'Is that so?' Catherine looked quite animated. 'Would these be incursions by the English or supporters of my brother? Or is it more peaceful now because it would have been more likely to be Burgundians?'

A flush spread over the young man's face. 'Madame is pleased to tease,' he remarked. 'Is it permitted to return the compliment should the occasion arise?'

Catherine tapped her lips with her fan, as if pondering her reply. 'Monsieur would have to make that decision for himself I think,' she responded sweetly. 'I imagine that a man of action is not afraid of taking a few risks.'

I was quietly amused by this exchange. I had never heard Catherine flirt in this way before, but then I did not very often observe her conversing with courtiers, let alone one so close to her own age.

Her ladies arrived to report that the accommodation in the constable's house was acceptable and I left them in a fluster of fan-fluttering brought about by a male presence, although I thought it unlikely that the Flanders mares would stand any chance with Monsieur de Mussy while Catherine was about.

That night, as she was preparing for bed in her new chamber, she gave me a detailed description of her sister's installation as Abbess of Poissy.

'It was a simple service of dedication but very moving,' she concluded. 'I am so impressed by Marie's achievements, Mette. She made me realise that intellect and learning are not a strictly male prerogative; that women fulfill God's purpose by using their brains as much as men do. And yet, when I try to discuss any literature other than romances or legends, men tend to give me the strangest looks. Why do they assume that no one in a skirt has ever read Aristotle?'

'I wonder how many men have done so,' I remarked, wondering myself who Aristotle was. 'Perhaps educated women make less educated men feel inadequate.'

Catherine considered this as she applied the frayed rosemary twig I had handed her for teeth-cleaning. As she returned the twig she frowned and asked, 'Do you think Guy de Mussy has read Aristotle, Mette?'

'Now I wonder why you mention *him*?' I responded, mirroring her look of innocent inquiry.

'Well he is quite attractive, you know he is!' she exclaimed, turning a little pink.

'He certainly seems to think so,' I agreed. 'Would you like him more if he had read Aristotle, or less?'

She laughed at that. 'I am not sure. More I think, as long as he was prepared to discuss it rather than explain it. Why do you smile?'

'Because I am pleased to see you happier than for some time and because I do not believe you really want to discuss Aristotle with Monsieur Guy,' I said, moving to discard the used twig in the waste pail which stood inside the guarderobe arch. 'I think you would rather flirt with him.'

'I would not! How dare you! I think he is rather big-headed actually and he is almost certainly a spy for the duke.' She stood up and wandered towards the bed. 'Anyway, what of it?'

I began to turn down the sheets. 'Nothing,' I shrugged.

'And what would you know about flirting, you wrinkled old hag?' She shot me a wicked look, threw off her robe and climbed naked into bed.

With a poker face I bent to arrange the pillows comfortably. After a moment she reached up and touched my cheek. It was a small gesture of contrition and I allowed myself a sly smile. 'Good night, Mademoiselle,' I said, drawing the curtains around the bed, 'May God grant you sweet dreams.'

'Good night, Mette, God bless your dimpled cheeks.'

I was walking away still smiling when her head suddenly popped through the curtains. 'By the way, what is that palliasse doing propped up behind the big linen chest?'

'Ah.' I hesitated, not wishing to start a dispute at bed time. 'Now that your ladies are not within call, Alys and I will be sleeping outside your chamber door. The mattress is for us.'

She gazed at me thoughtfully for a second and then shook her head. 'No, Mette. Outside is not safe for you. Bring it in here. There is room at the foot of the bed.' She disappeared briefly, then opened the curtains again to push two pillows through the opening. 'And take these. You will be more comfortable.'

18

Catherine's leisurely morning rides along the river with Guy de Mussy were taken in the company of her ladies and a sizeable escort of men-at-arms, but nevertheless the two of them quickly established a flirtatious friendship which spilled over into other social activities. A group of Burgundian squires and one or two young knights joined picnics organised in the river meadow below the castle cliff or, when occasional summer storms swept in from the Vexin, lively dancing sessions in the great hall, with court musicians inveigled into playing foot-tapping jigs, instead of the queen's preferred stately *salt-erellos*. Being frequently involved in lengthy meetings of the council, Queen Isabeau held court only two or three times a week, so on other days Catherine invited selected gentlemen to her salon, where poetry was read or songs sung to a lute or harp. Since she had not started to play until she left the convent, her skill on these instruments was rather rudimentary, but Guy de Mussy was quite a talented musician and proved a willing accompanist to Catherine's sweet renderings of popular songs and lays.

Obviously I did not take part in these entertainments, but

I eavesdropped shamelessly. The chamber was small and lent itself well to intimate conversations and much shared laughter and artless teasing, particularly between Catherine and Guy. If he was only doing it on Burgundy's orders, then Guy was playing his role to perfection, but then Catherine was hardly keeping him at arm's length. I knew there was more to their friendship than just teasing and flirting when I caught them returning from a ride ahead of the others and snatching a kiss on the stairs. I did not let them see me, nor did they show any sign of being aware of anything other than their own ardent embrace, but I had the distinct impression that it was not their first.

I confess I was slightly shocked. For some reason I had liked the idea of Catherine enjoying some harmless flirtation, but had not considered the inevitability of it turning into something more meaningful. Protocol at the Hôtel de St Pol had always been so strict that there had been little opportunity for covert kisses, especially for a princess who was always surrounded by her ladies and who had seemed to find more satisfaction in the company of her brother than any of the young gentlemen of his affinity. But Catherine was nearly seventeen. Had she been married to King Henry when it had first been mooted, she would have been bedded two years ago and might even have produced an heir by now. I should not have been surprised that she was answering the natural call of youth. The question was should I do anything about it and if so, what?

Catherine's waking and retiring ritual was still private between us and she had made it clear to the Flanders mares that their presence was not required in the bedchamber, so there were opportunities to broach sensitive subjects. However, I kept putting it off, thinking that a romance which had flared so quickly would probably falter just as soon. It occurred to me that if Guy de Mussy had been placed as a spy in close proximity to the princess, then a manipulative character like the duke might well have reckoned on the possibility of a romance developing and even have encouraged it. And if that were the case, the young squire would be under strict orders not to take advantage of the royal virgin, not that there would be much opportunity to do so. And then, if Catherine became aware of being manipulated in this respect she would probably bring it to an end herself, so there would be no need for any interference on my part. Meanwhile, displaying a no doubt morally lax attitude, I could see no harm in Catherine enjoying a *petit amour*.

After one particularly lively afternoon gathering, the princess sprang a surprise when Agnes and I were preparing her for bed. She opened a small silver-bound trinket box which lay on the toilet table before her and took out a folded paper.

'I have been presented with an ode to my swan-like throat,' she said coyly. 'It is not exactly the *Roman de la Rose* but then the author is more a man of the sword than the word. He must be quite in thrall though, do you not think, to have chewed his quill for me?'

I exchanged glances with Agnes, who took the paper from Catherine and unfolded it to reveal a page of beautifully presented script.

'He must have had a clerk copy it,' Agnes remarked, smirking as she perused the lines of verse. 'Where are all the blotches and scratches of the truly lovelorn?'

'Yes, perhaps it smacks more of strategy than impulse,' agreed Catherine reluctantly. 'But then he is a military man, given to precise planning. Does that make his feelings less genuine?'

I completed unlacing her gown and stood back. A glimpse of the verse over Agnes' shoulder had showed me a series of flowery phrases in high-flown language, linked by a few clever rhymes.

'I would want more than a few lines of doggerel before I trusted such a man,' I said briskly, 'especially a Burgundian. You should be careful how much you confide in him, Mademoiselle.'

Catherine took offence at what she obviously considered my over-protective attitude. 'Oh, Mette! Credit me with a little intelligence. I would not trust him with a tinker's sou. Nor do I think he believes I am a naïve schoolgirl. Yet it is the dream of every ambitious young squire, is it not – to win the love of a princess?'

'That might be every young squire's castles-in-the-air dream, Mademoiselle,' I said. 'But I doubt if they ever expect to live it.'

'Hah!' Catherine scoffed. 'That is all you know! I can tell you there are several young men about the court who think they have the looks and wit to do just that. Guy de Mussy at least has the grace to realise that our dallying is for the moment only for amusement.'

'Or for the Duke of Burgundy,' I muttered darkly but not loud enough for her to hear as I gathered up the voluminous gown and took it to hang in the garderobe.

Catherine took back the poem from Agnes and refolded it,

changing the subject and speaking loudly over her shoulder at me. 'Guy tells me that when supplies run out here, the duke intends to move the court to Beauvais, but first the king will hunt in the forest of the Vexin, so his hounds will be coming to Pontoise shortly. I imagine that means your son Luc will come with them, Mette.'

'That is welcome news, Mademoiselle, and Alys will be very happy to see her brother,' I beamed, returning to her side.

Catherine sighed. 'As I would be to see mine,' she observed, her brow knitting in a frown. 'Sometimes I wonder if I will ever see him again.'

At least Catherine's confidences about her relationship with Guy de Mussy had lessened my worries; it was an amusement; a romance of the mind but not of the heart. However, it turned out that my insouciance was not shared by everyone.

There had been a distinct shift in the relationship between Catherine and her mother. In all the years that the princess had inhabited the tower behind the Queen's House at the Hôtel de St Pol, her mother had never once set foot there, for it was her entrenched belief that, as Queen of France, people came to her and not the other way around. But Queen Isabeau's life was very different now that Burgundy was in charge. No longer did she have a dozen or so personally chosen ladies constantly around her, ready to indulge her every whim and fancy, for the duke abhorred such large groups of women, declaring them to be spendthrift and licentious. Instead, with the exception of one faithful German companion who had been with her for years, the queen had to make do with a small group of rather straight-laced and sober Flemish and Burgundian noblewomen selected from among the wives of the duke's retainers. I imagine it must have irked her to hear sounds of mirth and music coming from Catherine's apartment, so the day came when she simply turned up there without warning, causing me to duck off into a doorway at the bottom of the stair as I returned from fetching wine and sweetmeats for the afternoon salon.

I had not seen the queen at close quarters for some time, and I was surprised at the change in her. It was not that she was grossly fat like her son Louis had been, but her body had become padded in a soft, bolstered way. As she ascended the stair, dressed in a full-skirted cream silk houppelande gown, she resembled a ship in full sail; or perhaps a treasure-laden pirate galleon would be more accurate, for her head, hands and breast were laden with gold and gems. When her page threw the door open and she found Catherine with only a small group of ladies gathered about her, she looked disappointed.

'Ah, I had thought to find you entertaining, daughter,' Queen Isabeau said, puffing heavily from her climb.

The little company rose hurriedly and dropped to their knees, flustered by this unheralded visit. Catherine instantly offered her canopied chair to her mother. 'You are very welcome, your grace. I thought you were deeply involved in affairs of state.' She watched the queen lower herself gratefully onto the cushions adding, 'I understood you would not hold court today.'

Queen Isabeau fanned herself energetically. 'I let it be known that I was busy on purpose,' she announced, a smug smile hovering around her painted lips. 'I was told of the merriment to be heard coming from your chamber on council afternoons and I thought I would discover its cause. Am I to be disappointed?'

I had followed the royal personage unobtrusively into the salon and placed the wine and wafers quietly down on a table before slipping away to the garderobe to fetch the gold hanaps from Catherine's strongbox. The queen could not be expected to drink out of cups made from base metal!

'We do occasionally enjoy the company of some of the duke's retainers, Madame,' Catherine agreed hesitantly. 'We discuss literature of mutual interest and we read poetry and sing a little. I have been told that you and the king used to enjoy such entertainment in the early years of your marriage. A Court of Love, I believe it was called.'

'You foolish girl!' I heard the queen exclaim. 'You have made your point without understanding it. The difference is that we were *married*, Catherine. You are not – nor ever will be if you insist on ruining your reputation by flirting in an unseemly fashion with a *squire*!' She made the word sound like a blasphemy, enunciating it as if it left a nasty taste in her mouth. 'Such a lowborn creature is clearly unaware that the Court of Love was an entirely innocent pastime,' she added vehemently. 'Courtly love is platonic love. It does not involve furtive fumbles on staircases and grubby verses laced with innuendo.'

Catherine gasped and swayed, as if she might topple in shock, and I understood why. How on earth did the queen know of the snatched kisses with Guy de Mussy or the flowery poem to Catherine's snow-white throat? I glanced at Agnes, whom I had thought was the only other person privy to these details, and saw that she looked as astounded as I felt. Had someone else seen the kiss or read the poem? It did not seem possible. And then I remembered that one person in particular was party to both – Guy de Mussy himself! Did he report even such intimate details to the Duke of Burgundy? And did the duke whisper them in moments of equal intimacy to the queen? If thoughts of this nature were rushing through Catherine's mind, as they were through mine, it was no wonder she had gasped with shock.

'I think you had better sit, Catherine,' observed the queen, indicating the nearest stool. 'You look as if you might fall down otherwise.'

As her daughter found her way to a seat, I hastily poured wine into the two jewelled cups I had fetched and edged my way towards the queen's chair. Queen Isabeau lifted one from the proffered tray. Her previously sour expression had altered to one of pleasant anticipation. 'I hope this is some of that pale-green wine my lord of Burgundy has delivered from his vineyards in the high Loire,' she remarked conversationally. 'It is so light and delicious.'

Catherine rallied her forces, took the second cup and said faintly, 'We drink whatever the cellarer has to offer, Madame. Mette has some spring water to add if you prefer that. I know I do.'

'Well, I would not dream of watering his grace's wine, but yes, on this occasion perhaps I will,' Queen Isabeau conceded, correctly concluding that the wine was not from a Burgundian vineyard.

I caught myself staring at her in disbelief, astonished that she could be so malevolent one minute and so benign the next. Then I hastily dropped my gaze to the water-jug on the tray, pouring some of its contents into her cup. At the same time I offered honeyed wafers and she took one. In the tense silence I saw Catherine roll her eyes briefly at Agnes, sitting close at hand in silent support.

'I hear you go out riding, Catherine,' her mother remarked. 'Is the countryside well-tended here?'

As I distributed refreshments among the other ladies, Catherine obliged her with a description of the woods and pastures along the banks of the Oise.

'You might take an excursion in your barge, Madame,' she suggested, 'and see for yourself.'

The queen shrugged. 'Perhaps I will, as long as there are no ugly sights. I cannot bear to see deserted villages and untilled fields. The duke tells me that this desolation is due to outlaws and bandits and that in his territories all is neat and well-ordered. I have told him that if we must travel outside Paris, I long to go east into Champagne and he has promised that we will do so, as soon as we have welcomed Charles back into the family circle.'

This lightning bolt struck as I offered the wafers to Catherine. 'And w-when does he expect that to happen?' she stuttered with surprise, and at the queen's next words the wafer she had taken snapped in her tense fingers.

'In a week or so,' her mother said casually. 'Negotiations are at an advanced stage. Will it not be wonderful, Catherine, to see Charles and the duke working together to rid France of the pernicious English?'

'Have the two of them met?' asked Catherine, unable to conceal her incredulity. 'I did not think the duke had left Pontoise.'

'Oh no, he has not been conducting negotiations himself. That is not how these things are done, my dear,' explained the queen condescendingly. 'Envoys and lawyers from both sides have been closeted for days somewhere and they have drawn up an agreement, which has only to be signed and then Charles will come back to us.' Queen Isabeau smiled thinly at her daughter. 'I am sure you will be delighted to hear that this document does not make any reference to a marriage between you and that libertine Henry of Monmouth. So now we will have to start looking elsewhere for a husband for you.'

Catherine lowered her eyes, noticed the crumbs of wafer in her lap and brushed them off distractedly. 'Do I understand, Madame, that there is no longer any question of a marriage between me and King Henry?' she asked breathlessly.

Her mother pursed her lips. 'Let me put it this way; the chances of you marrying Monmouth are about as high as the chances of you marrying that young squire you seem so enamoured with.'

Catherine was unable to stop the blood rushing to her cheeks but at least her chin was up. 'I would like to point out that my being so much in the company of Guy de Mussy is entirely down to the Duke of Burgundy, Madame. It was he who appointed the squire my personal protector. If you

273

have any objection to it I suggest you broach the subject with him.'

'There is no need to ride a high horse, Catherine,' the queen retorted swiftly, although her tone was amused rather than angry. 'Personally I think there is little harm in a mild flirtation at your age, without the kisses of course, but I think I should warn you that his grace is not so lenient about such matters.'

Catherine drew in her breath and paused before responding. 'I would have thought the Duke of Burgundy had more important things to worry about than my leisure activities, especially if, as would seem to be the case, I am no longer a useful pawn in his great plan to rule France.' She said the last few words with special emphasis.

The queen frowned. 'You mistake the duke's intentions,' she said sternly. 'Burgundy's chief aim is to bring peace to France by reconciling your brother with the king. He has said so a dozen times in council and written personally to Charles to assure him of the fact. Of course Charles is very young and does not know who to trust. So far he has put his faith in the ragged remnants of the faction which supported Armagnac but, thanks be to God, that devil now rots in hell and his grace of Burgundy will soon be in a position to advise and guide Charles how to go about ruling France, expelling the English and bringing us back to peace and prosperity.' After this neat summing-up the queen refreshed herself by draining her cup and then closed her fan in a gesture of quiet satisfaction, while she gazed around the awed young ladies, absorbing their eager murmurs of appreciation.

'Well, Madame,' Catherine said with icy politeness, 'if I am mistaken in my interpretation of his grace's intentions, I will have to make reparation, but I must tell you that I am not willing do so until I see my brother kneel before the king and embrace both you and the Duke of Burgundy.'

The queen smiled and nodded indulgently. 'You will not wait long, Catherine, I assure you,' she cooed. 'That happy day is very close.'

That night I woke with a start, convinced that someone had entered Catherine's chamber. The room was inky black.

'Who is there?' I whispered, my heart racing. I sat up, reaching for my shawl and felt Alys stir on the mattress beside me. I could see nothing but I distinctly heard the sound of careful, muffled footsteps, followed by the clunk of the chamber door closing. Whoever had been in the room had left as stealthily as they had come.

'What is wrong, Mette?'

Catherine was out of bed, standing over me, tying the girdle of her robe. I scrambled up, pulling the shawl around my shoulders.

'I do not know, Mademoiselle,' I whispered. 'I could not see, but I am certain there was someone in the room.'

'How could that be?' Catherine responded. 'There are guards at the door of the building.'

'Guards can be persuaded not to see things,' I replied. 'But I will go and ask them if anyone entered the tower.'

'You had better wear more than a shawl and chemise if you

do.' I heard a rustle of rich cloth as Catherine shed her robe. 'Here, wear this and I will go back to bed.'

Naked without the robe, she plunged back under the bedclothes and I wrapped the robe around me and felt my way through the door. In the passageway a single lamp burned on a bracket, allowing me gingerly to descend the first flight of the spiral stair. At the bottom it opened out into a ground floor lobby before continuing down into the undercroft below. Another lamp burned at the main entrance, where two men-at-arms sat playing cards in a small guardroom alongside the barred door. They seemed very surprised by my arrival, but assured me that they had orders to admit no one to the princess' apartments.

Back in the bedchamber I said, 'I must have been mistaken, Mademoiselle,' as I drew back the curtain to return her robe. 'No one has been admitted. I am sorry to have woken you.'

Nevertheless, before I lay down again I moved a stool across the chamber door so that there would be a noise if it opened. I had no proof, but I was still utterly certain that someone had been there.

—ξξ—

From the Princess Royal, Catherine of Valois, Daughter of France,

To my beloved brother Charles, Dauphin of Viennois,

Yesterday I received from the queen's own lips that you and the Duke of Burgundy are about to sign an agreement that will bring you back to the king's side. If this be true, I am desperately praying that you will not to do it. Do not put yourself within reach of the Duke of Burgundy. Whatever his promises and assurances, he is not to be trusted. In following the advice and counsel of Tanneguy du Chastel, you have always shown yourself to be wise beyond your years and I firmly believe he will always keep the vow he made to you on the dreadful day of our brother Louis' death.

I now have proof that the duke has his spies closely and intimately surrounding me. It is only in my own bedchamber that I feel free of his malevolent influence and I greatly fear his ability even to invade that sanctuary. I pray daily to God's holy Mother to keep me safe from his evil intentions, but now that he has withdrawn all embassies to the English, I realise that I no longer have any value as a virgin bride to dangle before King Henry. How long will it be before the devil duke violates every code of honour and steals that state of purity for himself, as he constantly and lewdly insinuates is his intention? And what defence do I have? I would marry Henry of England or anyone else tomorrow if it would remove me from this vile entrapment.

I cannot trust the queen to defend my honour, for she seems totally in Burgundy's thrall. I have no protector other than you, my brother. How I wish I could saddle a horse and ride to your side! Yet I cannot reach you and I am urging you under no circumstances to come to me. I thank God

*daily that you are free and pray to the Almighty to give me
the freedom that you enjoy. Do not squander it!*

I am, as always, your loving sister,

Catherine

*Written at the Chateau Pontoise this day, Friday August
19th 1418.*

19

Several days went by and there was no sign of Prince Charles coming to kiss his father's hand. Having no other form of respite from the stifling confines of the castle, Catherine continued to ride out in the company of Guy de Mussy and his band of spies and gaolers, but there were no more Courts of Love and no more kisses on the stairs. As far as harmless flirting was concerned, the veil had been lifted from her eyes and my heart ached for her. The green leaves of youthful passion shrivelled under a blazing autumn sun.

The heat-wave took its toll on the king. Early one scorching morning, just before Mass, he ran out into the inner bailey screaming at the top of his voice that no one should come near him. Rushing down to investigate, we were greeted by the sad sight of King Charles cowering bare-headed in the centre of the courtyard, his grey hair wild and his skinny white limbs sticking out below his chemise. Several of his body squires and guardians had dashed out of the keep after him, but each time one approached he screamed more hysterically and flailed his arms to keep them off. He seemed utterly terrified of anyone touching him.

Catherine turned to me, her eyes wide. 'Oh dear God, Mette, I remember . . .' she whispered and her hands flew to her mouth to stifle a cry of horror. I knew what she remembered, even though she had only been three years old; that stifling day in the rose garden at St Pol when we had encountered her father in the throes of a similar sudden madness.

'He believes he is made of glass,' I nodded, speaking as steadily as I could. 'We must not frighten him any more than he is already frightened.'

There was general air of helplessness among the royal household because all the king's previous guardians had been replaced by Burgundians and the new men had not experienced this most extreme form of his illness. None of them seemed prepared to risk subduing him physically.

'I think we need some padding, Mademoiselle,' I suggested. 'Perhaps if Alys was to fetch a quilt . . .'

'Yes, yes,' nodded Catherine. 'Please Alys, find some quilts. I will try and talk to him – see if I can get him to calm down.'

'There are quilts in the chests in the room where you sew,' I told Alys and she hurried off.

Catherine began carefully to approach the still-screaming king who was turning in a slow circle, glaring with bloodshot eyes at the ring of curious people gathering around him. When he saw his daughter coming nearer, he clamped his elbows to his sides and flung up his hands like claws, sticking out his chin and baring his teeth at her like a wild animal at bay. His scream became a desperate screech and I wanted to run and pull Catherine back to safety, but she just kept walking towards him, speaking slowly and softly as if he were a no more than a naughty child.

'It is Catherine, your grace, your daughter. You know I would never harm you and I will not touch you. Please do not scream. You are frightening everyone and they do not know what to do. But I do. I know you are made of glass and will shatter if we touch you, so I will be careful not to. Can you hear me, my father? Surely you know me. It is Catherine. We go to church together nearly every day, do we not? We hear Mass and we pray. Shall we pray together now? Shall we kneel together and ask the Holy Mother to protect you so that you do not break?'

She was now only a few feet from the king and he had gradually stopped screaming to listen to what she said. Slowly and carefully she knelt before him and clasped her hands together. Then she began reciting the *Ave Maria*, murmuring it just loud enough for him to hear and repeating it over and over again until he too actually knelt and began to join in. It was a heart-touching sight, the wild-haired man and the veiled young lady kneeling three feet apart and reciting the words of the prayer while a growing crowd of palace inhabitants looked on. After a few minutes, one by one they all began to recite and the familiar words became a soothing chorus, resonating off the high grey walls of the castle courtyard.

When Alys arrived with the quilts, I thought it best that she take them to the King, since she was the least threatening figure among us, small, sweet-faced and solemn, laden with her downy burden which clearly could not harm the most delicate pane of glass. When she and Catherine held out a quilt between them, the king did not move and his lips continued to mumble the prayer as they gently wrapped him in its feathery softness.

I spoke to a man I took to be the captain of the king's troop of guardians, a tall, surprisingly mild-looking character who was watching Catherine's handling of the king with open admiration.

'You need plenty of quilts,' I suggested. 'The king thinks he is made of glass and will break at the slightest touch.'

'But the princess knows what to do,' the man marvelled. 'How does she know that?'

'Perhaps because she is his daughter and she loves him,' I said. 'And he knows it.'

He shook his head slowly. 'Amazing,' he murmured. 'It is a miracle.'

Without demur the king rose and trotted between Alys and Catherine up the steps of the keep and the chastened group of guardians fell in behind the unlikely trio.

'We will go to the chapel,' Catherine told them quietly over her shoulder. 'He will be content there while you prepare a padded room for him. But make sure it is well aired. If he gets too hot the madness seems to get worse.'

A loud clapping sound was suddenly to be heard echoing around the courtyard. The Duke of Burgundy had appeared at the entrance to the keep and was slowly applauding the incongruous procession climbing towards him. The percussive noise was generated not by his hands which were gloved as usual, but from clapping together the pages of his Book of Hours, which he was carrying to Mass, and it brought King Charles abruptly to a halt.

'Congratulations, Princesse,' the duke drawled, his lip curling. 'It seems you know how to cozen demons. We shall have to send you out to catch a unicorn.'

Chillingly, the king began to scream again. Then everything happened in quick time. At Burgundy's peremptory signal, the guardians moved swiftly forward and Catherine was forced to watch, powerless, as they bundled her father up in the quilts and carried him, thrashing and screeching, into the keep. The duke bowed as the king was carried past him.

'God be with you, father,' Catherine called in a high, choking voice. 'I will pray for you, to keep you safe from demons.' She almost spat this last word.

Then she turned on her heel and ran down the steps. She did not attend Mass that day.

In the late afternoon a long procession of carts and closed wagons, packs of hounds and mounted huntsmen trailed through the gatehouse, escorted by a phalanx of armed guards. Within minutes word had spread that the king's hounds and hawks had arrived from Paris in readiness for the autumn hunts. As soon as I could, I hurried down to the kennel in the hope that Luc might have come with them. The long wooden lean-to erected against the curtain wall in the furthest corner of the outer bailey had been a quiet place before this, holding only a few resident hounds, but now it was overflowing with excited dogs, barking and yapping and rushing about sniffing their new quarters. And Luc was there, helping to sort them into their allotted enclosures; one for the hounds, one for the terriers and one for the stocky brindle alaunts with their wet jowls and fierce jaws. Pleased though he was to see me, he was clearly flustered by my arrival and kept casting anxious glances at a senior huntsman, a stubble-chinned individual who wore a Burgundian badge on his leather jerkin and glared at me through one of the woven-willow panels that divided the long shed into cages.

'I'll be free once the dogs are fed and bedded, Ma. I'll come and find you then,' he said

I took the hint. 'Come to the princess royal's chambers in the inner bailey,' I murmured, pushing off a couple of friendly terriers and backing away with a placatory smile at the huntsman. 'Anyone will tell you where they are. I'll warn the guard to look out for you.'

Though Luc's behaviour worried me a little, I took comfort in knowing I would find out later why he was being so wary, but before I reached the tunnel where the guard stood, I was accosted by a royal page. I recognised him, for he came frequently to deliver messages to Catherine. Perhaps alarm bells should have rung because he had never before been accompanied by two men-at-arms, but his pleasant smile beguiled me.

'You are bidden to the grand master's office, mistress,' he said. 'I am to take you there now.'

I assumed it must be Guy de Mussy who wanted to see me. 'What does he want?' I asked, following as he set off towards the gatehouse.

The page shrugged. 'He did not say. I am just to fetch you.'

'With an escort?' I queried, startled by the loud clomping of nailed boots as the two soldiers fell into step behind us. 'It must be important.'

There was no response to that, but the page quickened his pace and we trudged across the rest of the bailey in silence. In the grand master's chamber there was no sign of Guy de Mussy but another, older squire was there, a man who did not look at all friendly. He had wiry salt and pepper hair, a red beard and a scar splitting one eyebrow and he, too, wore the Duke of Burgundy's St Andrew's cross on his shoulder. His severe expression and aggressive attitude sent tingling waves of apprehension down my spine.

Clearing his throat he said gruffly, 'There is a discrepancy in the inventory of goods that were brought from Princess Catherine's apartment in the Hôtel de St Pol. You are responsible for the princess' furnishings and chattels and I would like you to account for one missing jewel-studded gold hanap.'

I stared at him in astonishment, for having made my own inventory I knew without doubt that there was nothing missing from among the goods that had been transported from Paris. 'The princess has two jewelled hanaps, Monsieur,' I gulped. 'Which one of them is said to be missing?'

The grizzle-haired squire unrolled a parchment, which I

recognised as the inventory taken by the grand master's clerk when the carts were loaded for the journey to Pontoise.

'The missing hanap is of chased gold with inset stones of onyx and beryl,' he said, reading from the parchment and then glaring at me from under a pair of bristly eyebrows. 'Worth several crowns, Madame.'

'And it is not missing,' I protested. 'I myself served wine in it to the queen only a few days ago.'

'But has it been seen since?' persisted the squire in a hectoring tone.

'Not since I locked it away afterwards, no. The princess only uses the gold hanaps for important guests and I do not check all the items in the strong box every day.'

'But you do have charge of the keys, do you not, Madame?' The man's gaze dropped to the heavy iron chatelaine which swung from my belt, not quite hidden by the flap of my apron. 'And no one else has a copy of the strong-box key.'

'The grand master has copies of all the keys. I do not think you could call him no one!' I exclaimed in heated riposte.

'And where do you keep the strong box?' persisted the unpleasant squire, the threatening nature of his questions becoming more intense with every query.

'In the garderobe of the princess' bedchamber,' I replied and, as I said it, events suddenly began to slot together, like cogs in a winding gear. There *had* been someone in Catherine's bedchamber the night after the queen's visit. Someone who had crept to the garderobe, opened the strong box, removed the hanap and locked the box again. It had been the clicking of the

286

lock that had woken me. Meanwhile, the intruder had made his exit as swiftly and silently as he had come.

'The king's men will be searching your quarters at this moment, mistress,' added the squire with a sneering grin, 'and the grand master himself wants to speak to you afterwards, but until then you will wait here. These men will show you where.'

He indicated the two men-at-arms behind me, who put their hands meaningfully on their daggers and stepped up very close, giving me a none-too-gentle shove in the direction of a spiral stair set in the corner of the chamber. My heart began to pound, but there was nothing to do but comply and after a short climb I found myself in a small, round turret room furnished with a single bench and, ominously, a wooden pail. As soon as I stumbled through the door, assisted by another shove from one of the guards, the door slammed shut and I heard a bar being dropped into slots on the other side.

There had been no opportunity to plead my case, but if there had been, what could I have said? I knew I was the victim of a set up and as to *who* had set me up, that was easy – the Duke of Burgundy, or someone at his behest. But what I did not know was why? It was that mysterious 'why' that set my heart pounding with fear.

I had plenty of time to think about it and nothing else to do. I had no light and as night fell it soon became almost pitch dark in the little chamber. Only a faint gleam of starlight filtered through the one tiny window high up in the wall and a stray beam from the stairway lamp trickled through a knot-hole in the planking of the door. I heard the Compline bell and when it stopped tolling I tried hammering on the door but quickly realised there was no point, nor was there anything but shadows to see through the knot-hole. Investigating the wooden pail, I discovered a jug of water set down inside it and realised that my imprisonment had been carefully planned. There was water to drink and a pail to relieve myself in. I would be there all night – maybe longer.

Slumped miserably on the bench, I set my mind to considering the situation. I remembered the wiry-haired squire's statement that someone was searching my quarters and wondered whether they realised that, in fact, I had no quarters. I slept in Catherine's chamber and I kept my belongings, such as they were, in a small wooden chest in her garderobe. There was only one key to this chest and I had it swinging on my belt, so they would have to smash it to search it. That they would do so, I had no doubt, if only to leave evidence of their visit, for I knew full well that although it had not been in my locked chest, the gold hanap would be 'found' there and produced and I would be accused of stealing it. And the only fate that awaited someone who robbed the royal family was the hangman's noose.

Despite the warmth of the night I sat in the darkness shivering. I racked my brains trying to figure out how I could prove that I had not removed the cup from the princess' strongbox, but could not come up with a solution. I knew that Catherine would vouch for my honesty, but in the present circumstances she was as powerless as I was to influence proceedings. For some unknown reason the Duke of Burgundy wanted me out of the way and for him an accusation of theft was as easy to arrange as a day's hunting. He gave an order and it was done.

Then I began to worry about Alys and Luc. Would they find out where I had gone and come looking for me? I hoped they would not, for at all costs I did not want them to be involved in any way with this monstrous lie. Dear God, I thought in panic, would they have to see their mother hanged? Even if they did not, they would suffer as the children of a proven thief, would be stripped of their posts and left to fend for themselves as best they might and in the dead of night I imagined such terrible consequences for both of them that I had to bite my fist to stop myself from crying out in despair.

As a distraction I continued asking myself questions, for although I now understood the how, what and who of my situation, I had not fathomed out the why. Why was the Duke of Burgundy doing this to me? I was a nobody who made no impact on his life whatsoever. Was it possible that he remembered me from that awful morning in the nursery all those years ago? Surely not. He had not encountered me since and, even if he had, there was no chance that he would recognise me. Why would a great lord who ruled the lives of thousands remember the violence he had inflicted on a nursemaid fourteen years before? It might still prey on my mind, but it surely would not trouble his. No, it was something in the present, in the here and now, some reason he needed me out of the way.

Not one to invoke heavenly aid very often, at this point I fell to my knees and began to pray, burbling frantic entreaties to God and his Holy Mother and all the saints I considered relevant.

For suddenly I knew what it was that I prevented the devil duke doing and I was praying that I was wrong, praying that it would not happen, praying for a miracle. Yet all the time I knew that I was right, that the thing that I feared so much was probably happening at that very moment and that there was absolutely nothing I could do about it.

20

I was released from my confinement before dawn by a bemused-looking soldier, who shoved me down the stairs and out of the grand master's office without ceremony or explanation.

'Why am I being released?' I asked, almost tripping on my skirts in my haste to quit the gatehouse.

'Do not ask questions,' he growled. 'Just thank God you are free, for by all accounts you are lucky your neck is not to be stretched.'

Back at the tower I found Alys curled up in a corner of the entrance lobby, hugging her knees. She sprang up to greet me with exclamations and tears of relief. 'I thought you were dead, Ma!' she sobbed. 'Some soldiers took me to the guardroom and would not let me leave. They said you were a thief and would be hanged and I was to be thrown out of the castle as soon as the gates opened. Then, suddenly, they let me go. What in heaven's name is happening? Have they accused you of stealing?'

'Yes, but I do not know why I have been released,' I said. 'Have you seen Luc?'

Alys shook her head. 'No. Why, is he here?'

291

'The hunt arrived last night,' I told her. 'But I am glad he has not been here. That means they do not know he is in Pontoise. Can you run to the kennel and see if you can speak to him without anyone seeing? Tell him not to come here. I will meet him later. I must go the princess immediately. Come back as soon as you can.'

It was too early for any of the ladies-in-waiting to have come from the constable's house, so I found Catherine quite alone, huddled not in her own bed but on my mattress, wrapped tightly in one of her linen sheets so that she almost looked like a corpse. When she heard my voice she hurled herself into my arms and hugged me so tight I could barely breathe.

'Oh, Mette, Mette, thank God you are here – and free! He said he would not harm you if I did as he ordered but I was terrified he would go back on his word!' Catherine's face was swollen from crying. I stroked her tangled hair and uttered all the soothing words I could think of. I did not ask what had happened because she would tell me in her own good time – and anyway, in my heart I already knew.

When she grew calmer I sat her down in a chair, still stroking her hair and said gently, 'Stay here, Mademoiselle. I will tell everyone you are unwell and have a bath set up in the salon. You will feel better when you have washed him away.'

She stared at me for a long time, her sapphire eyes dull and red-rimmed. At length she asked hoarsely, 'You know, Mette? You know what he did to me? He told me to tell no one. I am so frightened for you if he thinks you know.'

I put my finger to my lips and shook my head. 'We will not

talk about it now. The most important thing is for you to get clean. Can you bear to be alone for a few minutes while I order the bath?'

—ξξ—

From Catherine of France to Charles, Dauphin of Viennois,
Oh my beloved brother,
I cannot write my name and yours at the head of this letter without bewailing the fact that both have been dishonoured and besmirched by the actions of one man – that vassal of the devil, Jean who calls himself The Fearless. You and I are children of France, the son and daughter of the king, scions of Valois as he is himself, and yet he has treated us both like the lowest worms that crawl on the earth, making you a bastard and me a whore. He is a son of Beelzebub, whose hellfire is not hot enough to consume him. Against all Christian principles of loving thine enemy, I hereby declare that I hate and abhor Jean, Duke of Burgundy, more than I hate and abhor those who crucified Our Lord.
I cannot write what it is that Burgundy has done to me because there is still enough remaining of my innocence that I am ignorant of the words to describe it. Suffice it to say that I believe I remain a virgin, in the precise nature of the term, but even so he has destroyed every vestige of the purity of my soul. He threatens imprisonment and even death to my dearest friends and companions if I do not submit and I

293

must remain constantly under the same threat and coercion as long as Burgundy holds the position he presently occupies beside the king.

For our father's sake I must not give in to despair. He is at present in the grip of the worst form of his affliction.

You once told me that you thought I would never take my own life because I am too stubborn and too devout, but that one day I might wish I had. That day has come.

Pray for me I beseech you,

Your sister beset by evil.

Catherine

Written at Pontoise Castle, in the early hours of Tuesday, September 30th, 1418.

—ξξ—

Those were dark days, when we all learned what it was to be powerless in the grip of evil. The Duke of Burgundy came often to Catherine's chamber before the court left Pontoise and on each occasion she would warn me to keep away.

'I do not on any account want him to see you, Mette. He would not hesitate to kill anyone he thought might threaten his position.'

Burgundy would signal his intention during dinner, by carving a choice piece off his own portion of meat and having it presented to her by an attendant. I saw it happen the first time and initially thought nothing of it because the code of good manners among the nobility held it to be a gesture of esteem for food to be shared in this way between occupants of the high table, but I noticed that when the page bent his knee beside Catherine's chair and offered the duke's gift, she went as white as the manchet bread from which the royal trenchers were cut. When I mentioned it later she tearfully revealed the significance of the action.

For a time I wondered how the duke entered Catherine's lodgings without passing the guards at the entrance, but I soon solved that riddle. The stair which led up to the salon and bedchamber also led down into a vaulted under-croft where supplies were stored against the possibility of a siege – barrels of salted meat and fish and sacks of flour. Armed with a lamp, I ventured down into the dark recesses of the vault and in a far corner discovered that some barrels had been moved to expose a mildewed door with freshly-greased hinges. I remembered what the carter had told me on the day of our arrival, about the castle being built on the remains of an ancient fort and I guessed that the duke was making use of some underground connection between the keep and the tower, as the intruder must also have done who removed the incriminating gold hanap from the strongbox. So Burgundy had planned his evil predations well in advance and ensured that Catherine was given her particular lodging on purpose, with its convenient underground access and lack of accommodation for inconvenient ladies-in-waiting. When Burgundy discovered that Alys and I were sleeping in the princess' chamber, it must have irked him considerably, but it also showed him the high regard in which Catherine held us and thus the means whereby to exert his will.

On the nights when she returned from the great hall hard-eyed and grim faced, I would explain to Alys that the princess was entertaining privately and we would help her to disrobe, then take ourselves off to the attic wardrobe where, working by candlelight on her sumptuous robes, I tried not to imagine the dreadful wrongs being inflicted on the one who wore them. I had suggested that perhaps she would prefer it if we no longer slept in her chamber, since the reason for our being there, to give her protection from just such a predatory intrusion, was sadly redundant, but she would not hear of it.

'No please do not abandon me, Mette,' she begged. 'I need your comforting presence now more than ever. I will put a lamp outside my door when he is gone. Come to me as soon as it is safe.'

He never stayed long. Whatever sordid gratification the duke found must have come entirely from asserting his dominance. There was no other interaction between them, for Catherine's way of preserving her sanity was to withhold all communication. She spoke not a word, kept her eyes averted and responded to his orders like a puppet-doll, as if by refusing to acknowledge his presence he did not exist to her and therefore the abuse inflicted on her was not happening. I know all this because I was her release valve. Somehow while the devil was with her, she managed to keep control but, afterwards, anguish flowed from her like wine from a split barrel.

'I say nothing to him but he speaks all the time he is there – filthy words to go with his filthy actions. He maintains that he is satisfying my secret needs, Mette! Can you believe such diabolical arrogance? When he touches me, I want to shriek like my father that I am made of glass and I will shatter. But I do not, I refuse to give him that satisfaction. As soon as he leaves, I am physically sick. I try to purge myself of him but I cannot. He is constantly there in my head, poisoning my mind. Even my body is no longer my own. I pray and pray to the Virgin to show me a way to be rid of him but She gives me no answer.'

'If Alys and Agnes and I were to leave your service, he would no longer have a hold on you,' I suggested tentatively, but her reaction was one of horror.

'No, no, no! I could not bear it! I need you all, Mette. They took me away from you once when I was too young to fight, but I am determined that nothing shall separate us again.'

She spoke so resolutely that I said no more about it, but I felt a terrible guilt that I was Burgundy's prime lever of coercion. My only comfort was that had it not been through me, Burgundy would have found some other way to control Catherine.

21

In early October a welcome change in the weather brought cool autumn winds. The afflicted king recovered from his terrible glass phobia and emerged from his padded chamber to play again in the fresh air and enjoy his favourite pastime – hunting. Royal hunts took place three or four times a week and Luc was kept so busy that Alys and I hardly saw him. However, I was asked to attend a meeting with the surly-looking head huntsman who had glared at me on the day of Luc's arrival, to discover that my son was being offered an apprenticeship, which I as his parent would have to approve. I had no opportunity to ask Luc whether or not he wished to become tied to the royal hunt for the next five years, but he nodded enthusiastically enough when he was quizzed formally in my presence by the master so I gave my consent. He was issued with livery consisting of a boiled leather jerkin, a distinctive green huntsman's hood and tunic and some strong leather bottins and I was extremely relieved to see that the badge on his shoulder was the royal fleur-de-lis and not a Burgundian saltire. Seeing Luc in his new garb for the first time brought a proud lump to my throat and I wished that Jean-Michel could have seen him too. Our little knobbly-kneed boy had developed into a sturdy and capable lad and his handling of hounds and hawks was a joy to behold. I only had Alys' word that he wanted to defect to the dauphin's cause, and he himself had no opportunity to make mention of it as the hunting season went into full cry.

Eventually the intensive hunting took its toll on the supply of game and, with the granaries and gardens of Pontoise almost totally depleted, the Duke of Burgundy at last gave the order for the court to move on.

Christmas was spent at the bishop's palace in Beauvais and we welcomed the Christ child in the breathtaking surroundings of the cathedral of St Peter, where the nave soared up to the highest ceiling vault in Christendom. Catherine spent long hours on her knees in this awe-inspiring church and believed that it was the answer to her prayers that the duke's unholy visitations ceased. Personally I put it down to the fact that there were no secret passages in the bishop's palace. However, Beauvais did supply an answer to my own prayers.

One damp day when low, swirling fog prevented hunting, Luc brought one of the bishop's dog handlers to meet me outside the stables and introduced him as Hugh.

'The bishop hunts far and wide in this area, Ma, and Hugh found something in the forest that I think you should see,' said Luc. I could tell from the look in his eyes that he was seriously troubled and my heart started to beat a little faster.

The huntsman was a big man with brawny shoulders and hands like hams. He wore the boiled leather jacket common to most outdoor retainers and the badge on his shoulder was the bishop's red lion rampant. But he also carried another leather jacket over his arm and when he shook it out to show me, I felt a jolt of recognition.

'It's Pa's, I am sure it is!' cried Luc. 'You recognise it, don't you, Ma?'

I felt my knees begin to tremble. The jacket did indeed look like the one Jean-Michel had received when he was promoted to the job of charettier at the palace and there on the shoulder was the royal fleur-de-lis, very frayed and faded but unmistakable. Instinctively I reached out, but I could not quite bring myself to touch it.

'How did you come by the jacket, Monsieur?' I asked faintly.

Hugh flushed bright red and mumbled something.

'I heard you tell the others you got it off a dead man,' Luc said ominously.

Hugh growled, 'All right, it is true. The jacket was on the body of a man who had been dead for some time. We were hunting boar and one of the hounds found him under bushes in a thicket, as if he had crawled there and then not been able to get up again. Wild animals had taken any flesh that was exposed. It was really a skeleton with clothes on . . . a skull with hair, brown hair.' When he saw me blanch he shrugged apologetically. 'I am sorry, Madame.'

There was a mounting block outside the stable entrance and I stumbled over to it and sat down. My mouth had gone dry and I swallowed on what felt like a stone in my throat, but after a minute I managed to croak.

'Did you find anything in the jacket? Anything at all?'

Hugh shook his head. 'The pockets were empty. I think he must have been set upon and the thief or thieves took anything he had.'

'But surely a thief would have taken the jacket,' Luc protested, adding accusingly, 'You took it.'

The huntsman bristled. 'I took it because of the royal badge. Perhaps the thieves were disturbed or even injured in the fight. There was another man with me who will confirm that we treated the body with respect. We did not strip him, but took only his jacket and boots. Then we buried him and said a prayer. You said you thought you knew whose jacket it was, but if neither of you can identify him I will take it to the royal hunt master. Sometimes there is a reward.' He made to go but I put out my hand to stop him.

'Wait,' I said. 'There might be something. I gave him a St Christopher medal for protection and I sewed it into the lining. Let me look.'

The leather was mouldy and water-marked, but the padded lining was still intact. I felt around the left armpit area, nearest the heart and my own heart missed a beat when I felt a small, hard lump.

'Have you a knife?' I demanded shakily.

It was Luc who produced his hunting knife, his face solemn and his bottom lip clenched between his teeth.

I could see where my stitches had repaired the original slit and I cut them. The medal popped out easily, still bright and shiny. I peered at it.

'See, there is the fault in the mould that made the saint appear to be smiling.' I held it out and Luc gave a choking sob. 'It is definitely Jean-Michel's. He has been missing for two years. He was injured after Agincourt and spent several months with the monks at Abbeville. I heard that he left there alone, heading for Rouen. Where exactly did you find him?'

The huntsman crossed himself and regarded me sorrowfully. 'In the forest of Neufchâtel, Madame, on the road from Abbeville to Rouen.'

'Thank you,' I said with a nod. 'I am glad to know the truth at last. I shall see to it that there is a reward.'

'I want to go there – to where you buried him!' cried Luc, grabbing the jacket from my lap. 'And I want to keep this.'

'I will take you there if we get a chance,' Hugh agreed. 'And the jacket is yours by right. But first we must take it to the Hunt Master and register the death with the royal household.'

I gave the gruff huntsman a rueful smile. 'At last we can pray for Jean-Michel's soul to find heaven. You have done us a good turn with a sad truth, Monsieur.'

Then I hugged Luc to me briefly before he wrenched himself away and turned to hide his tears as boys will do.

Before we left Beauvais, Luc did have a chance to visit the place where Jean-Michel was buried and he dug the St Christopher medal into the disturbed earth of the grave. 'It is in a beautiful place,' he told Alys and me on his return. 'You would both have liked it I think. Right under a great big oak tree and no animals have been near it so they must have dug really deep. I said a prayer like you told me, Ma, but I did not know any Latin ones.'

I smiled at that. His face was so solemn and earnest and I felt a great tug of love for my gangling young son. 'That is good, Luc. At least your father would understand your prayer and he would be proud of you. He may not be in consecrated ground, but he is in a place he would have liked himself. It is well done.'

In mid January came the devastating news that the English had taken Rouen. Having endured six months of siege without relief from either the dauphin or Burgundy, the crumbling and disease-ridden town had finally surrendered, effectively handing Normandy to England. There were reports of desperate refugees straggling into Pontoise, fleeing the raping and looting of the victorious English soldiers. Then we learned that King Henry had left a garrison at Rouen and moved the rest of his army up the Seine, receiving the capitulation of successive towns and castles en route. He was reported to have made his headquarters at Mantes, less than a day's march from Pontoise and only two days from Paris.

'By all that's holy, I despair!' stormed Catherine, letting off steam to me as she always did as soon as the bedchamber door closed. 'Will Burgundy march to confront Henry and prevent him laying siege to Paris? No he will not! Instead he says the king must avoid the threat from the English and move to Troyes, where he can be properly protected.' She paced angrily, slapping her palm against her fist in frustration. 'So pack the chests, Mette, we are running away. How far is it to

Troyes? Remind me to consult a map. God save us! If somebody does not confront Henry soon, he will be crowning himself in Paris before Easter.'

Catherine showed me the map she had acquired from the bishop's library and together we traced the route we would take to the famous 'Hot Fair' city of Troyes, made rich from centuries of trade with the east. It looked like a mammoth journey for the winter months, skirting Paris to the north and east, staying at a series of establishments still loyal to the crown, including the royal abbey of St Denis and Charles' birthplace, the castle of Vincennes. Then, however, we were to stay at Brie Comte Robert, the devil duke's own fortress, in his own territory. Who could know its labyrinthine passages better?

Catherine's face was pinched with fear as she confessed, 'I will not feel safe there, I know, as I do here in Beauvais, and hope to feel in the royal domains of St Denis and Vincennes . . .' Then, as though to put off a rising panic, she changed the subject. 'The queen is fuming because we cannot go to Melun – here . . .' Catherine's finger stabbed down at the point on the map where a little tower, delicately drawn, commanded a bend of the meandering middle reaches of the Seine ' . . .because it has been overrun by Charles' forces.' I saw a tear come to her eye. 'Charles might be there himself – so close by and yet I cannot visit him!'

—ξξ—

From Catherine of France to Charles, Dauphin of Viennois,
Dearly beloved brother,

This night we stay in the Duke of Burgundy's castle of Brie Comte Robert, less than a day's ride from Melun. I feel certain that you are there, so close, but I cannot come to you to beg your help.

Surely God cannot expect me to bear this!

He came to my chamber again, the devil duke in his most evil guise. He enters my bedchamber like a black spectre, mouthing filth, even though there should be guards at my door. How many people does he threaten and compel to look the other way? Why does my own mother not intervene? I cannot believe she knows what is happening, but still sings Burgundy's praises and sits him at her right hand where our father should be seated.

Nor do I know what devilish schemes are being hatched between Burgundy and the queen, although I have heard that couriers are still coming and going from Normandy, despite the English occupation. Are they dealing with King Henry again? Are you, Charles? Why do none of you raise an army and throw him out of France? Is everyone frightened of the victor of Agincourt?

I often ponder what manner of man this Henry is. Louis said he was a libertine, but even if there is any truth in this I am certain he would spurn me if he knew what has been done to me, as any man would. But, truly, I cannot think of Henry as the enemy when my real foe is right

here in our midst, using me as his whore. I struggle to find
faith in God when Beelzebub has stolen my true self.

I am forever your loving sister,
Catherine
Written at the castle of Brie Comte Robert at dawn this
day, Wednesday February 8th 1419.

—ξξ—

There were three occasions while we were in Brie Comte Robert
when Catherine sent me, Alys and Agnes away from her
chamber after we had made her ready for bed and Alys and I
shivered in the freezing attic room where the travelling chests
were stored, praying for a miracle that might keep the duke
away from her but knowing all the time that she was suffering
the violence of his lust. After the first time I gathered that she
had written another of her letters because ink had been spilled
over one of the tables in her chamber, leaving an indelible stain
and there were black marks on her fingers which we had to
scrub to remove. However, she did not tell me what it was she
wrote or to whom it was addressed. Sometimes I was tempted
to offer to find a way to get these letters delivered, but I thought
better of it, knowing that there was only Luc who might be
trusted to smuggle them out and not wishing to put him in
danger.

Being lodged in the devil's castle meant that we were severely
restricted in the service we could obtain from the Burgundian
household. More than once we were refused hot water for

bathing and Catherine had to cleanse herself in freezing water, straight from the well. To my surprise she actually welcomed the discomfort.

'It is like a penance, Mette,' she confessed, 'as if I am being tested, just as Christ was in the wilderness, and I must pray that God will release me from my suffering when He is pleased with me. If I did not believe that, I should run mad like my father.'

As it was, instead of losing her mind, she began to lose her looks. She grew thinner by the day and her hair began to come out in handfuls when I brushed it. With every brush stroke I cursed the Duke of Burgundy. At least communications with the English, which Luc learned of through the stable grooms, began to bear fruit. Instead of laying siege to Paris, King Henry apparently wanted to parley with the king's council and proposed sending his most trusted general, the Earl of Warwick, to Troyes for an Easter meeting. After two weeks at Brie Comte Robert, the great royal procession set out again and the queen finally got her wish to travel into the lush pastures and neat vineyards of Champagne.

The undulating upper valley of the Seine could not have been more different from the river's lower reaches, where marching feet and iron-shod hooves had trampled the life out of the land and the heart out of the people. Here an early spring sun shone down on verdant fields with well-fed peasants busy raising crops and tending flocks. From the high seat of a baggage cart, I viewed sights I had never thought to see. Prosperous villages rang with the sound of the blacksmith's hammer and the laughter of carefree children and boasted decent little timbered cottages, well-pruned orchards and a nice clear pattern of strip-fields clustered around churches built of stone with leaded roofs. I firmly believe that Paradise must be just like that well-watered vale; a land studded with sprouting crops and well-stocked farm-yards, where the advent of spring did not signal the onset of hostilities, but marked the beginning of a season of warmth and plenty.

22

Walking the streets of Troyes was like going back to the Paris of old, before the 'Terrors' had rendered it mean and vicious. For in many ways Troyes was a smaller version of its downstream sister-city, but without the domineering guilds and rival gangs. Unlike the sprawl of Paris over both banks of the Seine, Troyes neatly occupied one loop of a meander on the west bank of the river, its protective stone curtain studded with gates leading to trade routes in all directions. Ingeniously, some of the fast-flowing water had been diverted into a series of canals which pierced the curtain wall under portcullises and wound through the town, enabling heavy goods to be carried in and out by barge. One of the first things I noticed was that the main hazards to pedestrians were horses and hand-carts, not the huge ox-wagons which had daily claimed lives and limbs in Paris. The canals also carried away waste, causing some of the backwaters to smell like latrines. However, the April downpours, which had frequently drenched the royal progress, had also washed away most of the winter filth and refreshed the canals.

This was a blessing because the palace of the old counts of

Champagne where we were to stay was located on a canal at the centre of the town. It was built to an old-fashioned plan, consisting of a long great hall with royal apartments at one end, reached by a curving stone staircase. I had become quite used to adapting Catherine's furnishings to a variety of apartments that were cramped or difficult of access, but I was pleasantly surprised by the large and comfortable quarters she was given in the great gothic palace. Once again her ladies were to be housed in a separate building but, to her intense relief, we learned that the Duke of Burgundy had a mansion of his own in Troyes and would not be lodging with the royal family.

'What is more, he will not be alone,' Catherine announced with an air of triumph. 'His duchess has travelled from Dijon to act as hostess to the English embassy. The blessed Virgin has answered my prayers again.'

As a result of all this, the tension in our little household eased considerably. Catherine recovered her appetite and with it some of her zest for life. But Lenten meals were meagre, consisting of pottage, vegetables, bread and a little fish, designed to chasten the body rather than build its strength. So, anxious to put some flesh on her bones, I went daily to market, looking for tasty tit-bits to tempt her with. Basket on arm, I watched the town shake off its winter hibernation. With the great Easter festival approaching, amulet-sellers had set up stalls in the cathedral square offering everything from icons and relics to potions and pardons. Peddlers roamed the streets crying their wares in loud, musical calls which echoed among the timber-framed, step-gabled houses. These crazily-overhanging gables were brightly painted or decorated with tiles and pargeting and the wooden shutters which secured the ground-floor shops at night were lowered by day to form tables laid out with colourful arrays of food and household necessities. This alone was something to marvel at, for in thief-ridden Paris such tempting goods would have been snatched in the blink of an eye.

Although the Duke of Burgundy had sent the Earl of Warwick a letter of free-passage for his journey to Troyes, it only gave protection in royal and Burgundian territory and when the cavalcade of two hundred English knights and men-at-arms strayed uncomfortably close to Prince Charles' new garrison in Melun, an eager troop of dauphinists galloped out to ambush them. They were easily driven off however, and during the banquet held by the Duke and Duchess of Burgundy to welcome him to Troyes, the Earl of Warwick gleefully regaled the high table with a description of the incident. Seated at the earl's right hand, Catherine was well placed to absorb every detail of his amusing account and returned full of indignation which, to my surprise, was directed more at Prince Charles' supporters than at Warwick.

They were laughing at Charles at dinner and it is not a pretty sound to my ears,' she said angrily to Agnes and me, as I helped her take off her headdress. 'I think he cannot be at Melun after all, because he would never have agreed to such an ill-advised attack on an English troop as was launched from there two days ago, not if he has Tanneguy du Chastel by his side. The attack was a fiasco! To send out only fifty against two hundred does seem foolish, to put it politely. The earl was full of glee as he described how he sent his rearguard to take the little troop of dauphinists from behind before they could even draw swords. I imagine Charles can ill-afford to lose the ten men who fell before the rest fled.'

But her indignation did not last long for she was bubbling with excitement about Richard Beauchamp, Earl of Warwick. From her description he was a knight of the kind that the Troubadour of Troyes must have pictured when he wrote his poems of Camelot and the Court of King Arthur – tall and russet-blond, a true Norman, broad-shouldered and straight-backed, with muscular arms and legs and eyes like a hawk.

'And he dances!' Catherine added breathlessly. 'Well, enough not to step on my toes. But I think his best asset is his conversation. He is fluent in Latin and Greek as well as English and French, as is King Henry, apparently. So, of course, I had to ask him what King Henry is like and he told me that he is an übermensch. I asked him what that meant and he said it was German for a super-man. So he speaks German as well! When I asked if his king is good-looking, he laughed and said he could not be a judge of that, but I should rather ask if he was a good leader. So I did and he replied: "A good leader creates followers, a great leader creates leaders. Henry is a great leader."

'I think I am becoming a little frightened of Henry of England, but then I think Richard of Warwick intends that I should be; that we all should be. It is a good tactic, is it not? And I would rather be frightened of a great leader than of a disciple of the devil like Jean of Burgundy.'

At this, Agnes put a finger to her lips as a sign of caution, and the subject reverted to the entertainments the evening had provided . . .

Easter came and the streets of Troyes were decked with green boughs and crowded with people following the statues of patron saints and their relics as they were carried out of their churches and paraded through the town. In their wake, young men and girls paired off to sing and dance in the squares. With a lump in my throat I watched Alys set off to meet her new beau, a tailor named Jacques, whom I knew by sight having secretly been witness to Alys' first meeting with the young man when we went marketing together one day. Though she still had not admitted to any assignation, the care with which she fashioned a rosette of lace and coloured ribbons and pinned it to the bodice of her Sunday gown, told me all I needed to know. She left the palace with a group of fellow servants, but I suspected she would slip away from them at the first opportunity and I whispered a little prayer to St Agnes, asking the patron of young girls to protect my little daughter and give her a happy day.

After High Mass in the cathedral, the royal family was due to attend an Easter feast at the Hôtel de Ville and, once more, the Earl of Warwick would be there. I wondered what the earl would tell his king about the girl who was being offered as his wife. Despite Alys' hasty alterations, Catherine's pretty green and red houppelande gown still hung loosely on her too-delicate figure and although in my eyes she could never be anything but beautiful, having become so thin, she hardly looked the ideal fecund consort for a king who must be anxious to sire an heir for his ever-expanding empire. However, there was no mistaking Catherine's opinion of the earl, for she was once again full of him when she returned from the banquet in high spirits.

'I danced with the Earl of Warwick again today, Mette!' she crowed, twirling around me with exaggerated grace. 'I have decided that he is the most accomplished man I have ever met! He even described the fashions at the English court and confessed that they tend to follow the French styles, only several years later. The men have not yet started wearing folly bells, although the earl himself has acquired some while he has been in France and was wearing them tonight. He is the first man I have seen who does not look silly in them!'

'And did you only dance with the Earl of Warwick?' I enquired with a raised eyebrow.

'No, of course not. That would set the tongues wagging, would it not?' Catherine frowned. 'I was forced to dance a *salterello* with the Duke of Burgundy and then the treacherous Guy de Mussy had the cheek to ask me to dance a *ballade*. As if I would dance anything with him – least of all a *ballade!*'

A *ballade*, I assumed, had some connection with love or romance. Clearly there was no forgiveness for Monsieur Guy!

At this point Catherine abruptly changed the subject.

'Are you going into the town again tomorrow, Mette?' On hearing that I was, she declared her intention to accompany me. 'I will not be recognised in Troyes as I would in Paris and if I borrow a maid's dress from Alys, I am sure no one will know me. We could go shopping together. What fun that would be!'

'I would be very happy to have your company, Mademoiselle,' I responded readily, 'but I cannot imagine the queen approving of such an expedition.'

That gave her pause for thought, but she did not hesitate long. 'You are right. So I will plead a headache. The queen must know I have my monthly course at present?'

She regarded me meaningfully and I found myself blushing. Until then I had not been aware that Catherine knew I obeyed her mother's instructions to provide evidence whenever her daughter suffered the 'curse of Eve'. I did not like doing it, but I had no choice. During the process of the treaty under negotiation, reports had to be made of Catherine's regularity in this matter, as a guide to her fertility.

She smiled wryly. 'It is all right, Mette, I know you are obliged to do it and it gives me an excuse to say that I am keeping to my chamber. But instead, you and I will slip down the servants' stair and take to the streets. Agnes can keep the other ladies occupied so they do not suspect anything.'

Even in Alys' serviceable brown wool and unbleached linen, it was still hard to believe that Catherine was a servant girl until she put on the coif with its plain turned-back front, when she immediately lost her air of sophisticated nobility and became a simple maid.

We did not go arm in arm as Alys and I had done but, otherwise, we might have been mistaken for the same mother and daughter who had walked to market the week before. As we crossed the canal behind the palace and headed towards the labyrinth of shops and stalls around the main market place, Catherine was delighted to find herself totally anonymous among the passers-by. A number of people offered neighbourly nods and smiles and she smiled and nodded back, one of the crowd yet lost in it.

We dallied in the Rue du Chaperon, looking at all manner of hats and headdresses. In the Rue des Orfèvres we watched a goldsmith and his apprentice hammer out a sheet of gold-leaf so thin you would think it might blow away.

For nostalgic reasons the Rue des Pains was my favourite place because the sight and smell of freshly-baked bread transported me back to the days of my childhood, when my parents had fed their Paris neighbours in peace and harmony. I told the princess this, and we lingered there thoughtfully for a few moments.

As we entered the main market square, we came upon a wedding party on the steps of the church of St Jean. A solemn-faced young couple stood before the priest in the portal surrounded by their families, while hangers-on added to the crowd in the square; beggars expecting alms from the newlyweds, musicians ready and waiting beside the grooms who were holding horses festooned with ribbons and plumes in readiness for the wedding procession.

Passing the shop on the Rue de l'Aiguille where Jacques was a tailor, I pointed out Alys' new beau to the princess. He was sewing black silk edging on a brown velvet sleeve, and Catherine was as impressed as Alys had been by the speed and neatness of his stitching.

'He looks very earnest. Not one to wear his heart on his sleeve!' She chuckled briefly at her own joke. 'Would you not like to meet him, Mette?'

She wanted to go into his shop and order something, forgetting that she was dressed as a servant who could not afford even half a yard of that brown velvet.

So it was that next day that Jacques was summoned to the palace to take a commission for the princess, and a sumptuous new gown was soon in progress with Jacques stitching industriously by daylight and lamplight in the house on the Rue de l'Aiguille. Unsurprisingly it was Alys who volunteered to attend fittings and run errands to the tailor. No mention was made of love or even friendship between them and she confided nothing about his character or circumstances, but I had never seen my daughter look happier or more comely. Her eyes had a deep, warm glow and she seemed to be constantly on the verge of smiling. The princess too had a spring sparkle in her eye and her cheeks and shoulders had lost their bony sharpness – early signs of a resurgence of her natural beauty.

As if to celebrate this new blooming, a costly and fragile Venetian mirror arrived, a gift from King Henry, and was presented after dinner in the great hall by the Earl of Warwick. Not being one to hold back on the charm, he soon had Catherine blushing prettily as he played proxy for his king.

'If his grace King Henry were here himself I know exactly how he would feel in the presence of such beauty as yours,

317

highness,' the earl began, gallantly casting himself down on one knee before the princess. 'His heart would beat faster and the royal blood would throb in his veins at the enticing prospect of calling you his queen.'

I heard a little snigger beside me and kicked Luc's ankle hard. He and Alys were sharing my allotted place at the trestle, squashed in on either side of me below the rest of Catherine's household. Strictly speaking, Luc should have been eating with the outside servants in the under-croft, but occasionally the stewards let me bring him into the great hall. I had to vouch for his behaviour though and sniggering during the speech of an honoured royal guest, however excessively flowery the language, did not pass as good manners.

'It is King Henry's hope that this mirror will be acceptable to the most beautiful princess in Christendom and that every time she views her reflection she will feel the admiration of the man who gave it to her and his desire to see for himself what the mirror sees.'

At this point the earl rose to his feet, pulled off his elegant green chaperon hat and swept Catherine a deep bow before continuing to address her with an expression of smiling sincerity. 'But not yet having had the privilege of meeting your highness, my sovereign does not know as I do that the mirror can never reflect your true beauty, which is of the mind and therefore invisible to eye or glass. When I return to his side, I shall do my humble best to describe to him the agility of your intellect, the depth of your compassion and the tenderness of your spirit, but I fear the words of a mere soldier can never do them justice.'

The high colour that stained Catherine's cheeks as she acknowledged the handsome earl's speech revealed her true youth and innocence. 'You underestimate your own eloquence, my lord of Warwick,' she remonstrated mildly. 'Please convey to his grace, your lord and king, my grateful thanks for his generous gift. I shall treasure it and reflect upon the peace which we all pray will soon benefit our two countries. And I also thank *you*, Monseigneur, for your kindness in bringing me to an understanding of the love and loyalty you and your fellow barons all feel for your liege lord.'

The looking-glass was immediately set up in Catherine's salon and became the vehicle of much excited self-inspection by her ladies and visitors. Even the queen came to view herself in it and immediately expressed a wish to acquire one for her own chamber. When, in a quiet moment, I sneaked a look at my own reflection, I was horrified by the image I saw of a sturdy, ample-bosomed goodwife, when I still remembered myself as the light-footed, pink-cheeked maid I had seen reflected in the pools of Montmartre as I teased the boys on May Day romps. I could not imagine why the queen wanted to own such a cruel reminder of passing time. Perhaps she was blind to her own physical decline.

On the last day of April, the clerks and lawyers put down their quills and a formal truce was signed by the Duke of Burgundy and the Earl of Warwick, who immediately rode away to rejoin his sovereign in Mantes. At his leave-taking he bowed low over Catherine's hand, murmuring as he favoured her with one of his brilliant smiles, 'Until we meet soon again, Madame.'

23

'I hope King Henry is as charming as his general,' Catherine confided to me that night. 'Even though he is old enough to be my father, I have to confess that Richard of Warwick makes my knees tremble! But it is not all good news. There is to be a peace conference to finalise the treaty and I am to be presented to Henry.'

'But why is this not good news?' I exclaimed. 'You will meet him at last! You have often said that marriage to King Henry would be your only escape from Burgundy.'

She clasped her hands together anxiously. 'Yes, but I am worried about the eventual terms of the treaty. At the peace conference Burgundy will serve Burgundy as he always does and Henry will obviously serve England, but who will serve the interests of France? What will be left of her when they have finished parcelling out her territories? And where will that leave Charles?'

'Let Tanneguy du Chastel worry about that,' I insisted. 'Your brother has scores of advisers to look out for his interests, whilst you have only you.'

'And you, Mette, I am glad to say. And we will soon be on

the move again you and I, for this meeting with King Henry is to take place within a month at Meulan.'

Seeing my face she nodded ruefully. 'Yes, Mette; we are going all the way back to very near Pontoise, where we came from.'

Remembering the aches and bruises of the outward journey, I was far from thrilled at the prospect of a return trip, but my main misgiving was for Alys. When I told her the news I thought she might at last confess to her relationship with Jacques, but she did not. Instead she went very pale and she must have slipped away from the palace at the first opportunity. She had not returned when it was time to help Catherine dress for court.

The princess was unconcerned. 'Do not scold her when she comes, Mette,' she told me, 'for I will not.'

'You are too kind, Mademoiselle,' I protested. 'She is shirking her duty.'

'All too soon she will only have her duty to do,' said Catherine. 'The court is due to move in three days.'

—ξξ—

From Catherine of France to Charles, Dauphin of Viennois,
Greetings, dear brother,
Everything has changed again and now the inglorious
alliance of the queen and Burgundy informs me that there
is to be peace between France and England after all and I
am once again offered in marriage to King Henry! I am now
quite glad that you have not read my previous letters because

I am not certain whether you would keep the secret of my cruel treatment at the hands of the devil duke. But I pray fervently that this coming peace conference will prevent any repetition of it and that I may yet achieve my birthright, which is to become a queen and, at the same time, a bride who does not shrink from her nuptial duty in fear and loathing.

However, I do question how a peace treaty between England and France may be achieved without entirely destroying what I have always maintained is your legitimate claim to be the Heir of France. How much sovereignty will King Henry achieve over our territories and how treacherously will Burgundy conspire to expand his own fiefs, leaving little of France for you even to fight for? I only hope that you remain free from the yoke of Burgundy, and are at least in control of your own destiny. I hope you will not blame me for the fate to which I am delivered. I have no choice but to embrace it or else descend into madness.

And so, however things may transpire, I remain as always, your devoted and loyal sister,

Catherine

Written at the Palace of the Counts, Troyes this day Monday May 2nd 1419.

—ξξ—

To her credit, Alys did not moan or grumble about having to leave Troyes and, in truth, there was no alternative, for once the court departed, other than Jacques, she would be without friend or succour. Even Luc was due to make the journey because hunting was the king's chief pleasure and whatever kept King Charles amused made everyone's job easier. In Troyes at least he had been calm and content and there had been no return of the distressing 'Glass King' episode. It remained to be seen how he would be affected by a return to Pontoise.

To everyone's not altogether delighted surprise, Queen Isabeau chose to pay a visit to Catherine's salon shortly after Maître Jacques had delivered the completed gown. The ladies-in-waiting had carefully brought out the looking glass and Catherine had invited Jacques to wait while she retired to don her new purchase.

'You must see it in the mirror, Maître Jacques,' she insisted, 'for this is a silvered glass from Venice and I have been told that artists see the effect of their work more clearly in such a mirror.'

'I have never seen such a fine looking-glass, Madame,' acknowledged Jacques, peering at his own reflection in amazement. 'I am honoured to wait.'

While Alys and Agnes helped Catherine into the new gown, I was pleased to note that Jacques had seized his once-in-a-lifetime opportunity and designed something very different from the high-waisted houppelande which presently dominated court fashion for both men and women. Together he and Catherine had selected a deep turquoise brocade, figured in gold, for the body of the gown and a rich cream satin for the high collar and lining of the sleeves. Out of these the tailor had devised a gown that was cinched low at the waist with a

323

skirt that opened in an inverted V, showing what Jacques called a *petit-côte* of heavy cream silk, fabulously embroidered in gold thread, with a design of flowers and leaves. I am no expert, but I do not think anything like it had ever been seen at the French court. When she finally stood before the mirror, Catherine gazed at her reflection long and silently, turning this way and that to get an all-round view.

Perturbed by her silence, Maître Jacques hastened to make explanations. 'It is a development of the gown I submitted to the guild for my final apprentice piece, Madame,' he said. 'At the time the masters called it "fresh thinking".'

Catherine turned to him with a dazzling smile. 'I think it is stunning, Maître Jacques – a masterpiece. It is a gown I shall treasure. You are undoubtedly a craftsman of great talent and I shall sing your praises to the whole court.'

'Whose praises shall you sing, daughter? And what in the world are you wearing?' The queen's voice broke clearly over the murmurs of congratulation that had risen among the small gathering, whose backs were to the door while they gazed into the glass.

All instantly swung round and dipped to their knees as Queen Isabeau entered the room, closely followed by two of her ladies. At a gesture from her mother, Catherine rose first, her face flushed with surprise.

'You are most welcome, your grace,' she said faintly, indicating her own chair. 'Would it please you to sit?'

Waiting until her ladies had arranged the substantial train of her spectacular emerald and ruby gown, the queen sank into the cushioned seat and we all held our breath as her vertiginous padded headdress narrowly avoided being toppled by the tasselled canopy. The queen's headgear had become increasingly exaggerated lately perhaps, as her daughter had mischievously suggested, with the aim of drawing the eye from the increasing network of wrinkles on her face.

'You may all sit,' her mother allowed graciously, 'except you, Catherine. You may not sit until you have explained this extra-ordinary garment. I hope you are not intending to wear it at court!'

'Not without your grace's approval of course,' responded Catherine, frowning. 'But I cannot imagine what objection you could have to such a beautiful gown.'

'It is outlandish!' exclaimed the queen. 'More like a chamber-robe than a court gown. What can have possessed you?'

Catherine must have recalled some of the bizarre outfits that the queen herself had worn over the years and for Jacques' sake, she did not entirely guard her tongue.

'Well, I consider the gown delightful and I fully intend to wear it, though not in your presence if you object to it so much, Madame. Nevertheless, I predict that there will be a dozen copies made at court before the year's end.' She beckoned Jacques forward and he rose from the kneeling posture he had main-tained even after the others had sat down. 'May I present the master tailor who made this wonderful creation, your grace? Maître Jacques of Troyes.'

His face pink with awe and embarrassment, Jacques bent his knee before the queen's chair. She favoured him with the briefest of glances and an instant hand-flick of dismissal, exclaiming, 'A tailor of Troyes! That explains all. Be gone! I will have no ugly provincial styles ruining the reputation of my court.'

Crestfallen, Jacques backed off and made a hasty exit, closely followed by Alys who slipped away as only a servant can, without the queen ever having noticed she was there. I sighed ruefully. Catherine addressed her mother through gritted teeth. 'I fear you may soon have threadbare courtiers, Madame, for I see no prospect of an imminent return to the ateliers of Paris.'

'Now there you are wrong, daughter. My lord of Burgundy declares that once we have a treaty and a marriage contract, we will make a triumphant entry into Paris for your wedding to King Henry.' Her gaze swung majestically around the assembled company. 'And I assure you that the bride will *not* be wearing a gown made by any Maître Nobody of Troyes!'

Undertaken in balmy May weather, the return trip to Pontoise was much quicker and easier than the outward trip had been. It may be that Prince Charles had given orders for his parents' procession to be left strictly alone, for we saw no evidence of hostile troops and it would have been a foolhardy band of outlaws that would risk attacking the six hundred men-at-arms who rode with us, so the journey passed uneventfully. The king and his courtiers even managed to do some hunting, which kept the cooks supplied with game. Luc complained (though not to anyone that mattered, I am glad to say) that it was bad practice to hunt in the breeding season, but he was soon made to understand that no one told the king, however feeble his mind, when he could and could not hunt.

To Catherine's great relief, Burgundy and his duchess had hurried away to Dijon on business of their own and he had delegated royal escort duties to one of his senior nobles. Unhampered by Burgundy's insidious presence, Catherine suddenly became unexpectedly charming to her mother, actually talking with her in her litter for hours at a time, a ploy which successfully achieved a change in the accommodation arrangements at Pontoise. Declaring that she would need the queen's guidance on her forthcoming meeting with King Henry, she suggested that her former lodgings outside the keep should be allotted to Burgundy and the quarters in the keep which he had previously occupied be given to her.

'It is more fitting that you and I and the king should lodge together as a family, do you not think, Madame? And when he comes to Pontoise, my lord of Burgundy will be able to keep his own state and security in the separate lodging.'

During all our recent confidences Catherine and I had avoided one thorny topic; whether the Duke of Burgundy's lust for dominance and self-gratification had led him to a perversion which some might consider even more heinous than sodomy – to whit, lying with the queen as well as her daughter. I think we both suspected the worst and, certainly, Catherine's relationship with the queen, never warm at the best of times, had remained punctiliously formal, irreversibly soured by her childhood experience and more recently by Burgundy's nauseous habit of presenting them both with succulent morsels at meals. Being young as she was, I suspect she considered her mother unforgivably guilty of promiscuity, assuming that a queen must have possession of her own will, but for myself I wondered.

This queen struck me as a very different person from the one who had swayed majestically into the garden at St Pol and almost casually sailed off with Michele, Louis and Jean. That queen had been captivating and confident in her own magnificence; this queen was petulant and insecure, aware of her fading powers and desperate to preserve her position. Burgundy represented her last hope of retaining a glimmer of her former glory, of clinging to the reins of the realm. If she wanted to occupy her throne, she had no choice but to give Burgundy whatever he wanted to support her.

However, Queen Isabeau declared the accommodation change perfectly acceptable, seeming almost grateful for the apparent thaw in mother-daughter relations. Perhaps she hoped for an ally in her dealings with Jean the Fearless, whom she must have found a fearsome adversary on occasions, despite her apparent zest for contention. At all events, by the time the duke reached Pontoise, the swap was a fait accompli and, lacking any publicly acceptable reason to reverse it, he was obliged to accept it.

We spent ten days in frantic preparations for Catherine's meeting with King Henry. Since the queen had grandiosely dismissed the notion of 'provincial stitchers' as she so disdainfully called them, no tailor in Pontoise was deemed capable of preparing Catherine's robes for this all-important encounter, with the result that the queen's chief seamstress and Alys were saddled with the task of altering the priceless cloth of gold gown worn at the infamous tournament four years before. At the time I had thought that the heavy gold fabric swamped Catherine's delicate features but, to my delight, when she tried it on again I saw that the intervening years had lent her beauty a maturity and strength which could not be overwhelmed. And when the queen produced a priceless diamond collar and a ceremonial mantle edged with ermine and emblazoned with royal heraldic symbols, Catherine's appearance achieved a regal splendour which could not fail to impress.

Excited though she was at the prospect of at last meeting the man she had fantasised about for so long, she grew increasingly nervous as the day approached. 'The mantle gives me nightmares, Mette,' she confided. 'I cannot refuse to wear it, but I am horribly conscious that I could easily trip over it, which would jeopardise the whole treaty. King Henry is said to put great faith in omens and portents.'

I found it hard to believe that an all-powerful conqueror would pay any heed to a simple stumble and I said so, but Catherine was adamant, shaking her head.

'You are wrong. History is full of great generals who will not raise their standard if their horse tramples a toad or if a single swan flies overhead,' she said gravely. 'Were a Daughter of France to trip over the symbols of her nation it might blight the entire peace conference.'

'But you will not,' I assured her briskly. 'You are all nimbleness and grace. Anyone who has watched you dance knows that.'

'Perhaps,' she shrugged and gave me a little smile. 'But there are a dozen other things that could sour this meeting.'

'None that will be laid at your door,' I declared roundly. 'If anyone blights the very air he breathes, it is Burgundy! Mark my words, if anything goes wrong it will be his doing.'

24

I n this pernicious war, peace could not be made within walls.
Any castle, palace, church or even cathedral was considered
too dangerous, too conducive to treachery on either side. Meulan
was suitably situated halfway between Pontoise and King
Henry's headquarters at Mantes, but there was no question of
the two kings meeting in the town itself. Instead, a site was
chosen well out of bowshot range on an island in the Seine
called Le Pré du Chat, or the Meadow of the Cat, where elaborate preparations were made.

At one time the island had been used by the local seigneur
to contain the pet leopard he had acquired on a crusade to the
Holy Land. No one had told him that the leopard was the one
cat that did not fear water and, before long, the beast had swum
to freedom, whereupon it had proceeded to terrorise the local
flocks and herds for several years until it was hunted down and
killed. However its fame lived on in the island's name. The Seine
was fast-flowing at this point and access was only possible by
boat and so, when surrounding woods had been cleared and a
defensive stockade built, the island was considered suitably
secure. Separate gates and landing stages were set at either end;

the French would approach from the north bank, the English from the south. Inside the stockade a large central pavilion was erected for the formal proceedings and two smaller ones for each side's private retreat. Maps of the conference ground had been drawn for the principal participants, together with a comprehensive list of Rules of Behaviour. Catherine brought hers to her chamber so that she could study them carefully.

'Burgundy's hand is clear in this,' she said, intently perusing the rules. 'Every drink and dish is to be sampled by tasters of both sides and no arms are to be worn in the main pavilion, even by the kings. Blessed Marie, does he think King Henry might draw his sword on him?'

'He judges everyone to be like himself,' I observed tartly. 'Does your royal father even wear a sword?'

'Yes, on formal occasions, but the tip and the blade are blunted,' Catherine revealed. 'His squires have done that ever since he set upon a member of the council years ago.'

'How is his grace?' I asked gently, vividly remembering that occasion and the awful neglect that had resulted for the royal children. 'Will he attend the conference?'

Catherine made the sign of the cross. 'He is still quite well, God be thanked.'

I fanned myself with my hand. 'I wondered, because it is very hot for May. In the past he has been badly affected by the heat.'

'That is true, but I pray he will remain in reasonable health, because even if he makes no contribution, his presence seems to curb Burgundy's worst excesses.' A heavy sigh punctuated these remarks. 'The duke drew me apart at dinner tonight. From his expression an observer might have thought he was whispering words of encouragement, but what he said was: *Monmouth cannot have you yet but I can, however much you try to hide behind your mother.'*

I saw tears welling in her eyes and tried to quell the flow. 'Dear Mademoiselle, you must be strong. These are just words. He is angry because the apartments were rearranged. He is a bully and bullies do not like to be thwarted.'

Catherine nodded, a tear running down her cheek. 'And he is such a powerful bully! But you are right, I must be strong.' She brushed away the tear and drew herself up. 'It may make him even angrier, but I want you with me at the conference, Mette. I need you there. I am allowed two ladies to accompany me. Agnes will be one and you are to be the other. Will you do this for me?'

I was now blinking tears from my own eyes and I coughed to clear the lump in my throat. 'Well, of course, I would be honoured, Mademoiselle, but will I be permitted?'

Catherine threw back her shoulders, suddenly businesslike. 'No question of that, for we will not ask. We must find you some clothes. By the time you are wearing a fine gown and jewels and one of those horrible headdresses with templettes over the ears you will look just like one of the Flanders mares.'

This was not a comparison I treasured, but at least it meant that two days later I found myself among the distinguished party which embarked before Tierce on the royal barge bound for Meulan. On some pretext Agnes had managed to persuade one of Catherine's Flemish attendants to supply her finest gown – a grandiose garment of murrey wool which made me perspire freely under the growing strength of the sun. Fortunately the heavy black headdress also rendered me unrecognisable. At the last minute the unseasonably stifling heat had brought on a recurrence of King Charles' glass delusion and he had been hurriedly conveyed to his padded chamber. Therefore, to Catherine's intense disappointment, it would not be her father but the hated Duke of Burgundy who presided over her presentation to the English king.

Shaded by a tasselled gold canopy, she sat with the queen and the duke in the waist of the gilded barge while Agnes and I were packed into the stern with the queen's ladies, finding what shade we could in the lee of the barge-master's great tiller. Music from a small band of musicians seated in the bow lent the journey a melodious formality. Behind the royal barge three more galleys followed, carrying parties of chosen knights, clerks and counsellors.

As the procession approached the wharf, the Meadow of the Cat presented a magnificent display of welcome. At a blast from a line of trumpeters drawn up on the battlements of the timber gatehouse, rows of weighted silk banners in blue and red broke open in unison and avalanched down the side of the stockade to undulate gently in the warm breeze, revealing the heraldic badges of France, Burgundy and Valois embroidered in threads of azure and argent, gules, vert and or. The other landing stage was hidden from our sight but an answering call of trumpets indicated that King Henry's barge was approaching simultaneously at the other side of the island and banners showing the lions of England and the swans of Lancaster were performing a similar stately gavotte on the playful wind. On the river banks multi-coloured lines of billowing standards identified the knights of the English and French encampments, gathered in their hundreds and cheering lustily as the two royal parties arrived. I recalled the Rules of Behaviour, stipulating that any unruly conduct would be punishable by instant imprisonment and concluded that they must be grateful to be able to let off a bit of steam. Compared with waging war, making peace was a dull process.

After disembarkation the crush of retainers in the French pavilion rendered the atmosphere suffocating, but a small ante room had been partitioned off for the ladies, with doors opening onto a patch of meadow, screened from prying eyes by a copse of willows. There we were served cold drinks and honeyed cakes and I helped Catherine make the final adjustments to her appearance for this all-important meeting with her potential lord and husband. As I adjusted her headdress, I noticed to my consternation that she was pale and shaking and I led her hastily to the open door and fanned her with my veil. My instinct was to give her a reassuring hug, but my disguise as a Flemish noblewoman held me back and, anyway, I judged that now was not the time for tears and sympathy.

'Pinch your cheeks, Mademoiselle,' I urged her in a whisper. 'This is the moment you were born for. The lieges may have lost at Agincourt, but you can conquer their conqueror. Go and retrieve the pride of France.'

Surprised by my fierce expression and rallying tone, Catherine stared at me wide-eyed, then straightened her back, raised both hands to her face and pinched her cheeks. In that flash of time she changed from a trembling girl into the heart-stopping beauty of every knight's dreams.

'Sweet Jesu, Mette, you should have been a general!' she exclaimed wryly and turned to take her place in the procession to the main pavilion.

Catherine of France faced Henry of England for the first time across a wide expanse of priceless Persian carpet. In its central medallion a crouching golden lion confronted a kneeling white unicorn, a design worked into the rug by the skilled weavers of Esfahan. Heralds sounded a fanfare; Henry advanced to the lion, supported by his brothers, Thomas of Clarence and Humphrey of Gloucester; Catherine glided serenely to the unicorn, her mother and the Duke of Burgundy at her side.

'I have the honour to present her grace Queen Isabeau of France and her daughter Catherine, the Princess Royal,' intoned the whiplash voice of Burgundy as I watched Catherine sink into a deep obeisance, skirts billowing, head lowered, eyes modestly downcast. At the sight of her I felt my stomach knot with suppressed pride.

Braided into nets of gold filigree the bright hair I had brushed so vigorously shone like polished silk, encircled by a jewelled coronet. Sunlight streaming through the open sides of the pavilion reflected off the gleaming folds of her gown, while behind her stretched the purple mantle displaying her dynastic pedigree; the fleur-de-lis of France, the crusader's cross of St Louis and the three toads of Clovis. At this pivotal moment I could not help wondering what the English king would do if he knew that this beautiful and noble princess, offered to him in all her magnificent and costly finery, was the victim of the vile abuse of the man at her elbow and the daughter of a promiscuous queen and a king who thought he was made of glass?

King Henry bowed punctiliously over Queen Isabeau's hand, kissed her whitened cheek briefly and then turned to raise Catherine from her curtsey. My mind jittered with jumbled questions. Surely no red-blooded male could fail to be stirred by the sight of her, but how would she react to him? Would she be impressed with his tall, athletic figure arrayed in a sable-trimmed doublet that blatantly trumpeted his claim to the French throne – the lions of England quartered with the lilies of France – or captivated by the noble outline of his profile and the proud set of his cropped head under its heavy gold crown? Or would she be devastated by the mangled scar which almost obliterated his right cheek?

Descriptions of King Henry had mentioned the scar, the result of a Welsh arrow which had nearly killed him at the age of sixteen while he was helping to quash a rebellion against his father, but none had ever portrayed the full extent of the damage. A whole flap of skin was missing from the right side of his face so that where there should have been a clean-shaven cheek to match the left side, there was just tight, white scar tissue stretching from his cheekbone to his jaw. Some guardian saint must have been protecting him when that arrow struck, I thought and wondered if all the damage was visible or whether the arrow had also scarred his mind. It was not easy to tell because the blemish lent the affected side of his face a gaunt immobility and gave more than a hint of the skull beneath the flesh.

Catherine gave no outward sign of anything untoward as she rose like windblown thistledown from her low crouch. His first words to her were heavy with meaning and audible to the whole gathering. 'I have waited a long time for this, Catherine,' he said, then swiftly bent and kissed her lingeringly on the mouth.

I almost felt the kiss myself; the firm, dry pressure of those hard soldier's lips against her soft, smooth mouth and the electric silence as the assembled company froze at the audacity of it. Burgundy had his back to me but I could see his shoulders go rigid with anger. Then the pages found themselves scrambling to manoeuvre Catherine's train as King Henry swept her imperiously across the carpet to a line of three thrones which had been placed on a flower-decked dais. Queen Isabeau was escorted to one of them by Burgundy while the English king, having seated his putative bride, took the middle one himself and waved at the heralds to start proceedings.

I understood nothing of the ensuing debate, since it consisted of a series of long speeches given in Latin, starting with the two principle negotiators, the Earl of Warwick and the Duke of Burgundy. So I spent the time watching Catherine and her royal suitor.

For the most part King Henry's attention remained on the speakers, but every so often I caught him stealing a sidelong glance to his right, where Catherine sat poised on her throne, chin high, hands resting quietly in her lap. I wondered if it bothered him that protocol had placed Queen Isabeau on his good side, whereas Catherine was presented with the scarred eloquence of his damaged cheek. If so, she gave him no visible cause for concern, presenting an image of calm containment. But I knew that Catherine was like the swan she so gracefully resembled; all regal serenity above the surface and frantic mental paddling beneath.

If I could glean nothing of King Henry's reaction to her from his own expression, that of his brother Humphrey was more revealing. The Duke of Gloucester was the youngest and, by repute, the most impetuous of Henry's brothers. He had travelled from England for the peace conference, swapping roles with the third and most statesmanlike brother, John of Bedford, who took on the regency in England. Shorter and swarthier than Henry, Humphrey had a handsome, expressive face and was seated at the forefront of the English nobles. His appreciation of Catherine's beauty was obvious in his unashamedly admiring gaze and I noticed him give a knowing little smile when he caught one of his brother's sidelong glances, as if he recognised a male reaction similar to his own.

There were two hours of speech-making, at the end of which I was intrigued to note that, as if to make a point, King Henry spoke briefly in English, a language I understood as little as the others' Latin. Then trumpets sounded a break in proceedings and both sides retired to their respective quarters while the central pavilion was prepared for the banquet.

The minute the doors closed on the French pavilion, Queen Isabeau turned to Catherine excitedly.

'Well, daughter, are you happy with our choice of bridegroom for you? Did you not thrill to King Henry's splendid appearance? Those broad shoulders, his well-muscled thighs and the way he kissed you? That was so naughty of him, but so indicative of his ardour! I did not understand what he said – English is such an outlandish language! – but he was obviously very taken with you. I think all is going very well.'

During this outburst the Duke of Burgundy hovered nearby with a sardonically curled lip, before disappearing into a huddle with his advisers. Listening from a judicious distance to protect my disguise, I marvelled at the queen's apparent blindness to the scar, which manifestly prevented King Henry's elevation to the Adonis status she seemed to be awarding him.

Catherine was noncommittal in her response. 'It may be a little early to celebrate, Madame,' she murmured, keeping one eye on Burgundy whose black brows were knitted in anger as he harangued his lawyers. 'The Earl of Warwick made no mention of territorial concessions in his speech and a great deal hangs on that, as you know. May I have your permission to retire to the ante room? I am sorely in need of air.'

At a curt grunt and a nod from her mother, Catherine managed to escape so that we could press cold napkins to her brow and remove the heavy mantle for some temporary relief from the heat and strain. Ever the practical one, I suggested that she use the close stool and took her to the far corner where I had set it up behind a privy curtain. In her elaborate apparel any call of nature was unanswerable without considerable assistance and as Agnes and I lifted her voluminous skirts, Catherine dropped her voice to whisper, 'How did I do, Mette? I was so shocked when I first saw his face. That awful scar – the poor man!'

'You gave no sign,' I assured her. 'Not by one twitch of a muscle. But the scar is a dominant feature. Are you very dismayed by it?'

'No, no!' she exclaimed. 'If anything, it makes him seem less daunting – less perfect. But why was I not told? Did they think I would throw a girlish faint if I knew I was to be given to a battle-scarred warrior?' She gave a hollow little laugh. 'And his kiss! That was a surprise. Did I blush? The trouble with battle-scarred warriors is that they always seem able to hide their feelings.'

'Then you are a warrior yourself, Mademoiselle, because I could read none of this in your face.' I jerked my head in the direction of the main pavilion. 'In there everyone is acting a part.'

'And now I have to talk to him at table!' she fretted. 'Sainte Marie, what shall I talk about? For all that Louis called him a libertine, they say that now he is pious. That he reads St Augustine and St Gregory. Shall I talk to him about them or will he think that too pretentious? Does he have a sense of humour? And if I make him laugh, will he think me frivolous?'

'You are not frivolous,' Agnes protested.

'Laughter is an attractive trait, surely,' I interjected.

'Not in a queen, Mette,' observed Catherine despondently. 'It is not for queens to be amusing, but to be discreet. Perhaps I should remember that he is the conqueror who still holds my

341

cousin of Orleans to ransom and not be tempted to tease or flirt.'

'Just be yourself, Mademoiselle,' I advised, thinking privately that a little flirting might not do any harm. 'Do not forget that beneath the crown there is a man.'

'After that kiss, how could I forget?' She sighed and stretched her neck uncomfortably. 'And beneath this coronet there is only a girl. It is hideously heavy!'

When the privy curtain was drawn back and Catherine was restored to her state of regal elegance, I could not help reflecting that King Henry's sense of humour might be severely tested if he was ever to know on what kind of throne his character had been discussed!

Despite her vow of restraint, during the banquet I heard the bright ring of Catherine's laughter more than once, even from the farthest reaches of the table where Agnes and I shared a cup and trencher. To my relief it was not a place where the queen or duke deigned to glance, so I remained undetected in my Flemish masquerade but from that distance it was hard to glean any real clue as to progress between Catherine and the king. However, I thought it a good sign that they did not appear to stop conversing throughout the long meal. From a distance, King Henry's puckered cheek was barely discernable and he looked much younger than his thirty-two years. I thought they appeared a well-matched couple. Of course the likelihood of happiness resulting from such a union was another matter entirely and one to which I was probably the only person present who gave any thought at all.

I could see that Catherine found the return trip to Pontoise nearly as taxing as the oarsmen who pulled against the flow of the river. Sandwiched between the queen and the Duke of Burgundy, who appeared to argue long and intensely, causing the duke's expression to turn blacker and blacker as the journey progressed, she spent the time fiddling with the rings on her fingers and casting despairing glances back at Agnes and me. Nor did she gain any respite when we reached Pontoise, for Queen Isabeau insisted that Catherine accompany her to the great hall where eager courtiers were gathered to hear an account of the day's events. The candles had burned low when she finally stumbled up the grand staircase to her bedchamber.

I had shed my sweaty finery with heartfelt gratitude and I knew that Catherine must be exhausted in her heavy gold gown and weighty headdress. Her body swayed as she stood in silence while we undressed her and I rubbed unguent of camomile into the angry red chafe marks left by the heavy coronet. However, it was not until all the ladies had departed and she and I and Alys were left alone that I discovered her inertia was due not to exhaustion but to despair.

She sank down onto a stool by the hearth, wrapping her chamber robe tightly around herself and I noticed that she was shivering violently.

'Shall I light the fire, Mademoiselle,' I asked hastily. 'I did not do so because it was very hot today, but if you are feeling chilled . . .'

She shook her head. 'No, Mette, I am not shivering with cold, but shaking with anger. As the queen and I left the hall tonight,

Burgundy bent his foul mouth to my ear and whispered. "*I can see that you pant for him, but you shall not have him.*" By all that is holy, how dare he?'

It felt as if an icicle was sliding down my back. 'Sweet Mother of God!' I breathed as my hand flew involuntarily in the sign of the cross. 'He is Beelzebub himself.'

Catherine dropped her head into her hands and clutched at her hair in desperation. 'Surely God will not allow it?' she cried.

'The duke cannot threaten you here, Mademoiselle!' I protested. 'There are guards and courtiers and servants everywhere and the queen is in the next chamber.'

'You may be right, Mette, but do you know what he has done? He has banned me from the peace conference. He told the queen that King Henry should not be allowed to see me again until he reduces his exorbitant claims on French lands and monies. He is using me like a carrot, as if King Henry is an ass! But he is not. He will never back down. Despite all the elaborate preparations and high-flown speeches, the *Pré du Chat* will end in deadlock and I shall never get away from Burgundy's evil grasp!'

—ξξ—

From Catherine, the Princess Royal, to Charles, Dauphin of Viennois,
  My dear and beloved brother,
  I go from hope to despair in the space of a moment. Today I finally met King Henry, for so long the object of my fears

and fantasies. And, believe it or not, Charles, I liked him! I know he is the enemy of France and that you despise him as a glory-seeking warmonger, but he does not strike me like that at all. If anything, he is too thoughtful and analytical to put his faith in the sword alone. I see him as the antithesis of Jean the Fearless. Not a man who consorts with the devil, but one who puts his hand in the hand of God.

And I believe he liked me. He does not wear his feelings on his face like his brother Humphrey, who eyed me like a stag after a hind, but his manner was warm and his conversation lively, so I think he found me interesting. His kiss was certainly warm! Oh, he kissed me like a man putting his mouth to a fountain after a long, parched ride. I have never felt so thoroughly embraced at first meeting. And the conference seemed to go well. When we took our leave he kissed me again and I was happy that a peace treaty might come about.

However, I foolishly forgot the interference of a third party. The Duke of Burgundy! All the way back in the royal barge I was forced to listen to the poisonous outpourings of fearless Jean and the querulous protests of the queen, whom I find it more and more painful to call my mother. By the time we reached Pontoise, my feelings of optimism had been overwhelmed by a sense of utter despondency. Burgundy refuses to allow me to attend any further sessions of the peace conference until King Henry reduces his territorial demands, which is as likely as snow in August. Jean the Fearless cannot stomach the idea that another man might achieve more by honourable conquest than he has done by pusillanimous thuggery.

I write this at the Hour of Matins, when monks and nuns stumble sleepily from their cells to offer the first prayers of the day to the Almighty, but sleep does not come to me. My mind is overcome with fear that I am destined to live constantly under the threat of Burgundy's evil abuse and that France is destined to wither under his insidious malevolence.

Unless you do something about it. You are my only hope, Charles! Can you not broker a peace with Henry and rally your forces against Burgundy? That way we will all have what we want and Jean the Fearless can be left to fester and fulminate in Flanders!

I will pray for this outcome every day as I will pray for you to stay free from harm and free from HIM.

Your ever-loving sister Catherine,

Written at Chateau de Pontoise in the dark hours of morning on Tuesday May 31st, 1419.

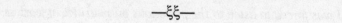

25

Catherine's absence did not bring the peace conference to an end. It stuttered on through a gloriously sunny June while she waited impatiently at Pontoise, nursing a flicker of hope for a return visit because she thought it inconceivable that a man like King Henry would waste his time talking unless he felt there was some point in it.

During these balmy days she resumed her practice of taking regular rides along the river to escape some of the heat trapped within the castle walls. Her old sparring-partner, Guy de Mussy, was still entrusted with command of her security, so it was he who arranged for the horses to be saddled and the escort assembled. On the last day of June, Agnes had begged to be excused from the excursion, and took to her bed in the Constable's House suffering one of her recurring sick headaches. However, over recent weeks Catherine had managed to form a working relationship with the two youngest of her 'Flanders mares', and they were more than willing to take fresh air and exercise.

Although Catherine felt safer living in the royal apartments, there was only one (admittedly quite large) chamber, in which she was obliged both to sleep and entertain and the afternoons when she and her ladies rode out were the only chance I had to get the tire-women in to clean the place. Time was when the actual scrubbing and sweeping would have been my job, but I had progressed from such drudgery, I am happy to say.

On this particular day, once I had supervised the cleaners' work and shooed them out, I began to arrange Catherine's change of clothes for the evening meal, taking the previous night's weighty court gown from its hook in the guarderobe and hauling it up a narrow stair to the attic chamber which contained both the queen's and her daughter's wardrobes. It was a long, low-beamed room packed with chests and boxes in which the royal ladies' many gowns and mantles, hats and headdresses, veils and shoes were stored, layered in lavender-scented linen; a quiet place with a distinctive smell that was part moth-repelling spices and part stale sweat. To my alarm I found Alys there alone and weeping. Her eyes were swollen, as if she had been crying for some time, and I rushed to comfort her. For my self-contained daughter to give way to tears meant something must be seriously wrong. 'Alys, my Alys. Come on now, my little girl. It is quiet here. There is no one except me. Whatever it is, I am sure I can help.' I pulled a kerchief from the sleeve of my bodice and gave it to her, which inspired a new bout of weeping and she buried her face in it, turning away.

'Is it Jacques?' I asked finally, in as mild a tone as I could muster.

'I think I am pregnant,' she said abruptly.

'Ah.' I stared back at her, unable for a moment to gauge my own reaction. Then I felt a great surge of warmth and sympathy.

How could I have felt anything else? I leaned over to take her hand. 'And you are frightened, yes?' She nodded mutely and I saw tears spring afresh in her eyes. 'But not of me, surely? You know that I have been in the same position as you. It is not so uncommon. Are you frightened of what Jacques will say? The baby is his, I suppose?'

Her chin jutted and she glared at me indignantly, as if I had suggested that the Virgin was a whore. 'Yes, of course it is!' she retorted. 'I have never been with anyone else.' Then she blushed and slumped, shaking her head miserably. A tear fell onto her restless hands. 'I am so far away from him,' she whispered.

'Yes.' I frowned and did some quick mental calculation. 'And you are sure you are pregnant? It is not long since we left Troyes.'

'I have just missed another of my courses. The first time I thought it could just be a mistake, the second time I am sure.'

I felt a pang of guilt that I had not noticed, as I certainly would have if Catherine had missed her monthly cycle. 'Well, you are not far on at least. It will not show for a while yet.'

'But the princess may not go back to Troyes,' wailed Alys. 'And I must go there, Ma. I must.'

I put my arms around her, hugging her tightly. She was so young and small and I hoped fervently that she had not misjudged Jacques.

'You shall, Alys. I promise. We will find some way. How do you think Jacques will react when you tell him?

Alys shook her head and whispered. 'I do not know.'

'Does he have any family?' I asked, remembering how my father had reacted when I fell pregnant as an unmarried girl and realising how lucky I had been to have him on my side, despite his initial anger. My little girl did not have a father to take her part. I would have to be both mother and father.

She blew her nose on the kerchief. 'His parents both died last year in an epidemic of spotted fever. It used to be his father's shop in the Rue de l'Aiguille.'

While I was genuinely sorry for Jacques' sudden loss of his parents, at the same time I recognised a promising situation. The young man had inherited a flourishing business and had the talent and training to pursue it successfully. This baby need suffer neither the stain of bastardy nor the privations of poverty. I must find a way for Alys to return to Jacques as soon as possible.

'He said I reminded him of his mother,' she whispered.

'I have a good feeling about this, little one. You must not worry any more. It is bad for the child . . .'

How could I have known that while I was busy comforting Alys, Catherine was riding into danger? Not that there was anything I could have done to stop it. Of course she confided in me later – how could she not? – but the full depth of her distress was only revealed to me many years afterwards in one of her undelivered letters to her brother.

Catherine, ruined daughter of France to Charles, 'bastard' Dauphin of Viennois,
   Greetings brother, as one victim to another.

Now the devil duke has done everything he can to ruin us both. You are labelled bastard and I can no longer call myself virgin. As I write this I feel distraught and on the verge of madness. Shame and dishonour have been visited on me by the brute force of Jean, Duke of Burgundy.

Yesterday, during my exercise ride outside the walls of Pontoise, he waylaid me in the forest, dismissed the vile creatures who were supposed to be protecting me and raped me. The words seem so simple to write, but the deed is so terrible to record!

The nuns at Poissy instilled in me a deep reverence for the Virgin Mary. Having found no honour in my own mother, She has always been for me the purity of the Church. She brought her virginity to Her contract with God, just as I should bring mine to my contract with my husband. But now that can never be and I must either begin any marriage I make with a lie or else retire into the religious life for which I know I was never made. My virginity is gone and the loss is unbearable.

Equally terrible is the fact that the people I was riding with, the treacherous Guy de Mussy and two of my Flemish ladies-in-waiting, could each have prevented it if they had not been cowards and traitors. They turned away when I told them to stay. Burgundy actually gloated about it. 'De Mussy wears my badge, Princesse. He is my squire. None of them will obey you. They are all my creatures.'

Even the women – for I can no longer call them ladies – must have suspected his wicked intention, but they were too cowed. There is no doubt that the devil is among us.

If you wonder why he chose to destroy the virginity he had so perversely preserved until now, I can tell you, for he took unnatural pleasure in telling me.

'You may be surprised to hear,' he said, 'that this morning your precious Harry Monmouth abandoned the peace conference in a fit of pique, declaring that he will have you and all the territories he claims, even if he has to drive me, King Charles and your bastard brother out of France.' Then he bent my arm cruelly up my back and snarled, 'There is as much chance of you becoming his wife now as there is of your baseborn brother becoming king. But he lusted after you like a rutting ram, I could see that. The arrogant fool really thought that he, the scar-faced son of a usurping dog, was worthy to couple with a royal daughter of France!'

That was when he forced me down to the ground and pushed his face into mine with words that made my blood run cold. 'And I saw that you lusted for him. Despite your prayers and delicate airs, beneath your skirts you throb with heat. You are just like your mother, panting for a man between your legs. Well, now you shall have one.'

I screamed then, but I knew it was pointless and he raped me, Charles. There in the dirt beneath the trees he pulled up my skirts and forced himself into my virgin flesh, as he must have done a hundred times to helpless girls across the land, as if it was nothing – just one of the spoils of war.

Afterwards, he told me that it was my own doing, that I wanted it as much as he did and will welcome him again whenever it pleases him to pleasure me! Ah, dear God, I shudder when I write it but I must, for I want it clearly understood, whenever it may be made known, that I was not willing, that I loathe and detest the beast that is Burgundy and I would be a virgin still if he were not the very devil incarnate.

How I wish I could tell you of all this face to face, then you could see my distress and know my true innocence of the horrible things he accused me of. But I am so completely at his mercy that I cannot even find a way to get this letter to you!

Our poor father cannot help me, for when he is not raving under some terrible delusion he is little more than a child in adult clothing. One does not have to look very far to determine the source of his bewitchment. As for our mother, I would prefer to think that she, too, is under some form of enchantment rather than believe, as I am afraid I do, that she knowingly and voluntarily turns a blind eye to what is happening to me. She may do it from her own necessity, but that does not make it excusable in my eyes. I feel as much at her mercy as I am at his. I believe that the deaths of Louis and Jean can ever more certainly be laid at the door of these two devilish conspirators and that when you escaped from Paris you narrowly avoided a similar fate.

May God and the Blessed Virgin deliver me from this living hell! I never thought there would come a time when I would

353

feel murder in my heart, but I cannot deny that I want him
dead. Do you think it possible that God would forgive anyone
who revenged the ravishment of the ill-used creature that is
your sister?

Catherine

Written at Chateau Pontoise in the dark morning hours
of the first day of July, 1419.

—ξξ—

Just as I had forced myself to my feet and run from the
scene of my violation, Catherine had forced herself to rise from
the forest floor and walk away from the devil duke. Somehow
she had ridden home. When she entered her chamber I was
alone there, laying out her apparel for the evening, and with a
cry of anguish she collapsed in my arms.

I suppose every woman or girl feels differently about virginity.
I admit that before I lost it I never gave much thought to mine.
I follow the teachings of the Church more from expediency than
belief and, looking back, I can see that I was lucky not to suffer
the possible consequences of my rather devil-may-care attitudes,
both to chastity and the Church. I was not publicly denounced
by the priest or disowned by my family and thrown onto the
streets, although some might say that the stillbirth of my first
child was a pretty severe form of divine retribution, if that is
what it was.

For Catherine however, virginity held a mystical significance. Reared by the nuns with an intense reverence for the Virgin Mother of God, the notion of her own purity was of great importance to her, not only because in a young royal princess the assumption of pre-marital chastity was an essential element of any marriage-contract, but also because of her personal belief in the Church's teachings on the sanctity of the human body. She had been able to withstand the Duke of Burgundy's earlier assaults because they had left her with a fragile thread to cling to; the belief that she could still consider herself both spiritually and physically intact. However the brutal destruction of her virginity was severely testing her previously unshakeable faith in God.

After she had soaked long and gratefully in a hastily summoned hot tub and was lying white-faced in her bed, one of my first tentative suggestions was that I provide a herbal poultice. 'It will heal the wounds and ease the bruising, Mademoiselle, and also, God willing, prevent any more serious consequence of your ordeal.'

Her frown deepened and her dull eyes sought mine. 'What do you mean, more serious consequence . . .? Oh!' As realisation of the possibility of pregnancy dawned, she made the sign of the cross and clasped her hands together at her breast, clutching the sheets around herself like a protective cocoon and shivering, despite the late afternoon heat and the recent warmth of the bath. Then she suddenly reared up from the pillows and glared at me where I stood at the bedside.

'I want him dead!' she exclaimed. 'If God will answer my

prayers, he will strike down Jean of Burgundy and send no spark to ignite his devil spawn,' she cried and then turned once more to me. 'But, just as I cannot kill the duke, neither can I poison his seed. Make your poultice for my wounds, Mette, but no more.'

Muttering my own curses against Burgundy, I prepared the poultice and also a soothing draught and watched for a good while until the tense lines in her brow smoothed away in sleep.

A little later, a message came in response to one I had sent in Catherine's stead, excusing her from dining in the great hall due to a sudden rheum. The queen declared her hope that her daughter would quickly recover and her intention to visit her the following day if she had not.

The Compline bell woke Catherine an hour or so later, its plaintive note echoing from the chapel beside the castle keep. The light of the setting sun tinged the shadows in the room blood red. Hastily I lit candles to dispel the gathering gloom.

'I cannot prevent the queen visiting,' said Catherine with resignation, when I relayed the message, 'but I cannot guarantee that she will like what she hears when she does.'

'The Flemish ladies came too while you slept, Mademoiselle, but I sent them away.'

'Tell them to stay away!' she exclaimed, 'ugly, traitorous wretches that they are.' Flinging back the covers she winced as she swung her legs over the edge of the bed, but I was gratified to see that no more blood stained the linen. 'Bring my gown please, Mette. I want to talk to you. Let us sit together.'

She perched in her canopied chair, the folds of her velvet

chamber-robe pulled tightly around her and I brought a bowl of the warm broth Alys had fetched and set it on a table close by.

'Please sup a little before you begin, Mademoiselle,' I said. 'It will restore your strength.'

Obediently she lifted the bowl and took several sips, regarding me solemnly over the rim while I pulled up a stool and settled myself beside her. Then she set the bowl down and said, 'With regard to my mother's visit, I have a plan. It concerns you.'

As I listened to her plan, I was torn with violently conflicting emotions. So much had happened in the last few hours that my mind was already reeling and Catherine's expressed intentions only added to the confusion. I could see that her plan was ingenious and would undoubtedly relieve her own deplorable situation, but in conjunction with my other concerns it put me in a quandary, which I pondered through the long sleepless night as I listened to the scratching of her quill.

By dawn Catherine had returned to bed and fallen into a deep sleep. Alys and I crept into the little turret oratory off the bedchamber to talk privately. Once again I did not tell her of Burgundy's attack on Catherine, but I did explain that there would be changes in the princess' life that would enable us to make a journey to Troyes very soon.

She gave me a troubled look. 'You are not leaving the princess' service for my sake, Ma?!' she exclaimed. 'You must not do that!'

I laid a warning finger on my lips. 'Ssh, we do not want to wake her. She was up half the night praying and writing. No, I am not leaving her; it is she who is leaving us, but only temporarily. I will explain everything later today, but what I need to ask you now is your permission to tell her about your baby. You can be there when I do and, of course, we will swear her to secrecy, but I think we owe it to her to tell the truth. What do you say?'

Alys thought about it for a minute then nodded. 'Very well, but do you think she will disapprove? Tell me to confess my sins and do a penance? She is much more saintly than you or I.'

I laughed. 'No, Alys, she will be happy for you, believe me. Hard though you tried to hide it from us, she knew about your friendship with Jacques and you know she likes him. She will wish you good luck and offer to pray for you.'

Alys shrugged. 'Yes, you are right, she will. That is what I mean about being more saintly.'

When Agnes knocked at the chamber door at the usual time, she was greeted by an emotional Catherine, who recounted her ordeal to her horrified friend. The headache which had plagued Agnes the previous day had retreated, but her brow was now knitted with deep concern, especially after Catherine revealed her plan to outwit Burgundy. The bell rang to summon them to Mass, which Catherine usually attended, but she made no move to go and instead bade us array her in one of her most ornate gowns and headdresses and a full set of jewels in preparation for the queen's visit.

'She will come after Mass, I have no doubt,' Catherine said, nervously pacing the floor, the strain of anticipation drawn in the tight set of her jaw and the thin line of her mouth. 'I must rehearse what I am going to say.'

Queen Isabeau did arrive direct from the chapel as expected, accompanied by her faithful German lady companion, Baroness Hochfeld.

'You were not at Mass, Catherine, so I thought you would be in bed, but I see you are not,' she said accusingly as she swept across the room, barely acknowledging the curtsies of its two visible occupants. The Flanders mares had put in an appearance again earlier but Catherine had told Agnes to send them away, refusing even to lay eyes on them. So it was apparently only Agnes who supported Catherine, as I was well hidden behind the curtains of the big bed. Nevertheless, out of habit, I still dropped to my knees at Queen Isabeau's arrival. The Queen seated herself comfortably in Catherine's canopied chair, signalling that Catherine, Agnes and the Baroness Hochfeld should dispose themselves on stools, which they did.

'If you are not ill, daughter, why were you not in church?'

Her mother's direct question seemed to disconcert Catherine, as if this was one answer she had not prepared. 'I – I did not feel well enough to leave my chamber, Madame. I thank you for taking the trouble to visit me.'

'You do not look ill,' returned the queen. 'Come nearer, child, so that I can see you.'

Reluctantly, Catherine rose from the stool she had deliberately chosen some distance away and allowed Agnes to set it closer to the queen's chair. 'You seem in good spirits yourself, Madame,' she said as she sat down again.

'Well, of course I am in good spirits. This morning his grace of Burgundy rode off to Melun, declaring that he will return with Charles. During all the time that he has been talking and talking with the perfidious English king, he has also had ambassadors talking to Charles and soon there will be an agreement. Henry of England will be forced to flee back to his foggy little island and our beloved cousin will unite France as she has not been united for years. The Virgin be praised, it is the answer to our prayers!'

I could imagine the thoughts that were spinning in Catherine's head. Burgundy the Peacemaker! Our beloved cousin! How could her mother mouth such adulation of the duke when only a month before she had sung the praises of King Henry as if he stood ranked with the saints?

'You really believe that Charles will be reconciled with Burgundy?' cried Catherine in disbelief. 'That is madness. Charles would not trust the duke to stroke his dog, let alone kiss his hand. I fear you are sadly mistaken, Madame, but then Burgundy is very good at misleading people.' She must have jumped up as she spoke, for I could hear her voice come and go as she paced the room in her distress.

There was a note of cold but contained anger in the queen's response. 'No, Catherine, it is you who is misled. I command you to sit down. We can talk about this calmly together. I know you are disappointed about the marriage to King Henry, but there will be another match. We will find you a worthy bedmate, never fear.'

I could hear the swish of Catherine's skirts as she continued to move about, ignoring the command to sit; a deliberate solecism since it left her head higher than the queen's. 'My *fear* is that this will stir King Henry into greater belligerence,' she persisted. 'And can you truly imagine Charles taking counsel from Burgundy, Madame? He abhors Burgundy, or why did he flee from Paris when the duke's forces arrived?'

'That action was ill-advised, but he is wiser now and he understands his position. It is not easy to bridle a spirited young stallion, but Burgundy is the ablest statesman in France and Charles has at last recognised that fact and taken the bit.'

The swish of silk skirts halted. 'And you, Madame? Will you give Charles the support he needs? Or will you cross him and differ with him at every turn as you did with Louis? Charles is sixteen now. He should be regent of France. He is no longer a boy to be ordered about by his cousin and his mother!'

Catherine must have advanced close to the queen's chair, for I heard a sudden rustle and thump as the baroness rose to protest. 'Princess, really! This is too much.'

'Thank you, baroness, I will handle this,' Queen Isabeau broke in, her voice sharp, like the cracking of ice. 'I do not need reminding of the age of my son Catherine, nor of my duty towards him as the dauphin.'

I almost choked and revealed my presence. Suddenly Charles was her son again and she was calling him dauphin! Catherine was right; the queen's mind was veering without a rudder, totally unable to steer a true course!

But she continued remorselessly. 'And I will not ask again that you sit down. Now!' There was a pause when Catherine must have obeyed. 'Thank you. I will overlook this outburst on the grounds that you are overwrought and anxious for the

361

future – your own petty future I would point out, rather than the future of France, which must always be my first concern.'

Catherine's tone was deceptively sweet when she resumed her discourse. 'And in this newly reconciled France, Madame, I take it that the man who was to have been my future is to be driven back over the Sleeve as soon as possible. Will that also be Burgundy's first concern?'

'Well of course,' declared the Queen with satisfaction. 'Burgundy and the dauphin together will hound the English back across the sea.'

'Now that will be impressive,' remarked the now apparently docile Catherine. 'I must say that I despaired of ever seeing Burgundy raise the Oriflamme, but I suppose he might prepared to do so now that he will be able to hide behind Charles.' Her voice turned suddenly icy. 'Where do you think he will be "unavoidably delayed" this time when battle is joined?'

Queen Isabeau's patience all but snapped. 'Mother of God, Catherine, you tread very dangerously! Burgundy has never hidden behind anyone. He is the mainstay of France. If it were not for him, we would be at sea without a sail.'

From her confidences of the previous night I knew that Catherine would not stop now and the anger in her voice intensified as she pursued her theme. 'If he is the mainstay of France, it is only because so many others more worthy were killed or imprisoned at Agincourt. Burgundy is unchallenged now because he failed to fight then. I shall never forgive him for that. And what makes you think that Charles will ever forgive you and Burgundy for declaring him a bastard and stripping him of the dauphincy? Are you conveniently forgetting that? Do you not see that Burgundy duped you into signing an edict which publicly made you a traitor and an adulterer, just as he will attempt to dupe Charles into a truce which he, Burgundy, has no intention of keeping. It is a trap! Madame, I beg you to consider the precious life of your only remaining son. Support him and cease to put your faith in Burgundy!'

When she stopped speaking, a hush descended on the room, as if no one dared to breathe. Then Queen Isabeau's voice snapped out, vibrating with fury.

'Enough! You speak treason, Catherine, nothing less! I should have you arrested but you are deranged by the failure of your marriage treaty, so I will be lenient. However, you clearly need some time to reflect on your duty and your position. Baroness, I think a spell with the nuns at Poissy will curb the princess' wayward spirit. See to it for me, would you? And it is to be no cushioned retreat. This is an opportunity for a sadly misguided girl to learn the error of her ways. I will ask your sister, Abbess Marie, to devise a regime of prayer and chastisement that will bring you to true penitence, Catherine. There will be no communication with the outside world, no visitors and no books. Prayer, hard work and silence are the cure for disobedience. You will not leave this room until arrangements have been made. Guards will be set and you should thank God that they do not come to remove you to a prison cell.'

No one spoke but there was much shoving of stools as the occupants of the room fell to their knees once more and a rustling of silk as the queen and her companion made their exit. I emerged cautiously from my retreat to see Catherine rise and sink into the cushions of the chair her mother had just vacated, a satisfied smile tilting the corners of her mouth.

She caught my eye and gave me a conspiratorial little wink. 'Well, Mette, I wonder what Burgundy will say when he hears I am sent to a nunnery?'

I frowned. 'Sadly your guess was right, Mademoiselle. Now that there is finally to be no marriage to King Henry, the queen has no more use for you.'

'I am a thorn in her flesh,' nodded Catherine. 'She wants me out of her sight, as she does everyone who dares to defy her. At least I am to be sent to a convent and not to my grave! How will you like life in a convent, Mette?'

I drew a deep breath and knelt down beside her chair. 'I fear that I will not be coming with you, Mademoiselle,' I said softly. 'Agnes must be your companion, and she is more familiar with Poissy anyway.' A glance behind me at Agnes' gentle face told how glad she would be to go, but Catherine's lip was trembling. She had become desperately vulnerable since the vile actions of the duke and I felt my heart lurch. 'I never wish to leave you, Mademoiselle. And it is not for ever but only for a short time. Firstly, my own family has need of me . . .'

'Why, what has happened to Luc, or is it Alys?'

'Yes, Mademoiselle, it is Alys. She needs me now as she has never needed me before and, as a mother, I cannot desert her. She is pregnant.'

'Oh!' Catherine's hand flew to her mouth in surprise and I

could see a succession of thoughts register on her face before she spoke further. 'Is it Jacques'?'

I nodded. 'Of course it is Jacques'. We conspired to foster their friendship and we succeeded beyond our expectations.'

Her eyes widened, her expression settling into one of resigned comprehension. 'We did, did we not? And what does she want to do?'

'She wants to go back to Troyes and tell Jacques. I have promised that I will go with her. So you see, I cannot come with you to Poissy.'

'Yes, I see that you cannot.' Catherine sighed and folded her hands in her lap. 'Will you come with me to Poissy, Agnes? It may well be bread and water and sore knees for some weeks.'

Agnes moved nearer and knelt beside me, smiling up at her old school-friend. 'That will be heaven, compared to the hell you are escaping by going there, Catherine,' she said simply.

Throughout this exchange we had heard the sound of heavy footsteps outside the door, where the guard was being reinforced on the queen's orders. Proof that Catherine was officially under house arrest. It might be only a matter of hours before she was escorted to a barge and rowed away to Poissy.

'There is a second reason I want to go to Troyes that I must discuss with you, Mademoiselle,' I whispered hastily, conscious that we might not be left alone for much longer and that ears might already be pressed to the door. 'Shall we pray together for your safety?' I rolled my eyes towards her turret oratory as I said this and Catherine was quick to grasp my meaning.

'Yes, indeed, and for little Alys as well,' she whispered back, standing up and raising her voice for the benefit of any listeners. 'We will go to my oratory now and prepare ourselves for the weeks ahead.'

In the little chapel there was hardly room for three of us to kneel before Catherine's triptych of the Virgin, so we abandoned the idea of 'prayer' and stood together to discuss the plan I had hatched during the previous long sleepless night. At first Catherine was adamant that it was too dangerous, but I gradually managed to persuade her that it was, in fact, the best chance she had of rescue from a future which now looked bleaker than ever before.

At the end of our conversation she grasped both my hands in hers and, with tears in her eyes, bade me take the greatest possible care of myself. 'Oh, Mette, we are to be parted again and I must be grown up and sensible about it,' she said miserably. 'We will not even be able to write to each other, so I will not know whether you have been successful in any of your endeavours – not until I leave the convent and who knows when that will be.' She squeezed my hands so hard it hurt and then kissed me on both cheeks. 'May all the saints protect you and keep you safe until we meet again, however long it may be before we do.'

26

Reconciliation! The church bells of Corbeil were ringing a joyful peal and passers-by shouted the news. 'The king and the dauphin are reconciled! Peace is declared!'

I exchanged dismayed glances with the boy at my side before we both hastily altered our grimaces to smiles as we noticed the triumphant grin on the face of the charettier perched on the driver's seat of the covered wagon in which we were travelling. He had turned his gaze from the road ahead to share his delight at the news.

'Burgundy's done it! God be praised!' he yelled above the crunch of the wagon's iron-bound wheels on the cobbled street and the answering rattle of its load of barrels and baskets. 'Now Paris will eat again.'

Despite the sick feeling in the pit of my stomach, I managed an enthusiastic nod, grateful that the noise prevented any further conversation. The charettier was doing us a big favour by letting us ride on his wagon and we did not want to offend him.

Yves was the good-hearted fellow who, four years previously, had rescued my badly wounded husband from the carnage of Agincourt and taken him to the monks at Abbeville. He knew the whole sad story. Luc asked him and he agreed out of sympathy to take me and Alys in his wagon, which was to carry supplies after the royal hunt was summoned to meet the Duke of Burgundy at Corbeil.

We had left Pontoise almost a week ago, on the now-familiar route around the north of Paris, and every time we had passed through habitation we had taken care to hide away from prying eyes. Royal convoys were not authorised to carry passengers. When we reached our destination, we took care only to view the scene through peepholes in the cart's canvas cover.

Corbeil was another walled town on the banks of the Seine bustling with activity centred on the castle. As we passed through the narrow thoroughfares, fights and scuffles seemed to break out every few minutes, as if no one had told the participants that peace had been declared between the two warring factions. Prudently, most of the citizens had retreated behind closed doors and the shopkeepers had put up their shutters. But the bells still rang out relentlessly.

'What does this mean?' breathed Alys in my ear, almost unrecognisable as the boy who was my travelling companion. 'Will Prince Charles really put himself in Burgundy's hands?'

'Only God knows,' I whispered back. 'We must wait and see.'

In the interests of her safety, I had persuaded my daughter to disguise herself as my son, wilfully ignoring the Church's diktat against women wearing male clothing. Even accompanied by her mother, a young girl was vulnerable on the road in a way that a boy was not. Wearing the jacket and hose which Luc had abandoned when he received his huntsman's livery, Alys made a convincing lad and had even managed to perfect the loose-limbed walk of a youth never hampered by skirts.

It had taken two days for the Baroness Hochfeld to obey the queen's orders and arrange Catherine's internment. We had wished her and Agnes a tearful farewell and they had departed for Poissy in a heavily guarded barge. Then we had begun the familiar task of packing the contents of her wardrobe and household, ready to go wherever the court went next. I had ensured that the small chest containing our own belongings was tucked away anonymously with the rest and had carefully sewn my small treasure of gold crowns into a pocket in my chemise and put the remaining deniers and sous into a purse, which I tied around my neck with a leather thong and kept hidden inside my bodice. But I hoped our greatest protection would be our insignificance. Why should any sneak thief or cutpurse imagine that a woman in drab working garb, in the company of her adolescent son, might be in possession of gold or silver?

We had reached Corbeil without incident, and Yves hauled on the reins to bring his team of oxen to a halt in the busy courtyard of the castle. 'I am going to report to the Intendant's office,' he told us. 'If you jump out now, no one will notice you. Mind the ox teams. They are clumsy at manoeuvering. I think the kennels are at the far corner of the main bailey.'

I grabbed the bundle containing the few belongings I had brought with me and eased myself over the driver's seat. Indeed, the big cobbled courtyard was so jammed with wagons that the queen herself might not have been noticed emerging from one of them. The noise was deafening, magnified by echoes off the

369

surrounding walls. Castle servants shouted orders, drivers yelled at their teams and tired beasts bellowed for food and water and, above it all, the bells continued pealing. I threw my bundle down to Yves and negotiated the awkward descent from the wagon. Behind me, Alys made easy work of it in her hose and boots, grinning at me cheekily from under her hood as she swung down.

'May God bless you for your kindness, Yves,' I said to the charettier, pressing a silver denier into his hand. 'Drink a toast with your companions tonight.'

Yves looked a little sheepish to be taking money off a woman, but only a little. As we meandered off between the carts and oxen, I glanced in wonder at the boy beside me. Male dress seemed to have brought out a new side of Alys' character, but she confessed she was still frightened of being found out.

Her fear was justified. The penalty for defying the Church's dress code was, at best, a day in the stocks and, at worst, a public whipping, but as long as I remembered to call her 'Alain', the disguise seemed to me to be fairly foolproof. Under her russet hood we had even taken the precaution of cutting her long chestnut hair into a boyish bob.

Halfway across the huge bailey we passed an encampment of people whose colourful garb was in stark contrast to the drably dressed servants, soldiers and carters who made up the majority of people crowding the space. Judging by the paraphernalia of balls, stilts, costumes and instruments they were unloading from their carts, I took them to be entertainers who would not spurn an approach from strangers. I spoke to

370

the man who was directing proceedings. He wore a bright-yellow tunic and parti-coloured green and red hose and carried a viol-bag carefully slung over his shoulder.

'We have just arrived, Sir, and wonder why the bells are ringing. Is there a celebration of some sort?' I asked him.

'Indeed there is, Madame,' he replied, favouring me with a grave nod of acknowledgement. 'There is to be a feast tonight to celebrate the new peace treaty between the dauphin and the Duke of Burgundy. They say it was negotiated in the saddle.'

'So are they both here then?' I could not believe my luck in having arrived at the very place where Prince Charles was staying, if it were true.

The entertainer smiled at me patiently. 'It would hardly be a feast without the principal guests, would it, Madame? We hope to entertain both the prince and the duke tonight. We take our chances where we can.' He made a flourishing bow. 'Ivo Player at your service, Madame – and yours too, young man.' This last was directed at Alys who grinned and attempted to copy his bow, which caused a surprised smile and a raised eyebrow in return.

'Thank you for your kindness, sir,' I responded, making him a polite bob and pulling Alys' sleeve to take her away. 'Be careful,' I hissed. 'Boys do not smile at men! Now, let us find the kennels.' Instinct had made me avoid giving him my name.

We eventually located the hunt quarters by following a pack of hounds returning from the day's sport. When Luc ran out to the cistern to fill a pail, I gasped with dismay, for there was a dark bruise on the side of his face. Of course it was possible that he had received it during the course of his work – a hunt was fraught with all kinds of danger – but his doleful expression led me to suspect he had been in a fight. He was astounded when we approached.

'Holy saints – Ma! What on earth are you doing here? And, Alys!' he exclaimed, suddenly penetrating his sister's disguise. 'I would not have known you.'

'Shh!' we both hissed at once, glancing round nervously. I pulled him into the shadowy cover of a buttress. 'Speak softly, Luc, and greet your brother Alain.' I laid stress on the name, then raised my hand to touch Luc's cheek where the skin was swollen and blue. 'And you are hurt. What happened?'

'It is nothing. A disagreement, that is all. Why have you come here?' His tone was sharp with anger and concern. 'Is something wrong?'

'Nothing serious,' I reassured him. 'Was this disagreement over the dauphin by any chance?'

A flush rose to meet the blue bruise on Luc's cheek. 'How did you know? One of the other lads was bad-mouthing him and we got into a fight. Since the reconciliation, at least we are now allowed to speak of the dauphin, but Burgundy's men still call him "the bastard" and it angers me.'

'You should try to bottle your anger, Luc,' I scolded. But I was heartened by his loyalty to the dauphin, which confirmed the wisdom of part of my intention. I drew him further into the shade of the buttress and asked Luc if he knew the Seigneur du Chastel by sight.

'Of course I do,' he said scornfully. 'The dauphin has been

hunting all week with the Duke and du Chastel never leaves his side. He is like a black leech!'

'Good,' I said. 'He needs to be! I have a letter I want delivered into Seigneur du Chastel's hands and no one else's. It is for his eyes only and it must be done tonight. Can you do this?'

My solemn tone of voice wiped the grin off his face. 'I can try. What does it say?'

'Part of it asks the seigneur to find a position for you in the dauphin's hunt,' I told him, watching closely for his reaction.

He looked amazed and excited all at once, as I had hoped. I hurried on, 'But the rest of the letter concerns the princess and it must be placed into his hands, no one else's. It must be given directly to Tanneguy du Chastel or the dauphin himself. Is that clear, Luc? It is very important. And it must be delivered tonight; the sooner the better.'

I could tell that he was becoming quite enthralled by the intrigue of the letter.

'Well, I could try and catch him now if you like,' he suggested. 'I know where he is. One of the dauphin's falcons was injured and he took it to the mews on returning from the hunt. He was very concerned about it. Shall I run now and see if he is still there?'

This was better than I could have hoped for. 'Yes, yes. Go now. Here is the letter.' I took a folded and sealed packet from the front of my bodice where it had been hidden away since we left Pontoise. It was a bit crumpled but still presentable. I thrust it into his hands. 'Tuck it in your jacket immediately. Do not let anyone see it. Tell Tanneguy it is from Madame Lanière. I think he will accept it. If you cannot deliver it, bring it straight back. Come straight back anyway. Go!'

Luc stuffed the letter away and sped off across the bailey, soon becoming lost among the crowd. I gave Alys a reassuring look and put my finger to my lips. 'I'll tell you later,' I said. She did not know I had been planning to contact Tanneguy du Chastel, nor did she know the content of the letter. Only I knew that. It was better that way.

I had penned the letter on the night before we left Pontoise, using some writing materials Catherine had left behind. She had taken few of her possessions to Poissy, but she had personally packed up her travelling altar with its secret compartment and she still wore the key hidden around her neck. It had taken me hours to compose my epistle to Tanneguy and as I paced about waiting impatiently for Luc to return, I went over its contents in my mind.

To the Seigneur du Chastel, Secretary and Counsellor to the Dauphin Charles,

Greetings, Most Honoured Seigneur,

I hope you will remember me as the Princess Catherine's faithful nurse.

As you will be aware, owing to the malady of her father the king, the princess has lately been living under the protection of the Duke of Burgundy and I feel it imperative to inform you that he has subjected her to appalling and dishonourable treatment. In recent months, by coercion and terror, he has forced her into acts of unspeakable depravity. To speak plainly, he has robbed her of her innocence and wickedly destroyed her honour and the honour of the Crown of France

I beg you to reveal this situation to the dauphin alone and I am confident that when you acquaint him with it, His Royal Highness will be moved to redress the dreadful wrongs done to his sister. I also know that, in view of the abuse she has suffered at Burgundy's hands, Princess Catherine would urge her royal brother to spurn all the duke's spurious offers of friendship and to reject any treaty of reconciliation into which he might be tempted to enter. The dauphin is the one remaining kinsman she feels she can trust, but only as long as he remains free of the terrible power of Burgundy.

This letter is carried by my son, Luc, who is a servant of the king's hunt. He was honoured to care for the dauphin's favourite deerhounds in the years before you and he were forced to flee the Hôtel de St Pol, and if I could beg it as a favour, my lord, he would be honoured to serve him again.

I remain always a loyal and humble servant of the King and earnestly pray for my lord Dauphin's health and success.

Signed: Guillaumette Lanière

Woman of the Bedchamber to the princess royal

We waited near the cistern and it seemed an age before Luc returned, but when he did he was jubilant.

'I did it, Ma!' he exclaimed. 'The Seigneur du Chastel took the letter from me but he did not read it. I said who it was from and he tucked it in the purse on his belt and told me to tell you to come to the dauphin's apartments after the feast. He will tell the guards to admit you.'

I stared at him aghast. 'But, Luc, where are the royal apartments? How will I even get into the keep?'

'You and Alys could come to the feast,' suggested Luc. 'There are so many extra servants drafted in from the town that you would not be noticed. And you might even get something to eat.'

Alys piped up eagerly. 'That is a good idea, little brother. I am hungry!'

Luc tweaked the sleeve of her grubby jacket. 'It serves you right for wearing my côte! Come on. People are gathering already. We will have to fight for a place.'

The great hall at Corbeil castle was crowded to bursting point, resounding with the clamour of merriment. Those lucky enough to rate a seat at the trestles were busy supping from wine jugs and grabbing portions of meat from heaped platters placed at intervals on the boards by perspiring varlets, who had to fight their way through the throng to perform the service. Those without places piled trenchers of bread with roasted meats and wolfed it where they could, leaning against the walls, propped back to back on the benches or even tucked away under the trestles with the dogs

By dint of some skilful pushing and shoving, Luc acquired three thick trenchers of bread from a service table and we scrambled to lift dripping slices of roast boar from a fresh platter carried past us by a staggering porter. The trenchers absorbed the meat juices and spicy sauce and the smell was mouth-watering. Luc managed to purloin a jug of wine from some fellow-huntsmen and we all drank deeply from it. Before long, he handed it back empty, grinning cheekily at the loud protests, which diminished when a passing server bent to re-charge it from the large wine-skin he carried on his back.

Reeling a little from the strong drink on our empty stomachs, and struggling to prevent our trenchers from tumbling into the rushes, we pushed our way to a position by the wall from where we could view the tumblers and jugglers over the heads of the seated diners. I saw Ivo, the viol-player, bowing away in the centre of the hall, accompanying his fellow entertainers with dramatic flourishes as they displayed their various skills and acknowledged ribald comments and sporadic bursts of applause. Having satisfied my gnawing hunger, I flung the crust of my trencher to the dogs which roamed under the trestles, wiped my fingers surreptitiously on my underskirt and lifted my eyes to the row of figures seated behind the garlanded table on the dais.

There in the centre, like two ill-matched birds of prey, sat the Duke of Burgundy and Prince Charles. Burgundy, considerably the broader and taller of the two, resembled a great sea eagle in his black houppelande gown, edged with gleaming sable and embellished in silver with a pattern of his personal emblem of carpenter's planes. At his throat the white linen of his chemise showed like the snowy feathers of the eagle's breast. Beside him, in a slate-grey doublet with apricot-coloured dagging at the shoulders, the dauphin put me in mind of the merlin that Catherine had sometimes carried to the hunt. Small and restless on his gilded throne as if constantly poised for flight, Charles' eyes roamed the room. The only visual similarity between the two men was the hawk-like beak which both possessed, displaying the high bridge and distinctive Valois hook at the nostrils. For two royal princes who had just struck a peace deal together, they seemed to have very little to say to each other and most of what was said came from the lips of the duke, with Prince Charles looking surly and uncomfortable, eating little and drinking less. It made me think, optimistically, that perhaps he was having second thoughts about the bargain he had apparently made.

When my gaze slid away to the other high-table diners, I immediately spotted the pale, lean-cheeked profile of Tanneguy du Chastel. Garbed in his habitual plain black gown, he was seated in the shadows beyond the canopy, less than an arm's length from the young prince's shoulder. Behind him, to his left, was an arch fitted with iron-studded double doors and guarded by two sturdy pike-men in fleur-de-lis livery. I concluded that this must be the entrance to the royal apartments. It looked quite accessible and so it seemed that all we had to do was wait until the dauphin quitted the table before approaching the guards. In the meanwhile we kept an eye out for passing platters of fruits and sweetmeats and settled back to enjoy the spectacle. My fingers began tapping out the rhythm of Ivo's merry viol music.

'Curse you, clumsy fool! Mind what you do. Men have stomached steel for less.' A cold, hard voice rang out over the ambient noise.

A tumbler had mistimed his cartwheel and cannoned into one of a number of Burgundian retainers who were patrolling the packed hall to keep order. Nothing unusual in such crowded circumstances, except that the voice made my blood turn suddenly to ice. It belonged unmistakably to Catherine's treacherous *amour-faux*, Guy de Mussy. In horror I turned to find the squire standing on the other side of the trestle, his handsome face distorted by an angry scowl. His hand was on his dagger, but several of the mummers saw the ruckus and gathered to rescue their quaking friend and hustle him out of trouble. Taking advantage of this distraction, I grabbed Alys and Luc and we all dived down behind the diners in front of us. I hoped that de Mussy had not seen us, but when I cautiously raised my head to check, he was staring straight at me.

—ξξ—

From Catherine, Princess Royal of France to Madame Guillaumette Laniere,

   Greetings to my beloved Mette,

   I cannot tell you how much I miss you so I will have to resort to writing you a letter, even though I know I cannot have it delivered since I am held without communication as part of my penitence, as my mother calls it. But I cannot help wondering what you would have to say about an incident which occurred just before I left Pontoise. I had not realised until I was starved of them, how highly I valued our regular tête-à-têtes.

I was permitted to visit the king in order to bid him fare-well and I found him unusually buoyant. If it were not lèse majésté, *I would even say he was quite 'perky' – but it is only to you I would say that! However, he called me Isabelle, which as you know was my late sister's name and so when he mentioned Charles I thought at the time that he meant the other dauphin, Charles, the one who died the year I was born. But now I cannot be sure. He actually came up and kissed me on the cheek – the first time he has ever done so – and then he whispered in my ear, 'Tell Charles not to come. It is dangerous.'*

What would you make of it, I wonder? Did he mean the first Dauphin Charles or did he mean the present one? And, if so, was it a warning he was trying to convey through me without Burgundy knowing? One assumes that the king is constantly weak-minded, but perhaps he is sometimes cleverer than we think. There were tears in his eyes, Mette, when I kissed him back. I was so moved I could hardly see my way out of the room. Is there still a spark of royal vigour there in the poor shell that is my father? I do hope and pray that there is and yet perhaps it is better if he does not understand the humiliation of his present sad condition. I fear that while I am gone no one will ensure that his needs are met with proper respect and due honour.

I am keeping well, if a little tired of broth and bread, which diet is another aspect of my 'penitence'. My sister Marie is kind but remote. We have only met twice in the ten days I have been here; once so that she could read me the terms of my enclosure and once so that she could inform me that our sister Michele has written giving her intention to visit the abbey. Is she coming specifically to see me? And will she fill me full of the glory of Burgundy? I admit I am apprehensive.

Meanwhile, I keep the Rule of St Dominic and the hours of a novice in his order. The regime is arduous but the best part is that I do not have to fear any further assaults from the Duke of Burgundy. Incidentally, he is regarded here with the honour and respect due to a wealthy patron of the abbey! Clearly the devil duke is attempting to buy his way into heaven. I trust in God and His Saints to see that he fails.

I pray for you daily, dear Mette, so if my prayers are heard you will find an eternal seat close to the Mother of God. But please not yet, for I long to see your dimpled cheeks again in this world.

I am your loving daughter of the breast,

Catherine

Written at the Royal Abbey of Poissy this day Wednesday July 13th, 1419.

27

'We have got to hide somewhere!' I shouted into Luc's ear as we shoved our way through the crowd, trying to get as far from Guy de Mussy as possible. We could not approach Tanneguy while he was still in such an exposed position at the high table, but I knew that Guy would report having seen me to the duke at the first opportunity. He would be wondering what on earth I was doing in Corbeil and when the duke found out about it, the conclusions he might come to spelled danger for all of us.

'You and Alys go back outside and I will come and get you when the dauphin and the duke leave the hall. That squire does not know me from the next huntsman so I will be fine.' Luc yelled back.

'Very well, but keep away from him,' I warned. 'He may have noticed you and, believe me, he is dangerous!'

Darkness had fallen completely before Luc found us huddled together in the kitchen yard, hiding behind a barrel. Although the evening was far from cold, we were both shivering with anxiety.

'You have been ages,' Alys accused her brother. 'We thought something had happened to you.'

'I found out that the Duke of Burgundy was leaving Corbeil tonight, riding to his castle of Brie Comte Robert, so I hung around outside the hall while they were mounting up,' said Luc. 'It is all right they did not notice me, but I overheard that squire de Mussy talking to the duke. It was about you, Ma! He said he had seen you and the duke seemed really angry about it. He said you were dangerous and ordered the squire to find you at all costs and bring you to him.' I could see moonlight glinting off the whites of Luc's eyes. 'What does it mean, Ma? Why would the duke call you dangerous?'

'Something to do with the princess,' I said grimly. 'But I have no intention of being found. What is happening in the hall now, Luc?'

'The dauphin has left the feast and the hall was starting to clear, but I expect there are quite a few drunks still there, settling down to sleep it off. Shall we go now?'

We took the precaution of approaching the great hall via the kitchen stair and peering cautiously around the servery screen. All the trestles had been stacked away and the great chamber lay open to us, but the entrance to the royal apartments was at the other end and we would have to make our way through two score and more of household servants, male and female, who were settling down on the floor for the night, full of food and drink. To my surprise, wandering among them was Ivo the viol player with two of the tumblers in their garish coloured costumes. They were collecting discarded balls and other pieces of equipment left behind when they had made their exit earlier. They did not pose a problem, but another group definitely did.

Moving from person to person and shining a sputtering torch in each face were three men-at-arms wearing the cross of St Andrew. One of them was Guy de Mussy.

'How are we going to get past him, Ma?' muttered Luc glumly. 'We'll have to wait for him to leave, but then he might come this way.'

Seeing a ball under the servery table, I picked it up and waited for one of the entertainers to move closer to us before rolling it across the floor. It was Ivo who approached where we hid, and as he bent to search under a stack of trestles close to the screen, he noticed the rolling ball and strolled across to peer into the servery. Fortunately he did not seem very bothered when a random woman suddenly pulled him close and whispered in his ear, 'I am the one who asked you why the bells were ringing, remember?' The player nodded, his teeth gleaming in the beam of his lantern and I spun him my not-entirely-fictitious yarn. 'Good sir, I need your help. I have an assignation with the guard on the royal apartments, but I do not wish to meet the squire with the lantern. There is a denier for you if you can get me there without him noticing.' I had reached into my hidden purse for the silver coin and now I slipped it into his palm.

'Consider it done.' Ivo made me his best showman's bow. 'On my signal you run up the hall along the wall and at the same time I will cause a distraction – or rather my boys will. Here, lads, I have work for you.' The two tumblers, who I guessed were his sons, had followed him into the servery out of curiosity and he went into a huddle with them, issuing swift instructions.

They were still wearing their tumbling costumes and eagerly

leaped around the screen one after the other, the second one shouting, 'Give it back, it is my coin, I saw it first!'

'Come and get it then – if you can!' yelled the first boy, clenching the silver denier between his grinning teeth and immediately starting to climb the intricately carved screen, nimbly hauling himself from one projection to another on the way up to the minstrel's gallery on the top. His brother followed close behind, still protesting his ownership of the coin.

We did not stop to watch them, but everyone else in the hall did, turning to face the action and away from the entrance to the royal apartments, while Alys, Luc and I ducked along the wall in the dark shadows, speeding as fast as we could towards the studded doors where the guards stood with their pikes crossed.

'My name . . . is Madame Lanière,' I panted as I halted before them. 'The Seigneur du Chastel has told you to admit me and my children.' I felt Alys and Luc rush up behind me.

Tanneguy had been as good as his word and the message had obviously been received. Nodding at each other the guards drew back their pikes and pulled the double doors open. I heaved a sigh of relief and smiled my thanks. Alys and Luc immediately ran through like bolts from a crossbow. As I followed them, I heard a shout but I also heard the intensely welcome sound of the doors slamming shut behind us. If it was Guy de Mussy who had shouted, he would have to convince the guards to open the door again before he could pursue us.

'Quick!' I urged the children, glancing feverishly around. 'We have to find the dauphin's chambers.'

We were in a vestibule where a carved arch framed an

impressively wide staircase leading upwards. Exchanging nods, we charged up the stairs two at a time, stumbling out into a wide passage at the top. The sound of raised voices reached us from below, spurring us down the passage to a set of massive double doors flanked by yet more liveried guards, who instantly crossed their long pikes against us as we ran towards them. 'Stop them!' At the sound of de Mussy's voice yelling and the ominous thud of footsteps on the staircase, I covered the distance faster than I ever thought I could.

Gasping for breath, I gave my name to the new set of guards. 'Please let us through,' I panted, 'The Seigneur du Chastel is expecting us.'

'Do not let them pass!' shouted de Mussy over the thunder of boots on the wooden floor as he and his henchmen pounded towards us. 'I arrest them all on the authority of the Duke of Burgundy.'

The name of Burgundy inspired doubtful glances between the two guards. 'Do not listen to him,' I urged desperately, unable to bear the thought of failing so close to our goal. 'Call the Seigneur du Chastel! He will vouch for us.'

Suddenly I felt my arm caught in a fierce grip. In his ferocious expression there was no sign of the charming gallant as Guy de Mussy swung me round so that my face was directly under the leaping light cast by a flambeau on the wall. 'Madame Lanière! I have you!' I could see triumph in his face as he barked at the guards with great authority, 'You can leave this to me. The dauphin will not wish to be disturbed, especially by a mad servant and her two snotty children.'

I tried to wrestle my arm free but he was too strong for me. 'We are bidden to meet the Seigneur du Chastel,' I blurted to the confused guard, trying to summon what I hoped was a reasonable and sane tone of voice. 'He will be wondering where we are.'

The guard's eyes rolled wildly with indecision and Guy's creepily disarming smile made its inevitable appearance. 'I'm sure the seigneur has far more important things to worry about,' he said firmly, his grip on my arm vicious as an eagle's claws. 'And I have no time to waste.'

I planted my feet stubbornly against him, but he was strong and easily pulled me off balance so that I stumbled as he dragged me away, beckoning to his two henchmen, who had unceremoniously collared my children. But they had reckoned without Luc who, craftily employing a sharp elbow in a vulnerable part of his would-be abductor's anatomy, managed to wriggle out of his shock-slackened grasp, dive under the crossed pikes of the guards and hammer loudly on the timbers of the door.

'Seigneur! Seigneur du Chastel!' he yelled at the top of his voice. 'Call the seigneur!'

Soon there was a blade at his throat and he was hauled backwards, but his shouts had been heard and the door was thrown open to reveal the imposing figure of Tanneguy du Chastel. The guards sprang to attention, raising their pikes.

Still struggling in de Mussy's grip, I cried, 'Seigneur du Chastel, God be thanked! I am here as you requested. Princess Catherine's nurse.'

Tanneguy peered at me, an expression of bewildered enquiry

on his long, lean face. Around the shoulders of his neat black gown he wore a heavy gold collar and looked grander and more dignified than I remembered him, but his fingers still bore ink-stains.

'Madame Lanière? Ah, yes, I see that it is you.' His gaze swung to Guy de Mussy and closed in a stern frown. 'Remove your hand, sir. This lady is here at my invitation. It is your presence that is not required.' He snapped his fingers at the guards. 'Escort these men from the keep,' he ordered, indicating the three Burgundians. 'And hold their weapons until they are off the premises. Only royal guards may bear arms in the royal apartments.'

As the sentries moved to obey, Guy de Mussy released me and drew himself up, returning his short sword to its sheath and keeping his hand defensively on the hilt. 'That will not be necessary, my lord. We are leaving. I will personally report this incident to his grace of Burgundy.'

Tanneguy smiled icily. 'I do not doubt it, sir.' He stood back and gestured me to enter the apartment. 'Come in, Madame, and bring your young companions.'

We hastily stumbled past the guards into a wide panelled passage containing only a few carved benches and a series of imposing doors set in deep stone arches. As Tanneguy firmly closed the door behind us, I stuttered my thanks, rubbing my bruised arm, and explained that my companions were my children. But before he had time to respond, a liveried page came through one of the doors. The noise of our altercation had evidently penetrated even these thick walls in the very oldest part of Corbeil castle, which had for centuries offered stout protection to the kings and queens of France as they journeyed from Paris to the eastern parts of their kingdom.

'His royal highness was alarmed by the noise, Monseigneur,' said the page. 'He sent me to investigate.'

Tanneguy shrugged. 'If the dauphin is awake, perhaps he would favour us with his presence,' he told the page. 'There are some visitors I think he should see.'

'I will give him your message, Monseigneur,' nodded the lad and hurried back through the door.

'I have not yet shown the dauphin your letter,' Tanneguy murmured to me swiftly. 'It contains news that will be hard for him to bear – I can quite see why the duke wanted to prevent your seeing the dauphin. How is the Princess Catherine?'

'Better, I think, since she managed to get herself sent back to Poissy Abbey, Monseigneur. She should be safe there,' I told him. Moving out of my children's earshot, I added, 'My children do not know what is in the letter. It is safer that way.'

'I understand,' nodded Tanneguy. 'I met your son earlier, but I thought you had a daughter in the princess' service.'

'Yes, sir, my son Luc. The smaller one is Alys . . .' I looked across at Alys in her frayed jacket and russet hood and explained somewhat uncomfortably, 'I thought it prudent for her to travel as a boy, but she was a seamstress for the princess.'

Tanneguy gazed benignly at me. 'You are a resourceful woman, Madame Lanière – but I always knew that.'

A light, reedy voice broke in. 'In the name of God, what is happening, Maître Tanneguy?'

The voice had a lower pitch than when I had last heard it, but the distinctive impediment and peevish tone of Prince Charles were instantly familiar to me. I turned and dropped to my knee, motioning Alys and Luc to follow suit. The dauphin stood outside the door of his chamber, swamped by a magnificent fur-trimmed chamber-robe of crimson silk figured with dolphins. He had grown taller, but was still undeniably a puny youth.

'Why do these strange people dare to look at me? Tell them not to do so.'

In my consternation I had forgotten the correct protocol. I immediately lowered my eyes from the prince's face, hoping the children would do the same.

'This is your old nursemaid, Madame Lanière, your highness,' said Tanneguy bracingly. I noticed that he had done no more than dip his knee briefly to the dauphin. 'Princess Catherine's woman of the bedchamber – and these are her children.'

'Why are they here?' asked Charles, his lip curling fastidiously. 'It is late at night.'

'We have brought news of your sister, the princess royal, your grace,' I told him boldly, attempting to seize some of the initiative. A prince he may be, and I owed him due deference, but the fact remained that I had blown his nose and wiped his bottom and I considered that gave me some right to be treated with respect. 'It was urgent and we had to run from the Duke of Burgundy's men who wanted to arrest us.'

'I do not understand. Why would Burgundy want to arrest my sister's servant?' Charles was still ignoring me, directing his questions at Tanneguy, so I let him answer.

'Because of what she knows,' the seigneur answered, pulling my letter from the sleeve of his robe. 'She wrote me a letter. I think you should read it, my lord.'

'Why do you not read it to me?' demanded the prince irritably, moving to sit down in the only chair available, which happened to be positioned with its back to us.

'I think you will see why when you read it,' Tanneguy said pointedly, offering the letter to Charles. 'The contents are private and must remain so.'

'Let me see it then!' The dauphin snatched the letter and unfolded it impatiently. There was a heavy silence as he scanned its contents. Behind his back Tanneguy and I exchanged doubtful glances and then I sprang to one side in alarm as the dauphin's chair came crashing over, propelled by his violent push as he rose and turned furiously to confront me. The letter shook in his hand.

'By God's Holy Bones, if this is true . . .! But how do I know it is true? We have only *your* word for it.' The word of a mere servant was the clear implication.

In Charles' sudden rage I had seen a flash of his brother Louis and I knew how to handle it. In times of stress, both princes found comfort in the things they had never had as children. Food had always calmed Louis, but with Charles it was flattery.

'Your grace, how would I, a humble servant of the king, dare to lie to the Heir of France?' I said, clasping my hands together and moving on my knees towards him, eyes carefully avoiding his angry gaze. 'When you come into your kingdom, I beg you to bring me before the holy relics of St Louis and I will swear on the crown of thorns, stained with the blood of Christ, that I have written the truth.'

Charles remained still for a moment, considering the weight of my words, then he turned away to wave the letter under Tanneguy's nose. 'This is treason, Maître Tanneguy. Treason and treachery! What are we to do about it?' I was disappointed, but not surprised, that the dauphin seemed more concerned with Burgundy's crime against the crown than with his sister's terror and distress.

Calmly, du Chastel took the letter from him, folded it and tucked it away in his sleeve. 'Let us consider that question tomorrow, highness. Right now, I think we should reward Madame Lanière for her bravery and loyalty in bringing this matter to our notice. Nor should we forget that it was she who warned us to leave the Hôtel de St Pol before the murderous butchers came to do Burgundy's dirty work.'

Charles grimaced at his secretary, but Tanneguy nodded insistently and the dauphin shrugged. 'Very well, if you think so, Monseigneur. What do you suggest?'

'Madame Lanière has made her wishes clear in the letter. She would like her son to be appointed to your household. I see no reason why that cannot be done immediately,' replied Tanneguy. 'The boy is here. He can swear his allegiance and I will arrange the rest.'

Prince Charles screwed up his face, remembering. 'Oh yes, the hound boy.' He turned abruptly on Luc. 'What happened to my white deer hounds, boy?'

I saw tears spring involuntarily to Luc's eyes as he recoiled in trepidation. 'Th-they were killed by Burgundy's thugs, highness. I b-buried them in the orchard.'

'They killed my dogs, but they did not kill you! Did you run away, boy? Did you abandon them?'

The dauphin was no taller than Luc, but he was on his feet. I could see that Luc was cowed and frightened, and I could not stop myself interjecting, 'No, your highness, he did not. He was not there. You left them in my care, remember? But I could not hold them and they got away.' I choked on the last words as my mind flashed back to that horrific night and the appalling violence of the butchers.

'You may look at me,' declared Charles suddenly, scanning our faces as we raised them to his curious speckled gaze, so different from Catherine's vivid blue. 'You both have tears in your eyes. Why?'

'I think, highness, that you are frightening the boy,' suggested Tanneguy. 'Everyone is upset by the memories of that terrible night.'

'I am not,' said Charles flatly. 'It was the beginning of my freedom. But I did regret having to leave my faithful hounds.' He held his hand out to Luc, a big jewelled ring prominent on his first finger. 'If you buried them, you must have cared for them. You may kiss my hand and swear to serve me loyally and faithfully.'

Luc grabbed the hand and planted his lips on the ring. 'I swear,' he said hoarsely.

'Very well.' The dauphin withdrew his hand and moved it towards me. 'And you? Will you serve me too, Mette?'

It was the first time he had used my name and I softened towards him. He was not easy to love but if he remained sane, perhaps he might make a better king than his father. I let my lips brush the ring lightly. 'I am a loyal servant of the king, your highness, and serve you as his son and heir. But my first duty will always be to your sister, Princess Catherine.'

'Why are you not with her now then?'

His question took me by surprise although, on reflection, I should have expected it. I could not tell him the real reason why we were apart, but I gave him a version of the truth. 'The princess is in retreat at Poissy abbey. My daughter and I are travelling to Troyes to wait for her.'

'Poissy will be good for her; she has much to pray for,' he remarked, moving restlessly to and fro before us. 'But you think she would not approve of the reconciliation treaty?'

'I know she would not,' I replied firmly. 'But not for the reason you might think from the letter. She has only your interests at heart, highness, and those of the king. You said a moment ago that escaping Burgundy was the beginning of your freedom. She, of all people, would not want that freedom to end.'

Charles studied me for several seconds before signalling me to rise. 'You are right. Catherine understands. Thank you for reminding me. I believe you are to my sister what Maître Tanneguy is to me,' he added thoughtfully. 'He did not want me to sign the reconciliation, but I was persuaded.' He turned to Luc. 'What is your name, boy?'

'It is Luc, highness.'

'Well, Luc, serve me as well as your mother serves my sister and I will be well content.'

'I will, my lord,' said my son fervently.

'Good. See that he gets some livery, Maître Tanneguy.' The dauphin put his hands to his eyes and rubbed them. 'Now I will return to bed. Come to me at first light.'

'I will, highness.' I saw a smile flicker briefly over Tanneguy's lips before he opened the bedchamber door and bowed his young master through. 'God give you good rest.'

I gathered my two children into my arms. It had been a tense and frightening evening and I was proud of the way they had handled it.

Tanneguy approached us, pulling my letter from the sleeve of his robe. 'We should burn this,' he said solemnly, unfolding it and holding the paper to the flame of a nearby candle. We watched it flare and dissolve to ashes. He smiled grimly at me. 'God be praised, the reconciliation is over. Now, Madame,' he continued, 'we must find you all somewhere to sleep. Tomorrow we will put young Luc to work and arrange for you and your daughter to travel safely to Troyes.'

28

Mid-July was not a good time of year to come to Troyes, unless you were a merchant making money. The Fair of St Jean, known as the Hot Fair, was in full swing, the largest of the six famous Champagne Fairs which attracted trade from all over the known world and turned the city into a human antheap. Balmy breezes on the Seine had relieved the intense summer heat as we travelled upstream from Corbeil on a riverbarge, but when we walked through the town gate and into the maze of narrow streets, the turgid urban fug hit us like a rank blanket. The thoroughfares were crammed with people, horses and hand-carts, and in the stifling gloom beneath the overhanging gables the air smelt second-hand, as if it had been breathed by a multitude before us, while from the clogged central gutters of the roadways, the acrid stench of dung and garbage rose like the fumes of hell. Market stalls gathered crowds at every junction, creating frequent bottlenecks, and it was hard to push a path through the throng of shoppers, traders and scampering couriers who elbowed slower-footed pedestrians recklessly aside as they hurried samples and messages from one merchant warehouse to another.

We finally fought our way down the Rue de L'Aiguille to Jacques' workshop, where we found the door barred and the shutters closed. Our anxious knocks were eventually answered by a dull-looking youth who raised the top shutter a few inches and poked his head out to declare that his master had forbidden him to open the door and would not be back until evening. A deflated Alys burst into tears, causing the lad's jaw to drop in surprise, though not as much as it would have done if Alys had not changed out of her disguise as a boy while on the barge.

Throwing a comforting arm around her, I told the apprentice to inform his master that we would go to the church and return at nightfall. I did not hold out much hope that the message would be delivered, for the lad seemed to me to be a few stitches short of a seam.

Mass was underway in the church of St Jean au Marché, but despite the nave being crowded, it was much cooler among the lofty pillars, and in fragrant contrast to the foulness of the streets, pungent clouds of incense rose above the worshippers. Reaching a dark corner we flopped down on the stone floor, propping our weary backs against the tomb of some long-dead Troyan worthy and I hugged Alys to me as her shoulders continued to shake with silent sobbing. It was not like my long-suffering daughter to let her feelings overwhelm her in this way, but I knew she had been fretting for weeks that her lover might reject her, and now she was having to wait even longer to discover if her worst fears were to be realised.

However, my doubts about the reliability of the daft-looking apprentice proved unfounded. Jacques came to find us just as the Vespers bell was ringing and I was beginning to think we should seek shelter for the night. Alys had fallen asleep with her head in my lap and the church had become a shadowy cavern of dwindling twilight and flickering candles. Cowled priests and lay-servers flitted about the aisles, emptying offertory boxes and snuffing candles, occasionally stopping to ask if we needed help. I shook my head at each of them and they left us alone. So I was not greatly startled when Jacques emerged from the gloom, a finger to his lips. Without speaking he knelt down beside Alys and softly stroked her cheek.

As soon as she opened her eyes to find him there, she whispered abruptly. 'I am pregnant. It is your child.'

Not a very subtle approach, I thought wryly, but that was her nature – I do not believe there was a coquettish notion in her head – and Jacques responded with such warmth and acceptance it was clear he loved her for it.

'God be praised,' he said warmly.

He was rewarded with a radiant smile from Alys and they both got a hug from me. 'God be praised indeed and may He bless your union,' I said, 'preferably sooner rather than later.'

So began a new life for Alys – and for me, while my mistress was kept at Poissy. At first we were dauntingly over-crowded at the house in the Rue de l'Aiguille, for Jacques had let the two upper rooms to a Milanese thread merchant, leaving him and his apprentice to work and sleep in the tailor's shop, amidst the bales of cloth needed to complete a bulging order-book of garments. But there was an empty cow-byre in the back yard and an outhouse kitchen that had not been used of late. Soon we had evicted the mice and spiders and had somewhere to sleep and cook.

At the beginning of August we heard that the reconciliation between Burgundy and the dauphin had so angered King Henry, that he had ordered a sudden night assault on Pontoise and the garrison had been taken completely by surprise. Bitter blow though the loss of that royal stronghold was to the French cause, as least the duke had escorted the king and queen away from the town a few days before and the retreating court arrived in Troyes a fortnight later. However, there was no sign of the dauphin coming to kiss his father's hand. No announcement was made, but the reconciliation was dead in the water, as Tanneguy had said it would be.

Once the excitement and distraction of our journey was over and Alys was safe and happy, I found I missed my little mistress sorely. Of course I missed the activity of royal service – the physical work of running her apartment, the constant robing and disrobing and even the intrigue and machinations of the court – but, above all, it was Catherine's presence that I missed most, though I hoped and trusted that Alys was unaware of my longing to be elsewhere.

—ξξ—

From Catherine, Princess Royal of France to Madame Guillaumette Lanière,
  Greetings to my beloved Mette,
  Once again I fervently wish that you were here with

me so that I might confide in you. It is only to you that I can express my true opinions and innermost hopes and fears. Perhaps if I write down my latest concerns I will be able to imagine what your wise and sensible counsel might be.

My sister Michele recently paid a visit to Poissy. I do not think there was any question of it being a chance visit because no journey in this part of the world is easy at present with King Henry's forces now in control of the gateway to Paris. Here in the convent we heard about the extraordinary storming of Pontoise and gave thanks to God that the king and queen were safely away from there. So although she did not specifically refer to it, there was no doubt that my sister came as an unofficial ambassador, prompted either by the queen, the duke or his son, her husband Philippe.

I was summoned to Marie's parlour to greet Michele, a rather formal meeting considering it was between three sisters. We were served with a meal (incidentally the most nourishing meal I have eaten whilst here), over which we conversed formally about the health of the king and queen, the state of the country and the prospect of Charles' return to court. It was excruciating, Mette! There were my two older sisters, expounding the virtues of reconciliation between our brother and the Duke of Burgundy, and I could hardly prevent myself from screaming out against it.

After the meal Marie left us to attend to her duties as abbess and Michele immediately started to reproach me for my lack of gratitude towards the duke. Her father-in-law was a great man, she said, who only had the interests of France at heart, which included giving careful consideration to my future as the only unmarried daughter of a king who was incapable of fulfilling his role as a father.

How is it, Mette, that two children sprung from the same womb can have so little in common? She was born only six years before me, but she seems already old and shrivelled in her mind. There is no joy in her.

Towards the end of our meeting she asked me if I would like her to convey a message to our mother and suggested an apology and a desire to make amends. I knew that obtaining this olive branch was the whole purpose of her visit, but I said that I considered it sinful to tell lies in a House of God and therefore I could offer no such message, but that I would like her to understand that I remain a loyal and dutiful Daughter of France. To tell the truth, I was surprised at how animated she became at that. There is more spark in her than I first thought, for she looked as if she would like to slap me. However, her self-control prevailed and she merely said that she pitied me and could not think what my future might be.

What do you think, Mette? Should I have been more contrite? Would it have served my purpose better? The trouble is, I am not really sure what my future might be either. Perhaps the devil duke was almost right about one thing; I do hanker after King Henry and I wonder if he still thinks of me. After all, when I consider the possible candidates for my hand in *marriage, none of them quite measures up to him and, if there is one thing I have definitely decided as a result of being here at Poissy again, it is that I do not wish to be a nun.*

I pray for you, Mette, and I hope you pray for me.

Your loving daughter of the breast,

Catherine

Written secretly in my cell at the Royal Abbey of Poissy, this day Sunday August 7th 1419.

—ξξ—

At the end of August the thread merchant vacated the upper floors of Jacques' shop and departed for Milan. Now Jacques could offer Alys a proper home, he went to a priest at St Jean's and made arrangements for their wedding, possibly anxious that they should make their public vows before Alys' pregnancy began to show.

The banns were read and the wedding feast was prepared, much of it by me and Alys.

I also ordered a carpenter to make a new cradle for the baby but, not wishing to tempt fate, I delayed its delivery until the child should be safely born.

In early autumn sunshine, standing proudly beside the bride and groom under the imposing portal of the church of St Jean, I realised that I could not have wished for a better outcome for my daughter. But how much my life had changed in these six months! In April I had been a royal servant and friend of a princess, now, in September, I was jobless and homeless, with only my daughter's new husband to give me a roof over my head. My store of gold coin would not last forever and the prospect of becoming dependent on Alys and Jacques did not appeal.

But, a week later, everything changed. 'Come quick, Ma! Luc is here,' Alys called.

There, in the middle of the workshop, wearing travel-stained but anonymous clothing, Luc stood grinning sheepishly at me. 'Hello, Ma,' he said, allowing me to enfold him in a big hug. 'Surprise!'

'You certainly are!' I exclaimed, holding both his cheeks and gazing searchingly into his eyes. 'What has happened? Have you been sent away?'

Luc extricated himself indignantly. 'No! The Seigneur du Chastel sent me from Melun in the train of the dauphin's Viennois Herald. I do not have long. We must leave soon because we may not be very welcome in Troyes after the news gets out.'

'What news? What has happened?' Jacques asked the questions that were on all our lips, having descended from his sewing-table to greet Luc when he arrived. It was the first time the two had met.

'The Duke of Burgundy is dead – killed.' Luc was unable to keep a note of triumphant melodrama out of his voice as he made this announcement.

'Praise be to God!' I exclaimed impulsively, crossing myself then biting my lip, for I knew I should have been more restrained in my reaction. 'But how killed, son? And where?' I asked.

Luc made a face and felt in the leather satchel that was slung slantwise over his shoulders. 'It is a long story and I will tell you as much as I can, but there is a letter for you before I forget.' He handed over a well-folded paper and I saw the embossed shape of a castle on the seal. 'It is from the seigneur.'

'I will read it later,' I said as I pushed the letter carefully into my sleeve and took Luc's arm. 'Come, we will sit in the yard and you can eat and talk at the same time. You must be hungry.' I smiled reassuringly and beckoned Alys to follow. I wanted the details to be between us three. Later she could tell Jacques as much as she thought he needed to know.

As dusk fell over the city, the growing darkness only added to the drama of Luc's tale.

'Yet another parly was arranged between Burgundy and the dauphin,' he began, talking between mouthfuls of cheese and griddle cakes, 'at a place called Montereau. There is a bridge there – a very long bridge which spans two big rivers where they join – the Seine and the Yonne. The two parties were to meet in an enclosure which had been built in the middle. Burgundy came from one side and the dauphin from the other. I think the duke was nervous because he had cancelled a meeting a few days before. Apparently he does not like bridges. Can you believe that? But the dauphin insisted that it was the safest place.'

'But how do you know all this, Luc?' I asked. 'Were you there?'

Luc gave me a patient look. 'Well of course I was there, Ma. I look after the dauphin's dogs. He has two new deer hounds and he never goes anywhere without them. But I was not in the party that went into the enclosure. Only ten men were allowed from each side. It was all very cautious.'

'So you did not actually witness the killing of the duke?' I remarked with relief.

'No, I was waiting with the escort party at our end of the bridge. We heard a shout that sounded like "Kill! Kill!" and some of the escorting knights made a rush to the enclosure and went inside, which was strange because the gate was supposed to have been bolted against entry. Then the dauphin was hurried out by the Seigneur du Chastel and a couple of other lords. Inside we could hear a big fight going on – swords clashing and men shouting and several of Burgundy's retinue were wounded before they were all eventually arrested by the dauphin's knights. Then my lord and the seigneur mounted up and rode into the town and I had to follow with the hounds so I did not see any more, but later it was confirmed that the Duke of Burgundy had died.'

'Was the duke the only one killed then?' I asked, feeling slightly sick at the thought that it might have been my letter to Tanneguy that sparked this violence.

Luc frowned. 'Yes I think so, although some say that another Burgundian died later of wounds. No one really seems to know exactly what happened. The dauphin has written a statement which his herald is presenting now to the king and queen. According to the Seigneur du Chastel, it says that the duke tried to draw his sword and take him – the dauphin – prisoner and it all kicked off from that, but one of the other knights is supposed to have claimed that Tanneguy himself hit the duke on the head with his battleaxe.'

I crossed myself again. 'My God!' I breathed. 'Did Tanneguy murder the duke?'

'Ssh, Ma!' hissed Luc. 'Nobody knows exactly what happened and it seems that your friend Tanneguy is determined that nobody ever will. Perhaps the letter will explain, but I do not want to know.' He stood up. 'I had better go. Viennois Herald will be returning to Melun very soon. I do not know when there will be another opportunity to get together, but if there is one I will take it.' To my surprise he gave me a big hug. 'Read the letter, Ma,' he urged and was gone.

From the Seigneur du Chastel to Madame Guillaumette Lanière,

Esteemed Madame,

I am sending this letter with your son because I know he cannot read. Do not share it with him and when you have read it please destroy it.

The dauphin was deeply shocked by the content of your letter to him and it is primarily due to that that you are hearing the news today of the death of the Duke of Burgundy. Having learned of the dreadful crimes perpetrated by the duke on the person of his sister, his highness decided he could no longer treat with Burgundy while Duke Jean remained alive. Therefore my lord and I agreed that he should not. It is done. And if France is ever to become united under the dauphin's rule, how and by whose hand he was killed must remain a mystery. I trust you understand this.

I would also like you to know that your son Luc has become an important member of the dauphin's entourage and contributes much to the well-being of his future king.

Take good care of your mistress for I fear that many ripples will flow from the death at Montereau.
May God in his mercy forgive us all.
In haste,
Tanneguy Seigneur du Chastel

Do not forget to burn this.

I read the letter twice, holding it in a trembling hand. Tanneguy had more or less admitted that he had murdered the devil duke and in doing so effectively condemned his soul to hellfire. As I committed his letter to the kitchen flames, I could not decide whether he was a man to be deplored, admired or pitied.

From Catherine, Princess Royal of France to Madame Guillaumette Lanière,

Greetings to my beloved Mette,

The devil duke is dead! I cannot believe it. The whole convent has gone into mourning, while I feel like throwing

407

off my novice's habit and dancing around the cloisters in my chemise!

Oh, Mette, previously Poissy was my refuge but suddenly I cannot bear the restrictions of my enforced enclosure. Nor can I rid myself of thoughts of King Henry, which continually intrude at inappropriate moments, such as when I am kneeling in penitence before the Virgin or trying to assemble my list of sins before confession. Perhaps I should confess these thoughts and then I might be given absolution and they would go away, but in truth I do not want them to go away, so I do not confess them.

My sister, Abbess Marie, says she has heard from Michele that her husband the new Duke of Burgundy has vowed to bring to the scaffold every traitor that was party to the killing. I do not know whether that includes our brother Charles, but I do know that if Philippe is going to wage a war of attrition on the dauphin's affinity, he cannot fight the English at the same time. Also, Montereau is still held by Charles' forces and while the late duke's body lies buried there, Philippe cannot take it to Dijon for interment in the Burgundian basilica. Question; who is the leader most likely to storm Montereau successfully and enable Philippe to retrieve the body? King Henry. And what conditions will the English King set on any treaty of alliance? I think I can safely say that marriage to me is one of them. While my mother was in thrall to Jean the Fearless, she no longer had any use for me, but now I predict that if she is to keep the support of the new Duke of Burgundy, she will find that she needs me once more.

So I am hoping that you and I will be reunited very soon. Try praying to St Jude again if you like, Mette, but truly I think this time ours is not a lost cause.

May God and His Holy Mother bless and keep you safe,

Catherine

Written secretly in my cell at Poissy Abbey this Sunday the 18th of October 1419.

29

The citizens of Troyes had held the Duke of Burgundy in awe as the powerful leader who had managed to preserve enough peace in their world to protect the commercial trade that was the source of their wealth. Dirge bells tolled over the town for days, sharp reminders that I should conceal my elation even from Alys and her new husband, who echoed the general Troyan view that the death was murder and that the dauphin, if not a murderer himself, was guilty by association with murderous individuals.

'But then he is only sixteen,' Jacques observed in mitigation, with the benevolence of a man six years older.

'Huh!' ejaculated Alys, not so demure a wife as to approve her new husband's every utterance. 'I am sixteen too, but I do not expect others take the blame for my actions.'

Jacques pointed out, 'But you are a married woman and cannot avoid it, for a husband takes responsibility for the actions of his wife. I do not know about Paris, but that is the law in Troyes.'

His reply gave Alys food for thought. She shifted slightly on her stool as if the babe in her womb had given her a kick, but I suspected it was her thoughts that made her uncomfortable.

'So if I steal a loaf from the baker, you are to blame,' she postulated. 'How does that work?'

'The baker holds me responsible,' replied Jacques. 'If the theft is proven, I must reimburse him and I must ensure that you suffer the punishment.'

'Which would be?'

Jacques shrugged. 'Theft is serious. It might be a whipping, it might be the stocks.'

'And who would whip me, pray?' Alys demanded indignantly.

'I would,' he told her gravely and then his lips twitched as he repressed a smile. 'But I promise I would not enjoy it.'

—ξξ—

From Catherine, Princess Royal of France to Charles, Dauphin of Viennois,

My dearly beloved brother,

I freely admit that I cannot regret the death of Jean the Fearless, yet I earnestly pray that you have not endangered your soul in the way it came about. Marie says you have made a statement claiming it was an accident due to a misunderstanding and I accept your explanation, while remaining extremely glad that such an accident occurred. God knows the truth but I fear the world may not so easily accept your innocence in the matter. For myself I am grateful that I no longer fear Burgundy's malign presence, nor do I need to worry that you might be drawn back into the Burgundian web, because however much you deny responsibility for the death, Philippe will never forgive you for it. Now you and I must both follow our destinies in the best way we can.

Marie tells me that Michele is on her way to Poissy again and I admit that I anticipate her visit with mixed feelings. Judging by the way she sang her father-in-law's praises the last time she was here, I am in for a tirade of anger at his death, most of which will doubtless be aimed at you. We children of Valois are destined never to enjoy a close family relationship!

I rather hope that Michele's imminent arrival signals the end of my enclosure here, even if I have to suffer her outbursts against you throughout my journey to Troyes. How I wish you could be there to greet me. Nevertheless, may God advance both your cause and mine, dear brother.

Affectionately,
Catherine

Written secretly in my cell at Poissy Abbey this Thursday, the 20th day of October, 1419.

When a royal messenger rapped on the door of the workshop in the Rue de l'Aiguille early on the morning of Catherine's eighteenth birthday, my mind flew back to the Paris bake house and the day my life changed for ever. Now my destiny was once more to change on that memorable date. This time, however, it was no high-nosed individual with an ebony stick who enquired for 'your girl' in haughty tones, it was a cheerful young page with a gold fleur-de-lis on the shoulder of his blue doublet and an apologetic smile on his face. The princess was arrived in Troyes and requested that I attend her that afternoon.

The royal palace was decked out with ritual mourning black everywhere, reminding me of the days after Agincourt. However, dressed in the neat brown houppelande gown Jacques and Alys had made for me to wear at their wedding, I felt comfortably neutral – hoping neither to appear to mourn the man I abhorred, nor to stand out as one who did not. I was shown into an anteroom and, in a matter of minutes, Agnes arrived and we embraced with great fondness.

'We have only been back for a day,' she informed me. 'The princess is with the queen at present, but I know she is aching to see you. Will you come and wait in her chamber?'

'Gladly,' I replied.

'She wanted to ignore the queen's summons in order to wait for you, but I thought it politic to persuade her to go,' said Agnes, leading the way from the room.

'How is the queen?' I asked.

Agnes made a face. 'They say she is torn. She mourns openly for Burgundy, yet she yearns for reconciliation with her son.

413

Now the new duke has come, demanding that his father's killers be hunted down and brought to justice.'

'What, all of them? Including the dauphin?'

Agnes nodded and whispered, 'All of them.' She cast a troubled glance at the guards lining the passage to the royal apartments and I understood the need for discretion.

'Have no ladies come to wait on the princess yet?' I asked as we entered her chamber, noticing the absence of the usual group of stools gathered around her canopied chair.

'She insisted that none be appointed without her approval,' replied Agnes. 'She seems to have acquired a new assertiveness since the Duke of Burgundy's death. See what you think. I hear her now.'

I swung round, expecting to see a familiar figure but for a breathless moment I thought a nun had entered the chamber. Then I saw that it was Catherine in a black habit and white wimple.

'Oh, Mette, thank God!' she cried and before I could make more than a half bend of the knee, she was rushing headlong into my arms – more impulsive than assertive I thought, eagerly returning her hug.

'Have you taken holy vows, Mademoiselle?' I asked as we drew apart.

Her laugh was as girlish as ever. 'No, Mette. This is the dress of a tertiary nun. I have been accepted as a lay member of the Dominican community of sisters at Poissy and I wore the habit to attend the queen because it is my way of avoiding court mourning garb.'

Agnes remarked with a smile, 'I see you also managed to avoid bringing any court damsels back with you, Madame.'

Catherine made a dismissive gesture. 'There were several candidates there, but I refuse to consider them at present. Now, I want to talk to Mette – alone please, Agnes.'

My eyes widened in surprise at her firm tone as I watched Agnes curtsey and make her exit looking a little crestfallen.

I made no comment but said, 'Well, Mademoiselle, let me immediately wish you a very happy birthday,' and offered the little package I had kept tucked in my sleeve pocket. 'I hope that eighteen will be a momentous age for you.'

Tears sprang to Catherine's eyes as she took the package. 'Thank you, Mette. I spent an hour sitting beside my mother and she never once mentioned my birthday. She was much too busy extolling the virtues of a marriage to King Henry – again! I have never known anyone who could change their mind as often as she does. This is so very kind of you.' She tugged the ribbon off the present. 'What have you brought me – Oh!' Unwrapping a remnant of beautiful brocade which Jacques had used to make a gown, she found an enamelled gold reliquary bearing an image of crossed keys.

'It is meant to contain a relic of St Peter, who as you know keeps the keys of Heaven,' I explained hastily. 'But I thought you could put the key of your altar inside. It would be safer. People will not be so curious if they see a reliquary hanging around your neck.'

Catherine lifted her eyes to my face and gazed at me for a long moment before kissing me on both cheeks. 'What a thoughtful gift, Mette, thank you. You are right, it would be safer. Will you help me to do it?'

When it was done and the chain tucked back into the neck of her habit, she took my arm and led me towards the hearth, where a bright fire burned. I sat beside her chair on a stool. 'First of all, Mademoiselle, how are you? You look thin.'

She made a face. 'I knew you would say that! In my strict repentance regime, prayer and atonement came much higher up the list of priorities than food. But from the moment I heard that the devil duke was dead, I knew that your daring plan must have worked – but I did not know if you were safe. What risks you must have taken. How I wish we could have shared the news of the death of Burgundy, our joint nemesis, for I could have given vent to my true feelings of justified euphoria with you as with no one else!'

It was wonderful to be in her company again and our talk lasted more than an hour as we exchanged all the details of our time apart. Finally there were tears of emotion when I recounted the story of Jacques and Alys' reunion and eventual marriage.

'Oh this is wonderful!' Catherine exclaimed. 'They are happy, you say. Then possibly, Mette, you will be willing to return to my service?' She looked earnestly at me and went on quickly. 'I want to offer you the post of my Keeper of the Robes. You already do the job anyway, but this would be a proper court post. Not quite Mistress of the Wardrobe, but at least it means that you will have a department and quarters of your own and the rank of a court official. I do so very much hope that you will accept.'

I gulped and stared at her wide-eyed. I was very conscious that what she was offering me was an enormous favour. The post of Mistress of the Wardrobe to the princess royal was always conferred on one of her nobly born ladies-in-waiting, for it held high status within the court hierarchy, but even an appointment as Keeper of the Robes would make me a courtier – as far above a menial household servant as a count was from a commoner. I would be allocated my own bedchamber, could wear bright clothing and speak directly to other courtiers without avoiding their gaze and generally be treated as a human being rather than like palace vermin. I could hear my mother's words when I was appointed Catherine's wet-nurse; '*It is a good opportunity, Mette. It will be hard at first, but who knows where it could lead?*' Even she could not have envisaged this.

My silence must have made Catherine think I was seeking a way to say no, for she gave me an encouraging smile and went on, 'There will be twenty crowns and three suits of clothing a year. You could order them from your son-in-law if you wish.' She clasped her hands tightly in her lap and her manner lost its new authority as she ended rather lamely, 'I think it is a good offer.'

'It is a very good offer, Mademoiselle,' I responded, tears springing to my eyes. 'I am honoured by it and of course I accept. I only hesitated because there is one proviso I must make, with your permission.'

'Yes, Mette. What is it?'

'I have promised Alys that I will be with her when her baby

417

is born, so if the court leaves Troyes and you go with them I fear that I cannot. At least, not until I have seen her safely delivered.'

A look of relief spread over Catherine's face. 'That is not difficult to grant, for I believe the court will not be leaving Troyes for some time. Philippe of Burgundy has assumed his father's position as joint regent with the queen and I must say I wish him the joy of her! She drove Louis mad, as you know. I have yet to meet Philippe, but Michele insists he is a good man. Hard to imagine with a sire like that! However, he is implacable about bringing his father's murderers to justice, so he intends to treat with the English. That is why the queen is singing King Henry's praises once more, because she wants to keep Philippe sweet. So the court will be staying in Troyes for the time being. Personally, I think Philippe wants the queen here because it is between Dijon and Arras and he can disappear to either Flanders or Burgundy whenever she begins to annoy him beyond bearing!'

'But if you are surrounded with people who speak against your brother and praise the memory of your tormentor, it will not be easy, Mademoiselle,' I felt bound to point out. 'How will you manage?'

Catherine reached forward and took my hands. 'With your help, Mette. Outside this room I can be whoever they want me to be, as long as I can come back to you and be myself.'

As she said this, there was a scratching at the door. Catherine gave my hands a little squeeze and nodded for me to investigate. It was the same page that had come to the shop in the Rue de l'Aiguille, but in my smart clothes and draped hat he did not recognise me.

He looked nervous and spoke in a whisper, proffering a sealed letter, 'For Madame, the princess. It is from the Duchess of Burgundy. The messenger said it was urgent or I would not have knocked . . .' His voice trailed off apologetically. I smiled reassuringly and shut the door.

'What does it say, Mette?' asked Catherine. 'Open it please.'

It was a brief note which I read aloud. 'Sister, my lord and I must depart tomorrow for Burgundy, to deal with his father's estate. I am bidding farewell to our mother the queen and will afterwards come to your chamber, where I understand you have retired, but I trust will be ready to receive your sister, Michele, Duchess of Burgundy.'

I looked up to see Catherine pursing her lips and rolling her eyes. She rose hastily and took the letter from me. 'Call Agnes, Mette. She should be here. I think you will find Michele much changed from the girl you looked after in the nursery!'

Michele, Duchess of Burgundy was indeed an altogether different creature from the shabby little girl who had followed the queen timidly out of the rose garden at the Hôtel de St Pol. After a few months in Jacques' workshop, I could easily distinguish fine and costly cloth from its cheap and shoddy imitators and I knew instantly that the fabric of Michele's black gown was extremely fine and extremely costly and its jet-beaded trimming had travelled all the way from a distant part of Castile only recently freed from Moorish rule. Clearly nothing but the best would do for the new duchess.

Michele paused on the threshold, gazing around the chamber in a leisurely fashion. Her black veil drained her pale complexion of colour but her large blue-green eyes glittered shrewdly as she took in every detail. 'I am pleased to see you are alone, Catherine,' she said, evidently categorising me and Agnes as nobodies. 'But I hope you will acquire some more suitable mourning garb soon. That hideous habit hardly fits your rank and status.'

I shrank back against the hangings, hoping to meld into the mythical scene woven into the tapestry, and marvelled how someone could so vividly resemble her mother when she had spent almost no time in her company. Not that Michele looked like Queen Isabeau – her features were too plain and severe for that – but her carriage and attitude echoed those of her mother so closely that she inspired the same shiver in my spine as I felt in the queen's presence.

Catherine refused to be intimidated however, remaining seated in her canopied chair and gesturing towards the carved armchair she had ordered to be placed beside it. 'Welcome, sister,' she said gravely, 'please sit down. Actually I consider the habit of a tertiary admirably appropriate for the circumstances. I am sorry to hear you are leaving. I thought the duke was waiting until his father's body could be conveyed to Dijon for burial.'

Michele crossed herself piously. 'It is shameful that the body has not been released to us!' she exclaimed. 'It is another instance of Charles's cowardice. Not only does he deny any involvement in the murder of his cousin, he even refuses to admit to knowing where the body has been buried.'

'Perhaps if your husband had not condemned him to the scaffold out of hand, he might have been more amenable,' suggested Catherine mildly. 'But let us not argue. Will you return to Troyes once these exequies have been completed?'

'I expect so. Philippe wishes me to keep you company while he urgently pursues a treaty with the English.' Michele shook her head at the cup of wine Agnes offered in refreshment. 'I would prefer a little spring water,' she said primly. 'I drink wine only if a toast is required.'

'Or when the priest offers the blood of Christ, surely?' observed Catherine slyly.

Michele's brow knitted. 'But then it is no longer wine, sister, is it,' she snapped. It was not a question. 'I take it you have been made aware that this approach to the English will renew the prospect of a marriage between you and King Henry.'

'Is that why you are here?' Catherine enquired. 'To see if I am willing? What if I object? That would seriously affect the chances of a peace treaty, would it not? And I hear Philippe desperately wants one.'

Michele forced a smile. 'I think desperately is too strong a word. He considers a treaty with the English is the best way to bring our recusant half-brother and his accomplices to book. Anyway, I hardly think you will refuse a marriage that would make you a queen.'

'I have met King Henry only once,' Catherine responded, 'but he seems acceptable.'

Michele's snort was almost unladylike. 'Acceptable! My little sister finds the King of England and conqueror of Normandy

421

only "acceptable"! Who would be irresistible then, Catherine? Emperor Sigismund?' She accepted the spring water Agnes brought and sipped it neatly.

'Oh no,' responded Catherine blithely. 'Too old – and I hear he has already taken a new wife. The second empress' name is Barbara, I believe.'

'It is not wise to be flippant about marriage,' said her sister pompously, setting down the cup.

'Oh I am not flippant about marrying King Henry,' Catherine assured her. 'The match has been dangled before me for so long that it has ceased to excite me, that is all.' She leaned forward earnestly and went on, 'But if we are to be companions, on your return you will be able to educate me in the advantages and disadvantages of matrimony. Tell me, *is* marriage exciting, Michele?'

A dark flush spread across her sister's throat and face and for a few moments she was lost for words. Then she frowned with irritation. 'Marriage is a contract which carries certain obligations, Catherine. You know that. Being excited is not one of them.'

'But bearing children is,' said Catherine gently. 'How awkward it must be if they do not come along.'

I counted the years. Her sister and Philippe of Burgundy must have been sharing a bed for at least seven years and so far there had been no offspring.

The duchess stood up suddenly and smoothed her skirts. 'As I said, you should beware of flippancy, Catherine,' she admonished. 'It does not sit well in a queen. I will take my leave now. There is much to do before my lord and I depart at dawn tomorrow. I am sorry I have no time to help you to select some noble companions, but I advise you to do so without delay.' She cast an eloquent glance in my direction. 'You will find them better company.'

Catherine rose to kiss her cheek. 'I will remember that, sister,' she murmured. 'And so, I am sure, will Madame Lanière. God protect you on your journey.'

30

Shrewdly, Catherine had appointed six new ladies-in-waiting by the time Michele returned from Dijon. They were all younger than herself and the daughters of lesser knights and barons; girls who would do as they were told without causing any ripples. 'Now, if Michele brings someone forward to act as her spy in my camp, I can legitimately say there is no room for her.'

Michele did indeed produce not one but two candidates, the sisters of one of her husband's close friends and advisers, and she was much irritated when Catherine sweetly thanked her and told her that the six companions she had already selected were quite enough.

'But they are all so young!' exclaimed an exasperated duchess. 'You will never manage a decent conversation with any of those bubble-brains and I do not suppose they have any skills with a hairbrush or a needle.'

'I do not need those skills for I have them already in Agnes and Guillaumette,' Catherine pointed out, smiling at us both as we sat quietly with our embroidery. 'My girls can dance and sing and play games. They entertain me. What could be better than that?'

'These are frivolous reasons for choosing your maids of honour,' Michele observed. 'You do not have a good history in this, Catherine. The commoner, Madame Lanière, for example; you have let her get much too close to you. I am sure that will not go well with King Henry.'

Catherine frowned and gestured in my direction. 'Madame Lanière is sitting over there, sister. Is it good manners to talk about her without acknowledging her presence? As for King Henry, he personally told me at Meulan how he has introduced English as his official language. He is of the opinion that as many commoners as possible should be able to read and understand their laws and ordinances. How many commoners does Philippe have among his advisers? I know that King Henry encourages likely young men who show intelligence and ability, whatever their birth.'

Michele looked affronted. 'I do not need a lecture from you about my husband's court,' she said. 'Although, for your information, Philippe intends that it will be the most culturally advanced in Europe. He has already attracted artists and scholars of all classes and nationalities to work in Flanders. However, what is most important here and now is your preparation for marriage and I feel bound to point out that packing your household with commoners and dizzy daughters of minor nobles is not building the right image as a consort for a king. Besides, what am I to say to the brother of my two ladies, who is one of Philippe's closest councilors?'

'I should tell him to hasten the peace negotiations,' suggested Catherine. 'In the last month King Henry's forces have overrun every Seine stronghold up to the gates of Paris. Even Poissy fell last week. If they had arrived there a fortnight earlier, King Henry might have claimed conqueror's rights and swept me to the altar in Poissy Abbey without need of any treaty! Philippe needs to arrange a ceasefire quickly or the St Germain gate will open to the English just as it did to your father-in-law last year. The Paris guilds are notoriously fickle. They cannot be relied on to continue supporting Burgundy.'

Michele's lip curled. 'Do not pretend that you know anything about these matters, Catherine,' she retorted. 'All those towns and castles on the Seine are – or were – royal garrisons. Our Burgundian strongholds remain solid.'

'Oh, I see,' cooed Catherine, feigning enlightenment. 'So the Burgundian allegiance to the crown does not include help in relieving beleaguered royal garrisons? Nothing has changed then since Jean the Fearless failed to turn up at Agincourt. Like father, like son.'

For a moment it looked as if Michele was going to explode with anger, but her immense powers of self-control held good and she merely closed her eyes and put both hands to her temples, rubbing gently as if to ease a sudden headache. Then she said slowly, 'I think if you and I are going to spend our time pleasantly together, Catherine, we had better avoid certain topics. What have you been reading lately?'

It was a great relief to us all when, in mid-December, Michele set off for Flanders to spend Christmas with her husband.

From Catherine, Princess Royal of France to Charles, Dauphin of Vienne,
 My dearly beloved brother,

It is nearly Christmas and the season of rejoicing. I hope you will be making merry at your court, wherever it is – Bourges or Tours or Chartres? – and with people who love you. I often wonder how you do with Marie and whether you two have been blessed and bedded yet. Perhaps you will spend the festive season in Anjou with her family.

Sadly I do not believe we shall ever spend Christmas together again. I do not yet know exactly how things stand between the English and Burgundian negotiators, but it is probable there will eventually be a marriage between me and King Henry. After Montereau there will be no goodwill towards you, my brother. Therefore it is inevitable that you and I must become enemies. How I wish it were not this way, but so it is.

Would that we could have remained children, ignorant of and unaffected by all these political differences! Do you have any memories of Michele? You were very young when the queen spirited her out of the Hôtel de St Pol, but let me tell you that she and I do not find each other easy to love!

It has been made abundantly clear to me that royal

offspring are never really children at all, being rather 'assets of the kingdom'. What an uncomfortable state that is!

Nevertheless, in so far as I can, I remain your loving sister,
Catherine

Written at the Palace of the Counts, Troyes, this day Tuesday the 20ᵗʰ December 1419.

—ξξ—

Christmas at court was a subdued affair. Mourning prevailed ,and most of the major courtiers were anyway involved in treaty negotiations, busy travelling between Troyes, the Burgundian court in Arras and the English king at Mantes. King Charles and Queen Isabeau were unable or unwilling to undertake the planning of seasonal celebrations, so it was left to Catherine and her ladies to arrange what entertainment they could. For my own part I heard Mass at the Church of St Jean with Alys and Jacques, and shared a celebration meal in the workshop in the Rue de l'Aiguille. At the end of January I moved back there to await the birth of Alys' baby.

Her labour started in freezing weather in the middle of February and by the afternoon of the following day I was becoming extremely concerned, for although I could tell from the writhing of her body and the agony in her eyes that the birth pangs were fierce, her cries of pain seemed to be growing weaker. The midwife, a normally cheerful and positive soul called Grizelde, took me out of the chamber and confided that the baby seemed to be stuck.

'We must pray to the Virgin and St Margaret that she and the child be saved.'

I stared at her aghast. 'She has been so well during her pregnancy,' I protested. 'She is strong. I am sure she will manage to push the baby out eventually.'

'Alas it is not a case of how strong she is, but whether she opens to release the baby. Your daughter is young. Sometimes a young mother's body is not ready to stretch and, so far, my ointment of comfrey and yarrow has had no effect.'

My voice rose in panic. 'But are there no old methods, no ancient lore to guide us? I beg you to use anything you can to help her!' I saw hesitation in the wise woman's eyes and I clasped her hand eagerly in both of mine. 'Please, Grizelde! You do know of something. I can see you do. Tell me!'

'Sometimes a mother is responsive to the house being opened up around her. Every door, every shutter, every drawer, every knot should be untied, every lace undone. And – well, there is also the power of jasper. Even the smallest piece of that stone can be effective, but I do not know where any is to be found.'

'Jasper? A magic stone? What does it look like?'

'The most powerful type is a gemstone, coloured deep red. Some call it bloodstone. .'

'I know of one set in a ring! I can get it. Go back to Alys,' I told the midwife. 'Tell her I will be away for a short time but when I come back I will have relief for her pain. Oh – and open everything, Grizelde – all the things you said – and tell Alys why you are doing it.'

In the workshop Jacques was sitting at his tailor's table but his needle was lying loose on the cloth and his lips were moving in silent prayer. Another heart-rending cry of pain sounded from above and his face turned a paler shade of white.

'You can help as well as pray, Jacques,' I said, my sharp tone making him jump. 'Open the shutters and the doors, even the cupboards. Pull out all the drawers, untie every knot or remove it from the house. Everything must be opened to free the baby's way into the world. There is something important I need to fetch for Alys.' I took down my cloak from a peg near the door and departed hastily.

Having attended Catherine almost every day for the past five years, I was very familiar with the contents of her jewellery casket and had been in possession of the keys, which I had consigned to the care of Agnes while I was away.

When I gained admittance to Catherine's chamber, half running down the room, I dropped to my knees at her chair. 'What is it, Mette? What has happened? Have you news of Alys?'

'Yes, but all is not well, Mademoiselle. May I beg your high-ness' leave for a word in private?'

A brisk word and a wave of Catherine's hand sent the ladies scampering to the door. I tried to speak calmly, but anxiety made my words tumble over each other. 'The baby is stuck. Alys grows weaker and weaker. It is torture to watch her. We have prayed for a miracle but time is running out. Our last resort

430

may not be acceptable to the Church and so you may not like it but I must beg your help nevertheless.'

I kept my gaze fixed on Catherine's face, hoping that I would not see doubt reflected there.

'I cannot know what to think until I hear what it is you want, Mette,' she prompted gently.

'The midwife says there is power in a certain gemstone called jasper that can draw babies from the womb when all else fails. The practice might be considered sorcery by the Church, but I am desperate. Mademoiselle, there is a ring in your jewellery chest that you seldom wear which is set with that stone and I beseech you to let me take it to Alys so that we may try this ancient cure. Of course I will return it straight away, whatever the result.'

My heart gave a jolt when I saw Catherine frown and I feared she was about to refuse, but the frown was one of perplexity. 'I do not know of such a ring, Mette. Are you sure I have one?'

'Oh yes, Mademoiselle. The stone is a large red one, a cabochon set in gold, but you may know it as bloodstone.'

Her face cleared. 'Oh yes, I know the one you mean. Of course you may take it to Alys. I understand your concern about Church opinion, but the stone may be the vehicle through which God answers our prayers. Bring the chest here, Mette. The sooner you take the ring, the sooner God can begin to work his miracle. And, meanwhile, I will be praying for her constantly. I will not stop until I hear that she is safely delivered.'

As I retraced my steps through the town, the ring was in a small leather pouch tucked into the bodice of my robe.

Approaching the house I heard Alys cry out and paradoxically the agonised wail gave me comfort since it confirmed that her strength had not failed her completely.

Jacques pounced on me as soon as I entered. 'The midwife will not let me in!' he complained bitterly. 'Alys is likely to die and the hag will not let me say my farewells! She says it is bad luck for a man to enter the birthing chamber.'

I thought of Queen Isabeau's gilded labours, surrounded by fur-trimmed noblemen and mitered bishops and wondered at this latest Troyan superstition. Then I silently scolded myself for inconsistency – I was desperate to try Grizelde's bloodstone remedy and yet I was ready to sneer at her fear of men tainting a birth. I hastened to reassure poor Jacques. 'Alys is not going to die,' I told him firmly. 'Have faith and keep praying and I will call you as soon as the baby is born.'

As I climbed the steep stair I wondered at the confidence I had managed to inject into my voice, for it had no firm foundation.

With the shutters wide open the room was freezing, but Alys' face and throat were glistening with a slick of oily sweat. Her eyes were closed and she looked utterly exhausted. I hastily threw a couple of logs on the fire before hurrying to the bedside.

As my hand touched hers, Alys's eyes flickered open but another pain seized her before she could speak. She arched back against its onslaught, the mound of her belly like a swelling wave pushing up the quilted coverlet. 'Gently, my little one,' I crooned, stroking her clammy brow. 'Try not to fight it.'

'You went away,' whispered Alys hoarsely, when she could speak. 'Did the princess need you for something?'

'No, darling girl. She had something you need.'

Grizelde came to stand beside me. I took the heavy gold ring from its leather pouch and heard the midwife gasp. The smooth round stone glowed like a pool of blood in the lamplight as the midwife took Alys' hand and nodded for me to slip the ring onto her middle finger. As I did, I said urgently to Alys, 'This is a very special ring. It will ease your suffering and bring the baby safely out. Here, let the baby feel its strength.' I lifted her hand and laid it on the mound of her belly while she struggled to lift herself to see it. I helped her, feeling the slightness of her shoulders as I held her up. Dear God, she was so young and frail! How could she withstand the fierce forces of nature that battered her so mercilessly? Then a thought struck me.

'Why do you not sit upright,' I suggested, my maternal instincts surging to the fore. 'Perhaps the baby wants to fall down from you and Grizelde will catch it!' I gave a little laugh to encourage her. 'You could sit on my lap! Like when you were a child. Come, let us try it. Before the next pain comes.'

But she was already in its grip and it was minutes before she could catch enough breath to put her arms trustingly around my neck and be lifted. With Grizelde's help, I carried her to the big wooden armchair which had been set by the fire and I lowered myself onto it, holding Alys in front of me, her hand with the bloodstone ring still held firmly against her belly.

When the next pain came she suddenly sat bolt upright, as if infused with a new and purposeful strength. Her cry was not of pure agony but of mingled pain and effort. 'Blessed Saint Margaret,' I prayed aloud, throwing all my religious scepticism to the four winds, 'intercede for these two young lives and give them both the strength to overcome this trial.'

We will never know which of the desperate measures worked the miracle – the wide open house, the red power of the jasper, the change of position or the saint's intercession – but after only two more convulsive contractions of her womb, Alys let out a great sigh and my hands felt the pressure lessen in her belly. Hot, sharp-smelling liquid burst from her and she fell back against me with a deep moan, as if a dam of suffering had been relieved in a single moment.

'God is good.' I murmured, watching steam rise gently from the flood of birth fluid that soaked my fine woollen skirt. I saw Grizelde's smile and delighted nod and shouted out with glee. 'The baby is coming. Push!'

Within minutes we were welcoming the new infant into the world, crying and laughing at the same time while the baby sent up a squalling yell of protest. Grizelde gently sponged the child and wrapped it in a warm shawl while I carried Alys back to the bed and arranged the quilt over her before hastening to close the shutters and heap wood on the fire. Jacques hurtled through the open door as Grizelde placed the baby in its mother's willing arms.

'I heard a cry!' exclaimed Jacques. 'I thought there would never be one.' He flung himself down beside the bed and reached out to smooth a lock of Alys' damp hair back from her forehead. 'Jesu, Alys, I thought I was going to lose you!'

Eyes wide, he reached out and drew back the shawl, but he was rendered speechless by the sight of the small, pink, bawling scrap of human life that was revealed and looked up at me in bewilderment.

'It is a girl,' I told him gently, 'a tiny, beautiful, healthy girl.'

An hour or so later, Alys and the baby were sleeping and I wended my way back to the palace, very happy, but anxious to return the ring as soon as possible, and conscious that Catherine had promised to pray until she heard of Alys' safe delivery.

'She is at her prie-dieu,' Agnes confided. 'She says she is not to be disturbed unless you come.'

I hugged Agnes impulsively. 'Well here I am!' I exclaimed. 'And there is good news.'

Not wishing to startle Catherine, I poked my head quietly around the door. She was kneeling before the gilded Virgin triptych, her solace through so many of her troubles. When she turned her head at the noise, I noticed that she had been weeping and was touched that she should be so deeply affected by Alys' plight.

I bobbed a curtsy. 'Mademoiselle,' I said gently. 'All is well.'

In an instant she had covered the distance between us, her arms spread wide. 'Oh God be thanked!' she cried, closing them around me. Then, releasing me quickly, she raised a hand and laid her fingers on my cheek. 'But you are frozen, Mette! Come and warm yourself! I will ask Agnes to mull some wine.'

'Do not call Agnes yet, Mademoiselle,' I warned. 'First I must give this back to you.' I drew the leather pouch from my bodice and pressed it into her hands. 'The baby is born, a beautiful girl, and Alys is safe, thanks to your kindness.'

She looked delighted at that, but she said solemnly, 'No, Mette, I believe it was the power of God.' Then she said, 'I would like to stand as godmother to the child. I feel a certain responsibility towards her, which you and I will not disclose to them. What do you think?'

It was some seconds before I could reply for a big lump came to my throat. To make a vow at the font to protect and nurture a child was of enormous significance, she would become one of its guardians, and for a little girl to number the princess royal among her sponsors was to provide her with an enormous advantage in life. 'This is a great honour that you do us, Mademoiselle,' I said, swallowing hard. 'I do not need to ask the child's parents if they will accept, for I can tell you their answer.'

Catherine raised an admonishing hand. 'Nevertheless, it is only right that they have the choice. I will send a page first thing tomorrow morning to fetch their answer and to discover the time and place of the baptism. And now we will call Agnes to mull the wine and drink the baby's health.'

Next morning I carried the baby, carefully wrapped against the biting cold, to the church of St Jean au Marché, with Jacques walking proudly by my side receiving the blessings and congratulations of his neighbours and fellow tailors. Behind us, Grizelde carried the traditional christening cap, a tiny cream silk helmet which Alys had embroidered with Christian symbols, and beside her strode Jacques' apprentice, who would be the child's godfather. Alys, of course, was not allowed to take part in religious activity or prepare and serve food to others until she had been 'churched' in a week or so. Although she protested against this ruling, I thought it sensible that she should concentrate on her own recovery and on her baby and to leave the domestic chores to others, which in this case would be me.

Although the market was not yet busy, a substantial crowd had gathered around the church door, attracted by the glamorous group waiting under the portal; Catherine in full court regalia accompanied by Agnes and several royal guards carrying pikes and wearing the distinctive fleur-de-lis livery. As I had predicted, Alys and Jacques had been overwhelmed by the princess' offer to be godmother for the baby. For the occasion Catherine had abandoned deep mourning and wore a beautiful white velvet gown and jewelled headdress. A formal crimson mantle trimmed with ermine clearly demonstrated her regal status. It would be only a matter of hours before every burgess of Troyes knew that royalty had stood at the font for Jacques and Alys' baby.

The priest was ready, but he was only a junior member of the clergy and he was so overawed by the magnificence of Catherine and her train that he tripped clumsily on his soutane and almost fell flat on the floor as he bent his knee before her.

'Y-you do our church m-much honour, your grace,' he stammered, staring fixedly at the hem of Catherine's gown, too abashed to raise his eyes further.

'It is a beautiful church, Father,' she said graciously. 'Please rise and let us proceed with the ceremony. I am anxious about the baby in this cold weather. Is the Holy water warmed?'

The priest clambered awkwardly to his feet and put a hand

on the side of the large ewer that stood beside the font. 'I asked the housekeeper to put it by the fire, Madame, and it is indeed warm.'

Steam rose from the font as he poured the warm Holy water into the cold stone bowl and I quickly unbound the baby's blanket and swaddling and passed her to Catherine. Wriggling and screaming at shock of being suddenly naked in the chill air, the little infant also sprayed urine over the princess' beautiful velvet gown but Catherine was unperturbed.

'I am sure that is a sign of good fortune for us both,' she said, smiling and handing the baby gently to the priest. 'I have been baptised again.'

Blushing, the priest plunged the protesting baby into the water, gabbling the Latin words of the baptismal service, barely audible over the sound of the infant's vexed cries. 'Who names this child?' he shouted finally and, without hesitation, the princess announced loudly and clearly, 'I do. Catherine. Her name is Catherine.'

PART FOUR

From Troyes to Paris
The Fateful Year
1420–21

31

Towards the end of March, the outline of a peace treaty between Burgundy and England had been agreed and the Duke of Burgundy brought it to King Charles for ratification, riding to Troyes with a retinue a thousand strong to demonstrate his paramount status as regent of France. Six months of mourning for Jean the Fearless' death was officially over and, despite Lenten restrictions, the French court was to be *en fête* to greet the young Duke's arrival.

The prospect of grand events stirred the queen out of her prolonged depression. She sent a hundred royal knights with heralds and trumpeters to accompany Michele out of Troyes to meet her husband at the Seine Bridge and escort the ducal couple through the town to the palace. Along the route damsels strewed armfuls of scented spring flowers before their horses and an elaborate welcome feast had been prepared in the king's great hall.

Now that I had an official court post, I was among the courtiers who gathered in the royal ante-room waiting for the royal party to come and warm themselves and take refreshment before beginning the long ceremonial of a public banquet, at which I was also entitled to a place.

Duchess Michele wore as flamboyant a display of wealth and status as her ultra-fashionable husband, managing to eclipse both her mother and sister in the magnificence of her appearance. Requiring the assistance of three ladies-in-waiting to manage her train, she moved majestically into the room gowned in gold-figured scarlet beneath a sable mantle so voluminous it must have touched the ground as she rode her palfrey. Her chestnut hair was held in a neat cap of gold filigree studded with glittering jewels and framed by a veil of crystal-scattered silk-gossamer, cunningly folded and wired into points. Such sumptuous and sophisticated attire outshone anything seen since the French court had left Paris and I could almost hear the queen's teeth grinding. Michele's facial features were not as fine as Catherine's, but her shrewd sea-green eyes were piercing and the exaggerated shaving of her hairline heightened her brow and emphasised the nobility of her long Valois nose. Collaring Catherine at the hearth, she immediately launched into the topic that was uppermost in her mind.

'Are you aware of the terms of this treaty, sister?' she enquired over the head of an attendant who knelt to brush mud off the hem of her gown.

'No, not in detail; I do not have the advantage of being married to one of the chief negotiators,' Catherine responded, matching Michele's businesslike tone.

'But my lord has written to you concerning the marriage contract, has he not?' Impatiently Michele tugged her skirt from the grip of the kneeling attendant. 'Take care not to pull me over, Madame!' she snapped. 'Enough.'

442

The lady with the brush rose and backed away, murmuring an apology, but I noticed that she had left a dark smear of mud to mar the costly sheen of the fabulous gold-figured fabric. Catching her eye, I fielded a conspiratorial twitch of the mouth which told me this neglect was not entirely accidental. Serving royalty was not without its little moments of triumph.

'I know that King Henry specifically insisted that the treaty be sealed with our marriage,' agreed Catherine. 'But that is all I know. Why do you ask? Is there something you wish to acquaint me with particularly?'

Michele glanced about her as if suddenly aware that this conversation was not private. 'We cannot talk of such matters here. We will discuss it later.'

Catherine shrugged, making it obvious that the prospect did not exactly thrill her. 'As you wish, sister. However, I would prefer that you had not aroused my curiosity if you do not feel inclined to satisfy it here and now.'

In view of this frosty exchange it was perhaps fortunate that at the ensuing banquet Catherine's high-table place was some distance from her sister's, on the other side of the king and queen, so she was able to converse instead with the Archbishop of Sens, an unusually good-looking prelate whom I knew she found pleasant company.

'He is such a charming man,' she had told me after first meeting him a few days before, 'not at all like a priest!'

I had not the heart to tell her that one consequence of his grace's handsome worldliness, was that he maintained a mistress in Troyes and it had been during an extended visit to her a few weeks previously that he had left his city and cathedral of Sens inadequately defended, allowing the dauphin's forces to overrun it. Now he was an archbishop without a See, but evidently he still had his charm.

When the tables had been cleared and the sweetmeats set out, the great hall was silenced by a fanfare for Montjoy Herald, who began a public reading of the draft treaty, which the king was due to approve the following day. Since it was in Latin I did not understand it, so I watched Catherine's reactions closely. After only a few sentences I saw her flush angrily and cast a black look down the table at Philippe of Burgundy. From that moment on, the treaty's content appeared to infuriate her more and more. When another flourish of trumpets marked the conclusion of the reading and a wave of animated conversation filled the hall, I saw her immediately treat the archbishop to a whispered tirade, while he made futile attempts to pacify her.

My attention was diverted by the arrival of the stewards, who wanted to clear the lower trestles for dancing, so I moved from my bench and when I glanced back to the high table I saw Catherine push back her chair angrily and make a whirlwind exit through the privy door. The queen and the duchess turned to glare disapprovingly, but this was unlikely to cut any ice with Catherine. Clearly my princess was in no mood for dancing.

Hurrying to her chamber, Agnes and I found her pacing up and down, pounding her clenched fists together and muttering, 'Treachery! Treachery! Holy Mother of God, I have been utterly betrayed!'

Seeing us, she stopped and spread her hands in desperate

indignation. 'How can they do this to me? Philippe, Michele, my mother – they have all betrayed me! The treaty is impossible – poisonous!'

'Agnes, you understand it. How can I possibly agree to its terms?'

She blinked back tears and her voice hardened into sarcasm. 'Oh, but my consent is not necessary! Agreement has already been reached. All I have to do is marry the enemy, betray my brother and defy the will of God!' Shaking with fury and frustration, she threw herself into her chair and sat staring into the banked-up fire, biting her knuckles, stopping only to add, 'I was prepared for the marriage – even welcomed it, but to force me into treason and heresy and total betrayal of my brother is inexcusable – unbearable! I will not – cannot – do it!'

Agnes tried placatory words. 'France is to make peace with the English and you are to marry King Henry. Is that not what was always intended?'

'No!' Catherine exclaimed. 'You have not understood. This is not a peace treaty between France and England; it is Philippe's revenge on the dauphin for the death of his father. It creates a triple alliance between France, England and Burgundy, the sole purpose of which is to destroy Charles and revoke his claim to the throne. It is an evil and pernicious document which, after our marriage, will make Henry the Heir of France, to rule in my father's stead until he dies when, if you please, the French crown is to pass to King Henry of England and to HIS HEIRS!'

Her voice rose hysterically as she yelled the last two words. Then she continued in a calmer but icier tone, 'The treaty is illegal and immoral, but that is not the worst of it. It is also against the divine will of God, which the Church has ruled to be that, when the king dies, the French crown passes to the next male heir in line, who is not Henry or any son that he and I might have. It is Charles. He is the king's son, recognised by him from the moment of his birth, whatever rumour otherwise may have been spread at the time. This heinous treaty contracts me to marry a man who is to be rewarded for destroying my brother with the very crown that should be his. And I am required to provide the usurper with a son who will inherit the throne which Charles' son should inherit. Now do you understand?'

'But the queen and Burgundy have both agreed to this,' Agnes reminded her. 'They must have good reason.'

Catherine rose, brushed past the kneeling Agnes and started to pace the floor once more. Her anger seemed to have been replaced by bafflement. 'You are right. They have their reasons, but they are not good ones. Philippe wants the men who killed his father brought to justice and King Henry will help him do that. In return he gets the throne of France, *if* he can drive Charles from the southern half of it. Obviously this is to Burgundy's advantage, for it means that the English will concentrate on uniting France and stay away from Philippe's Flemish border. As for the queen – what can be her reason?' She seemed to be thinking aloud now. 'I believe she is frightened. She fears Charles because she knows he hates her – with good cause! She is afraid of what will happen to her if he becomes king, and she thinks that if she supports Henry's claim to the throne, she will retain the regency in his inevitable absences.'

Suddenly there was an unexpected interruption.

'Why have you dishonoured my lord by walking out of his welcome feast?' Michele had entered Catherine's chamber unannounced and unobserved.

Catherine stared balefully at her sister for several seconds before dropping to one knee. 'Madame of Burgundy! You are not welcome in my chamber and your lord is not welcome to my home. Nevertheless, I bow the knee to you because that is your due – for the time being.' This sharp reminder that their positions were soon to be reversed was accompanied by a falsely sweet smile.

Head high, Michele stalked past Catherine and pointedly sat down in her sister's canopied chair. 'You may not welcome me, sister, but I should have thought you would welcome my husband with open arms, for it is he who has negotiated a marriage for you that will bring you not one crown but two. You should kiss his feet,' she added with bitter emphasis. 'His efforts have ensured that your children will sit on the throne of France when, by the law of primogeniture, it should be mine.'

Catherine rose gracefully from her obeisance. 'Actually, strictly speaking, if Charles is not to be king, it should be our older sister Jeanne's son, Francois of Brittany, but let us not quibble over laws which evidently no one takes any notice of. Anyway, your jealousy is misplaced, since neither of us has children; though I at least have the excuse that I am not yet married.'

Michele shook her finger reprovingly. 'Tut, tut, sister! You are unkind to mention my lack of children yet again, but do not make the mistake of assuming that God will instantly bless your union, or that he will not one day bless mine. The point is, now that it has been established that Charles is not our father's son, our children will be in line to the throne of France.'

Catherine paused and took a deep breath before responding. '*Has* that been established? Or has our mother perjured herself for her own ends? She is protecting her own position, just as she did when she failed to save you and Louis from your forced Burgundian marriages.'

Michele gave a harsh laugh. 'Ha! In all your eighteen years have you learned nothing, Catherine? A dynastic marriage is what every girl of the nobility is born for. At the age of nine I may have hated being taken away and bound to a boy I had never met, but now I thank God that I am married to Philippe of Burgundy. It has given me wealth and position and a role in life. If the marriage was made to some purpose and brought my lord's family more power and status, so much the better. You should wake up, sister, and realise that Charles is not your concern. He is a man who must fight his own battles, and you are a woman who must save your loyalty and love for the lord and husband whom God has chosen for you.'

I could see that Catherine was aching to answer this tirade with an enlightening lecture of her own. It was less than a year since the devil duke's depravity and violence had defiled her. While Michele proudly professed herself the beneficiary of Burgundian power and privilege, Catherine was very much its victim. But whatever Catherine may have been thinking, her response, when it came, was a measured one.

'You are to be admired for making so much of what fortune has offered you, Michele,' she acknowledged, 'but, like the rest of your husband's family, you speak without insight or compassion. However, much of your advice is good and I will try to follow it, particularly the part about building dynasties. So let us return to the feast and show our royal mettle by dancing the night away!'

And that is what they did. There had been no settlement between them but feelings had been aired, points of view established and some form of truce achieved. I thought it remarkable that both sisters showed a diplomatic ability to set personal animosity aside and present a united front, which caused observers of these momentous events to comment on the love displayed between two divisions of the de Valois family. When these reports later reached the ears of the dauphin I could easily imagine his reaction.

—ξξ—

From Catherine, Princess Royal of France to Charles, Dauphin of Viennois,

    Greetings, brother,

    You will not be surprised that I am struggling to come to terms with the treaty which the Duke of Burgundy has agreed with King Henry. Part of me wants to throw it back in Philippe's face and tell him that I cannot agree to it, although I know such an act of defiance would condemn me to the cloister, but another part of me likes the idea of a marriage to King Henry because I believe it is a perfect match. I wish I could explain this to you face to face, but simply writing it down may at least clarify my thoughts.

I cannot rid myself of the idea that the marriage is divinely ordained. King Henry believes he is obeying God's will when, as heir male of his great grandmother Queen Isabella, he claims to be the rightful King of France. On that basis, a son born of our marriage would be doubly God's chosen ruler and I believe the Almighty would be bound to bless such a marriage with a son. If I confessed these divine presuppositions to Michele, she would accuse me of wild and fanciful notions but then she finds the whole idea of my becoming Queen of France very hard to swallow. You and she have that in common no doubt.

When you read the treaty I expect you will rage against it and then you will consult your astrologers. You and I always differed about that. I still consider astrology to be an insult to God and His Saints, who steer the fortunes of us all, and I cannot deny that I feel that He and They are sanctioning this union with Henry. I have met the King of England only once, but there was a spark between us then which I believe ignited his desire for our union and lit an ember in me which has smouldered ever since. Because of this I cannot bring myself to halt the present course of events, but please believe me when I say that I do greatly regret the enmity it will create between you and me. Easter is upon us and provides an opportunity to seek divine guidance. I hope God will show me that my intuition is an indication of His will.

I will also pray for Michele, that she may be blessed with a child. I have heard that Philippe has already recognised several children as his baseborn offspring, which cannot be easy for her to bear and may account for her sourness of mind. While I am loath to take after our mother, I do hope to be at least as fertile as she was! Meanwhile she continues to change her mind with the tide of events and Henry is once more her Leander, or at least she would like him to be. I think she is nearly as jealous of me and my place in this treaty as Michele is – but I should stop writing before I become too uncharitable.

Despite all I am still your loving sister,

Catherine

Post Scriptum: I have just received a summons to the queen's chamber. She rarely holds court these days because most of the bright young knights and damsels flock either to Michele and Philippe's Hôtel or else to your court at Chinon, and that infuriates her, as you can imagine. These private meetings are hard to stomach because she usually has some bone to pick with me. I think this time I will take Mette. I have given her a court position as my Keeper of Robes and it does not please the queen (or Michele for that matter) to

451

see a commoner wearing colours and carrying my train.
Such small triumphs make the tedium of waiting for Henry
bearable!

Written at the Palace of the Counts, Troyes, this day
Thursday 28th April 1420.

—§§—

I was aware that Catherine found her meetings with the queen
hard to bear, but my heart sank when she asked me to accompany her on a private visit to her mother's chamber. It was
usually Agnes' role to carry her train, for the queen expected all
who paid court to wear formal dress, even if they were only
coming from the next room.

'Are you sure you want me, Mademoiselle?' I asked, hoping
she would see my reluctance and change her mind. 'I am clumsy
with trains. I may trip you.'

'I do not want you for your lightness of touch, Mette,' she
smiled. 'I want the queen to see you in your courtier's role, and
also there is invariably a hidden agenda to my mother's summons.
A shrewd witness is always useful.'

Despite my misgivings, I must confess that it was a memorable experience simply to enter the queen's chamber for, to my
great surprise, it was alive with birdsong and the flutter of
wings. As was to be expected, it was a large room containing
a fabulously draped bed in one corner, the usual array of chairs
and stools scattered about and a series of tables set against the

panelled walls, upon which stood a dozen or more beautifully wrought cages containing birds of various colours and types, most of which were singing their little hearts out. I had heard of the queen's passion for songbirds, but I had thought it only extended to one or two pet finches. In fact, her chamber could more accurately be described as an aviary containing scores of birds, some of which had never before been seen out of Africa.

Michele, Duchess of Burgundy, was present, sitting in a deep cushioned chair beside her mother's throne-like seat. Both royal ladies were magnificently attired, as brightly clad as the feathered creatures in the cages around them, and all their glitter and the frenetic singing and fluttering of the birds combined to create an atmosphere of nervous intensity. Even the ladies-in-waiting, supposedly relaxing with their embroidery, sat in watchful silence. Having made her curtsy, Catherine took the chair on the other side of the queen and I arranged her train carefully at her feet.

'Your birds are in fine voice this evening, your grace,' Catherine remarked, raising her own voice above the avian chorus. 'Have you some new recruits?'

'No. They sing loudly to repel interlopers,' replied the queen, staring pointedly at me as I retired backwards to the benches by the door, where Michele's lady in waiting perched placidly. 'Why have you brought your nurse, Catherine? Are you ill?'

'No, Madame,' Catherine responded, flashing an apologetic smile at me. 'You may remember that I am eighteen now and no longer need a nurse. I have appointed Madame Lanière my keeper of robes.'

'Keeper of robes!' echoed the Queen in a scathing tone. 'What on earth is that, pray? It sounds like a garderobe!'

'Keeper of the garderobe!' cried Michele derisively, 'how appropriate.'

The queen gave one of her hearty laughs. 'Ha, ha! Extraordinary! Next you will be appointing a Guardian of the Latrine! Ha, ha!'

Catherine frowned. 'Is our conversation to remain at this level, your grace, or is there some other reason for this summons?' she enquired in a sweet and sour tone.

The queen grew serious, leaned forwards and gave her a searching look. 'As your mother, I want to be certain that you are properly prepared for your marriage, Catherine, because King Henry is on his way. He left Rouen last week and has joined up with two of his brothers to come to Troyes to sign the treaty. So if you have any questions, you should take advantage of this tête-à-tête to ask them. There will not be many opportunities for raising delicate topics in private.'

Catherine's eyes swept the chamber. I knew what she was thinking. There were two pages tending the bird-cages with bags of seed and water-jugs, another was pouring wine into goblets and there were at least eight ladies-in-waiting arranged about the room. The situation was hardly tête-à-tête.

'How kind of you to offer your motherly advice, Madame,' she said earnestly, her gaze returning to engage the queen's. 'What questions would you suggest I might ask in the "privacy" of your chamber?'

'My goodness, Catherine!' exclaimed her mother impatiently, apparently unaware of the underlying note of irony in her daughter's enquiry. 'Can you not think for yourself? Are you familiar with the obligations of marriage, for example?'

'I discussed that very subject only recently with Michele,' Catherine answered blithely, turning her smile on her sister. 'Did she not tell you? We have been much together and have had plenty of chance to talk, have we not, sister?'

'Indeed,' agreed Michele with a slight frown. 'And I have expressed concern to the queen that you are too frivolous in your approach to this marriage.'

Queen Isabeau nodded complacently. 'There you are, Catherine. It is no light matter to become the bride of a king and I should know. You are chosen to be the pure and loyal mother of his children and his comfort and confidante, which means that much is expected of you. We – your sister and I – worry that you are not ready for these great expectations.'

I could almost hear the cogs slotting into place in Catherine's mind, as they did in mine. Now we knew the reason for this unusual summons. The queen was worried that Catherine would jeopardise the final and crucial stage of treaty by not presenting the image of the biddable, compliant virgin that they thought King Henry required.

There was no mistaking the sharp edge of anger in the princess' voice as she responded. 'Believe me, your grace, I have taken this marriage seriously for five years; ever since you brought me out of the convent as a girl of thirteen to dangle before the English king. I have met numerous English envoys, sat for successive tedious portraits and been paraded before King Henry as if our betrothal were already accomplished, only to be disappointed and humiliated time and again as negotiations faltered and failed. I think it could be said that my reputation, my integrity, my whole future rides on the success of this treaty and its resolution with my marriage, as I am only too aware; so I do not understand how anyone could believe that I find the matter frivolous. Actually, the fact that I still laugh at all is almost entirely due to Madame Lanière and my group of merry ladies, who keep me from becoming too despondent at the length of time I have spent in the hurly-burly of the marriage market.'

With her breast heaving, the queen burst into speech as soon as Catherine finished. 'I hope you are not accusing *me* of being dilatory in my pursuit of the marriage!' she exclaimed. 'I have done more than could be expected of any mother to bring you the best match in Europe. Am I to be met with gross ingratitude for my pains?'

At this outburst I clenched my fists so anxiously that my nails dug into my palms, but Catherine had long ago got the measure of her mother's ability to manipulate a situation. 'Have I ever expressed one iota of ingratitude, Madame?' she enquired, valiantly withholding all anger from her voice. 'I am intensely aware of the importance of this treaty and its significance for the future of France and I fully intend to be the perfect bride for the victor of Agincourt and to be his loyal consort and the successful mother of his children, if God wills.' With a flicker of her hand she crossed herself, reinforcing the seriousness of her declaration, and then clasped her hands together in her lap. 'Now, may I hear more about the arrangements for my wedding? Has a date yet been set?'

*

The following day Catherine asked me to meet her after Mass and bring her a plain cloak and one of my old servant's coifs. 'I want to visit my god-daughter,' she said.

Among the townsfolk Catherine's celebrity was now sky-high but, with a basket over her arm, the coif pulled down over her brow and an enveloping cloak, she could visit the Rue de l'Aiguille without being recognised. Her namesake was screaming when they arrived, but Catherine quickly crooned the baby to sleep, and seeing the young mother was very tired, insisted that Jacques hire a servant or a wet nurse. 'And you should do it now,' she said, removing a purse she had carried in her basket. 'There is gold here for my god-daughter's dower. I believe I will soon be leaving Troyes and I want to ensure that she is well provided for. Please use some to hire the help you need.' She placed the purse on the tailor's table.

Jacques bent his knee beside her chair. 'Thank you, Highness,' he said warmly. 'I will do as you say. I have been at fault, concentrating on completing all these orders and not noticing how tired Alys has been getting.' Catherine smiled indulgently at Jacques' fervent gratitude, but then she said thoughtfully, 'Actually, do not hire a servant, Jacques. I have an even better idea. Why do all three of you not come and stay at the palace for a while? I would be delighted if you would design and construct my bridal gown and all the necessary finery that a new queen might need.'

She suddenly laughed, as if amazed at her own cleverness. 'It is the perfect solution to all our problems!'

32

In the cathedral of St Pierre and St Pol, sunbeams pierced the clerestory, throwing shafts of light across the sanctuary and illuminating the seven people who stood before the high altar; the Archbishop of Sens in his gold-edged cope, King Henry of England supported by his two brothers, John, Duke of Bedford, and Thomas, Duke of Clarence, and Catherine, supported by her mother Queen Isabeau and Philippe, Duke of Burgundy. Gathered in the choir was a mixed group of courtiers and retainers, lesser clergy, lawyers and clerks, who had all just witnessed the final signing of the historic peace accord that would thereafter be known as the Treaty of Troyes. After the signing Henry and Catherine had moved into position facing each other at the altar, their faces solemn, their eyes locked, waiting to begin the betrothal ceremony. It was the second time they had met.

Catherine had wanted me to be there so I stood with Agnes and the maids of honour, craning my neck to see through a small gap between two buxom knight's ladies who kept putting their heads together to whisper comments, infuriatingly blocking my view. I could hardly believe that after five long years of hopes and fears, triumphs and miseries, my princess was finally standing before her king, ready to plight her troth. I wondered how she felt. Well, no, I *knew* how she felt, yet she managed to keep a faint smile on her lips and showed no sign of a tremor when the archbishop took her hand to join it with Henry's for the betrothal vow. As usual, the ceremony was conducted in Latin but even I understood the question '*Donec velit esse desponsata viro hoc?* Do you give yourself willingly to be betrothed to this man?' And Catherine's emphatic answer: '*Imo ego.* I do.'

The betrothal kiss was accompanied by a soaring psalm from singers positioned in the screen gallery and a muted murmur of approval from courtiers and clergy too polite to cheer. I watched their lips join and wondered if Catherine experienced the same surge of feeling as she had during the unexpectedly passionate kiss Henry had given her at the Pré du Chat. She would be disappointed if not.

Similar in sense and effect though the vows were, this was not a wedding, and after the ceremony was concluded the participants retreated to opposite sides of the altar. Two were not yet one. The main players on this occasion were those who had signed the treaty; so it was Queen Isabeau who paraded first down the nave, smiling archly between King Henry and Philippe of Burgundy, followed by Catherine and the archbishop and the two English dukes. I felt deflated, like someone who has come second in a race they thought they had won. It was a diplomatic event rather than a festive occasion. A banquet would follow to celebrate the treaty, but since the Church forbade weddings during Pentecost, the marriage would not take place until a fortnight's time, on the day after Trinity Sunday. Perhaps then there would be merriment.

At the banquet Catherine sat, apparently serenely, between King Henry and his brother Thomas of Clarence, while sandwiched between King Henry and the Duke of Burgundy. Queen Isabeau was more cheerful and animated than I had seen her for years. King Charles, as usual these days, was absent. I sat beside Agnes, both of us on edge.

'The Queen looks like the cat that got the cream,' I remarked, *sotto voce*. 'Does she see this as her finest hour, do you think?'

Agnes pursed her lips. 'She is seated between two handsome, powerful men in the prime of their life. Even though she is nearly fifty, that still makes her flirt like a courtesan!'

I looked at Agnes with surprise for she rarely passed adverse comment on anyone. 'King Henry does not seem dismayed,' I said. 'He has hardly exchanged a word with the princess and gives all his attention to the queen and the duke. If Catherine allowed it to show, I would say she was hurt and angry and I would not blame her.'

'The Duke of Clarence keeps her well engaged, though,' Agnes pointed out. 'He is said to be the most charming of the four brothers and he is working that charm on Catherine.'

I sighed and pulled a face. 'Yes, but it is not Thomas of Clarence who stirs Catherine's blood. I think we will have trouble boosting her spirits tonight.'

As I predicted, Catherine made her feelings about King Henry very clear at bedtime. She remained composed and gracious while her young ladies played their part in the disrobing, removing her heavy gown and mantle and carrying off the wreath of red roses she had worn on her headdress as a compliment to Henry's Lancastrian blood, to which in my sight her betrothed had not given so much as a glance, but as soon as they departed leaving only Agnes and myself, Catherine leapt up from her dressing stool and began to pace up and down the bedchamber, giving vent to the full blast of her Valois temper.

'What is the *matter* with that man? When I first met him at the Pré du Chat he could not have been more attentive, gazing into my eyes, asking my opinion, listening to my views. Afterwards, if you remember, he sent me the priceless Venetian mirror, presumably because he thought my appearance worthy of reflection. Now he favours me with barely a glance, turns his back on me at table and returns my smiles with frowns. Thomas of Clarence was kindness itself, trying to make up for his brother's discourtesy, but it was he who delivered the unkindest cut of all. Henry has asked Clarence to bring his wife from Rouen to teach me how to be a queen! Oh, he did not put it exactly like that, but the intention is clear. Henry does not think I know how to behave. How dare he imply that *I* am gauche, when he has such appalling manners himself?'

She swung round to glare accusingly at us as we stood dumbstruck by this uncharacteristic and violent explosion of wrath. 'Well? What do you think? Am I not right? Henry is a Janus. He is showing a completely different character from the one he showed before. How am I to handle this? Tell me please, for I am completely confused.'

Agnes spoke first, daringly taking Henry's part. 'Perhaps the king is tired, or even unwell. There have been reports that the ague is rife among the English troops.'

Catherine stamped her foot, although in her soft calfskin slippers she did not achieve the percussive thump she intended. 'No, he is not ill. Look at him! He is the image of a sleek, fat cat who has just made a kill. He is smug and self-satisfied and thinks he can do no wrong. I hate him!' She turned away as if to fling herself upon her prie-dieu, then changed her mind and strode to a table where stood a jug of wine and some cups. Her hand shook as she poured herself a drink.

Personally, I completely agreed with her. Even seen from my distant viewpoint, King Henry had displayed all the unpleasant qualities she had described and more. He had been haughty and rude but, worst of all, he had been unkind. Catherine was eighteen and inexperienced, but surely that was exactly what he wanted, a bride unstained and compliant. He was thirty-two and had the world at his feet. A man of honour and integrity would have held out a hand to help her, not crushed her eager attempts to please. He had shown every sign of being a monster and my heart bled for her, but I felt that at this moment Catherine did not need sympathy and comfort for that would make her weak. She needed all that Valois pride and anger bolstered, in order to keep her head high and her courage intact. So I played the devil's advocate.

'What did you expect, Mademoiselle?' I enquired with a shrug. 'This is a king who has persuaded his subjects to leave their lands and families and follow him over the sea, to risk their lives in a tenuous cause. He did not do that with charm and soft words, he did it with a steely will and vaunting ambition. He is not a fat cat but a sleek lion, like those on his banners. He is proud and fierce and cunning and utterly ruthless and the only thing that frightens him is something he does not understand – such as a beautiful, intelligent, courageous young woman like you.'

Catherine's frown deepened, but her expression changed from anger to intrigue. 'What do you mean, Mette? Are you saying *he* is frightened of *me*? No! That is impossible.'

I had been doing my homework on his English royal highness and I spread my hands to demonstrate my point. 'Consider for a moment. He has never been married. His mother died when he was very young. He has spent his life among soldiers and the only women he may have known are not the sort you have ever met or may ever wish to. He knows nothing of clever, educated, beautiful noblewomen. In fact, he has probably encountered precious few. You should not hate him. Perhaps you should feel sorry for him.'

I heard Agnes' sharp intake of breath and saw Catherine glare at me under beetled brows. Her head was moving slowly from side to side as if what she had heard was incomprehensible. 'No, he is a king,' she protested. 'Women of high birth throw themselves at him. I have seen the ladies at my mother's court, the way they flock around the men of power. Men like King Henry can take their pick. No, no, Mette, I cannot feel sorry for him; not at all.'

'Very well,' I agreed. 'But do not be frightened of him either.

Because, believe me, although he is a lion, when you are his wife you will be able to get close to him, get inside his regal shell and discover the real man, who is not a lion, but more like a pussy cat. For a king, someone who has perfected the role of ruler and soldier and conqueror, that vulnerability is terrifying and enticing all at the same time. He wants it, but at the same time he fears it because he fears that, like Samson, he will lose all his strength.'

Now Catherine's mouth had dropped open in amazement. 'Holy Marie, Mette – you are right! I do not know how you know this, but I instinctively feel that you are right. How *do* you know this?'

I had been concentrating so hard in trying to get my point across that I did not realise how tense I had become. My whole body was taut as a harp string and I had almost forgotten to breathe. Taking in a huge gulp of air, I let it out in a long, slow sigh, which ended in an apologetic little laugh. 'I do not know,' I confessed in bewilderment. 'I have never met a king and I have never been a princess, so you would be perfectly justified in ignoring every word I have just said. In truth, Mademoiselle, I do not know where it came from!'

It was Catherine's turn to laugh. 'Well, I wish I could have bottled it, but instead I will remember it. And I will not be frightened of the king. Every time he is rude or domineering, I will smile and imagine I am stroking his soft fur – and sooner or later, maybe one day I actually will!'

I clapped my hands in delight. 'Bravo, Mademoiselle!' I cried. 'When he first saw you at the Pré du Chat he did not know

464

you, but he realised that you were a prize worth fighting for. Now that he has won you, he worries that although Henry the king is more than worthy of you, Henry the man may not be.'

Catherine sat down on her dressing stool again and handed me the hair brush. 'All right, Mette, on the basis of your argument, Thomas of Clarence is nice to me because he is married and used to the close companionship of a lady.' She paused to consider this statement and seemed to find it satisfactory. 'I think that may be so. His wife's name is Margaret and he clearly holds her in high regard, even though sadly they have no children together. She is the one who is to teach me how to be a queen.'

I began to pull the brush firmly through her hair as I had done so many times. Agnes brought rosewater and sponged her face and throat with dampened linen.

'I think you may have misread that situation, Madame,' Agnes ventured gently. 'Might it not be a kindness to help you adjust to your new life? There must be many differences between the French and the English courts and it would be a shame for a new queen to make mistakes out of ignorance.'

'I expect you are right,' agreed Catherine, closing her eyes to allow Agnes to wield the facecloth freely. 'Perhaps I should have started to learn English earlier. Henry conducts all his court business in English so unless I learn quickly I will not know what is going on. Yes, I can see that I may have been too hasty in rejecting Margaret of Clarence's help. Maybe I will ask King Henry to also provide me with an English tutor.'

So her mood of anger and indignation diminished and in the

end we left Catherine kneeling calmly before her triptych and took ourselves off to the small adjoining chamber where Agnes and I shared a tester bed. Gone were the days of sharing a pallet with Alys. But finding sleep evasive, I lay considering the alarming possibility that history may be repeating itself; that I had engineered the death of one devil's spawn only to see Catherine shackled to another.

—ξξ—

From Catherine, Princess Royal of France to Charles, Dauphin of Viennois,

A final greeting to my beloved brother,

This will be the last letter in which I address my confidences to you, Charles. After my wedding to King Henry, it would be an act of disloyalty, perhaps even treachery, to continue sharing my thoughts with my brother, even though this correspondence is unseen and unsent and will, I suspect, remain so for ever. Perhaps in the future I will find some other recipient.

In the past I have indicated to you that I was struggling to accept that the treaty which brings about my marriage to King Henry also declares him to be the Heir of France and revokes your position as dauphin. While I will never believe that you are not the legitimate son of our father, I have come to believe that the Salic law which brought our grandfather to the throne is not divinely sanctioned and that the claim brought by King Henry's grandfather to be the rightful king of France was therefore legitimate. On that basis I will not be marrying a usurper, but the rightful heir to the throne of France.

Perversly, my intuition that King Henry pursued the marriage out of an emotional spark that ignited between us on first meeting has proved false. Even before we are bedded, I feel now that this will be a dynastic union and not one based on a mutual attraction. And so, while you and I must of necessity become enemies, it does not follow that Henry and I will become friends. This may be of some satisfaction to you, but I confess that it is none to me. Truthfully, I wish it were otherwise.

My wedding is in four days. I would like to believe that, should you have been here, you would have wished me well, but the first being impossible, I suppose the second is unlikely! However I do wish you well and hope to hear news of your continued health and the establishment of a brood of sturdy children with Marie.

Be happy, Charles, as I will try to be, and may God bless us both.
Your loving sister,
Catherine

Written at the Palace of the Counts, Troyes, this day Friday, May 30th 1420.

—ξξ—

I popped my head around the door of the oratory and saw Catherine placing another letter in the secret compartment of her triptych. She shot me a sly glance as she turned the lock and placed the key back in the reliquary around her neck.

'What is it, Mette?' she asked, tucking the reliquary away in her bodice. 'It must be important for you to interrupt me in here.'

'There is a message from the queen, Mademoiselle. She summons you immediately to the great hall. King Henry is on his way to pay his respects.'

Catherine wrinkled her brow, unimpressed. 'I do not think that an *immediate* appearance is necessary, Mette. Is not a bride permitted, no – expected – to keep her groom waiting? I believe I will change my gown. Please fetch the first one that Jacques made for me.'

'You mean the one the queen wished never to see again, Mademoiselle?' I enquired with a smile.

She returned the smile with interest. 'Exactly, Mette,' she nodded. 'And please prepare yourself to come as my train-bearer.'

I was intrigued. With one appearance Catherine intended to challenge two of her mother's expressed dislikes, her taste in gowns and her choice of companions, and she intended to do

468

it in front of King Henry, when the queen would be most annoyed and could make no direct comment. For once I was agog to be her train-bearer!

Personally, I thought Catherine looked wonderful in the aquamarine and cream gown with its unusual styling and beautifully embroidered front panel and as we entered the great hall I could see that King Henry thought so too. He cut short his remarks to the queen and took several long strides to meet the princess as she crossed the hall.

'Catherine!' he said, taking her hand as she curtsied low and, raising her immediately, kissed the hand he held and murmured, 'It lifts my heart to see you.'

'Your grace,' she said as softly as he, but not so soft that my service-trained ears could not hear.

From my position behind her I could not see her face either, but she must have looked up at him through her eyelashes in her inimitably dazzling fashion for I saw the blood rise in the king's good cheek.

'Where have you been, Catherine?' her mother called irritably from her canopied chair. 'His grace has been waiting.'

'But it has been worth the wait,' he said, smiling and leading her to another chair set beside Queen Isabeau's.

I arranged Catherine's train, fielded an angry glare from the queen and retreated to the stone bench on the wall beside the hooded, empty fireplace, close but unobtrusive. I noticed Queen Isabeau's ire increase as she recognised the gown Catherine was wearing and I debated how she might attempt to bring her daughter to heel. Did she know yet, I wondered, that she had already lost control of this last remaining member of her family, just as she had all the others?

'I have come to ask for your help, Catherine,' King Henry said, taking the third seat.

'Help, your grace? What help could I offer such a potent prince?' she responded, unable to hide her surprise.

'It concerns our wedding,' he continued, his eyes studying her closely as if doubtful of her reaction. 'I confess that I was less than satisfied with the ambiance of the cathedral during our betrothal ceremony and I wondered if you would object if we held our wedding somewhere else.'

Catherine inclined her head enquiringly. 'May I ask what it was about the cathedral that you did not like, my lord?'

The queen protested. 'His grace does not need to go into detail, Catherine. If he is unhappy that is all you need to know.'

Catherine ignored the interruption and smiled disarmingly at King Henry. 'I merely wondered if we were dismayed by the same things, sire. For instance the fact that the cathedral is still under construction and there are masons' tools and equipment everywhere and part of the nave stands open to the sky.'

King Henry's smile transformed his face, relieving the stern expression dictated by his scar. 'You felt it too!' he exclaimed. 'It spoiled the atmosphere. We need calm and beauty for this most important occasion, not ladders and scaffolding.'

'I completely agree,' Catherine said, nodding happily. 'Would you permit me to suggest another church?'

King Henry seemed a changed man that day. I swear I saw

a twinkle in his eye as he responded, 'As long as it is the one I was going to suggest.'

And together they both said, 'St Jean au Marché!' and burst out laughing.

'I have worshipped there several times since coming to Troyes,' added the king when their laughter subsided. 'I like the way it sits in the midst of a busy market and yet is a haven of peace.'

'And it has seen many weddings and masses and churchings,' continued Catherine eagerly. 'I myself attended a baptism there recently. I would love our marriage to take place there.'

'Then I will ask the archbishop to arrange it,' King Henry said, then hesitated before raising a new topic. 'But there is one more matter I must mention, which also concerns his grace – it is the matter of his See.'

Catherine raised her eyebrows. 'The Archbishop's See? I thought Sens had fallen recently.' I noticed she avoided mentioning that it was the dauphin's forces which had overrun the city. Her brother was still a thorny topic as far as she was concerned.

King Henry was impressed at her grasp of military progress. 'That is precisely the matter in hand. In return for marrying us, I have promised the archbishop to restore him to his city and his cathedral. I wish to lay siege to Sens immediately after our wedding, Catherine.'

I stifled a gasp and could only imagine Catherine's reaction to this announcement.

'When you say immediately, how soon would that be?' I had the distinct impression that her question was asked through clenched teeth.

471

King Henry had the grace to blush. 'I wish to leave the next day.' He held up a hand apologetically, 'I know – you are offended – but you are marrying a soldier, Catherine. June brings good siege weather and the Pretender is strengthening all his frontline garrisons by the day. We cannot wait.'

There was a tense silence and even the queen had the sense to hold her peace. When Catherine spoke her words were laced with irony. 'It must be frustrating for a soldier like yourself, sire, that the Church permits war during Pentecost but not weddings. Otherwise we could be married today and I could become a camp follower tomorrow.'

I sighed. There had been the stirrings of harmony, but discord had prevailed.

Nothing had changed about the marriage, however, except the location. There was still much to prepare, which now also included packing all Catherine's goods and chattels ready for immediate departure on what she ironically called her *'lune de siège'*. In their attic workrooms above the royal apartments Jacques and Alys stitched away on the princess' wardrobe, while a nursemaid rocked baby Catrine's cradle and I sneaked up for frequent grandmotherly cuddles and playtimes.

Michele of Burgundy kept us straight about the etiquette and form of a royal wedding, explaining the order of the ceremony, the distribution of alms, the programme of feasting and entertainment and the awkward bedding ritual, which apparently would involve the archbishop, all the family members present and even musicians.

'And that reminds me,' she added during this crucial planning meeting, actually turning to address me personally, 'it is time you got busy with your tweezers, Madame Lanière. No royal or noble virgin in France goes to her marriage bed looking less than smooth all over.'

This was a tradition I was familiar with, that young French brides of dynastic families must be brought to their deflowering in a state of hairless purity, a condition that did not of course extend to their crowning glory, which had to be worn loose and flowing as a magnificent statement of their nubility. In painful pursuit of this pristine state, Catherine endured hours of tweezing in intimate places and endured it without complaint – a stoicism which I anticipated might stand her in good stead.

'I suppose the dates of my menses were freely discussed in council when they were deciding on the wedding date,' she observed dryly, as she lay naked under a carefully arranged sheet while I worked as gently as I could on her right armpit. 'I assume you still keep the queen informed, Mette. It cannot be just coincidence that they managed to avoid my time of the month.'

'No, Mademoiselle,' I admitted contritely, 'it is not coincidence. But you can thank King Henry himself that you were spared the indignity of a virginity test. I gather he said that he was prepared to take it on trust.'

I stepped hastily back from my task as Catherine reared up, clutching the sheet around her, her eyes wide with shock. 'Jesu, Mette, I did not know such a thing was a possibility! Whatever would I have done?'

I shrugged. 'I do not think it would have been necessary to do anything, Mademoiselle. I took the precaution of making subtle enquiries. It seems such tests are not intimately physical; that would defeat the purpose, would it not? But I am glad King Henry refused it, for dignity's sake.'

'Yes, that was good of him.' Catherine gave me a troubled look. 'Did he really say that? That he was prepared to trust me?'

'So I am told,' I nodded, following her train of thought. 'And so he can,' I asserted firmly. 'God knows he can.'

33

'When we were girls at the convent we used to day-dream about what our husbands would be like. Do you remember, Agnes?'

Catherine's voice held a far-away note, which made me wonder if I had put a little too much poppy juice into the calming posset I had insisted she drink on rising. Outside the chamber window the early morning sky showed a milky haze and weak sunshine cast long, faint shadows across the waterside gardens. Despite an overnight downpour, it seemed unlikely that rain would spoil the royal wedding day.

'Of course I remember,' nodded Agnes, beckoning Alys to help her gather up a heavy under-skirt made of precious cloth of silver and hemmed with broad gold lace. 'We imagined you marrying a handsome, royal prince – and you are going to do just that, this very day!' Intensely aware of the bride's jangling nerves, Agnes' words were warm with encouragement. Carefully she and Alys lifted the silver skirt high and slipped it over Catherine's head. It fell about her with a rustling sigh and they set about arranging the folds and tying the points at the waist.

I knelt at Catherine's feet, proffering the pearl-encrusted satin slippers she would wear for her wedding. Jacques' exquisite gown lay like a lifeless puppet across the bed beside us and the tailor himself paced the ante-chamber, anxiously awaiting the call to come and make last-minute adjustments when the princess was dressed.

'But we imagined him kind and gentle as well as royal and handsome, did we not?' said Catherine wistfully. She appeared almost unaware of what her attendants were clothing her in. The prized Venetian mirror stood close at hand, but she had not so much as glanced at her reflection. 'I suppose little girls can never imagine any other sort of bridegroom.'

Gently I felt under the heavy gold lace hem of the under-skirt for one foot after the other and she put a hand on my shoulder for balance as I pushed them into the slippers. Helped by Alys, Agnes went to collect the filmy wedding gown from the bed. 'King Henry is chivalrous enough to satisfy any young maid's dream,' she observed. 'He will treat you with honour and respect, I have no doubt.'

'You may be right.' Catherine's voice was muffled by the folds of fabric as the gown was pulled down over her body. Obediently, she held out her arms to allow the two helpers to pull on the separate sleeves. 'But we did not dream of honour and respect. We dreamed of love. How young and silly we were.' Over our heads she gazed about the room as the three of us fussed around her. 'I may never sleep in this chamber again,' she announced, as if suddenly arriving in the present. 'Tomorrow we leave for Sens and who knows where King Henry will lead his army after that. I am just so thankful that you are all coming with me. I do not think I could have borne to be without you.'

The decision I had been mulling over for days had been made for me. I had not needed to choose between staying with Alys and going with Catherine, because she had invited Jacques to be her personal tailor and he and Alys had agreed to bring the baby and become part of Catherine's household, at least for the time being. It had been a massive decision, but for Jacques in particular it was an offer he could not refuse. So the apprentice was to keep the house in the Rue de l'Aiguille ticking over and my little family was to join the wandering caravan that formed the all-conquering English king's retinue. As to where it would lead us, only time would tell.

I did not attend Catherine's wedding Mass. Large though it was, the church of St Jean au Marché was no cathedral and by mid-morning it was so crammed with royalty, priests, lords, ladies and courtiers that although Catherine had put me on the guest-list, I knew there would be little chance of my seeing anything through the throng. So, along with Alys and Jacques and a thousand other citizens, I watched from the marketplace as the bride and groom met under a gold canopy at the entrance to the church and exchanged their marriage vows before the Archbishop of Sens and the people of Troyes.

A hushed silence fell while King Henry's deep, clear voice invoked the Trinity – '*In nomine Patris, et Filii, et Spiritus Sancti,* In the name of the Father, and of the Son, and of the Holy Ghost' – and performed the ritual of sliding the wedding ring over the first and second fingers of Catherine's left hand, before pushing it firmly down onto the third. I had not yet seen it but Catherine had told me that the ring was fashioned from rare red gold mined in the hills of Wales, Henry's first royal demesne, and studded with rubies to honour the scarlet and gold of the English sovereign's three-lion standard. I felt my heart thump in my chest as the realisation hit me that its solid presence on Catherine's finger symbolised her irrevocable union with this man of immense power whom she scarcely knew. One man of power had already done his best to ruin her life; would this one be the making of it or would the ring prove to be a shackle that fettered her to a future of fear and disappointment? Was the real Henry of Monmouth the kind and compassionate companion of her schoolgirl dreams or a slash and burn creature of the *chevauchée*? Crossing myself, I put up a silent prayer to St Catherine to protect her namesake from further harm.

As the ring slid home, a great cheer went up and the crowd surged against the crossed pikes of the guards ringing the church steps. 'Long live the Princess Catherine, long live the bride and groom!' they chanted, their voices swelling louder and louder on a tide of enthusiasm fuelled by the emotion of the ceremony and the spectacle it afforded. King Henry had given Catherine a wedding gift of six milk-white horses to carry her litter and the magnificence of this equipage, combined with the brilliance of King Henry's escort of knightly retainers, stirred the mass of onlookers into an emotional frenzy which the guards struggled to contain. It was an outward manifestation of my own inner turmoil. It was all so different from the quiet vows Alys and Jacques had exchanged on the steps of this very church not nine months before. Glancing across at them, I saw that their hands were clasped as they relived the moment. But of course the glamorous pair on the church steps today was not just any young couple. When Archbishop Savoisy lifted his hand and waited patiently for silence, he formally presented the newlyweds to the people, using the full list of their honours and titles and it became evident to all that this union was an event that would change the world.

'Citizens of Troyes, people of France, subjects of our most gracious sovereign King Charles the sixth,' boomed the prelate, well used to making his voice carry to large congregations. 'I present to you as man and wife Henry and Catherine, by divine grace King and Queen of England and Ireland, Heir and Heiress of France, Prince and Princess of Wales, Duke and Duchess of Lancaster, Duke and Duchess of Normandy and Duke and Duchess of Guienne. Let those who are joined by God be never divided by man.'

As the cheers erupted once more and the bells of St Jean sounded a joyful peal, I exchanged awestruck glances with Alys. The nervous girl we had dressed that morning and calmed with kind words and kisses was now the queen and consort of a man who could claim dominion over what seemed like half of Christendom.

'Jacques' gown looks superb, does it not, Ma?' Alys shouted proudly above the tumult. She turned to whisper something in her husband's ear, making Jacques smile and blush, banishing the tenseness and exhaustion which had shadowed his face for the past three weeks.

'You are indeed a genius, Jacques!' I declared at the top of my voice, causing several of those nearest in the crush to turn and stare at the bashful young tailor. 'The gown is a triumph!'

Alys was right, it was a glorious creation, and Catherine looked every inch the queen she had just become. Standing slender and graceful beside her broad-shouldered husband, she shyly acknowledged the crowd's ovation, her natural and striking beauty dazzlingly offset by the impact of her attire. Jacques' gown and the mane of flaxen hair spilling down from her jewelled gold coronet made her look like an angel in a gospel illumination.

In shape the gown was a classic houppelande, but the difference was that Jacques had tailored it in two layers. The outer robe was made of royal fleur-de-lis blue gauze scattered with gold and this delicate filmy fabric flowed in one seamless sweep from a tiny form-fitting bodice over the cloth of silver under-skirt. From afar the combination gave the impression of stars glinting against a moonlit sky and when Catherine lifted her skirt to walk, there were glimpses of the thick gold lace on the hem of the under-skirt, which caught the light like sunrise streaking in the eastern sky. It was a gown both demure and sensuous, and neither was it overshadowed by the massive jewelled clasp and grand sweep of her mother's royal mantle, which swung from Catherine's shoulders in majestic folds and spilled down the church steps in a river of vibrant scarlet.

I watched Agnes de Blagny and the rest of the young ladies move forward to pick up the heavy train and King Henry turned about and took Catherine's hand to lead her into the church for the nuptial Mass, but the crowd was not content. For them the marriage rites were not complete.

'The kiss!' they chanted. 'Kiss! Kiss! Kiss!'

With a brief smile and a wave of acknowledgement, King Henry complied with their demand and bent to plant the nuptial kiss on his new wife's lips. It was a gentle salute but a boldly possessive one and even from twenty yards away I could see the hot colour flood Catherine's cheeks. As they moved towards the door, the groom turned his head to flash another smile at the increasingly frenzied crowd. Manifestly King Henry understood the value of public approbation and knew exactly how to get it.

While the nobles and officials celebrated Mass with the newly married couple and Alys and Jacques went back to their baby, I slipped down a lane off the Rue Nôtre Dame and collected a phial of fresh chicken blood from a butcher's shop I knew. Then I hurried back to the palace, concealing my purchase in the pocket of my sleeve. I had told the butcher I wanted it for a poultice for my injured grand-daughter and felt that God would forgive me the lie.

The wedding feast lasted from noon until dusk and was conducted according to high court ceremonial, where royal bride and groom were served by their noble kinsmen. Therefore the opening presentation of the wedding cup of spiced mead was performed by Thomas of Clarence, acting as butler. King Charles had not been present at the church but he came to the feast and was corralled between the trestle and the arm-rests of his high-backed throne, placed between Queen Isabeau and the

481

archbishop. I spotted two of the king's 'minders' hovering in the shadows at the back of the dais, but there was no call for their attention because the child-like monarch was enraptured by one of the gifts presented at the start of the meal.

King Henry had given King Charles a gold and silver chess set but his gift to Queen Isabeau was an exotic red and blue popinjay in a gilded cage and it looked as if the chess set might lie untouched and tarnishing through the years but the popinjay would entertain the French king for many a beguiling hour. He insisted it should be placed beside him during the rest of the feast where it squawked and preened, vying for his attention with the tumblers and the jugglers.

Catherine had been in urgent discussion with the master of the king's household about the gift she had in mind for her new husband, but she had told no one elsewhat she intended until the previous evening, when she had shown it privately to Agnes and confided that the idea had been inspired by my birthday present to her. The gift lay, wrapped in cloth of gold, on the high table, where Agnes had placed it just before the meal began.

The ceremonial High Steward for the evening was the English Earl of Warwick, who had so intrigued Catherine during the build-up to her first meeting with Henry at the Pré du Chat. Now he came to the front of the dais to thump his gilded staff loudly on the wooden floor. 'Your royal graces, my noble Lords, Ladies and honoured Guests, pray silence for the Bride, our most gracious Queen Catherine!'

Catherine had confessed to me her utter terror at the thought

482

of making her first public speech, but she was determined to mark her personal and precious gift to Henry. An attendant pulled back the heavy bridal throne to give her room to stand and a tremor in her voice betrayed her nerves as she began.

'My royal parents pray forgive me if I address my remarks to my new husband and sovereign lord, King Henry.' She made a little bow to him and he nodded his head solemnly in return, curiousity creasing his brow. 'I believe it is not customary in England for the bride to make a gift to her groom on their wedding day, but in France we do so and I wish to acknowledge and express my gratitude for the great honour my lord has done me today in making me his wife.'

There was a burst of applause from the rest of the guests as Catherine picked up the gold-wrapped parcel with two hands and placed it carefully in front of King Henry who rose to acknowledge it. Catherine continued, her voice growing stronger as the words began to flow more freely.

'God the Father has greatly favoured your endeavours, my lord, and I pray that from this day forward the passion of God the Son will protect you from all bodily harm and that the grace of God the Holy Spirit will bless us throughout our marriage. This gift symbolises and invokes the power of the Holy Trinity, which I believe you hold in great reverence. It brings with it my vow of love, loyalty and fealty, until death shall part us.'

Sinking to her knees, Catherine clasped Henry's right hand and pressed her lips to his coronation ring in the tradition of oath-making and, in return, Henry raised her from her knees and kissed her cheek. Then he crossed himself reverently before opening her gift. He drew back the folds of gold cloth to expose a polished wooden box inlaid with gold and jewels. Inside this was a crimson velvet purse, and inside the purse lay what I knew was a small, brightly enamelled gold reliquary on a cunningly wrought chain. Lifting it out, Henry took several seconds to locate the hinge mechanism, but at last he found the trick of it and with surprising delicacy freed its interlocking halves. No one had dared breathe while this was achieved and now an awe-struck intake of air spread like a wave from where he stood, the reliquary held open to reveal a transparent crystal phial in which a vicious-looking thorn marked with a dark stain was encased.

'It is from the true crown of thorns that was brought to France by St Louis on his return from the Crusades. Allow me to put it on for you, my lord.' Catherine reached across to take the reliquary from him and he bent his head to let her fasten the chain around his neck. 'May it protect you from the devil and all his agents – injury, disease and treachery.'

'A prayer we all echo a hundredfold!' cried the archbishop, raising his hand in benediction.

Henry kissed the reliquary reverently before tucking it into the neck of his doublet. 'I thank you, my queen,' he said, clearly much moved. 'Your gift will never leave me; that I swear on the name of Him whose blood is on it.'

There was applause from the guests and then Warwick's staff thumped once more as the earl announced the first course. Catherine and Henry subsided back into their seats to begin the feasting. A surfeit of food and drink followed through course after course, when the bride and groom were served skilfully and gracefully by Thomas of Clarence and Philippe of Burgundy and shared a cup and trencher together with the traditional intimacy of newlyweds. So many were the toasts and so elaborate the speeches that accompanied them, that it took me by surprise when, shortly before darkness fell, the music suddenly stopped and Warwick's staff thumped loudly yet again. 'The bride and groom will now retire,' he announced.

There was a ragged cheer from the more circumspect guests and a chorus of cat-calls and suggestive remarks from the better-lubricated. A flush spread over Catherine's cheeks, but King Henry smiled indulgently at the lewd taunts and raised his hand for quiet.

'My good friends, you may carouse until the small hours if you choose, but we all depart early tomorrow morning for Sens. Therefore I and my bride salute your stamina, crave your indulgence and bid you good night.' With that he turned to take his bride's hand and lead her from the hall.

I had to scramble for the door but fortunately, even though she had removed the cumbersome mantle for the meal, Catherine's skirts were so voluminous and heavy that she could not walk far without her maids of honour to manoeuvre them for her. Consequently I managed to reach the grand solar before the bridal procession arrived.

I was setting a taper to the fire when the great double doors of the chamber flew back and King Henry led Catherine through, followed by his squires and her ladies. I sank to my knees, head bowed.

'And who is this?' asked the king. 'I think I have seen her before, carrying your train, Catherine?'

'You have, my lord,' replied Catherine. 'And I am happy to present her to you first and foremost, for this is Madame Lanière, my beloved nurse Guillaumette, who has been with me for most of my life. She is now keeper of my robes and has been like a mother to me.'

'Indeed?' King Henry made a flapping gesture with his hand. 'Rise, Madame Lanière if you please.'

I tried to rise smoothly, but nerves made me clumsy so I fear that I shook my veiled headdress slightly askew.

'My own old nurse still tries to treat me like a child when we meet. Are you guilty of that, Madame?'

I gulped, unable to think of an instant response. 'I – I hope not, your grace,' I stuttered. 'I am Queen Catherine's loyal servant.'

'My *most* loyal servant,' interposed Catherine with a smile. 'Who loves me well – as an adult, not as a child.'

'Good.' When he chose to aim it at one person, King Henry's smile was a knee-weakening weapon and I felt mine begin to shake under its aim. But his next remark was businesslike in the extreme. 'Then you will have prepared her well for her wedding night no doubt.'

I shot a glance at Catherine and saw her cheeks flare. It inspired a reckless anger in me for I could not bear her fragile confidence to suffer any dent.

'My dearest lady was born to be the wife of a great king, your grace,' I answered defiantly. 'There is no princess to match her in the world.'

'Ha!' King Henry's laugh was a surprise. 'I think your nurse is trying to tell me I do not deserve you, Catherine!' he exclaimed. 'She is indeed loyal and I prize loyalty above all things. I will leave you to her tender ministrations. We must make haste. The archbishop will be here before long to give us his blessing!'

An adjoining room had been prepared for King Henry to disrobe and he departed with his group of body squires. The ladies-in-waiting began to bustle about their various duties, chattering in low voices while Agnes issued them with instructions. For a brief few moments Catherine and I were able to embrace.

'I am so frightened, Mette,' she murmured. 'I wish you could sleep by my bed as you used to do!'

'Every bride feels like that but you have nothing to fear,' I tried to reassure her. 'The phial is hidden where I showed you and I will be right outside the door. If you call, I will come.'

Catherine drew back from our embrace, gazed at me soulfully and said, shaking her head, 'I do not have a good feeling about this.'

34

D ue to the influence of alcohol and excessive prurience on the part of the principal guests, the ceremony of bedding the bride and groom proved to be exactly the awkward and embarrassing episode Catherine had predicted.

When the archbishop arrived at the head of a procession of priests and family members, Catherine and Henry were waiting solemnly in their fur-trimmed chamber-robes on either side of the great bed. Each was ceremonially placed between the sheets by their closest relatives; Catherine by her mother and sister and Henry by his two brothers. Holy water was sprinkled over them by the queen's confessor, the Bishop of Beauvais, and then the worldly Archbishop Savoisy began his prayers, which were progressively salacious and seemed to go on forever. He prayed for the success of the union, for the gift of children, for the approval of Heaven, for the blessing of the Virgin, for the sanction of their individual patron saints, for the fertility of the bride, for the virility of the bridegroom, for the fecundity of their bodies, for the mutuality of their desires . . . on and on and on went the prayers, straying into such arcane realms of secular and canonical fancy that many in the room began to titter and smirk. It became very obvious that drink had been taken as freely by the priesthood as by the laity.

'We thank you, your grace, for your prayers and intercessions.' Eventually King Henry could take no more and interrupted, his tetchy tone commanding attention even when delivered from between the sheets. 'Now, since the night grows ever shorter, perhaps we may be left to our own prayers.'

'I trust it will not only be *prayers* you'll be about, brother!' exclaimed Thomas of Clarence, whose uncharacteristically boorish leer was a side effect of the bridal mead. 'You'll get no heir by wish and prayer. Ha, ha! I am a poet in faith!'

'And a very bad one, Tom!' cried Henry in exasperation. 'Get back to your wine and take the rest of this rabble with you. Can you not see that my wife is tired?'

'Not so quick to use the word "wife", brother! That has still to be consumed,' retorted his inebriated sibling.

'I think you'll find the word is consummated,' Henry told his brother flatly and turned to the archbishop. 'Can you not bring some order into these proceedings, your grace? Or you, Madame?' He aimed this at the queen, who wore a smug smile and did not appear to be standing too steadily on her feet.

'Ah, you are an eager bridegroom, my lord!' she exclaimed archly. 'Take care that you do not test my little daughter too severely. Remember her delicate virgin state!'

Seeing that he would receive no help from this source, King Henry turned to his younger brother John of Bedford, a quieter and soberer presence at his side. 'John, will you come to our aid? We appreciate all your kind wishes and advice, but enough is enough! And please, take those musicians with you when you go!'

A band of merry minstrels had jostled into the chamber at the tail of the procession and struck up a tune on their lutes and tabors that had some of the younger lords and ladies twirling merrily together at the foot of the bed. I began to understand why the queen had insisted on using the spacious great solar for the bedding ceremony. She clearly had foreknowledge of the extent of the high-jinks to be expected on such an occasion. Catherine and Henry, on the other hand, evidently had not.

I hovered as close as I could to Catherine's side of the bed and observed her become more and more dismayed by the volleys of innuendo. In the capacious bag-sleeve of my best gown lay the flask containing the calming potion I had dosed her with that morning and I berated myself for not giving her another nip of it as we were helping her to disrobe, but there had been too many of her ladies about and I had felt the moment too public. As the level of noise and distractions increased however, I managed to slip the rest of the potion into the jug of wine that had been provided to sustain the young couple during their overnight endeavours, considering it likely that after being the butt of so much coarse banter they would be more than likely to partake of it.

At length the honeymoon cup was administered and, with the tactful encouragement of John of Bedford, the rowdy party slowly and reluctantly vacated the chamber and returned along the passage to the great hall, leaving a fuming bridegroom and an agitated bride propped side by side on the bed in fraught silence. Whispering to Catherine that I would be just outside the door, I pulled the heavy curtain along her side of the bed and watched as Henry's body squire did the same on his. Then we both bowed at the end of the bed, drew the final curtains and backed away, closing the door behind us and leaving King Henry and his new queen alone together for the very first time. The squire and I rolled our eyes expressively at each other before settling ourselves on stools in the ante-chamber. Outside in the passage we could hear the guards on the exterior door stamping their feet to keep themselves alert.

Less than an hour had elapsed when I was startled out of a doze by Catherine calling through the door in a small voice. 'Mette! Mette, are you there?'

Responding to the squire's raised eyebrow with a shrug, I carefully opened the door and slipped into the chamber. It was in darkness save for a glimmer of light from the dying embers of the fire. Catherine crouched naked and shivering in its glow, hugging herself with her thin arms and sobbing silently. I ran to fetch her chamber-robe and wrapped it around her.

'Mademoiselle, Mademoiselle, ssh,' I soothed, rocking her gently from side to side. Quietly I led her towards a curtained archway which led to a small oratory off the solar, glancing towards the great bed as we passed. The curtains were closed but I could hear the sound of heavy breathing from within. Evidently her new husband was fast asleep.

In the meagre light of a sacred lamp, the agonised figure of Christ gazed down on us from the crucifix and we sank onto the prie-dieu before the small altar. I passed Catherine a kerchief from my sleeve and lit a votive candle from the lamp as she wiped her eyes and nose.

'What has happened, Mademoiselle?' I asked gently. 'Did he hurt you?'

She shook her head earnestly. 'No, no, Mette, nothing like that but I badly need your advice. In truth I do not know what to do.'

'About what?' I probed, relieved to hear that despite her maulings by Burgundy, apparently she had not taken fright at King Henry's advances, as I had feared she might.

Catherine did not answer immediately. 'I do not know how to tell you,' she whispered at length. Although his breathing had not sounded like that of a man on the brink of consciousness, we were both speaking in undertones, fearful of waking the sleeping king.

'Start at the beginning,' I suggested. 'What happened after we left? Did you talk?'

'A little,' she nodded. 'But he was angry. Very angry. Oh, not with me but with his brother and my mother. I think he is not a man who likes to be made fun of.'

'Ah yes, I can imagine. So what did he do?'

'He got up and prowled about, declaiming against the whole tradition of bedding the bride and groom, calling it a barbaric procedure. Then he poured some wine for us both. I took a small sip but he drank his in one big gulp and then took another cup and drank that. I think he was trying to calm himself down.'

What she said made my heart skip a few beats. If King Henry had drunk half the jug of the spiked wine in such a short time it was no wonder he was sleeping so soundly now!

'And did it calm him?' I asked, although I already knew the answer.

Catherine smiled briefly through her woebegone expression. 'Oh yes. In fact he got quite drowsy. Eventually he lay down beside me and I am sure he wanted – intended – to consummate our marriage, but instead he started snoring!' Despite her anxiety she giggled. 'He just fell asleep.'

I shared her mirth with a smile but also felt compelled to make a swift check on King Henry, so I pressed a finger to my lips and crept away to the next chamber. Cautiously I opened the bed curtains and by the light of the fire I scanned the sleeping figure lying amongst the rumpled bedclothes. The king's usually stern expression was softened by deep sleep and he lay on his side so that the livid scar on his left cheek was hidden in the dip of the pillow. He was breathing through his mouth which was slightly open and one naked shoulder protruded from the white sheet. He looked almost boyish in the peace of his slumber. I breathed a sigh of relief. Fortunately the potion had not been too strong for such a fit man, but I reckoned he would sleep soundly until morning.

I returned to the oratory to find Catherine in earnest prayer before the altar but she crossed herself immediately and turned to me when I entered. 'I was praying to the Virgin, but I think perhaps she is not the one to help me. What shall I do, Mette? He has not consummated the marriage, but I do not know whether he knows that. So should I use the blood to stain the sheet or not?'

I saw her problem. If Henry had taken her virginity, then

there should be blood, except of course that we knew better. But if there was no sign to show the world then he would appear impotent, which I doubted his pride could stand. There was risk involved but, after some consideration, I made my decision.

'I think you should use it,' I said positively. 'I am not an expert on mankind, but I think if you assure him that he consummated the marriage before he fell asleep, he will believe you. But you will have to do it sweetly and demurely, Mademoiselle, so that he is completely convinced. No tears or tantrums, just shyly but confidently. Can you do that?'

Catherine had recovered enough to twinkle at me. 'Oh yes, Mette. I can be really sweet and demure when I try, do you not think?'

'Yes, Mademoiselle, I do.' I gave her a lop-sided smile and a little hug. 'Have you found the phial?'

She nodded eagerly. 'It is safe. I will do it now and give the phial to you and then there is no risk of it being found. Wait here.'

'Use only a little, Mademoiselle, and just streak it on the bottom sheet, as if you have started your menses as you slept.'

In the light of the candle I saw the whites of her eyes. 'I do not think I shall sleep at all, Mette,' she sighed. 'I shall worry about Henry's reaction when he wakes.'

'But you need rest, Mademoiselle,' I told her. 'Take a little more of the wine. That will help you sleep.'

She glanced at me sharply then. 'Will it, Mette? Will it indeed? Then, after I have drunk some, I think you should take the jug and wash it.'

I wondered if she could see the blush that spread over my own face. 'Very well. I will wash it out before I leave and bring some more wine.'

'Be very quiet when you do,' she warned. 'I should not care to see you suffer the wrath of King Henry if you wake him!'

As I poured the contents of the wine jug down the latrine sluice in the guarderobe and swilled it out with water, it occurred to me rather too late that what I had done was a treasonable action. I remembered how the poppy juice had eased my mother's passing into the next world and put my hand to my throat. I could almost feel the tightening of the hangman's rope. It had been one thing to calm the nerves of a jittery bride and quite another to poison the King of England. I was lucky to have got away with it, if indeed I had.

I carried the now-empty jug past the curtained bed and listened intently to the steady breathing of its occupants. Unable to resist a quick peek, I opened a small gap in the curtains. Catherine's hair was spread across the pillow in a golden wave that gleamed in the dying firelight and several tresses trailed over Henry's outstretched arm. Should I ever have been asked to bear witness, I would not have hesitated in saying that they looked like a couple who had fallen asleep, sated after prolonged and successful love-making.

When I left the solar I handed the empty jug to the squire with a wink. 'They may require more wine when they wake,' I said meaningfully. 'It has been thirsty work.'

Knowing that there was unlikely to be another call from either of the newlyweds until morning, I felt able to pull the cushions from a window embrasure in the ante-room and lay them on the floor as a makeshift bed for myself. I was woken when King Henry's commanding voice summoned his body squire and told him to 'Send in the queen's woman!' I noticed that the original squire whom I had sent for the wine had now been replaced by several new arrivals plus a pair of clerks, armed with letters for their master's attention. King Henry obviously started work immediately on waking.

Catherine looked cheerful and refreshed when I brought her chamber-robe to the great bed. 'Have you slept well, your grace?' I asked, careful to use the correct form of address in the hearing of the king.

'Like a baby,' replied Catherine, stretching luxuriously. 'What is the hour, Mette? Has the Prime bell rung yet?'

'It has indeed, your grace, some time ago. Will you bathe before you dress?'

The curtains were still drawn around the bed, but with the room full of men she slid her arms into the robe before climbing out from under the covers. I caught a glimpse of the blood-stained sheet as she emerged and concealed a satisfied smile. A menial had brought warm water and placed it ready for washing.

Catherine glanced across at her new husband who was busy studying the correspondence his clerks had brought. 'I cannot very well wash while all these men are in the room,' she remarked loudly.

King Henry looked up at the sound of her raised voice. 'Indeed not,' he agreed, giving her what I could only describe as a complaisant look. 'I will withdraw and let you make your toilette,

Madame. It would please me if you would attend Mass with me as soon as you are dressed.'

Catherine made a small bow in his direction. 'As my lord wishes,' she said agreeably.

Agnes arrived when King Henry had left the chamber and we set about arranging bowls of water, wash-cloths and towels. For a time I speculated about the cause of the rather secretive expression on Catherine's face, but it was not long before she revealed it.

'I suppose I should tell you that you were right, Mette,' she began. 'He did believe me.'

Agnes raised an enquiring eyebrow in my direction but said nothing and I passed a damp cloth to Catherine before commenting. 'I am very glad to hear it, your grace,' I said, mentally willing her to say more but not daring to ask.

'But he decided that in order to satisfy himself he should repeat the process. So you can rest easy now for the marriage is well and truly consummated. No doubt the queen will be asking for the sheets.'

Catherine wielded the cloth with vigorous thoroughness and handed it back, while Agnes set about her with a soft linen towel.

'Madame will be sending one of her ladies to collect it as soon as she rises,' I told her.

'That may not be for hours yet, judging by her enjoyment of the wedding mead,' remarked Catherine a little sourly. 'I will be surprised if she ventures forth early enough to bid us farewell.'

But she misjudged her mother on this occasion. Both King Charles and Queen Isabeau were present in the Church of St Etienne when Catherine and Henry arrived for Mass. In a rush of circumspection the queen even waited until they were gathered for breakfast in the great hall to broach the subject that was uppermost in her mind.

'I hope we may conclude from your grace's cheerful countenance that all has been done according to God's holy ordinance,' she probed as King Henry washed his hands in the bowl of warm water offered by a kneeling squire.

'You may so conclude, Madame, as long as it is the last mention made of what should henceforth remain confidential between my wife and me,' responded Henry, drying his hands on a napkin. 'Suffice it to say that the terms of our marriage contract are fulfilled and the Treaty of Troyes is not only signed but sealed.'

'We shall need the evidence,' persisted the queen, who seemed miraculously to be suffering no ill effects from the previous night's festivities.

'And then I told her that you were at that moment delivering the nuptial sheet to the Baroness Hochfeld, Mette,' Catherine revealed later in private, as she described this exchange in gleeful detail. 'So you see, all your schemes and machinations have come to a satisfactory conclusion.'

'Excellent, Mademoiselle,' I responded with a conspiratorial smile. 'And were your other fears unfounded as well?'

'If you mean, did I shrink from my husband's touch, no I did not,' Catherine admitted. 'So at least I denied the devil duke his legacy. However, I can only conclude that what the nuns told me was correct. The marriage bed is a duty, not a pleasure.'

'Ah, Mademoiselle!' I sighed, struck by a sudden memory of those thrilling tumbles in the fragrant hayloft with my handsome Jean-Michel. 'I truly hope that one day you will discover that those purse-lipped nuns were wrong.'

35

From a military point of view, King Henry had been right to waste no time in laying siege to Sens since defence preparations by the dauphin's constable had been far from adequate and it was an easy victory. Consternation had grown among the townsfolk as Henry's formidable ranks of guns and bombards gradually assembled to blast their missiles at the city's walls, and after only twelve days these angry citizens managed to overcome the small garrison of knights and men-at-arms and throw the gates open to the attackers.

With tears in his eyes, Archbishop Savoisy celebrated Mass in his beloved cathedral of St Etienne and in the congregation, alongside the new Heir of France and his bride, were the King and Queen of France and the Duke and Duchess of Burgundy. King Henry had insisted that the people should be shown that behind the guns and soldiers their country now had a strong and united leadership, which would bring the rebellious pretender to heel like a naughty young puppy. So the combined courts of France and Burgundy had travelled from Troyes to Sens and the local populace had never seen such a glittering cavalcade of royalty and nobility.

The only person who was not happy with the swift surrender of Sens and the grandiose arrival of the rest of her family was Catherine. She had enjoyed her brief stay at the archbishop's summer palace, enlivened by some riding and hawking in the lush parkland around it and visits from King Henry, who rode the fifteen miles from Sens almost every evening. It had given the newlyweds a chance to get to know each other and I began to wonder if Catherine was beginning to feel a little more enamoured of her enigmatic spouse.

'Last night in our chamber he played the harp, Mette,' she confided one sunny morning, when she had invited me to walk with her in the grounds of the palace. 'He learned it as a boy in Wales, where he tells me there are many fine harpers. It reminded me of Charles. Do you remember him playing to us sometimes at the Hôtel de St Pol?'

I did remember, but not with much pleasure, for Prince Charles had tended to consider his skills rather better than they actually were. 'So you have a love of music in common then,' I remarked, dodging the question. 'That is good.'

'Oh, not just music; he has read widely as well – much more than I have – but we share an admiration for the meditations of St Gregory. I told him that I thought for a pope St Gregory was a very down-to-earth individual and he laughed and said he had never looked at him that way.' She halted in the dappled shade of an oak tree and fiddled with her betrothal ring, a giant sapphire that had belonged to Eleanor of Provence, an ancestor common to them both. She studied it so intently that I suspected her thoughts were actually elsewhere, but where they were took me completely by surprise. 'Even when we are alone he is still very formal, though.'

'Formal?' I echoed with a frown. 'How do you mean?'

Catherine blushed. 'Well I suppose it does not matter, but he never really touches me, even in bed. Oh, he takes me often enough, but it is very brief and perfunctory. I worry that I will not become *enceinte* if he is not a little more . . . er . . . assiduous.' Sheepishly she raised her eyes to mine. 'It is probably foolish of me, Mette, but I believe that I will not fall pregnant unless I feel more than I do. You are the only person I can talk to about this. Should I not feel some – how shall I put it? – some sense of union?'

I frowned, not entirely sure that I understood precisely what she was getting at, but aware that even mentioning the subject indicated that she was very concerned. 'That is a hard question to answer but I am glad that you feel able to ask me, Mademoiselle.' I paused, searching for a way to help her without embarrassing us both. 'I am no farmer, but I do know that if crops are to germinate it is important that the seed is planted in the right conditions and at the right depth in the soil.'

She thought about that for a minute then clearly decided she did not like my analogy and tossed her head dismissively. 'I do not think that planting is the problem, Mette. As I said, I am probably being naive, thinking that there should be more to the act of love than there is.'

She suddenly strode on in a rather agitated manner, as if the subject made her restless and I had to break into a jog to keep up with her. 'It is early days, Mademoiselle,' I said breathlessly.

'You hardly know each other. You may be worrying unnecessarily. Give it time.'

I almost cannoned into her as she stopped and rounded on me. 'But time is what I do not have, Mette! The treaty made King Henry the Heir of France and his issue will be his heirs. He needs a son and it is my duty to provide him with one sooner rather than later, do you not think?'

I looked at her anxious face and felt a surge of compassion. She was only eighteen and yet so much was expected of her. I nodded sympathetically. 'Yes, I do, but it has been but ten days. For all you know you may already be pregnant.'

Her face crumpled at that. 'No. I am not. I suppose I should send a message to King Henry that my courses have come. He will not visit me now, I expect.'

She looked so crestfallen that I impulsively laid a consoling hand on her arm. 'I will see to the message,' I said. 'But perhaps he will come anyway.'

He did not, which sent a message of its own, and when King Charles and Queen Isabeau and the Duke and Duchess of Burgundy joined them in Sens, that did not please her either.

'It is bad enough having to share my honeymoon with a siege!' she fumed. 'Now my entire family has arrived. I married the enemy to get away from them!'

However, partial relief was not far off. After the service of thanksgiving in Sens, the French king and queen stayed on with the archbishop, while Catherine and Michele travelled to the Burgundy stronghold of Bray on Seine, a few miles upriver from the crucial town of Montereau which had been held by the dauphin's forces ever since Jean the Fearless had been murdered there, and which King Henry and Duke Philippe intended to take back. Several of the knights involved in the murder were believed to be still holed up there and were high on the list of Philippe's wanted men.

During the journey to Bray, tension built between Catherine and Michele because the latter seemed unable to talk of any subject other than her husband's mission to find his father's body and bring his murderers to justice, a topic Catherine tried constantly to avoid since it always included robust criticism of Charles. At Bray, unfortunately, although comfortable and well situated among gardens and hunting parks, the castle was not large and the sisters were much thrown together. Nor did their husbands visit very often, being anxious to oversee every aspect of the siege at Montereau. So Catherine was almost relieved when a thousand knights and archers rode in as reinforcements for King Henry's siege army, because travelling under their protection was the Duchess of Clarence, the lady who was to introduce her to English ways.

Margaret of Clarence turned out to be a tall, beautiful woman in her mid thirties and possessed of a warm and gracious manner. She had brought her young daughter Joan with her, a copper-blonde cherub of a girl of fourteen who reminded me vividly of Catherine when she had emerged from the convent. During their introduction in the great hall at Bray, Catherine made her first attempt at speaking English but became so frustrated at not being able to make herself understood that she soon lapsed into French, which both ladies also spoke.

'Forgive me,' Catherine said, red-faced. 'I promise to work harder at my lessons and perhaps Lady Joan will help me. But, Madame, I understood from your husband that there were no children from your marriage, so naturally I am surprised to meet your pretty daughter. Were you married before then?'

Margaret of Clarence laughed. 'Yes, your grace. I was married at fourteen to the Earl of Somerset, one of King Henry's Beaufort uncles, and we had six children in the ten years before he died. Two of my sons are knights in the retinue of their stepfather, the Duke of Clarence, and my youngest son, Edmund, is one of King Henry's body squires. I am surprised you have not met him.'

'I have probably seen him, but the king does not introduce his squires by name,' Catherine said. 'And where are your other two children, Madame? Have you had to leave them in England?'

A shadow crossed the duchess' face. 'My eldest son Henry died two years ago at the siege of Rouen and little Margaret is too young to travel with me. She is living with my sister in England.' I got the impression that these were emotional matters for the duchess, who quickly changed the subject. 'But we cannot talk solely of me, your grace. I have not congratulated you on your marriage. I am sure you will make the king very happy.'

Catherine shrugged. 'I think his sieges make him happy, Madame. But they take a terrible toll. I am so very sorry to hear about your eldest son. May God rest his soul.' She turned to the young girl. 'You must be a great comfort to your mother, Lady Joan. I was not jesting when I said you might help me with my English. Do you like music? Perhaps you could teach

505

me some English songs that I could sing to King Henry. If you would like to, you could join me and my ladies and we could all make music together.'

Young Joan blushed. 'I can sing, your grace, and will willingly teach you the songs I know, but I play badly, I am afraid.'

Duchess Margaret nodded ruefully. 'She is right. We have tried numerous instruments but Joan is all fingers and thumbs.'

'I can play tennis though!' protested Joan defensively. 'I beat Edmund once.'

'That is settled then,' laughed Catherine, charmed by the rosy-cheeked indignation of the girl. 'You can teach me tennis and English songs both at the same time! That is if your lady mother agrees.'

The duchess looked a little embarrassed. 'Tennis is not really considered ladylike, your grace. Joan plays because her brothers have taught her, but at court it is the preserve of gentlemen.'

'But we are not at court!' cried Catherine. 'The king has a portable tennis pavilion which his carpenters erect for him when he stops long enough to use it. I will ask him if it can be erected here, then we could all use it.'

Despite the Duchess of Clarence's warning that tennis was a male preserve in England, Henry agreed to Catherine's request and allowed his portable tennis court to be erected in the garden at Bray. As what Thomas of Clarence called 'good siege weather' continued throughout June, Catherine declared the outdoor life greatly preferable to the stuffy heat of the castle rooms and the tennis court was well used. Under Lady Joan's lively guidance, she became passably adept at tennis and rather less so at English, but an added attraction was the fact that Michele stayed away. The Duchess of Burgundy disapproved of ladies playing tennis and hated the sun and the summer insects, which together made her hot and irritable.

I divided my time between my usual duties for Catherine and helping Alys and Jacques in the quarters they had been allocated in a small row of houses built against the wall of the huge castle barbican. Their neighbours were other craftsmen and their families, who were travelling with the royal entourage; armourers and blacksmiths, saddlers and grooms, cobblers and joiners. It was a busy enclave of workshops with living quarters above and there were always children playing around the doorways and running errands for their parents. Catrine was now a bonny baby of five months old, who slept less and less and enjoyed being carried on my hip to watch the craftsmen at their labours. She particularly liked me to stand outside the forge to watch the blacksmith make sparks fly from his anvil. I loved the fact that the noise and the heat did not frighten her and she would wave her hands with delight and giggle and wriggle in my arms. I became a split personality; at one moment a besotted grandmother and the next a courtier and confidante.

In late June Catherine and the two duchesses were sharing the high table at dinner in the great hall when a squire came from Montereau with a letter from King Henry. It was handed to Catherine, but I could see Michele fuming with impatience as the Duchess of Clarence smiled upon the squire and said to Catherine, 'This is my son, Edmund Beaufort, your grace. As I told you, he has the honour to be one of King Henry's squires.'

Catherine glanced down at the good-looking lad in royal livery who was kneeling before her. 'Greetings, Edmund,' she said, taking the letter from him. 'You must have ridden like the wind. I declare that the wax is still soft on the king's seal!'

Edmund's cheeks burned and he could not tear his gaze from Catherine's face. Even from the lower trestles you could sense the awe of a youth struck by beauty. 'It is not so far, your grace,' he muttered bashfully. 'The king said it was urgent.'

At the other end of the table Michele was drumming her fingers loudly. 'In God's name, sister, if it is urgent let us hear the news!' she exclaimed. 'Has the town fallen? Is my father-in-law's grave discovered?'

Catherine did not look up until she had perused the entire text of the letter, then she smiled. 'You will be happy to hear that the town *has* surrendered, sister. The king requests my presence in a victory procession tomorrow.'

'But surely that is not all!' cried Michele. 'Does he say nothing of the murderers of my lord's father? Have they been apprehended? Has his grave been found?'

Catherine waved the letter and shook her head. 'No. There is nothing here about that. Perhaps the duke has sent you news separately and his squire does not ride as fast as Edmund here.' The squire blushed anew as she bestowed another beaming smile on him.

Michele could not hide her frustration. 'I suppose that may be so. I expect at least to be invited to join the procession.'

And indeed, only a few minutes later, a messenger arrived in Burgundy livery bearing a letter addressed to her.

Michele scanned it swiftly. 'King Henry did not give you the full story, Catherine,' she boasted. 'One side of the town has opened its gates, but the castle holds out and has closed off the other side. The murderers are believed to have taken refuge there. Duke Jean's grave has been discovered in the abbey church of St Nicholas and Masses are already being said for his soul, but King Henry still has to reduce the castle to bring the killers to justice.'

'Which I am sure he will do,' responded Catherine calmly. 'Although I think having Masses said for the late Duke's soul is rather like closing the stable door after the horse has bolted.'

It took a few moments for Michele to comprehend the exact meaning of Catherine's remark, but when she did she erupted from her chair and spat angry words at her sister. 'Have a care, Madame Queen of England! Precedence may put you above me now but it does not allow you to slight the honour of Burgundy. Be sure that my lord will hear of this!' And with that she turned on her heel and swept from the hall.

The Duchess of Clarence coughed into her hand. 'Your sister is very loyal to her husband's family,' she observed neutrally, 'which can be an admirable quality in a wife.'

Catherine sighed. 'She and I view Burgundy from opposite sides,' she said. 'We will never agree.'

'You are not obliged to venerate your sister's family or your brother's,' pronounced the duchess. 'In fact, to do either would be unwise – now that you are, as she so forcefully reminded you, England's queen.'

Despite the victory procession there was still much business left to do in Montereau. The town straddled the confluence of the rivers Seine and Yonne and the castle stood in the middle of the long bridge which spanned them both, blocking access from one bank to the other. The men who were responsible for the duke's murder on that very bridge remained at large, probably in the castle but possibly in disguise on the north bank. The siege was not yet over and to reduce their chance of escape, Henry wanted to end it quickly.

He and Catherine were honoured guests at the Abbey of St Nicholas, which provided a victory dinner of sorts in the great refectory. We all sat at the polished wood tables where the monks usually sat and I could see King Henry and Catherine discussing something at length as they ate. I learned what it was when she came to prepare for bed in the abbot's chamber, which the abbot had obligingly vacated in their honour.

'Several prominent burghers have been taken prisoner, whose families took refuge in the castle,' Catherine explained. 'The king says that the constable of the garrison will surrender tomorrow when these prisoners are sent to beg him to do so. He wants me to be there to witness the arrest of the murderers when they emerge.'

'Must you do this, Mademoiselle?' I asked earnestly. This was a duty about which she was bound to have mixed feelings because the men her husband called murderers were those who had rid her of the evil threat of Jean the Fearless.

'Yes, I must,' she told me solemnly. 'But Henry says they are knights whom Philippe will treat according to the rules of chivalry. They will have a fair trial and he believes they will be proved innocent because there is only one man who is responsible for the devil duke's death and that is Tanneguy du Chastel.'

'Does he *know* that?' I asked, thinking that surely Tanneguy had not admitted as much to anyone.

'He says he has read the witness statements and come to that conclusion. And really, knowing what I know, it would not surprise me if it were true, Mette.'

However, King Henry had not revealed precisely how he planned to use the burghers to get the castle gates opened. After hearing Mass the next morning he and Catherine stood on the river bank, out of range of the archers on the castle battlements, as one by one the guns and arbalests of the siege army fell silent all around the emplacements. Then, at his signal, the prisoners were sent out onto the bridge under a white flag of parly, ten burghers in chains and with nooses hung about their necks.

'What are they wearing those for?' Agnes whispered to me, appalled. 'That is what condemned prisoners wear.'

I shook my head, my heart heavy with foreboding. We were there as Catherine's female support, which as a queen she was entitled to wherever she went. Above us the sky mirrored my dark thoughts; black clouds were piling up on the eastern horizon, heralding the end of an unbroken month of dry weather. King Henry's Windsor Herald, resplendent in his leopard tabard, cried out the king's demands to the castle garrison, but the wind carried his words to them and not to us, so we could not hear them.

The rain held off as we all stood in fraught silence, listening as the mournful wails of women and children drifted faintly down from the battlements, where we could see the veils of the burghers' wives blowing in the wind. The white flag flapped over the heads of their men-folk, huddled together on the bridge, waiting for the constable of the garrison to order the surrender.

'He will surrender,' King Henry assured Catherine loudly as the noon deadline drew near. 'Even the pretender will not expect his constable to hold out against such impossible odds. There is no reason to do so.'

Minutes went by and the sun disappeared behind the bank of gathering cloud but everyone knew that it had reached its zenith. Then the bell began to ring from the abbey for the Hour of Sext, the monks' noonday office. We all listened intently for the sound of surrender; a trumpet blast or a shout from the battlements or simply the noise of the portcullis being raised in the gatehouse of the castle. But as the bell stopped ringing not a sound broke the silence.

King Henry turned and gave a signal to men in the mass of troops behind him and slowly but surely they began to push a high-wheeled platform forward, such as might be used to scale a wall or protect an attack; except that on the top of this particular platform there was erected a ten-man gibbet.

'What is that for, my liege?' Catherine almost shouted at King Henry in alarm. 'You are not going to hang them?'

'I am showing the constable that I am a man of my word,' replied the king, his face set like stone. 'He will open the gates when he sees that I mean what I say.'

Then the wailing from the battlements began again, piteously loud as the gibbet was anchored in full view of the prisoners' families and the men themselves were hauled back by their chains, desperately protesting, and pushed one by one up the ladder. The rope tails of their nooses were thrown over the gibbet and fastened to the platform. It was then that I saw there was a lever at the end of the platform which would release the hatch on which the men stood. The gibbet was purpose-built.

'Your grace, my lord, my husband! You cannot mean to do this!' cried Catherine in great distress.

'The constable knows I am a man of my word,' King Henry said again. 'Calm yourself, Madame, the gates will open.'

But they did not. The wailing increased to a dreadful crescendo and the prisoners called to their families and to heaven again and again.

Catherine fell to her knees before Henry and clasped her hands together in supplication. 'I am your queen and I am begging you for these men's lives. They are not soldiers, my liege, they are family men, merchants and tradesmen who do not deserve to die. For your conscience and your soul do not do this.'

King Henry took her hands and gazed at her long and hard. 'I understand your feelings, Catherine, and if I could I would grant your plea, for the laws of chivalry allow a king to accede to the supplication of his queen. But this is a matter of honour. The constable harbours known felons. He is the one to blame, he and his commander, the Pretender. They both know that unless a relief army is sent, the castle will have to surrender. There is no sign of a relief army. The garrison should surrender now. The lives of these men will be on the conscience of the constable, not mine.'

His face was a stern mask as he raised his arm and gave the signal to the hangman. With one fatal pull on the lever, the hatch dropped and the ten men fell through the gallows' floor. Catherine buried her face in her hands and I rushed to comfort her. From the battlements the heart-breaking screams of the wives and children froze my blood. King Henry watched the ten bodies sway and jerk in a slow grisly dance then he turned and walked away as the rain began to fall in great oily drops. Within seconds the guns began to roar one after another.

'Jesu, Mette, I am married to a monster!' Catherine sobbed in my arms.

36

After the Montereau hangings relations between the newly-weds were frosty, to put it mildly. Nor was the ice any more likely to melt after the castle opened its gates only eight days later, proving what a waste of human life the whole sorry episode had been. The only thing the cold-blooded execution of ten men had achieved was a delay, time enough to allow the men held responsible for the devil duke's death to somehow spirit themselves away to Melun, another of the royal castles now held by the dauphin's supporters. Having achieved little except a serious dent in his reputation, the situation had left King Henry furious and frustrated. He was still bound by his vow to Philippe of Burgundy and so found himself unable to pursue his own primary aim, which was to confront the dauphin in his southern strongholds of Berry, Orleans and Touraine. Perhaps by way of distraction, he instead relentlessly pursued his other current endeavour – to father an heir.

Still haunted by the hangings, Catherine suffered Henry's regular connubial visits in sullen silence and he apparently made no effort to placate her. The siege honeymoon had become just that, with Henry firing frequent salvos but making no apparent breach in Catherine's defences. It seemed that she was almost back in the dark days of the devil duke, except that this time the violation was legal and sanctioned by the Church.

After a fortnight of this marital stand-off I received a summons from the Duchess of Clarence. She and her husband had a suite of rooms in a separate tower of the castle at Bray and I was escorted there by a page wearing the Clarence lions. I found the duchess alone and, cutting short my dutiful bend of the knee, she beckoned me forward to sit beside her in a low-backed chair. 'Thank you for responding so promptly to my call, Madame,' she began graciously. 'I know that you often visit your daughter and little granddaughter at this time of day. It must be a great comfort to you to have them here close by.'

I was faintly alarmed at the thought that my movements had been so carefully observed and reported on, but hoped that I hid my consternation. 'Yes indeed, your grace,' I agreed politely, wondering what was coming.

When Margaret of Clarence smiled, as she did then, it was easy to see why she had been considered one of the court beauties of her day. 'I know very well the joy that children bring for I bore my first husband six. Sadly however, that was not a happy marriage, whereas my present marriage was made for love but has produced no children. So I know the vicissitudes of the marriage bed.'

The duchess paused as if to gather her thoughts, smoothing the magnificent figured silk of her skirt with her ring-laden fingers. I thought it best to remain silent, waiting for her to continue.

'Also, as a result, I am both aunt and sister-by-marriage to the king and therefore one of the few women who know him well, all of which explains why it is to me that he has turned for help in a very private matter. Before I continue however, I must impress on you, Madame Lanière, that what passes between us from now on is to remain absolutely confidential. I know you have always had Queen Catherine's best interests at heart and therefore I can trust you not to repeat a word of this conversation.'

'If it concerns her grace then of course you have the promise of my complete discretion, Madame,' I declared. 'I will swear it on the bible if you wish.'

'That will not be necessary.' The gleam of a smile sprang once more to the duchess's thick-lashed grey eyes. 'Queen Catherine tells me you are her most trusted confidante and that is enough for me.'

'I am fortunate to remain high in the queen's regard, Madame. I owe her everything.'

She nodded, satisfied. 'Very well – let us get down to business. My task is this – to ask for your help on behalf of King Henry.' She shifted a little in her chair, as if settling herself to the job in hand. 'It must be obvious to anyone with sensitivity that the king is a complex character – a driven man with huge ambition for himself and his country. He also has great faith in God and a hungry intellect.

'However, it must be admitted that he lacks emotional depth. His mother died when he was eight and he was reared in a completely male environment to be a soldier and a king. If he has a soft side it has never had a chance to develop. However, he is sensitive enough to realise that something has gone badly wrong in his relationship with Catherine. The bright and beautiful girl he thought he was marrying seems to have vanished. Oh, she does not defy him or refuse him, but she is cold and silent. While she gives him her body, she has closed her mind to him. I thought that you might have some idea why this should be so. Apparently the first days of the marriage were quite satisfactory from his point of view. It is only in recent weeks that things have changed. He simply does not know what to do.'

I did not respond immediately, but sat pensively rubbing my palms together, thoughts tumbling in my head. Should I be tactful and vague, or should I be honest? I glanced up into the duchess's clear, searching gaze and opted for the latter, though nervously.

'Might I suggest more precisely that it has been since the unfortunate hanging of hostages in full view of their wives and children under the walls of Montereau castle, Madame, that her highness has changed towards her husband?' I offered.

Margaret of Clarence raised her eyebrows. 'Ah. Do you think that might have something to do with it?'

'More than that, I would suggest that it is the chief cause of the coolness between them,' I persisted. 'To speak plainly, it was unwise of the king to ask Queen Catherine to witness that event. She is young and has been protected from much of the violence of war. Any girl of her age and upbringing would be dreadfully shocked by such a gruesome, and might I suggest regrettable, sight?'

The duchess frowned angrily. 'I was not aware that she was there. I can easily imagine that she was very shocked. Is there any way you can suggest that he might redress this error, Madame?'

'Short of bringing the ten men back to life, no, Madame,' I said with a grim smile. 'However, I did indicate that was the main cause of the queen's withdrawal – not the only one. There is also the matter of the way King Henry treats her.'

The Duchess cleared her throat. 'Ahem. I hope she is not coy about her duty in the marriage bed. She is his wife and she is not a child. She cannot deny him his marital rights.'

I shook my head. 'No, no. She understands that and I note that King Henry has not implied that she does. But before the unfortunate incident at Montereau, she had expressed concern to me that the king was very formal in his manner at all times, even in bed. She said that he was polite and kind and did not frighten her, but nor did he offer any tenderness or intimacy.' I spread my hands. 'She may not be a child but she is still a young girl and all young girls hanker after a little romance, do they not? Even in a marriage that has been arranged by lawyers and fixed by treaty.'

'So you think I should teach the king how to be romantic?' One of the duchess' eyebrows had taken on a distinct upward slant and I detected a suppressed twinkle in her eye.

'Well – yes, Madame. At least someone should.'

'Hm,' she pondered. 'And you really believe that a little sweet-talking would help?'

'If King Henry is able to urge his army to victory against the odds I am sure he can cajole one young girl to come willingly to his arms.'

The duchess looked a little doubtful. 'Perhaps, but those are two very different tasks. However, I will tell him of your advice.'

It was my turn to look doubtful. 'Would you not prefer to offer it as your own, Madame? After all it was to you he turned, not to the queen's servant.'

From under the arch of her fine brows those shrewd grey eyes studied my face for a long moment and then she nodded. 'You are a wise woman, Madame. I can see why Queen Catherine values your advice.'

I smiled ruefully. 'Not always, your grace. She has a strong will. King Henry should bear that in mind also.'

'I think he has discovered that already,' the duchess remarked dryly, reaching for the little bell that stood on the table beside her. 'Now that our business is over, Madame, let us take a little refreshment together. If you are willing to tell me, I would be fascinated to hear how you became such a pillar of Queen Catherine's life.'

I do not know when the Duchess of Clarence managed to speak to King Henry, for the next day news came that we were to move on. The Duke and Duchess of Burgundy were to follow Jean the Fearless' catafalque back to Dijon, where the murdered duke would finally be interred in the family basilica. The Duke of Clarence had already begun the laborious process of laying siege to yet another town, this time the formidable stronghold of Melun and, much to her dismay, Catherine was to join her parents at the castle of Corbeil, whence King Charles had been taken to enjoy some hunting.

I found the return to Corbeil castle unsettling, which is not surprising as it reminded me of my meeting with the dauphin and all the things, bad and good, that had happened as a result of that meeting. For her part, Catherine instantly hated the place; hated its thick walls and small, defensive windows and the heat which seemed to clog its cramped courtyards. And whereas in the past she had generally managed to keep her temper with her ever more fractious mother, she was now prone to exploit her equal status and argue with Queen Isabeau over the slightest difference of opinion. After only a couple of days she took to avoiding her mother's company as much as possible, taking her meals in her chamber and resorting to her usual solace of rides out into the surrounding countryside, but even they did not seem to lighten her mood. I began to worry as her appetite waned once more and then she became even more depressed when Eve's curse arrived, confirming for another month her failure to conceive an heir. When she woke to discover blood on the sheets, she sobbed in my arms. Gently I pointed out that it was not long since she had sworn to me that the idea of bearing an heir to a monster was abhorrent.

'You do not understand!' she cried in despair. 'I said that because I hate him for killing those poor men at Montereau but now I realise that the sooner I am pregnant the sooner he will leave me alone and not treat me like a brood mare. He is charm itself when he visits, now that Margaret of Clarence has shown him how to be – oh yes, I know about that! – but as soon as he gets into bed he becomes like a stallion in a stable yard. Mount, mate, off!'

She dissolved into a paroxysm of sobbing, burying her face in the bedclothes and punching the pillow. Her hair was tangled and damp with sweat as I stroked her head with motherly concern, racking my brains for some way to relieve her misery.

In contrast to Catherine's dejection, Alys was blooming in her new abode; a workshop and rooms that had been found for them in the town, on a street close to the castle entrance. There was a small garth at the back of the house and a young local girl had been hired to help with Catrine while Alys assisted Jacques to sew more of the light summer gowns Catherine needed so desperately.

To her surprise King Henry was not too disheartened by the arrival of Catherine's monthly courses, for nothing seemed to dampen his good spirits. Far from feeling drained as she was by the excessive summer heat, he was full of energy, riding frequently between Melun and Corbeil and even taking the trouble to send Edmund Beaufort to tell Catherine if he was not able to come. The siege of Melun was a complex one, but the difficult logistics only served to fuel his enthusiasm. So absorbed was he by his plans and strategies that he could talk of nothing else over the suppers he shared with Catherine in her chamber on the evenings of his visits. Unexpectedly he continued to come, even when he was kept from her bed by faithful observation of church strictures on the taint of menstrual flow.

I undertook to serve these meals, as I had during Prince Charles' visits at St Pol, and King Henry grew used to my discreet presence just as Catherine's brother had. It was as a result of one of their conversations that an idea came to me of how to relieve Catherine's despondency, inspired by something the king himself said.

'How do you think your father would fare if he joined the siege camp?' he asked her as she toyed with some rather rich venison stew. 'His presence could be very useful in parleys.'

Catherine frowned, pushing her bowl away. 'But where would he lodge? You know how intensely he fears being shattered. I do not think he could bear the insecurity of a tent and he would be terrified by the sound of the guns.'

'Yes, I realise that, but I believe my carpenters could build him a wooden pavilion similar to my tennis court, only with a roof and windows and even a padded chamber, just like the one he sleeps in now.'

'Would that not take a long time to build?'

Henry laughed. 'No, you do not realise how quickly my carpenters work. They can build a scaling tower in half a day. Such a pavilion will not take more than a few days, even with embellishment fit for a king.'

'In that case, I think it a good idea. He has never fared well in the heat and I am sure he would benefit from the fresh air. As long as he cannot hear the guns and can sleep in a safe place. But what would you expect him to do?'

'Just show himself now and then to the castle defenders. We would stop the guns while he did so. Their commander is one Seigneur de Barbasan, a doughty knight for whom I have great respect, but I fear he does not return the compliment. He declares that he will not parley with "the ancient and deadly enemy of France" but only with his liege lord, King Charles the Sixth.' The king shrugged. 'I can see his point of view, but I am sure that even if Barbasan does not immediately surrender, your father's presence there might encourage the townspeople to put pressure on him. King Charles and Queen Isabeau are still very popular in Melun and conditions within the walls are appalling in this heat.'

Catherine fanned herself with her hand. 'That I can believe,' she said with feeling. 'They are nearly as terrible here.'

I saw him regard her then with a surprisingly tender look and reach over to push a damp tendril of her hair back under the edge of her headdress. 'Why do you not take this off Catherine? Would it not be cooler?'

She blushed then, as hotly as Edmund Beaufort did when she smiled at him, and at that moment I knew that the hangings at Montereau had not entirely killed her feelings for him. However he did not remove the artfully wired veil that hid her hair. 'If it would please you, my lord, I will leave it off the next time you come,' she said softly.

He chuckled at that, a rich, throaty sound I had not heard before. 'It would please me as much as it obviously pleases you to tease me with waiting, my lady!' he smiled.

The next morning I screwed up my courage and sent a page with a message to request an audience with the Duchess of Clarence. King Henry had already shown himself receptive to suggestions from her, so I hoped she might consent to plant the seed of my latest idea.

A few days later, Edmund Beaufort told us that carpenters had begun mysterious building works in a hidden green valley not far from the Melun camp.

'As the king has spent so many nights away lately, the men suspect he has a mistress and is preparing to accommodate her closer to hand,' the young squire said, adding indignantly, 'Such coarse, common creatures do not understand that a king with a queen as beautiful as your grace would not need a mistress.'

'Why thank you, Edmund!' Catherine appeared delighted both by the compliment and the shy devotion of the boy who delivered it. 'Pray do not disappoint them with the truth, which is that it is the queen's father not the king's mistress who is to be accommodated. Truth is never as fascinating as rumour, is it?'

To make the most of the cooler morning air, I usually rose at first light and attended to Catherine's wardrobe, and there before cockcrow a few days later King Henry's page brought me a summons to attend him. As I followed the messenger I was assailed by unpleasant memories of a similar summons two years before in Pontoise and became alarmed at finding armed guards at the door of the Corbeil Constable's chamber. On admittance however, I was reassured to find King Henry sitting alone at a table piled with letters and documents awaiting his attention.

With a brief nod he acknowledged my bend of the knee and gestured me to rise. 'I have dismissed my clerks for I wish to talk with you confidentially, Madame Lanière,' he began without preliminaries. 'The Duchess of Clarence speaks warmly of your wisdom and discretion.'

'Her grace is kind to do so,' I said, hoping this meant the duchess had also spoken to him of my latest idea.

I admit to feeling overawed in the king's presence, for even working at his desk at this early hour he cut a distinguished figure in his colourful doublet liberally embroidered with Lancastrian swans and roses, a gilt and silver-sheathed sword strapped to his hips and the spurs of kingship fastened to his highly-polished leather bottins. Despite his scarred cheek, he gave the impression of a supreme being, a demi-god at the zenith of his regal and physical powers, fit and lean and awesome.

'You are the keeper of the queen's robes, so I presume you can manage to pack what is necessary for a few days away without her being aware of what you are doing?' It was more of a statement than a question, posed in clipped, businesslike tones that did not invite a negative answer.

'Yes of course, your grace,' I replied.

'Good. Then after the midday meal today, Edmund Beaufort will bring her grace's horse and an escort and baggage train and convey you all to the special pavilion I have had built near the camp at Melun. Choose whichever of the queen's ladies you like, but there is only room for two and yourself of course. The queen knows nothing of this and I want it to be a surprise for her. Can I trust you to keep my secret?' He looked at me from under beetled brows.

'Yes indeed, your grace,' I responded, wondering fleetingly what he would do if I said no. 'But may I ask one thing?'

His hazel eyes narrowed. 'Ask,' he grunted.

'Is there any possibility of hangings at Melun?' My heart was in my mouth and I felt rather like a mouse caught in the swooping shadow of a sparrow-hawk, but I was still driven to pose the query.

'Why do you ask that?' he barked, his frown becoming fiercer.

'Because I do not think the queen has the constitution to withstand another such spectacle, your grace. Not if she is to bear you an heir.' In the folds of my skirt I crossed my fingers and put up a mental prayer to the Virgin that he would understand that I dared to say this out of love for her.

King Henry steepled his fingers and rested his elbows on the table, studying me intently. I held my breath and waited.

'If there are any, I will ensure that she does not witness them,' he said at length, suddenly favouring me with one of his crowd-pleasing smiles. 'That will be all, Madame.'

I bowed low and retreated, feeling the effects of that smile as goose-bumps on my skin. I was elated, convinced that a retreat from formality was just what this new and fragile marriage needed.

37

Catherine later called the place where the pavilions had been built *Le Vallon Vert* – the 'little green valley'. It was a deep, sloping rift a mile or so behind the siege camp, caught between two craggy outcrops of rock and completely hidden from the town, while the solid rock of the crags baffled and deflected the roar of the nearby siege guns. In its quiet fastness, a stream rippled over pebbles and stones, forming little pools and short, rushing rapids, filling the air with its cool music.

Just as aptly it might have been called 'the valley of the kings', for the building at the lower end, where the little stream rushed towards its confluence with the Seine, was furnished for the King and Queen of France and the other, higher up in a shaded green glade where spring-water bubbled over a rocky lip, stood waiting for the King and Queen of England. Each nestled behind a stout defensive palisade and consisted of two large and airy chambers, one above the other, with an entrance tower at one end containing a ground-floor service room and a spiral stair leading to the upper chamber and a small ante-room at the top. Tents for servants, sentries and latrines were pitched outside the palisades. Artists had painted the wooden walls to resemble stonework and decorative battle-ments topped the pavilions, bearing the lions and lilies of the two kingdoms, while the towers fluttered with banners and flags.

Shadows were lengthening when we arrived, entering the valley from the top without encountering the siege camp and so the journey had passed with laughter and the air of a joy-ride, unassociated with war or weapons. At the final stage I had to get out and walk because the path was too narrow for the carts, so I did not see Catherine's first viewing of the stream and the pavilion, but I could imagine her delight. With ash trees and ferns overhanging the fountain and the sound of birdsong loud in the branches, it was an oasis of peace and calm, seem-ingly untouched by the dust and noise of the siege being ruthlessly pursued on the other side of the hill.

Guessing that Catherine would enjoy the light-hearted amusement of Lady Joan's company, I had asked the Duchess of Clarence for permission to bring her along. While Agnes and I supervised unloading the baggage, she and Catherine explored the pavilion and I could hear their exclamations of surprise and delight as they discovered its camp-style furniture and silken cushions and hangings. Cooling breezes blew through the open shutters, catching the light fabrics and causing them to billow softly.

'Look, no stuffy curtains and heavy covers!' cried Catherine, twirling on the bed posts which the carpenters had embellished with gilded crowns. 'I believe I shall sleep well for the first time in weeks.'

On that first evening of our stay King Henry brought the Earl of Warwick to the pavilion for a meal and Edmund Beaufort had also been invited to join his sister. Cooks had been busy at the kitchen spits and a supper of roasted birds and salads was served at a trestle set up under a canopy by the stream. Torches thrust into the ground gave a dancing light and herbs had been strewn on small braziers to scent the air and deter biting insects. Agnes and I took our food to a separate spot a little distance away, but after the board was cleared Catherine sent Edmund to invite us to bring our stools to join them as they prepared to listen to the music of a harper from among the ranks of the Welsh archers, who had attracted King Henry's attention whilst playing at a siege campfire.

'His name is Owen Tudor,' the king announced, 'and he sings the legends of the hills and valleys of the land where I was raised. You may not understand his words because he mostly sings in his native tongue, but I think you will hear in the music the wild beauty of Wales and the strength and bravery of the people that produce the best archers in the world.'

'The king has a soft spot for Welsh archers,' Warwick told Catherine with a teasing glance at his royal friend, 'but in truth they are a bunch of ruffians!'

Henry laughed. 'They have saved your life enough times, Dick!' he retorted. 'And the whole world knows they were the reason we won at Agincourt. There may be a few rogues among them, but they are the pride of my army.'

'I thought it was a Welsh archer that gave you that scar on

your cheek, my lord,' said Catherine, surprised by his admiration of a people who had marked him so.

'Yes it was,' nodded her husband. 'And the wound that made it showed me how withstanding pain and disfigurement can build a man's inner strength and determination. It may surprise you, but I feel that I owe the Welsh bowmen a debt of gratitude, even the unknown archer who shot me in the face.'

At this point Owen Tudor made an unobtrusive arrival, going down on one knee at the shadowy edge of the canopy. He was a young man with the broad shoulders and fine physique of all longbow-men and a handsome face with dark features and deep-brown eyes, framed by a luxuriant mop of curly chestnut hair that was scarcely tamed by a soft-brimmed hat of green felt. He wore an archer's thigh-length belted leather jacket which had clearly seen active service judging by the grazes and bruises on its surface, hose of murrey red and long brown equally battered leather boots. Slung across his back was a leather sack which contained his harp.

'Ah, Owen,' said the king, catching sight of him and waving him to rise. 'Come and present yourself to the queen. Catherine, this is Owen Tudor. Despite being a Welsh barbarian, he seems to have acquired an education somehow and actually speaks French, do you not, soldier?'

King Henry's teasing tone was designed to put the young man at his ease and seemed to succeed because the archer smiled good-naturedly, moved forward and dropped gracefully to his knee again before Catherine. Bowing his head he replied using hesitant French, heavily accented and with a distinctive lilt. 'The king's grace may generously call it French but I doubt if Madame the queen would do so.'

Catherine smiled. 'I most certainly would, Master Tudor, for it far surpasses my feeble attempts at English. And if your music is as wonderful as my lord describes, then your talents doubly eclipse mine.'

As Owen Tudor raised his head and looked up into Catherine's face, I thought I saw a jolt of recognition in his eyes, as if a dream or a memory had resurfaced and taken him by surprise. But his voice was steady and his expression grave as he shook his head. 'Nothing of mine could eclipse anything of yours, my queen,' he said humbly. 'It will be an honour to play for you. With your permission, sire, I will begin at once.'

'Do so,' nodded King Henry and waved at his squire. 'Edmund, place a stool for the harper.'

Catherine watched the archer as he backed away and swung the bag off his back. 'He seems quite young, my lord, to be as accomplished as you say,' she remarked quietly to her husband. 'Where did he learn to play?'

King Henry shrugged. 'I do not know. He is one of Sir Walter Hungerford's men and he recruited in the north of Wales, I believe, but I have a mind to acquire his services myself, just for his musical skills. After you have heard him play you may tell me whether you think I should or not.'

Owen chose a spot where the firelight cast dancing shadows across the ground and settled himself on the stool which Edmund brought for him. A minute later the air was filled with humming vibrations as he skilfully tuned his harp strings. Then, after a short pause, he laid the calloused tips of his fingers on the strings again and began to coax from it music of quite astounding sweetness. When he sang his voice was like liquid gold and the vocal lilt which had coloured his French found its home in the melodic cadences of the Welsh lyrics of his song. The music he made seemed to take possession of the valley, floating out into the shadows of the crags and joining with the sounds of the stream so that we all became quite mesmerised by its rhythmic harmony. It was not a lullaby, but by the time it was over young Joan had succumbed to its hypnotic charms and Edmund had to carry her up to her truckle bed in the little tower ante-room.

After Owen Tudor left, King Henry had his own small harp brought from his saddle-bag and when he and Catherine retired to the upper chamber he sat playing it and humming softly while Agnes and I helped her prepare for bed. He was not as expert as the archer, but his music contained the same plangent evocations of legend and landscape. As I said good night I saw Catherine throw a cushion to the floor at his feet and sink down on it to listen. Agnes and I spread our pallets out in the lower chamber and I lay sleepless for some time but I did not hear the king call for his body squire.

When I went to Catherine in the morning she stretched luxuriously under the soft linen sheets and smiled at me with a cat-that-got-the-cream expression I had never seen before.

'Did you sleep well, Mademoiselle?' I asked unnecessarily.

'Like a newborn babe, Mette,' she cooed. 'And now I am

starving. King Henry rode off to the siege camp at dawn and said he would send his confessor to say Mass for us later but I do not think I can wait until after that to break my fast.' Rising with unaccustomed alacrity, she took her chamber-robe from me and pulled it on herself, crossing to where the king's harp lay where he had left it on the stool. She bent to pick it up, dreamily plucked a few random notes and turned to glance at me over her shoulder. Her hair was tumbled into curls about her face and I noticed a radiance about her, a glow to the skin on her neck and throat. It did not need a soothsayer to put two and two together and make four.

I said nothing but raised one enquiring eyebrow, which elicited a gurgling laugh. 'Might there be any hot water, Mette?' she asked. 'I would like a bath and one of your delicious rubs with attar of roses.'

'Would that be before or after breakfast, Mademoiselle?' I asked, poker-faced.

'Oh, after I think.' She sat down with the harp on her lap and there was a ripple of sound as she ran her fingers across the strings. 'It is a thrilling instrument in the right hands, is it not? That man last night – what was his name? – Owen, the archer – he was a magician.'

'He certainly knows how to play and sing, yes. He must have had a good teacher.'

'But I think my lord plays with equal feeling,' she declared loyally. 'And, what is more, he sings in French so that I understand the words.'

'Were they romantic words by any chance?' I asked slyly.

She gave me another of her sidelong looks. 'Yes, Mette, they were – very romantic.'

'I am glad, Mademoiselle.'

The archer did not come to play every night, but I noticed that when he did come, King Henry did not again invite any of his captains or generals to share the music, preferring to sink onto cushions with Catherine, where they would listen leaning close together, occasionally whispering comments to each other. During these concerts Agnes and Joan would sometimes play board games at a discreet distance, but I would just sit and watch the sun set and the bats begin to fly from the caves in the cliffs to hunt for night insects. Occasionally Edmund and Joan were asked to join Catherine and the king for supper, but most evenings the two newlyweds chose to eat and talk alone together for the precious hours that Henry could spare away from the increasingly complex logistics of the siege.

Apart from attending her on waking, I rarely found myself alone with Catherine during that time so we did not discuss her relationship with King Henry in any detail but it was easy to see that they had turned a corner. When King Henry rode in from the siege camp she would drop whatever she was doing and run to greet him and although she always stopped to make him a curtsy it was plain that it was mostly done for the pleasure of feeling his hands cup her elbows and raise her for a lingering kiss. Any formality in their relationship was now restricted to public occasions, of which there were very few in the *Vallon Vert*. Slowly and shyly I could see that Catherine was finding the man behind the king and he was beginning to love and trust her for doing so.

She had promised her husband that, with soldiers everywhere in the vicinity, she would not wander beyond the confines of the valley, but she and Joan explored every nook and cranny and everywhere they wandered men-at-arms shadowed their movements. There were also lookouts posted on the tops of the crags and substantial guards set at either end of the valley. Even in that quiet and peaceful oasis, danger was never far away.

King Henry had acquired several new giant guns from Germany to add to the considerable battery that already pounded the walls of Melun and one day Catherine proposed that we all climb over the steep side of the valley and take a look at the siege. I think she wanted to see just what it was that she was competing with for his attention and the king agreed that she could arrange it, but said he would send Edmund with a suitable escort of men-at-arms to ensure our safety.

King Charles and Queen Isabeau arrived at their own pavilion at noon on the day of our proposed expedition, having travelled most of the way from Corbeil by barge. We all gathered to watch them enter the valley, the queen in a chair-litter, carried by eight sturdy grooms and the French king, swamped by his full regal regalia of crown and mantle, mounted on a docile white pony. Catherine and King Henry met them at their pavilion and patiently waited while Queen Isabeau inspected the facilities and King Charles was gently discouraged from immediately taking a paddle in the stream. As soon as was decently possible, King Henry persuaded his father-in-law to remount his pony and join the procession of knights and heralds who had come to escort him through the siege camp for his first parley at the main Melun gate.

This whole process took more than an hour and meanwhile Catherine, Joan, Agnes and I met Edmund and our escort of men-at-arms and climbed the steep path up the side of the valley. It was the first time the four of us had ventured beyond its tranquil confines and it was a shock to breast the summit and encounter the roar of the guns as we descended steeply through the woods that covered the far side of the bluff. At the edge of the trees was a vantage point which gave a panoramic view over the siege camp, the town of Melun and the network of freshly dug earthworks that now surrounded it.

Until the dauphin had established his garrison there, the royal castle of Melun had been Queen Isabeau's favourite summer residence, chosen for its cool river breezes and glorious surrounding countryside. Its walls seemed to grow out of a sheer red sandstone bluff on the opposite bank of the Seine, which mirrored the one we stood on ourselves. Below the castle the walled town occupied flatter ground on an island in a bend of the broad, fast-flowing stream, which in itself presented a major obstacle to any besieging force. As the only river crossing was within the walled town, in order to coordinate their attack, the besiegers had built a new bridge upstream, just out of range of the defenders' arrows, and by so doing had joined up a ring of trenches and ramparts, which allowed them to move between gun emplacements without exposing themselves to the archers on the walls.

Scores of guns of different shapes and sizes were deployed at various strategic points and continuously hurled a variety of missiles vast heights and distances to crash into the walls of the castle and the town. There were also ranks of mangonels and arbalests, ancient forms of artillery which Edmund explained were now mostly used for flinging fireballs and quicklime over the town walls to set fire to the houses within. The squire also pointed out caves in the cliffs where sappers had started to build tunnels to undermine the walls of the castle.

However, surely the most daunting prospect for the defenders must have been the battery of huge new cannons that King Henry had deployed to attack one comprehensively pock-marked stretch of wall close to the main town gate. We had heard much of the English king's admiration for these bombards, which were cast in the belching foundries of the Rhine and manned exclusively by teams of specialist German gunners, who were paid a fortune to risk life and limb to aim and fire what were notoriously unwieldy and unstable weapons. I counted six of them; huge cast-iron tubes capable of projecting vast stones several hundred yards and I found it hard to understand how any defending constable could look down on that array of death-dealing monsters without immediately raising a flag of surrender.

As we watched, the guns fell silent and an eerie quietness descended on the valley, heralding the appearance of the French king, whose procession slowly snaked through the tents of the siege camp and headed for the new bridge. Two heralds in their brightly coloured tabards led the way carrying standards flying white flags, indicating their intention to parley. Having crossed the river they broke away to gallop up to the town gate, leaving the king and his entourage waiting at the bridge. The distance was too great for us to hear the words that were shouted up to the defenders on the walls, but there was a bustle of action visible on the battlements of the gatehouse.

In due course a knight, bare-headed but otherwise in full armour, appeared above the gate, his personal banner fluttering behind him in the hands of a bearer. From this Edmund Beaufort identified him as the renowned Seigneur de Barbasan, the garrison commander.

After a shouted exchange the heralds wheeled their horses and galloped back to the royal party on the bridge. Then a helmeted knight on a great black courser rode forward leading King Charles' white pony at a gentle walk towards the gate. I realised from the golden-fleece emblem on the knight's pennant that it was Philippe of Burgundy on the black horse, parading his liege lord and attempting to reinforce the symbolic supremacy of the pathetic, hunched figure at his side. My own opinion was that the contrast between the physical stature of the two riders and their beasts only served to underline the shrunken power of the French crown and the king's inability to exert authority over any of his lieges.

Several minutes of further shouted exchanges ensued before the duke and the king turned and walked their mounts slowly back over the bridge, breaking into a trot to cover the mile-long track back to our little valley. The Seigneur de Barbasan disappeared from the gatehouse battlements and presently, as the sinking sun began to turn the western sky blood-red, the noise and dust of hostilities began again, taking advantage of the last hour of daylight.

We saw men begin to swarm over the new cannon battery, like ants on an anthill. It took a dozen to aim, load and fire each gun and one after another the monsters gradually began to spew out their stone-splintering missiles, subjecting their target to a steady bombardment. Watching ragged holes blossom like gaping wounds in the solid masonry of the town walls made dreadful but compulsive viewing.

Then, as we watched, one of the heavy iron cannons seemed to backfire, lifting several feet off the ground and suddenly disintegrating in clouds of smoke and bone-crushing shrapnel. In a dreadful human shower it sent the bodies of its attendants flying high into the air, limbs separating from torsos and spiralling gruesomely into the river which suddenly flowed red with blood below the battery. A ragged cheer rose from the invisible defenders behind the town battlements. I buried my face in my hands, and when I had collected my thoughts enough to look up I saw that Catherine had turned away and was being violently sick in the nearby bushes. Lady Joan was with her, but I hurried over and together we half-carried her to a clearing further back in the wood out of sight of the bloodbath below, where we propped her up against a fallen tree and I sent Edmund to wet my kerchief in the nearest stream.

She was distraught, as we all were and Edmund was horrified that his queen had witnessed such dreadful carnage. 'Oh your grace, my lady, I am so sorry. I should have realised the risk and brought you back earlier,' he wailed. 'The king will be furious that I allowed you to be exposed to such a sight!'

He was right, I thought, echoing the squire's despair in my own mind as I pressed the cool cloth to Catherine's brow. Her face was chalk-white with shock and I prayed that such a close encounter with the full horror of war had not killed any spark of new life which might be growing within her. If such were the case King Henry would be justified in being extremely angry with those whom he had trusted with the care of his young wife.

38

I stood in the steep lane leading down to the bakery. The cobbles were slippery with rain and I clutched at the rough stone pillar of the Grand Pont for support. Above me the roadway and shops on the bridge were busy but the lane was quiet, few people venturing out of their cramped little timbered homes in the wet weather. At the foot of the slope the big wooden gate was shut that led to the bakery yard where the ovens stood. To my surprise everything looked much the same as it had six years before, when I had reluctantly handed the keys to one of my late father's former apprentices.

Beside me Jean-Michel's brother Marc shot me a worried glance. 'Are you all right?' he asked gruffly.

I nodded. 'It's just the pattens,' I said with a smile, hitching up my skirt to show him my feet in their clumsy iron over-shoes. 'It was never easy walking down here in these.'

He glanced down at his own feet, more secure in boots. 'It might not lift you out of the mire but you can rely on leather,' he grinned. I shrugged. He was a saddler, he would say that. 'Come on, give me your arm.'

I had walked to the Lanière workshop at midday and Marc

had volunteered to accompany me to the bakery. He and his family had continued to collect the rent from the tenant during my extended absence and I considered myself very lucky that they had remained loyal to Jean-Michel's memory and saved the money for me. The elder Lanières were dead and it cannot have been easy for the remaining brothers to support their families during recent years. In the desperate periods of scarcity and starvation that had struck the city of Paris latterly, it would have been understandable if they had used my rent money to feed themselves but they had not.

'Mind you, it has not always been easy to collect,' Marc had grumbled. 'With the shortage of flour there were times when your tenant was on the breadline himself!'

The joke was typical of the black humour of those dark times. Paris had lost fifty thousand souls in the plague epidemic, which we in the royal household had avoided by moving to Pontoise, and more had succumbed in the famine that followed it. Also, despite the nobles' reputation for not paying bills, many craftsmen had been forced to follow their patrons out of Paris, for want of customers. I had already noticed how many houses now lay empty and dilapidated in the city's once-teeming streets.

'I am very grateful for your kindness and good faith,' I had responded with genuine warmth. 'I intend to ensure that the money goes to your nephew Luc, for I think he, of all our family, will have most need.'

'But how will you get it to him if he has thrown his lot in with the Pretender?' Marc had asked. Luc's move had been greeted with dismay by Jean-Michel's family for the Lanières had always been Burgundian in their loyalties and had no time for the Dauphin or the Orleanist cause.

'I will find a way,' I assured him. 'Envoys and couriers often cross the lines. I will get a message to him and if he needs the money, which I am sure he does, he will contrive to come and get it.'

The royal households of England and France had arrived in Paris in early December. After an unexpectedly long siege, King Henry had finally managed to starve the Melun garrison into surrender, demonstrating to the French and Burgundian armies that siege-warfare could be won by patience as much as by headlong assaults on well-defended walls. Philippe of Burgundy had watched two of the murderers of his father hanged in the town square but when, outside the gates of Melun, the defeated garrison captain had kneeled to offer his sword in surrender, much to Catherine's relief King Henry had not condemned him to death but committed him as a prisoner until a heavy ransom was paid for his freedom. This had enraged Burgundy because Barbasan was also on the list of guilty men.

But the king was adamant. 'The seigneur is too formidable a knight to go to the scaffold,' he had declared. 'He has sworn an oath that he played no part in Duke Jean's murder and I believe him.'

Catherine experienced no physical ill effects as a result as a result of witnessing the gun explosion, but that had not lessened King Henry's anger and all her attendants had felt the lashing of his tongue, but fortunately it had gone no further than that. Perhaps Catherine had persuaded him that she was the one who had suggested the expedition or perhaps it was simply that in the little green valley the great warrior king had mellowed. Remarkably, a dynastic marriage forged in the violence of war had brought solace to two lonely and damaged people, who had now had a taste of the happiness that shared experience and mutual affection can bring. Henry and Catherine had found delight in each other's company and in the simple pleasures of conversation, laughter and music; especially music, for Henry's harp was often to be heard through the open shutters of their chamber and Owen Tudor's playing and singing had been a regular feature of their pavilion life. Owen's troop captain, Sir Walter Hungerford, was also Steward of the Royal Household, so it had been an easy matter to arrange a transfer for the archer from his troop to King Henry's retinue. Although, rather than issue an order, the king had cannily invited his steward to a slap-up dinner at the pavilion to make his request.

As a veteran of Agincourt and one of England's most celebrated knights, Sir Walter had nonetheless dared to grumble to his king, 'You are taking one of my best bowmen, sire!'

'You can have your pick of my royal archers, Walter,' King Henry had responded, signalling Edmund to pour more wine. 'And you will be doing the queen a great favour.'

Sir Walter had bowed his head a little tipsily to Catherine. 'God forbid that I, a humble knight, should refuse a great lady,' he said gallantly. 'But in future I must take care not to recruit any handsome, harp-playing Welshmen!'

The deal was done, as was inevitable.

While I was at Melun I had sorely missed my daily contact with Alys and Catrine, but once or twice they had managed to hitch a ride on a supply cart to visit me and it was a joy to see the baby squeal and laugh at the babbling stream and roll around in the soft grass on its banks. She was a pretty, merry little soul and Alys had made her beautiful chemises and kirtles out of remnants of fabric from Catherine's summer wardrobe. On one occasion both child and queen had chanced to wear kirtles of the same pretty flower-patterned linen and Catherine had proudly dandled her 'twin' goddaughter on her knee, showing her off to Lady Joan.

'If I were not a queen who must bear a son, I would pray for a beautiful little girl just like you!' she cooed, hugging Catrine tight.

The fair weather held through September and into mid-October, when the autumn storms at last arrived and drove us back to Corbeil. Within a fortnight the failure of Catherine's monthly course had us crossing our fingers and sending up pleas to St Monica and by the beginning of December we were certain she was pregnant. King Henry was understandably jubilant and would instantly have trumpeted the news to the world, but I urged Catherine to caution him to wait.

'It would not be wise to announce it yet, Mademoiselle,' I warned. 'This is such an important child that it would be as well to wait until after Epiphany to make it known, just in case it slips. You must take extreme care of yourself for although in the early weeks there is no obvious sign of the baby, that is when it is at its most vulnerable.'

Catherine gave me a worried look and instinctively put her hands to her belly. 'It may not be obvious to you, Mette, but it will not be easy to hide the sickness I feel every morning. I am sure that cannot be good for the child.'

'It will pass, Mademoiselle' I said sympathetically. 'I will make a tisane that you should drink daily on waking and you must eat white food to calm your stomach – little and often.'

'I hope it will pass *very* soon,' she fretted. 'How did my mother bear twelve children if she felt like this every time?'

'Not all babies cause this problem. You must pray for patience, Mademoiselle.'

'Pah! That is what a priest would say!' she protested. 'And what do they know about being *enceinte*? I do not expect you of all people to spout religion at me, Mette!'

Catherine had been so happy to leave Corbeil castle that she even consented to travel to Paris by barge with her mother, bowing to Henry's stipulation that she should not ride on horse-back in her condition. The barge was met at the Charenton Bridge and the two queens were carried shoulder-high by royal guards in gilded litters through the streets of a city that was *en fête* for the first time in years. After a Mass of thanksgiving at the cathedral of Nôtre Dame, the French king and queen were escorted to the Hôtel de St Pol, while King Henry and Queen Catherine set up their court in the fortress of the Louvre.

After my visit to the bakery I set myself the task of finding some way to contact Luc. I could not write to him, nor could I entrust any messenger with confidential information about money because that would be asking for trouble, so when I located a courier who carried official letters to the dauphin I simply asked him if he would seek out Luc and tell him that all his family, including his new niece, were now in Paris. I hoped the mere fact that I had bothered might indicate to Luc that he should respond.

It had not taken Jacques long to establish his credentials with the Paris guild of tailors and to rent a workshop and rooms in a narrow street between the Louvre and the Châtelet, where a number of other tailors had their premises, and close enough for me to visit them often. With the English queen as his patron he did not find himself short of work. In September King Henry had made Thomas of Clarence Constable of Paris, with the result that the warring factions within the city had been brought under control and it had become safe to walk the streets again, but the people were still hungry and when I visited the markets I noticed that, compared with Troyes, there was little fresh produce available. If the English court stayed for long there would be famine by spring.

Looked at it from the English point of view however, King Henry deserved his feasts and celebrations. In the five years since his extraordinary victory at Agincourt, he had established himself as the ruler of Northern France. Winter had brought an end to campaigning and he had an opportunity to sit back and count his triumphs, among them the tiny new life that he had not yet announced. No wonder he strode about Paris in his richest apparel and wore his crown at public banquets. He was and intended to remain, one of the most glorious monarchs in Europe, the focus of fame, fortune and fealty.

The grand master of the French king's household came to protest that King Henry was only the Heir of France and should place King Charles or Queen Isabeau at the head of all court ceremony but Henry dismissed the idea outright.

'Let King Charles hold his own court as he has always done and I will hold mine, as I have always done,' he declared.

'But no one attends his court, sire,' complained the grand master. 'They all flock to yours.'

'If that is what they choose to do, I cannot deny them,' Henry shrugged. 'Let the King of France call them back to him and see if they will come.'

Of course they did not, for it was Christmas, a time of giving, and King Henry was in a mood to be generous, handing out rewards of conquered titles and estates to all who had helped him attain his victories, while the King of France had none to give. I noticed too that Catherine made no effort to visit her mother at the Hôtel de St Pol and Queen Isabeau could not bring herself to come to Catherine's court. The old queen must have been lonely but I could not feel sorry for her. After Catherine's neglected childhood and abused girlhood, she deserved her days of glory. Let her display her undoubted beauty, wear her glorious gowns and sparkle with precious jewels, just as her mother had once done as the young bride of King Charles.

Catherine had bidden me spend the first two days of Christmas with my family, promising that she would not forget to take her herbal drinks and would not stay up too late at the court festivities. So I planned to celebrate the birth of Christ with Alys and Jacques, taking little Catrine to visit the crib at Nôtre Dame and listening to the choirs singing carols in the cathedral square. But before that I walked once more to the bakery under the Grand Pont where my tenant had promised to make me a special pastry of the Virgin and Christ Child as a Christmas subtlety.

It was a fine afternoon, crisp and cold under a clear sky and the river sparkled with reflected winter light as I walked along the old familiar path carrying my basket. With a lump in my throat I recalled my trips to visit Jean-Michel in the royal stables, in the days when I had been a carefree fourteen-year-old with not a thought for the future. Then I had worn my brown homespun kirtle and wooden-soled shoes and been proud that I had neat clothes and could read and write when so many around me could not. Now I wore a gown of blue Flanders wool, warded off the winter chill with a coney-lined heuque and had exchanged letters with princes. Yet although I mingled with kings and queens, inside I still felt like the rebellious baker's daughter who had thrown away her maidenhead on a handsome young groom with twinkling eyes.

The memories seemed so vivid and the surge of energy that accompanied them so sudden and uplifting that I gave a skip and a twirl of my skirts out of the sheer joy of being alive. Then I stopped dead in my tracks, pulled up short by the sight of a ghost. Ahead of me on the path, where the little gate opened from the back of the bakery yard stood Jean-Michel. My heart began to pound with excitement and disbelief, as if it would burst from my chest. There he was! Not dead but come to the bakery to find me and here I was skipping towards him as if I was still that fourteen-year-old-girl with tumbling brown curls and rosy cheeks.

Then I looked more closely and of course it was not Jean-Michel at all, it was Luc, looking so like his father it was uncanny. It was more than a year since I had last seen him and my son

550

had filled out into a broad-shouldered youth, with Jean-Michel's dark complexion and his swinging, loping stride. Tears filled my eyes, tears of joy at the sight of my son and, I confess it, a few tears of disappointment that it was not his father.

'Luc!' I shouted, ashamed at even momentarily wishing him to be another. 'You have come!' So much had he matured in mind as well as body that he did not protest when I ran up and hugged him, planting excited kisses on both his cheeks.

'I got your message,' he said when he could speak, 'but the courier found the dauphin in the middle of a hunt and my lord heard what the man said to me.' Luc looked a little sheepish as he said this. 'I know that if I had learned to read you could have sent me a private letter.'

'Never mind that!' I exclaimed. 'He found you and you found me and it is Christmas! What could be better? And it is pure chance that I came to the bakery to fetch a pastry for little Catrine. Did you expect to find me here?'

He shook his head. 'No. I came to see the tenant because I thought he would know where you were. But the point is that the dauphin himself sent me to Paris because he wanted me to carry a letter secretly for him to his sister, the princess.'

'The queen. She is Queen of England now,' I reminded him. 'The dauphin sent her a letter, you say?'

'Yes. He gave me leave to come and even let me take a horse so I rode back with the courier. I left the horse at the bakery and walked down the towpath because the baker said you would be coming.' He looked wonderingly around him. 'I remember playing on this path when I was a boy.'

'Oh, so at fourteen you are a man, are you?' I teased him. 'Not quite yet, I think.'

'I do a man's job!' he retorted. 'The dauphin thinks so anyway, or he would not have trusted me with the letter.'

'That is true,' I agreed, nodding thoughtfully. 'Can I see it?'

'You can take it,' Luc said, pulling a folded paper square out of the front of his jacket. It was sealed with a blob of wax on which a fleur-de-lis was boldly imprinted. Luc looked relieved to be rid of it and I noted that, wisely, he was not wearing any sign of his affinity to the dauphin.

'I cannot go to the palace, Ma!' he exclaimed. 'Can I stay with Alys? Does she have a place?'

'Yes, of course,' I said, tucking the letter safely away. 'We will go there as soon as I have seen the baker. You can meet your new niece. Catrine is a little beauty.'

'Catrine? Is she named after *her*?' Luc's mouth twisted.

'After Queen Catherine yes – who else?' I answered, frowning. 'She stood godmother to the child, Jesu bless her. Have you forgotten how much we owe her?'

He scowled and turned away. 'No,' he muttered. 'But things have changed. There was that treaty. I do not think the dauphin's letter will be a friendly one.'

I caught his sleeve, stopping him as he opened the gate into the bakery yard. 'Do not tell anyone about the letter,' I warned, 'and I beg you, do not speak of the dauphin, even to the family. It is Christmas. Let us celebrate in peace together.'

Luc nodded. 'You are right. After all, who knows if we will ever celebrate Christmas together again?'

His last words sent a chill through me and I wished he had not said them, for we cannot read the future but sometimes premonition strikes out of an empty sky.

So even now, as I write this nearly twenty years later, I treasure the happy hours we spent together as a family in the little house behind the old royal palace. Alys and Jacques had cleared the workshop and hung it with evergreens and ribbons and we had our own little feast of pies and puddings and roasted fowl washed down with a cask of wine sent by Catherine as a Christmas gift. We even had music because Jacques had clubbed together with other local craftsmen to share the cost of paying a little troupe of minstrels, who moved down the street from house to house singing carols and playing reels and jigs for dancing. Flushed with wine and mirth, I danced with Jacques and I danced with Luc and we all twirled baby Catrine until she shrieked with delight. Flopping breathless onto a bench and taking her on my knee, I sat and watched the young people kicking up their heels arm in arm, elated with the fellowship of laughter and the joy of the season. I was in the company of those I loved and the world seemed peaceful and in harmony. I could not remember being as happy as we were that night since Agincourt had wrought its terrible legacy.

Through all the days of Christmas the dauphin's letter to Catherine weighed heavy on my mind, exacerbated by the sadness of bidding farewell to Luc, when he rode off from Alys' house, with ten crowns of rent money under his belt, to return to the dauphin's court. Later, back at the Louvre, I locked the letter away in my private coffer, awaiting a suitable moment to deliver it to Catherine. She was by turns so elated by the excitement of the extended festivities and exhausted by the strains of her condition that I kept putting it off until she seemed ready to deal with its contents. Of course I did not know what the contents were, but Luc's warning had been enough to raise my fears.

Then, just after Epiphany, our worst fears were realised. Catherine began to bleed and although at first I hoped it might just be one of those peccadilloes of pregnancy, the bleeding persisted and grew more serious until we knew for sure that there would be no baby in the following summer, no heir yet for the Heir of France. While Catherine wept and railed at her bad fortune, I concentrated on making sure that the flow of blood was staunched and her condition stabilised. Above all, I wanted no repetition of the sad case of Bonne of Orleans who had bled to death.

I sent a message to King Henry who came to her chamber straight from one of his council meetings, still wearing his boots and fur-lined riding cloak. I sank to my knees as he strode through the door, fully expecting an explosion of anger and an outburst of blame, but he seemed quite resigned when I gave him the woeful news. In fact, surprisingly, he ended up reassuring me.

'Do not berate yourself, Madame, it is no one's fault,' he said. 'All that matters is that the queen recovers. She will recover, will she not?' There was a faint sign of tremor in his voice when he asked this and I realised for the first time that he genuinely regarded Catherine as much more than the bearer of his children.

'I am certain she will, your grace,' I replied earnestly, still on my knees, having expected to plead for his forgiveness for allowing this disaster to happen. 'She is mourning her loss but she is strong and healthy. There will be other children I am sure.'

'And so am I,' he said, nodding solemnly, 'for it is God's will that I shall have a son.'

His absolute certainty took my breath away. It was the same total confidence that had propelled him from near annihilation before Agincourt to his present state of glorious supremacy. And it was catching. The way he said it also made me completely sure that there would be another child on the way before too long and when he went in to speak to Catherine he conveyed the same sense of assurance to her. I began to understand what the Earl of Warwick had meant when he told Catherine that great leaders create leaders, for it takes supreme confidence to imbue others with self-belief and that was what King Henry did.

However I plucked up my courage and dared to warn him to exercise patience. 'I am not a midwife, your grace,' I said when he was leaving, having coaxed a weeping Catherine into healing slumber, 'but I do know it would not be advisable to get the queen with child too soon. Her body needs a few weeks to heal.'

He regarded me steadily with his tawny eagle eyes and then nodded curtly. 'I understand what you mean, Madame. My mother died from breeding – too young, too many and too soon after each other. I rely on you to nurse the queen back to health as quickly as possible. No, not for the reason you may be thinking,' he cast me a brief and rueful smile, 'but because we will be travelling to England soon for Catherine's coronation. I want her to be my true anointed consort before any son is born to us.'

At least my decisions were made for me. I could not leave Catherine while she was recovering from her miscarriage, nor could I show her the letter from the dauphin. And I could not bring myself to leave her while she was still anxiously waiting to become pregnant; waiting to display the fertility which was so important to the long-term success of the Treaty of Troyes. So I decided that I would have to leave Alys and Catrine instead. Jacques was happy working in Paris among the cream of Europe's designers and tailors and Alys did not want her children to grow up in a strange country across the sea.

'It will not be for ever, Ma,' she said when we discussed my leaving for England. 'People travel across the Sleeve frequently and I am sure you will be back in Paris before too long. I have always known that the princess would need you, wherever she went, and you can make sure she does not forget her god-daughter!'

I laughed at that. She was not without a good bourgeois eye to the future, my canny daughter! I did not believe that she and Jacques and Catrine would do anything but thrive together in Paris.

I had said I would follow Catherine anywhere, but that was before I saw the sea and the ship we were to sail in, bumping up against the harbour wall in Calais six weeks later. Oh, it was a splendid ship, there was no denying that; the best in King Henry's new royal fleet. It was sturdy and fat-bellied with bright-coloured pennons fluttering from every line and spa and it sat comfortably in the water like a prize hen on its nest, its three masts and upper decking painted royal blue and crimson and picked out in costly gold-leaf. But it was hardly as long as the great hall of the Louvre and it was supposed to carry two hundred people over a sea which looked grey and greedy and ready to swallow anything that ventured onto its restless, crested surface. However, when I whispered my fears to Catherine she just laughed and said, 'Really, Mette! Do you think God would have granted King Henry a glorious victory at Agincourt and the crown of France if He intended him to drown on his way back to England?'

I might have pointed out that her father was still living and therefore the crown of France was not yet on her husband's head, but I did not because she was by now totally persuaded of the fact that King Henry ruled England by divine right and that the Almighty also supported his claim to rule France. That was why he had won every battle and siege he had engaged in on French soil in the last six years and why there would be a son to inherit all that he had gained. In Catherine's opinion you could not, and did not, argue with God and only rarely with King Henry. And it was this confidence, born of the newfound love that had blossomed between them, that had persuaded me it was time to show her the letter Luc had brought from the dauphin.

I did it when the ship was halfway across the Sleeve and the coast of France had dwindled into a blurred line on the horizon behind us. The action of a stiff breeze on the triangular sails hoisted fore and aft had been enough to push us out to sea, but as we cleared the harbour the crew had broken out the huge square mainsail and I had gasped in wonder at the bright-coloured image revealed on its flapping canvas. The king's ship was called the Trinity Royal and there, in benediction over us all billowed the sacred figures of God the Father, God the Son and God the Holy Ghost. Perhaps Catherine was right. It really did look as if the Almighty did not intend King Henry or any of his entourage to drown on the crossing to Dover. I approached her as she stood on the deck of the forecastle, the wind blowing her veil off her face, which was turned resolutely towards the north and England. There was no one else nearby.

'I have a letter for you, Mademoiselle,' I said softly. 'I have had it for some weeks but now it seems the right time to give it to you.'

She took it from me and examined the seal. 'A letter from Charles!' she exclaimed in astonishment. 'However did you come by it, Mette?'

'It was brought to me by Luc, Mademoiselle. No one else knows of it.'

Her face fell. 'Ah, yes. I suppose it must be kept a secret, even from Henry.'

'Particularly from King Henry,' I echoed solemnly.

'Do you know what it contains?' She seemed suddenly reluctant to open it.

'No, Mademoiselle! As you see, the seal is intact.'

She shrugged. 'I thought perhaps Luc might have an inkling. He must be much in my brother's favour if he was entrusted with a secret document.'

'As you know, Luc cannot read, so he is a safe courier.'

'Ah, yes.' She pondered this then gathered her courage and broke the seal. As she unfolded the letter, one single word stood out, written in bold black ink at the top of the page.

Seeing it my heart sank and I turned away, not wanting her to feel that I was reading over her shoulder but I need not have bothered for once she had scanned its contents she handed me the letter without speaking, her face as pale as the paper.

It did not take more than a few seconds to read.

> *You were my sister but you are no longer.*
> *You have betrayed me and think to steal my throne but I warn you, when you go to England do not hope ever to return to the land of your birth. It is written in the stars that I and my heirs shall rule France and yours shall rule England. Our nations shall never live in peace. You and Henry have done this.*
> *The devil take you both.*
> *Charles*

The hand holding the letter dropped to my side and I crossed myself with the other. 'I am sorry to be the bearer of this, Mademoiselle,' I said.

She shook her head and bent to take the letter from me. 'Let us pretend it was never written,' she murmured with a sigh and dropped it over the ship's rail.

It was whipped away by the wind and the last thing I saw was that terrible word at the top, scrawled in the fiercest script and the blackest ink.

Traitor

Read on for an exclusive extract from the compelling
follow-up to *The Agincourt Bride*

The Tudor Bride

by Joanna Hickson

THE TUDOR BRIDE

1

The grey-green sea had a hungry look as it lapped and chewed on the defenceless shore, like the monsters that map-makers paint at the edge of the known world. With her sails flapping, the *Trinity Royal* idled nose to the wind under the walls of Dover Castle, a vast stronghold sprawling atop chalk cliffs which gleamed pink in the flat February sunlight. At their foot it was possible to make out flags and banners and a large crowd of people gathered on the beach. Unfamiliar music from an unseen band drifted towards us on a dying breeze.

Having almost completed my first sea voyage, I could not say that I was an enthusiastic sailor. Queen Catherine, on the other hand, looked radiant and unruffled after the crossing from Calais, even when faced with the prospect of being carried ashore in a chair by men bizarrely called the Wardens of the Cinq Ports; bizarrely because apparently there were seven ports, not five, as the title suggested. It may have been an English tradition, but I considered it barbaric that she and King Henry were expected to risk their lives being lifted shoulder high over treacherous waters to a stony beach when they could have made a dignified arrival walking down a gangway to the dockside. Besides, being keeper of the queen's robes, I, Guillaumette Lanière, would have the job of restoring the costly fur and fabric of the queen's raiment from the ravages of sand and salt-water. As one of her attendants, I stood a few paces behind the royal couple on the aftcastle deck, much relieved that the swell which had plagued my stomach all the way from France had now eased and the ship's movement had dwindled to a gentle rocking motion.

From our high vantage point we watched a gaily painted galley advancing fast over the waves, oars flashing in the sunlight and a leopard and lily standard proclaiming the approach of the King of England's brother, Humphrey, Duke of Gloucester, the man responsible for the coming chair-lift. That his grace of Gloucester thought himself a fine fellow was amply evident in the swashbuckling way he climbed the rope-ladder, vaulted the ship's rail and sprang up the companionway to reach us. A short green velvet doublet and thigh-high boots hugged his muscular physique and his broad shoulders admirably displayed a heavy gold chain from which hung a trencher-sized medal of office. His knee-bend showed practised perfection and he flourished his stylish chaperon hat in his right hand as he grasped his brother's with the left.

'A hearty welcome to both your graces!' Although Gloucester pressed his lips to the king's oath ring, he raised his eyes to Catherine. 'England waits with baited breath to greet its beautiful French queen.'

Catherine was indeed beautiful in her ermine-lined mantle, sapphire silk gown and sleek silver fox turban which spurned the playful breeze and accentuated the long, smooth line of her neck. A faint flush stained her cheeks but she remained straight-faced under the impact of Gloucester's dazzling smile. I believe few men of thirty can boast such a complete set of white teeth. If the duke's youth had been in any way misspent, it did not show. His clean-shaven face, smooth and unblemished, was like that of a youth compared with the scarred and care-lined visage of the king, only four years his senior.

King Henry raised a quizzical eyebrow. 'We hear you have a ceremonial welcome planned for us, brother. We are to be carried shoulder high through the surf.'

'As is customary for honoured arrivals, sire.' Gloucester appeared reluctant to drag his gaze from Catherine's face. 'Fortunately the surf has dwindled to friendly ripples and you may remember that when he visited England we welcomed Emperor Sigismund in this way. If the Warden's Lift was appropriate for the Holy Roman Emperor it is surely appropriate for the return of the glorious and victorious King Henry the Fifth of England and Second of France – and the advent of his beauteous queen.'

King Henry frowned. 'It is premature, not to mention unlucky, to place the crown of France on my head while the father of my "beauteous queen" still lives. I am as yet but the Heir of France, as you well know, Humphrey.' He made a brisk upward gesture with his hand. 'You may rise, but only to tell us how we are to enter these chairs of yours without getting wet. I have always avoided such mummery in the past.'

On his feet Gloucester stood almost as tall as his royal sibling, which was a head taller than Catherine. 'A simple matter, sire!' he declared, gesturing over the side of the ship. 'The litters are safely roped onto my galley. The captain will bring your ship as near to the shore as he may, the gangway will be lowered and you and the queen will walk regally down it. Once seated, you will be conveyed towards the shore until the water is shallow enough for us to take the litters on our shoulders and bear you ceremoniously to the beach. Trumpets will sound, the musicians will play and the crowds will cheer. When he can make himself heard the Lord Warden – my humble self – will make a speech of welcome. Then your litters will be lifted shoulder high once more for the short journey to the castle. I can assure you that the whole town is out to greet you.'

'And do I have your solemn word that there is no question of either of us receiving a ducking?' The king favoured his brother with a fiercely narrowed gaze.

Gloucester made an appreciative gesture in Catherine's direction. 'Her grace appears to be made of fairy dust, my lord. We could carry her from Dover to London without a stumble. As for your grace's royal person, it can surely rely on divine protection to remain dry.'

'Hmm.' King Henry grunted, unconvinced.

Catherine favoured Gloucester with one of her most regal smiles and surprised him by speaking in charming broken English, her voice light but firm. 'My Lord of Gloucester is gracious to honour us with this ceremony but should I not also

566

descend from the chair and set my foot on English soil? The people will expect it, surely.'

Humphrey bowed. 'There will be an opportunity for that your grace, when the Mayor of Dover humbly presents you with the freedom of the town. And I trust you will forgive the coarseness of the peoples' greetings. They will doubtless hail you as "Fair Kate!" It is not meant to offend. Fair is in praise of your beauty and Kate is a shortening of your name.'

'The king has told me this. If they think me fair before they have even seen me, such blind devotion cannot be deemed . . . how do you say? . . . an insult,' responded Catherine with another smile. 'And if they call me fair how can I then not like the name they give me?'

I watched Gloucester bow deeply in acknowledgement, as if he recognised that, like him, she possessed a keen appreciation of the importance of public acclaim. 'You are a lady of great wisdom, Madame. And you are to be congratulated on your grasp of English. Is she not, brother?'

King Henry directed one of his rare smiles at Catherine. 'You will find that my queen grasps many things quickly, Humphrey, including the relative value of flattery. Now, let us get this carnival started. I think you will need help in mounting the chair-litter, Catherine, however much my brother makes light of the matter. You should summon your ladies.'

There were only three of us to summon because Catherine's French attendants had been left behind with the exception of me and Agnes de Blagny, a devout and practical knight's daughter who had been orphaned and impoverished by her father's death at the Battle of Agincourt. The third attendant was a recent recruit, an English beauty and cousin of the King, Lady Joan Beaufort. At nineteen and fourteen years old respectively, I readily conceded that Agnes and Joan were better fitted than I to help Catherine down the gangway and onto the gilded litter. Being the same age as the king, I do not suggest for one moment that I was over the hill but the years had broadened my beam and made me less agile than my young companions. However my relationship with Queen Catherine ran closer and deeper than that of any teenage court damsel, for I had suckled her as a babe, nursed her as an infant and steered her through a profoundly troubled youth. She had left her mother, Queen Isabeau, in Paris with barely a second glance but she had raised me from the rank of a menial servant and given me a courtier's post in order to bring me with her to England as one of her closest companions. I had come a long way from my father's bakery on the banks of the Seine.

So I bustled behind, fussing, as Agnes and Joan did all the bending and tugging, easing the queen's silk skirts down the narrow gangway. The king and the duke handed her into the galley and the girls helped her into the litter, tucking her costly robes around her feet to keep them clear of the water. Once the royal couple had been lifted from the boat, the rest of us, including the king's personal squires, were to be rowed to a nearby jetty to be available if needed, and I was very nearly more greatly needed than I would have wished.

As the galley drew closer to the beach, seven men in short doublets and high boots began to wade out towards us, the wavelets lapping first at their ankles and then their shins as they strode deeper. The shingle shelved gradually and they were a good twenty yards offshore before we came alongside them, at which point the Duke of Gloucester stood up and leapt casually over the side into the ice-cold water. Muttering under my breath I brushed the splash-drops from Catherine's skirts as the rowers shipped their oars and began to untie the ropes attaching the chairs to the galley.

'Have no fear, my q ueen,' Gloucester said as the boat rocked alarmingly, unbalanced by their efforts to heave the litters over the side and onto the shoulders of the bearers. 'Archbishop Chichele was our last carry and he is twice as heavy.' He glanced over his shoulder at the other three men in his team and signalled with his free arm. 'Advance, fellow Wardens!'

Catherine raised her chin, stretched her mouth into a fixed smile and forced herself to lift one hand to wave to the crowd. On the other side of the galley King Henry was already shore-bound, unmistakable in his royally emblazoned doublet and jewelled gold coronet. The rowers returned to their oars and we began to swing away towards the jetty, giving me a clear view of the queen's chair as it suddenly tilted violently.

The huge cheer which had risen from the onlookers instantly turned to a collective gasp of horror as they saw Catherine lurch forward in her seat, clinging desperately with the one hand that was still on the arm of her chair. The duke appeared to have lost his footing, drastically tipping one corner of the litter, but he quickly managed to thrust his arm upwards to return it to the horizontal, throwing Catherine back into the chair just as it seemed inevitable that she must topple out of it into the water. There was no particular reason to think that his stumble had been deliberate, but I could not help wondering. Although he was soaked to his armpits, he did not look greatly troubled as he turned to speak to her. 'A thousand pardons, your grace. A loose stone attempted to trip me, but as you see it failed. All is well and your adoring public awaits.'

There were bright pink spots of anger on Catherine's cheeks but she ignored his glib apology and began to wave again. Relief redoubled the cheers of the crowd on the shingle as the boisterous mob of men and women waved evergreen branches and coloured banners and hailed their hero king and his trophy French queen.

'God bless Queen Kate! Fair Kate! Bonny Kate!'

'Welcome home, brave Harry! God bless good King Hal!'

There was the same tumult as they passed through the streets of Dover and it was repeated time and again during the following days as the royal procession crossed the county of Kent. At every village the populace turned out in their best clothes, carrying precious relics and statues out of the churches to greet them, while petitioners scrambled to catch the king's attention or beg the queen's blessing for their children. Even the weather joined in the celebrations, favouring the royal progress with unseasonal warmth, bright sunshine and blue skies.

During our stay in Rouen, before we took ship for England, Catherine had insisted that I take riding lessons. Being a girl from the back streets of Paris, I had never learned to ride, even though at fifteen I had married a groom from the royal stables, and until I began to travel around France with Catherine I had never felt the need but she had decided the time had come. 'You cannot accompany me on a royal progress if you have to ride on one of the baggage carts, Mette. I may need you en route and will not want to wait while someone goes to search for you at the back of the train. Besides, I assure you it is much more comfortable to ride a horse than to be bounced around on a cart.'

So one of the royal grooms had been instructed to find a docile cob and teach me the rudiments of horsemanship. It did not take long for all I needed to do was walk and trot and keep my mount safely following the horse in front. I was not intending to chase after the hunt or indulge in headlong gallops across moor and heath. However what I had not anticipated were the aches and pains that resulted from sitting on a horse for long periods of time. Even though I opted to ride sideways rather than astride, which Catherine favoured, I still found I was using parts of my body that had never been used before. However, by the time we reached Canterbury my rump was less saddle-sore and I had become quite fond of the sturdy brown mare which had been procured for me at Dover, reared and broken I was told, on the wild moors of England's South West. She had been named Jennet but I decided to re-christen her Genevieve after the patron saint of Paris and hoped she would look after me just as that virgin saint protected my home city.

It was concern for Genevieve that brought me to the stables of the Abbey of St Augustine, where the royal household was lodged in Canterbury en route for London. The queen and king were dining privately with the abbot and I had taken the opportunity to slip away and check if any of the grooms had tended my horse's front foot. The mare had begun to limp towards the day's end and having just got used to her paces, I was anxiously hoping it was nothing serious. However, when I led her from her stall I found that she was still lame and it being the dinner hour there was no sign of anyone to ask for help. On searching about, the only soul I encountered was Joan Beaufort, looking flustered and nervous and very out of place in her elaborate court dress and furred mantle.

'Sweet Marie, Lady Joan, a young girl like you should not be wandering about the stables alone when it is nearly dark! Whatever are you doing here?'

Apart from being the epitome of English beauty – strawberry-blonde, blue-eyed and apple-blossom-cheeked – as the king's cousin, Joan was one of the most eligible young ladies of the court.

'Searching for you,' said Joan, obviously very relieved to have found me. 'I have been looking everywhere.'

'My horse is lame,' I told her. 'I want someone to have a look at her foot.'

Her response astonished me. 'I know about horses. I always favoured the stables over my embroidery. Has the mare got a stone in her hoof?'

I shook my head. 'I have no idea. I know nothing about horses.'

'Let me take a look. Is that her there?' She trudged off to where Genevieve was tied back in her stall and I winced as horse dung and wet straw sullied the hem of her priceless brocade gown. Giving the mare a gentle pat she bent down and expertly lifted her hoof, peering at its underside. 'Yes, there is a stone.' She placed the foot carefully down and turned to me. 'I need something to prise it out with. A strong stick would do.'

I was about to go off in search of an implement when I suddenly realised that she must have been seeking me for a reason. 'Incidentally, Lady Joan, why were you looking for me?' I asked.

She frowned. 'Oh, I almost forgot. The queen wants you. She is in a frenzy.'

If Catherine had ever been in a frenzy it had died down by the time I got to her, but she was certainly angry.

'Where on earth have you been, Mette? I wanted you and you were not here.' There was a strident, peevish note in her voice that was new to me. She could be cross and critical at times, but was not usually given to petulance.

'I am sorry, Mademoiselle. I went to the stables to check on Genevieve.'

Catherine was pacing around the abbey's grand bedchamber, which the abbot himself had vacated in favour of the king and queen. 'Do you mean to say that you abandoned your queen in favour of a *horse*?' she almost snorted. 'Is there something wrong with your horse?' The sharp tone of this enquiry did not imply a sudden burst of equine benevolence on her part.

'She had a stone in her hoof,' I replied. 'Lady Joan removed it for me.'

This revelation brought Catherine's anger fizzing to the

surface again. 'This is unbelievable! I have three ladies to serve me and yet when I need their assistance I find that two of them are dancing attendance on a horse!'

Wondering what it was that could have brought on this uncharacteristic fit of pique, I decided that there was nothing for it but to act the truly humble servant. 'Forgive me, your grace,' I said, abandoning my usual, more familiar, form of address. 'I had no idea you were in such urgent need of me. How may I serve you?'

She turned her back and paced away across the room. 'Oh, it does not matter now. Clearly my problems are of no consequence compared with a stone in your horse's hoof!'

Agnes de Blagny, who had taken the brunt of the queen's initial outburst, was making faces at me behind her back. I found these facial gymnastics hard to interpret, but gathered it had involved King Henry in some way.

'Please, Madame – your grace – tell me what it is that has upset you. Does it concern the king? Was it something he said?'

She swung round at that, her eyes brimming with tears. 'All day people have been calling out my name, begging for my glance, holding out their babies for my touch. I am their beautiful queen, their Fair Kate, their Agincourt Bride! But my husband, the one who should have my glances and my touch and whose child I should be bearing, prefers to squander his attention on debating doctrine with the abbot and inspecting the abbey's library of dusty old books! And tomorrow – after he has prayed for an heir at the tomb of St Thomas à Becket – he says he must leave me here and hasten to Westminster to meet with his counsellors.

I ask you, where in the two thousand books the abbot is so proud to display to the king, does it say that there has ever been more than one Immaculate Conception? What is the use of praying for an heir if Henry does nothing about actually getting one?'

There was the crux of the matter. She may be the darling of the crowds right now, but she would soon be called a failure as a queen if she did not produce the heir that was so essential to securing the future of the crowns of England and France. Her marriage to King Henry was not only the embodiment of the unification of the two kingdoms, and the living proof of Henry's remarkable conquest of the better part of France, but also the joining of the two crowns, set in law by the Treaty of Troyes at their wedding eight months before. The treaty would be useless unless there was an heir born of the marriage and to the empire that Henry was still in the process of creating. On the surface Catherine was the ultra-beautiful, super-confident Queen of England and soon-to-be Queen of France, but inside she was a quivering mass of insecurity, centred on the imperative conception of that heir.

I hurried across the room to the abbot's carved armchair into which she had sunk with a heavy sigh. 'His grace will be here soon, Mademoiselle, I am sure,' I said, lapsing back into the intimate form of address I had used since her infancy. To me she would always be 'Mademoiselle', however many other grand titles she acquired. 'His grace rarely fails to wish you goodnight, even if he works into the small hours.'

Catherine gave me a withering look, far from mollified by

my attempt at consolation. 'A goodnight kiss is hardly going to sire the next King of England, Mette,' she said, fretfully, tugging at the pins that secured her veil to her head-dress. 'Henry could learn something from his subjects when it comes to enthusiastic outpourings of love!'

I gazed at her ruefully. What she was trying to tell me was that King Henry had not fulfilled his side of the marital contract recently and I was guiltily aware that I might be responsible for this lack. A month ago, just after Epiphany, Catherine had miscarried a child. It had not been a well-developed pregnancy but for a few joyous weeks she and Henry had believed the essential heir had been growing in her womb. Fortunately, on my tentative suggestion that it might be best to wait until a few more weeks had passed, they had not made any announcement to this effect. So Catherine had not had to suffer the murmurings of disappointment and doubts about her ability to carry a child. To my surprise the king had not been critical of Catherine or blamed any lack of care on the part of her attendants, which had emboldened me to advise him that it would be wise to allow her a few weeks to heal before making any further attempt to get her with child. The fact that I had not told her of this conversation was now coming home to haunt me. The king might be scrupulously following my advice, but the queen was misinterpreting his restraint, construing it as lack of interest.

I decided to try a fresh approach. 'I recall the king saying that he was eager that you should be crowned his true consort before any heir was born, Mademoiselle. Perhaps he has decided that it would be best even to delay conception until after your coronation, believing that God will bless your union once you are both consecrated.'

The feverish removal of hair-pins ceased and Catherine turned to meet my eye, a flicker of hope dawning in hers. 'Do you think that could be so, Mette? Really?'

I nodded vigorously, glad to have provided at least some crumb of comfort. 'Yes, Mademoiselle. As you know, King Henry lays great stress on divine approval of his actions. Truly, I believe you should not doubt his regard for you or his trust in God's holy will.'

She frowned. 'But if he is convinced that is God's intention anyway, why does he pray for a son at the shrine of every English saint we pass?'

I gave her a mischievous smile. 'Why do you attend Mass every day, Mademoiselle, when God must know that you worship Him unreservedly anyway? Is it not to demonstrate your faith to the world?'

Catherine's brow wrinkled as she considered this. 'Actually, I think it is to reinforce my faith, Mette,' she said after a moment.

'Well then, perhaps the king is reinforcing his faith in God's will by giving Him a little reminder now and then,' I responded.

She gave me a reproachful look. 'I have said it before, Mette, sometimes you are too flippant in your attitude to God and His Saints. However, we will soon see if you are right about my coronation. The date is set for February the twenty-third. That is just over a fortnight away.'

Agnes and I exchanged relieved glances. A crisis had erupted and now seemed to have subsided, but I did not doubt there would be many more over the next weeks. This had been a warning that for the foreseeable future we would be dealing with a vulnerable young queen whose growing popularity would continue to wreak its share of havoc with her mood. King Henry would not be the only one praying for an heir at the shrines of the English saints. I would very likely be creeping in behind him with my own fervent prayers of intercession.

**The thrilling sequel to *The Agincourt Bride*,
coming in Autumn 2013**

The Tudor Bride

**Follow Catherine and Mette as the French princess
becomes an English queen . . .**

King Henry V's new French Queen, Catherine, dazzles the crowds in
England, blithely unaware of court undercurrents building against
her. Her loyal companion, Guillamette, suspects that the beautiful
Eleanor Cobham, mistress to the Duke of Gloucester, is spying for
him. Her warnings are ignored though, for Catherine believes herself
invincible as she gives birth to an heir.

Tragedy strikes when King Henry is struck down by fever back in
France and Catherine suffers further tragedy trying to reach his
deathbed. A weak and weeping dowager queen follows the slow
funeral cortège through France and the King's Harper, Owen Tudor,
plays to comfort her.

Back in England, Gloucester persuades the regency council to remove
the new young king from her care, and a defeated Catherine retires
to her dower estates and asks Owen to go with her as Steward. At the
secluded manor of Hadham, a smouldering ember bursts into flame
and Catherine and Owen Tudor become lovers.

But their love cannot remain a secret forever, and when a grab for
power is made by Gloucester, Catherine – and those dearest to her –
will once again face mortal danger . . .